"*A gripping contemporary tale told with a rare elegance. Captivating.*"
C.F. Dunn, author of Fearful Symmetry

"*Perfect blend of gritty life and romance. Engrossing!*"
Carol A. Brown, author of Highly Sensitive

THE
HEALING
KNIFE

S. L. RUSSELL

LION FICTION

Published by
Lion Hudson Limited
Wilkinson House, Jordan Hill Business Park
Banbury Road, Oxford OX2 8DR, England
www.lionhudson.com

ISBN 978 1 78264 303 6
e-ISBN 978 1 78264 304 3

First edition 2020

Acknowledgments
Scriptures quotations are from the Good News Bible © 1994 published by the Bible Societies/HarperCollins Publishers Ltd UK, Good News Bible© American Bible Society 1966, 1971, 1976, 1992. Used with permission.

A catalogue record for this book is available from the British Library

Printed and bound in the UK, December 2019, LH57

ACKNOWLEDGEMENTS

It's been said before, but bears repetition: no book is the product of one mind alone. I am most grateful to my perceptive beta readers and my supportive family and friends, and for the skill, enthusiasm, and patience of the Lion team.

PART ONE

PORTON WEST

Death is everywhere, and it makes me angry.

Those months when I couldn't afford to live in the city, looking out of the bus window in the early morning, close-packed with other half-awake commuters – shoppers – whoever they were, with just the occasional cough or muttered word breaking the silence, I'd see slumped by the roadside a fox, or a rabbit, maybe even a badger. Something that had once had a purpose, however mysterious it might be to human understanding; something that had sight and hearing, could feel the wind in its pelt and food between its teeth, now pathetic in death, nothing but a broken body of no significance. I should be used to it by now – death – and I am, but I give my fury rein, because after all it's that hatred of death that drives me.

I'd never admit to it – of course I wouldn't – especially not to any of my colleagues. They'd raise their eyebrows and laugh. Do they feel it? Is it what drives them too, but they hide it for fear of ridicule, just as I do? Or is it just a job to them? Did they have it once, but now are fixated on their careers to the exclusion of all else? I don't know. I hardly know them, and I don't care to.

Of course I can't win – not ultimately; I know that. I'm not so deranged or arrogant to think that I can make much of a difference at all, not when I look at the vast numbers of living creatures dying every day. Everything that breathes comes to an end, and so will I. That miraculous pumping organ on which we all depend will wear out eventually, even if there is no disaster. But I can work, one day at a time, cut by cut, stitch by stitch, and give someone a bit longer to live and breathe and love and laugh – or not, depending on their circumstances.

I know I can't win the war. Death, with his scythe and grinning skull, always has the last word. But I can win a few of the battles. I can send a person out with the chance of a few more years of life. I can give the old tyrant something to think about. That's what keeps me going.

I was never much of a speculative thinker. More of a practical person, which is as well in my work. If I were to give in to "what if?" thinking I'd be paralysed. These last months, though, I've found myself taking a long, hard look at things. Life. Myself. My motives. My choices.

I didn't think in those terms that day, of course. I didn't know then – how could I? – that my ordered world was about to crack open like a melon under a hatchet. But since then I've wondered what would have happened if I'd ignored the phone, which I often do on my day off. Would Malcolm have called on someone else? He said there wasn't anyone, but that's not true. Someone could have done the job. If they had, would everything have come out differently? Useless to wonder now. The fact is, I did pick up the phone. I expected it to be something to do with the hospital, but I wasn't prepared for what came.

"Rachel? It's Malcolm. I'm in A and E."

"What? What's up?"

I heard a sheepish laugh. "I fell off my bike. Just coming into the car park. A lorry was reversing, I swerved out of the way, must have hit an icy puddle. The bike's a mess."

I could feel myself frown. "What about you?"

"That's just it. I've broken my arm – quite a nasty complex fracture. Must've fallen awkwardly."

"Oh, Malcolm! What were you thinking of, riding your bike to work in January? Have they patched you up?"

"Yes, I'm in plaster." He hesitated. "Rachel, you know I wouldn't ask if there was any other way. I was due to do the Rawlins op on Monday, first on the list. The other things can be given to someone else, or postponed. But not this one."

My frown was rapidly turning into a scowl. "Malcolm, I'm not a paediatric surgeon."

"I know. But you're the best choice, Rachel. Wesley's in the Caribbean somewhere. Sefton's got something infectious, and – this is off the record, by the way – Chan has put himself in rehab."

"About time too," I muttered.

"And," Malcolm pursued, "Craig Rawlins is hardly a baby. He's nearly thirteen."

"And undersized."

"Well, of course he's undersized! So would you be, if you'd had his problems. Look, Rachel, he has to have this operation now. It can't wait any longer. You know what a mission it's been getting his mother to agree to it. And it's his best hope of anything like a normal life. Or life at all, come to that."

I exhaled loudly, making sure he'd hear. "All right, all right, I'll do it. But you'll need to brief me."

"They're bringing me home by ambulance, so there'll be a wait. I should have time to get up to my office for the file. If you drive over to my place now you'll be there before me. Bridget will find you something to eat, I'm sure."

"Malcolm, did you fall on your head?"

"What? No, just my arm. They gave me all the scans – everything else is OK. Bruised to hell, but nothing worse. Why?"

"You're not thinking straight. If I have to get my car out, I can take you home. You don't have to wait for an ambulance."

"You're right." He sounded slightly bewildered. "Perhaps it's the shock."

"Have you rung Bridget?"

"Not yet. She wasn't expecting me home for hours, so she won't be worried. I've spent ages ringing round for cover. Scuppered today's clinics, obviously."

"Don't you have a secretary for all that?"

"Well, yes. She's been ringing people too. Had to cancel some routine appointments, and there'll be a few people having to wait a bit longer for their operations. But Craig Rawlins can't wait."

"All right, Malcolm – you win. Give me half an hour; I need a shower. Then I'll drive over and you can bring me up to speed."

"Yes," he said, sounding brighter. "We can go up to my office, and I'll show you the latest angiograms. They'll convince you if nothing else does."

"Half an hour, then. And for goodness' sake ring Bridget."

"I will. Thanks, Rachel. You're a good friend."

Standing under pounding hot water ten minutes later I reflected that Malcolm and Bridget Harries were the nearest thing I had to friends at the hospital – despite their being quite a bit older than me – even after two years, four if you counted the time I was doing locum work to finance my PhD. He wasn't exactly my boss; it didn't work that way. I had my own patients, my own clinics, my own preferred teams. But as a professor at a respected teaching hospital he was certainly a senior colleague. He was where I planned to be in a few years' time, if all went well. Unlike some, he treated me with professional courtesy and trusted my ability. The fact that I was a woman in a specialism dominated by men, many of them boorish sexist jerks, didn't seem to make a jot of difference to him. I didn't want to do the Rawlins surgery, but in a way it was flattering he'd asked me. As for Bridget, she did her best to mother me, for reasons I couldn't fathom. She'd eye me up and down and complain I was too thin. I ate whatever she put in front of me, even though it didn't seem to make me any fatter. I can cook – more camping cookery than haute cuisine, if I'm truthful – but I'd much rather not. So as I reversed my car out of its parking space that afternoon I was anticipating something hot and tasty when I got Malcolm home.

It was at least another two hours before we were on our way to the Harries' place, because I wanted to have a handle on everything to do with Craig Rawlins' case. Malcolm had talked about him, of course, and I had some idea of his background, but none of the details. If I was to operate on this boy in a few days' time I needed every last morsel of information that was relevant. Malcolm copied sheets from the paper file and we studied the latest angiograms, taken only the week before.

"There's an aneurysm forming here, I think." He pointed to the image on his computer screen. "As well as the enormous one that practically hits you in the eye here." He looked at me, the late afternoon sun glinting on his steel-framed glasses as he turned his head. "You can see why I'm concerned."

"So these developments are relatively recent?"

He sighed and shook his head. "We've been keeping an eye on Craig for years," he said. "You know he suffered considerable damage to his coronary arteries following that attack of Kawasaki's he contracted at age four. Undiagnosed till too late."

I nodded. This much I knew.

"Well, it was very much a watching brief until quite recently. Perhaps it's something to do with his age, with the onset of puberty, because believe it or not he's grown a bit over the past year. Perhaps he's been exercising a bit of adolescent rebellion, doing what he wants instead of giving in meekly to his mother's over-protectiveness. I don't know. Whatever it is, his condition has worsened. If I'd been able to convince his mother of the urgency I'd have done the operation six months ago."

"Why wouldn't she agree? Couldn't she see it was in his best interests?"

Malcolm shook his head. "You need to meet Eve Rawlins. She's no ordinary mother. But to be fair, if she has a dim view of the medical profession you can hardly blame her. If that dull-witted GP had made the right diagnosis Craig wouldn't be in this state now, teetering on a razor-edge, needing coronary artery bypass before he's even a teenager, poor lad."

"Kawasaki's not something you see every day, though, is it?"

Malcolm shrugged. "It's all academic now. Whether Craig gets his life back is down to you."

I frowned. "And the rest of the team. It's not just the cutter."

"I know that, you know that. The public, generally speaking, tend to think the surgeon's the hero – or the villain."

We were silent for a few moments, thinking our own thoughts.

Then I said, "You only ever mention Craig's mother. Doesn't he have a father?"

"Presumably so," Malcolm said. "But it's not a question I'm brave enough to ask. On that subject Eve Rawlins is fiercely private. Whatever the case, Dad's not in the picture." He glanced up at the window. "It's getting dark. Let me print these bits and pieces off for you, and then we can go home."

"Did you ring Bridget?"

"Yes. She says you must stay for dinner, if you're free."

"I was rather hoping she might say that."

I laid down my fork. My hostess was sitting across the table from me, her own meal finished. Malcolm had gone to soak in the bath, trying to ease his aching joints and purpling bruises.

"Keep that plaster out of the water!" I told him.

"Yes, yes," he muttered. "Don't nag."

I turned to Bridget. "You are a wonderful cook," I said. "That was delicious."

"Well, I think you need looking after," Bridget said. 'You work far too hard; I know you do. I don't think you get enough sleep. And I always say you're too thin."

"I'm perfectly healthy," I said, smiling at her. "I work long hours – we all do. But I love my work. I run most days. And I do eat, but it just gets used up. That's how I am."

She shook her head. "I worry you might – what's the word? – burn out. People do, you know."

"No need to worry. I thrive on pressure. And I don't need mothering!"

"That's a matter of opinion," Bridget muttered. "From all I've heard, your mother's not a lot of use."

I laughed. "Not as a mother, that's true. She wasn't really cut out for it. She agreed to one child, grudgingly, just to please my dad. But even with Martin she wasn't exactly hands-on. And I was an accident, as she never tired of reminding me."

"Honestly! What a thing to say to your child! It's amazing you had any confidence at all."

"My father was as good as two parents, if not better," I said quietly.

"I guess you must miss him."

I shook my head. "Not any more. He's been gone twenty-two years. But he's the reason I'm where I am, doing what I do."

She leaned forward, about to ask me more, but then we heard a faint yell from upstairs. "Hold on," she said. She pushed her chair back and left the room. I took the opportunity of clearing the plates and stacking them in the dishwasher. A few moments later Bridget came back. "You needn't have done that, Rachel!" she said. She seemed a little breathless.

"Is he OK?" I asked.

She laughed. "Yes, just couldn't reach the towel. Helpless Harries." She sat down again, sobering. "He'll be out of commission for weeks, won't he? What a good job he's got you to do the Rawlins operation. I know he's concerned about it."

"It's just a straightforward CABG, isn't it?" I said, puzzled. "I do them all the time – admittedly on older patients."

"As far as I can gather, it's not so much the surgery as the circumstances," Bridget said softly.

Malcolm poured himself a large brandy – medicinal, he called it, for shock. I declined. In his lamplit study, swathed in a huge velour dressing-gown in a startling shade of green, he sat at his desk, and I lounged in the one easy chair.

"Will I need to see Ms Rawlins and Craig before Monday, do you suppose?" I asked.

"It might be as well," he said after a moment's thought. "I'll ring her this evening and tell her you're doing it. Then I'll let you know. But if you do meet her, Rachel, tread softly."

"What do you mean?"

He took a deep breath, then exhaled loudly. "Well, she's not the easiest. As I say, it took me some time and effort to get her to agree to the op. Now she seems to think I'm some kind of surgical angel, so she might balk at someone else carving up her son."

I was beginning to feel slightly irritated by the whole scenario. I still wasn't best pleased at being dropped in it. Perhaps I might have felt differently if it had been some kind of groundbreaking procedure, something needing imagination and ingenuity as well as concentration and manual dexterity. But replacing someone's coronary arteries is bread and butter these days.

"Look, why don't I ring her now?" Malcolm said. "While you're here? Do you have your diary with you?"

I leaned down to where I had dumped my handbag on the floor. "Yes, I think so."

"We can set up a meeting if she wants one." He picked up the desk phone, dialled, and waited for what seemed a long time.

"Ms Rawlins? Malcolm Harries."

I heard him explain what had happened. He made himself sound like an idiot for having an accident; it seemed to me that he bent over backwards to persuade her to accept me as her son's surgeon. Surely it was me or no one, wasn't it? Wasn't her son's life worth more than her ignorant prejudice? It was nice to hear Malcolm telling her how very competent and experienced I was, but I felt my pride raise its head and snarl. I wouldn't have said so, but I was, even then, easily as good a surgeon as Malcolm, though I certainly didn't have his bedside manner – or his benevolent teddy-bear appearance.

Eventually he said goodbye and hung up. He blew out his cheeks. "See what I mean? Anyway, she'd like to meet you, and it wouldn't hurt for you to have a word with young Craig. He'll be scared, poor little chap. She'll be bringing him in on Saturday so they can keep an eye on him over the weekend. How are you fixed?"

I flicked the pages in my diary. "I've got clinics on Saturday.

I could call in on the ward at lunchtime." A thought struck me. "No, it'll have to be later. I've got my monthly duty visit to my mother: 'Two thirty and don't be late, Rachel!'"

Malcolm chuckled. "A weekend of problematic mothers for you, I see. Later will be fine. I have no doubt Eve will be there right up to the point where they ask her, I hope politely, to leave." He looked over at me, no doubt noting my raised eyebrows. "You don't have children, Rachel," he said gently. "I can put myself in Eve Rawlins' shoes. I remember a few worrying times when our lads were young. And Craig, I suspect, is all she's got."

By the time I made it back to the hospital on Saturday afternoon I was not in a good mood. Time spent with my mother was always likely to ruffle my feathers even if they had been perfectly smooth to start with, and I'd already had a busy morning full of the usual frustrations and no time to write anything up. It wasn't that I had any thrilling plans for the rest of the weekend, but I sometimes resented using up all my time on paperwork. On the other hand, it didn't do to let it pile up. I knew people who let it slide, but I like to have a clean slate and a sharp focus.

I had found my mother, as usual, in the communal sitting room of the warden-assisted apartments where she lived, surrounded by a gaggle of her cronies, holding court. I suspect she was bored much of the time, because her wits had not deserted her, and they were as acid as ever.

"Rachel, darling, how lovely!" she carolled as I entered the room. She liked to make out my visit was a surprise, when we both knew I was required to turn up once a month, on the dot, and heaven help me if I didn't. The cronies all fluttered and twittered as I bent over her chair and pecked her cheek.

"Hello, Mother. How are you?"

"As well as can be expected," she sighed. I should have been used to her theatrical ways, but they never failed to irritate. Her followers were all she had now of the adoring public of more than two decades ago, but even though her circle was restricted she made the most of it. Of course the other residents were of a similar age, and those that weren't senile could remember how she had been at the height of her celebrity: beautiful, elegant, perfectly groomed, and who could forget that voice! They just don't make them like Frances Chester any more. *And a good thing too*, thought her sour only daughter.

"Why, Rachel!" she trilled that afternoon. "Why the beetling brows?" She leaned forward, as if to whisper in my ear, but her voice lowered not a jot. "You know, dear, you really ought to have your eyebrows seen to. They really are – well, so bushy and black!"

I'd learned to ignore her little jibes, and the accompanying smothered giggles of her entourage, but I could feel my blood pressure rise a notch nevertheless. I smiled – oh, so false! – and said loudly, "Any chance of a cup of coffee, do you suppose?"

One of the nicer old ladies, Dorothy someone, jumped up. "Of course, Rachel. I'll make you some. I expect you've had a hard morning at the hospital, haven't you?"

"Do sit down, Dorothy," my mother snapped. "It's hardly the time for tea yet, let alone coffee." Dorothy subsided into her armchair looking quite stricken, and my mother leaned over and patted her hand, all twinkly smiles and powder-puff charm. "Perhaps a little later, all right, dear?"

So it went on, for a long, stretched-out hour and a quarter, the chat dominated by my mother's reminiscences of her sparkling career, and the other old ladies sighing as they recollected the elegant and glamorous figure she had once been. Finally she announced that it was indeed time for tea, and grudgingly allowed me to have coffee instead, muttering at my barbarity. We sat in silence and sipped out of flowery china cups. Sometimes, though not today, a man joined us, a tweedy octogenarian who called my mother "Dear lady!" in unctuous tones and played up outrageously to her need for adulation. Once he seemed to glance at me and I swear I saw him wink. *Good for you, Basil*, I thought.

If it wasn't such a monumental waste of time I might have found it funny, this ridiculous little charade of my mother's. But I'd had many grim years of her, and funny it was not. My watery coffee drunk, I made my "goodbyes" and "see-you-next-times" and escaped. The air outside smelled deliciously fresh.

By the time I parked back at the hospital a brisk wind was blowing round the building. I paused as I locked the car, seeing myself reflected in the driver's window, and was not encouraged by the shadowy vision of a dishevelled individual with a surly expression: perhaps, I had to concede, not the ideal image of the competent surgeon to present to an anxious patient and parent on a first meeting. I took the lift to the fourth floor where I shared a tiny office with Sefton Chalmers, a colleague as flowery and vain as his name implied, but a respectable craftsman nonetheless. I had little to say to Sef at any time but as it happened he was off sick with conjunctivitis and I had the cubbyhole to myself. An immaculate white coat was hanging on a coat hanger on the door, and I purloined it: Sef wouldn't be needing it, and if it was a bit large round the middle it was at least a cover for my workaday jeans. I rarely bothered with this traditional disguise but somehow, today, I felt it might be needed – to foster confidence, if nothing else (whose, I didn't ask). I found a lanyard with my face and name on it in a drawer, and smoothed down my unruly hair. I sometimes tell myself I will have it all cut short one day, but something holds me back, despite the inconvenience of having thick wiry hair that refuses to behave predictably. I heaved a sigh. Would I do? That's a question I can never answer, apart from when masked and gowned in theatre. Am I up to expectations? No idea.

Shaking off this unproductive self-doubt (probably the result of seeing my mother, who was uncannily able to undermine me) I took the lift back down to the ward where Craig Rawlins awaited his operation, and was buzzed in by a nurse yawning over a file at the desk inside the door. She directed me to the bay where his bed was.

The curtains were partly drawn across, but there was a gap and I could see that this was not for any medical intervention but just for privacy. I tapped politely on the metal strut of the curtain and cleared my throat before I entered.

Eve Rawlins was sitting on a hard chair beside the bed, at an angle to me, holding her son's hand as it lay unresisting on the white sheet. She turned her head as I approached, and it took all my years of medical training not to flinch when I saw her face. Malcolm had not prepared me for the large, vivid, port wine stain that spread, bumpy and deep red, from her hairline over her brow and her right cheek, bisecting her chin and splashing down across her jaw before it came to an untidy halt. I smiled, trying to mask my shudder, and I thought, *Why on earth haven't you had that seen to?* It seemed such a burden to carry.

"Ms Rawlins? Rachel Keyte."

I stretched out my hand, and she shook it as briefly as she could. Looking past that facial disfigurement, I saw a tall, thin woman, perhaps a few years older than me, sitting very upright. She had long, thick, surprisingly lustrous brown hair, tied back in a ponytail, and straight, regular features. But even if her appearance had been more arresting it would have been overshadowed by the birthmark. I looked away from her to the boy in the bed, and saw no resemblance to his mother. His smallness was due in large part to his illness. He was thin, apart from his enlarged chest, and very pale. His hair was black and stuck up all round his head, and his eyes had a slant to them: slight, but noticeable.

"Hi, Craig. I'm Rachel, your surgeon." He raised his free hand in a languid wave, and smiled faintly. "You heard about Mr Harries' accident, I guess."

When he spoke, his gruffness came as a surprise. He may have been the size of an average ten-year-old, but he was almost thirteen and his voice was changing. "Yeah. Fell off his bike, didn't he?"

"Mm. Almost under a lorry. But he's OK. Just sorry he can't do your operation, that's all."

Craig shrugged. Perhaps who held the knife didn't mean much to him. His mother clearly thought otherwise, and she cut in sharply, "Mr Harries said you had experience of this type of surgery?" Her voice was somehow both shrill and flat. I suspected the shrillness owed itself to a high degree of anxiety; the hand that wasn't clutching her son's was clenched tightly in her lap.

I spoke as gently as I could, though I felt little empathy with this woman. "Yes, I've performed many successful coronary bypass operations, though usually on older patients." She nodded. "Mr Harries will have taken you through the procedure, I imagine." She nodded again, pursing her lips. I battled on. "Has he made you aware of the risks and possible complications? I don't foresee any, but no operation is without risk."

"Yes. But he said it was absolutely necessary."

"Well, I agree with him. The sooner, the better." I turned back to Craig, who was watching me with those clear dark eyes. "Do you have any questions you want to ask me, Craig?"

He shook his head. I looked at his mother, my eyebrows raised enquiringly. "Is there anything…?"

She cut me off. "No. I just want to get this over with." Her voice was low, tense, almost grating.

"All right, so I'll see you both on Monday. Till then, just rest, OK?" As I pushed aside the curtain to leave, I turned back to Eve Rawlins. It seemed that something else needed to be said. "I'll do my best for him, Ms Rawlins," I said very quietly. "As I do for all my patients."

She stared at me for a long moment; then she nodded briefly, unsmiling, and I left them.

I was unlocking my car when my phone rang. It took a while for me to register my ringtone, buried as it was in the junk-heap I called my handbag, which I kept promising myself I would sort out. There were always more important things to do, and as it was I never seemed to keep up with my reading. Just as I found it the ringing stopped. I thumbed the appropriate key and saw that the caller was my friend Beth Walters. I said the Harries were my only friends at the hospital, because now it was true: Beth was my scrub nurse till she got pregnant (unplanned, I'd guess, but I don't really know). Now Beth was waiting for the birth, and living with her Ugandan boyfriend Jimmy, whose surname I could never remember how to spell. He was an anaesthetist, but he was not around the hospital that much, because like me a few years ago he was working on a PhD.

Beth had left a message. "Hi Rach, just thought I'd see if you were still alive. Want to come to dinner Sunday night?"

I called her number, and she answered straight away. "Hi, Beth, thanks for the invite. I'd love to, but I've got an op to do first thing Monday so I'll need an early night."

"I thought you didn't operate on Mondays," Beth said.

"I don't normally. This is one I'm doing for Malcolm." I explained the circumstances.

"Another time, then, OK?" Beth said. "But don't leave it too long, or I'll be much too busy."

"Can't think why," I said, smiling.

"Yeah, right – I can change a nappy one-handed while proof-reading Jimmy's latest pages and knocking up a four-course meal at the same time."

"Piece of cake, love."

"Ha!" Beth said. "I'd like to see *you* do it."

"Of course I could – I'm a surgeon."

"What you are is an idiot," Beth said with a fond smile.

"Probably. See you soon."

"Yep, hope the operation goes well."

I spent the rest of the weekend doing my laundry, going for a run when it wasn't raining, and reading some research papers I'd downloaded from the internet. I got takeaway food and didn't see anyone, which suited me fine.

Monday morning started as it had for the past week – cold, dreary, with patches of fog. Craig Rawlins' surgery was scheduled for 8:30, and at 7:30 I met up with the other members of the team. These were Malcolm's people: there hadn't been time to reschedule and anyway they knew the case and were therefore the best people to work with me. For various reasons Malcolm had decided to do the operation the traditional way, with the chest open and the heart stopped, so as well as the theatre nurse and the anaesthetist – a tall, gangly man I'd worked with on occasion – there was also the perfusionist, a garrulous Irishman I didn't much like but who, I knew, was good at what he did and trusted by Malcolm. Once we'd established that we'd got the right patient for the right procedure, and talked over some of the details, we were ready to begin.

Then came the part of every operation which, but for the fact that I am highly alert, has an almost hypnotic quality for me – perhaps because I have done it so many times before, following an exact sequence of actions. I have always preferred not to talk during the process, because silence is what takes me into the zone of total focus. Wearing a mask, hat and scrubs, with headlight and magnifying loupes in place, I chose gloves from the rack, size seven and a half; I peeled the packet open and placed the gloves beside my sterile gown on the trolley. At the long stainless-steel communal basin I turned the taps on with my elbows, waiting for the water to get to a comfortable temperature as I opened a new pack containing a nailbrush which I doused with antiseptic. For ten minutes or more I scrubbed: hands, nails, arms up to the elbows, brushing, rinsing, repeating; then, holding my clasped hands up, I dried them thoroughly on a paper towel, touching nothing else. My surgical gown, made of paper, was folded so that I needed to touch only the inside. I thrust in my arms and wriggled it onto the rest of my body, sleeves covering my hands, and waited for someone to fasten the ties at my back. With my hands still hidden in the sleeves of the gown, I put on the gloves, making sure each finger fitted with immaculate smoothness, and folded each glove over the cuffs of the gown.

I was ready. The team congregated around the operating table. Once again, for the last time, we checked who the patient was and what we were going to do. I looked down briefly at Craig's inert anaesthetized body, then I drew a line down his bony white chest, marking my intended incision.

After that it went as it always did, and on this occasion there were no scares, no unexpected hitches: it was like a well-rehearsed and perfectly executed dance. The patient's chest was painted and draped, the tubes of the heart-lung machine secured. Now I set to work with scalpel, diathermy, oscillating saw, stopping any small bleeds as I went. Then the retractor, the action that always seemed most invasive. The chest was open. I gently set aside the thymus and cranked the retractor a little more, exposing the pericardium. We were almost there. If anything my level of concentration rose. I was unaware of my colleagues, assuming they were doing their part efficiently as I focused only on my own delicate actions. Craig was just a skinny kid, and I was more used to burlier patients; I made a conscious effort to slow down. I incised the pericardium vertically, and stitched the edges away. There was the heart – that miraculous organ which has dominated my working life, practically my every thought, for almost twenty years. For a brief moment I remembered the first time I laid my gloved hand on a beating heart. I have never forgotten it, and it can still send a shiver through my whole body.

Four hours later it was all over. Following Malcolm's plan I bypassed all Craig's coronary arteries, replacing the damaged sections with a nice leg vein, and made the neatest of tiny stitches to attach the ends. There were still many things to do, much to check, before we could go into reverse, closing the wound layer by layer. But finally it was done. The team wheeled Craig away, and I was able to strip off the gloves and gown and flex my shoulders and wrists. Now it was someone else's job to look after him as he recovered from the necessary trauma we had inflicted on his fragile body.

"Nice one, Rachel," said the anaesthetist (I remembered his name – James), "as always. Malcolm will be pleased."

I nodded. "Thanks, everyone," I said to the team. "Good work."

Feet up in the coffee lounge, I rang Malcolm. He answered the phone after the first ring; obviously he had been on tenterhooks all morning. "You can relax for a while," I said. "Textbook operation. Now I'm going home."

I heard him heave a huge sigh. "Thank you, Rachel. Before you go, have a word with Eve, will you? She'll need to know from you that it went well."

"If I must. Yeah, OK." Privately I thought the nurses could tell her, but I went along with Malcolm's way of doing things, this once.

I found Eve Rawlins sitting in the side room next to the bay where Craig was being monitored, prior to taking him back to the ward. She was as upright as ever, her hands clasped in her lap, her face pale and expressionless but for a tiny telltale tic at the corner of her eye.

"Ms Rawlins?" She turned her head towards me. For a moment, seeing her face, I felt a pang of sympathy with this rather unprepossessing woman. The birthmark seemed to show up more raw and fierce in the white light of the room. "It's over, and he's as well as can be expected," I said. "The operation went smoothly. I have hopes of a good recovery."

I heard her swallow, and with some difficulty she said "Thank you" very faintly and immediately turned away from me. I waited for a moment before I left the room. *Odd woman*, I thought.

That was Monday. On Tuesday I called in on Craig to see how he was doing. I didn't much like the look of him, but he'd had major surgery the day before – it wasn't unusual, and I relied on the ICU team to let me know if anything developed. On Thursday I was on call, and I'd just gone up to my office to file some paperwork. I was thinking about going for a run; then I looked out of the window and saw it had started to rain. I don't like running in the rain: too slippery. I didn't want to have an accident that would stop me from working, certainly not while Malcolm was out of action. At that point my pager bleeped.

I rang the ICU straight away. A senior nurse I knew quite well, Julia Williams, answered. "Rachel, we may have a problem with Craig Rawlins," she said with admirable calm. "He'd been restless, complaining of chest pain, and there was some sign of infection in the incision site – nothing to worry about, but something to keep an eye on, I'm sure you'd agree. But then his condition suddenly, I mean *very suddenly*, worsened. Just this afternoon, within the last hour or less. Rachel, I've seen this before – I think it's mediastinitis. You're going to have to open him up again. Or someone must." She sighed. "Poor lamb."

I rarely swear, but I did then, and immediately apologized. "Look, Julia, I need to check the exact procedure, but I'm in my office in front of a computer now, so that shouldn't take long. I'll be with you as soon as I humanly can. Meanwhile can you get someone to organize a free theatre and the necessary people? Ideally the same team I had on Monday, but anyone who's free and sober."

"Yes, of course."

I'd been booting up my computer while I was speaking. I typed in mediastinitis and scanned the page. As I thought, it was a case of sternal reopening and debridement – clearing out the necrotic and infected tissue. Speed was essential, because an infection of this kind dramatically increased the chances of patient death. The question that remained now was just how I would approach the reopening. The best practice seemed to be to leave the wound open after I'd dealt with the infection, just in case yet more surgery might be needed subsequently. I shut down the computer and went to the door, but then a thought struck me. I decided to ring Malcolm – partly for a valued second opinion, but also to cover my own back in these days of "let's find someone to blame" litigation. I rang his mobile, and he answered after a few rings. There was raucous noise in the background; it sounded as if he might be enjoying a pint at his local.

"Malcolm, be prepared for this – I need your thoughts, and I need them fast." I told him briefly what Julia Williams suspected, and I heard him groan. Perhaps heartlessly I ploughed on, running before him what I was planning to do. "I'm going up to ICU now," I said. "As soon as a theatre's free I'll re-operate. Are you in agreement with what I've outlined?"

He sounded almost dazed, and I remembered that he too was not in good shape. But it was Craig that needed our best, and quickest, efforts now.

"Yes, yes," he said. "That's absolutely spot-on. Keep the chest open until you see adequate granulation tissue. Then use muscle-flap closure. That's what I'd do. Did it once, patient survived, but it was a while ago. Mediastinitis isn't something you see every day."

"No," I said, hearing the grimness in my own voice. "Seems young Rawlins is determined to be as unusual as possible. I'm going now, Malcolm. Thanks for your input."

"Yes, OK. Keep me posted."

Consulting the internet and speaking to Malcolm had taken little more than fifteen minutes – twenty at most. Now I power-walked down the corridor and rode two floors down in the lift: perhaps another ten minutes. At most it had been half an hour since I'd spoken to Julia Williams. But when I got to the ICU swing doors and was admitted, she stood in my way, her expression anguished.

"Rachel, I'm so sorry, but we're too late."

I felt my eyes widen. "What?"

She spoke with her usual calm, but there was a huskiness to her voice. "Truly, I've never seen sepsis race away so fast. We did everything we should, and more. But then Craig started to moan, complaining of chest pain. He said, 'I can't breathe.' It was difficult to hear him – like he was choking." She cleared her throat, swallowing down tears.

"Renal failure?"

She nodded. "I think so. He had a seizure, Rachel – quite horrible. And then it was over. Nothing we could do. It all happened so incredibly quickly."

That was when I swore again. Not loudly, but vehemently. "Sorry."

She patted my arm. "No, it's OK. We're all devastated, of course."

"Does his mother know?"

"Yes. Someone's with her. She's in the relatives' room – she wouldn't go home. Been here all day, every day. I told her you were on your way – that was before he died, of course. I'll go and see her now. Will you come with me?"

I made a face. "If I must. Not my favourite job."

"It's no one's favourite job, is it?" Julia said. "But you get used to it, working here."

"Yes. We do our best. I certainly did, all the team did, for Craig. But patients die." I shook my head. *Death is everywhere.*

She nodded. "Let's get it over with. However bad we feel, it's always worse for the family."

I followed her to the relatives' room, a short walk up the corridor. Inside, a nurse was sitting beside Eve Rawlins, her arm round the older woman's shoulders. The nurse looked up and wordlessly shook her head. Eve's head was bowed, her hands, as usual, clenched.

"Ms Rawlins – Eve," Julia said softly. "Ms Keyte is here. I

told you she was on her way, ready to do another operation. I explained that, didn't I?"

I stepped forward into the room. "Ms Rawlins, I'm so very sorry. We did our best. Sometimes things happen that are simply out of our control –" I stopped suddenly, because then Eve raised her head. I took in her eyes, red-rimmed with fatigue, staring, her hair greasy with neglect, scraped back from her forehead, the angry birthmark that dominated her face; but what forced me back, stumbling, through the open door, was the guttural sound that came from her throat, like a snarling dog, and the baring of her teeth, and the way she threw off the young nurse's arm as she half-rose from her seat. Julia saw it too, and stretched a protective arm across me.

"Go, Rachel. Obviously she's not herself."

I pushed open the door. "I'll tell Mr Harries," I mumbled. Then the door banged closed behind me, and I stood in the corridor, puzzled and shaken. A mother had lost her son. But her face had been almost demonic, her fury unmistakable. And I was the culprit.

**

Life returned to normal – normal for me, which is probably not normal for most people – and I forgot about Craig Rawlins. If that makes me seem heartless, I probably am. Of course no surgeon likes losing a patient, but it happens. By the time they get to us many patients are very ill and we're their last hope.

Everyone involved in Craig's case convened for a meeting and all the angles were thrashed out: what we could have done better, what we should learn from the whole experience. We weren't hopeful that the post-mortem would cast much light. A couple of weeks later I sat again in Malcolm's study, listening to Bridget downstairs as she practised scales – she was taking singing lessons – and Malcolm leaned back in his chair, nursing his plastered arm. "All it'll tell us," I said, "is that Craig died of mediastinitis – a massive bacterial invasion that his compromised body couldn't withstand. It'll mention staphylococcus aureus and staphylococcus epidermidis. What it can't tell us is how those little devils got into his system."

Malcolm looked down at his desk where papers were scattered. "It says here," he said, tapping the uppermost sheet, pushing his glasses further up his nose, "'… the origin of infection following open heart operations is not known in most patients.' And the fact is, even if it seems like a cop-out, the likeliest source of infection is the patient's own skin flora. The thing that surprises me, though…" He paused.

"What?"

"Well, how quickly it took hold. Just hours. But they must have been monitoring him constantly in ICU."

"Of course they were. But symptoms aren't always clear-cut. Full-on florid sepsis can be a galloper, and it can be very difficult to control. We know that. It's what we all dread, isn't it? But even when the PM is released there'll be no blame attached. There can't be."

Malcolm sighed heavily. "Try telling Eve Rawlins that."

"What? You've seen her?"

"Mm." He looked up at me. "Don't forget I had a lot to do with both her and Craig, over the years, not just pre-op. I felt, feel, a certain responsibility. She's a mess, obviously. Angry, grieving, bitter, just a bit wild. I don't know, possibly quite a repressed personality, and maybe all the more explosive for that." He hesitated. "I tried to assure her that Craig's death was not down to an individual, or a group, or the hospital. It was a tragic event, but these things happen: our knowledge isn't complete, our systems aren't perfect, however hard we try. But she wasn't buying it."

I sucked in my breath. "Is she going for medical negligence? I can't see she'd have a case."

Malcolm shook his head. "No. By the time I left she was

quite calm – cold, even. She said, 'I can't afford to sue. I'm not well-off; I can't risk incurring costs I won't be able to pay. But there are other ways. One way or another someone will feel my pain.' You should have seen her face – completely expressionless – especially with that awful birthmark of hers. I've never felt I could get anywhere near her. She's such a strange woman, but I feel very sorry for her all the same. She has nothing now. I just hope she gets some support from her church and they can convince her that her anger is destroying her."

"Oh," I said. "She's a churchgoer, is she? More brimstone than meek-and-mild, it seems."

Malcolm frowned. "Whatever your private opinions, it's better not to voice them. I hope she finds some comfort in her beliefs."

"Yes. Sorry, that was flippant."

Malcolm took off his glasses and rubbed his eyes. "Look, Rachel, once the PM comes through they'll release the body and they can hold the funeral. I can't drive at the moment, what with this arm, but I'd like to go – represent the hospital, at least. Bridget will be at work, of course. Would you consider driving me, maybe even go to the funeral with me?"

I felt my eyebrows shoot up. "Me? Are you serious?"

"It would give a positive message – that we're not heartless butchers but human beings with feelings, a conscience, whatever you like to call it."

"Well," I said dubiously, "I can't see what good it would do, but if you think so… if it doesn't interfere with something more important, like someone needing surgery."

"Understood. Maybe," Malcolm said thoughtfully, "maybe by then she'll have calmed down a bit. Had a chance to think it through."

As it happened it was less than a fortnight later that Malcolm rang me with details of the funeral. "St Joseph's, Thursday, eleven o'clock."

Thursday was my day off, a fact well known to Malcolm. I had no excuse. "All right."

"I'll buy you lunch afterwards."

"Better." I thought for a moment. "St Joseph's – isn't that a Catholic church? Is Eve Rawlins Catholic?"

"No, high Anglican. All the things you might associate with a Catholic church, but within the Church of England fold."

"Right. I'll pick you up at ten thirty, then."

I liked to give the impression of being, if not exactly an atheist, uninterested and dismissive of things spiritual. I had a reputation for pragmatism, for extreme self-belief, for impatience with sentiment. I read somewhere, probably in some old heart surgeon's autobiography, "Cardiac surgery is not for the faint-hearted." It may have been the same guy who claimed that surgeons tend to be psychopathic – something to do with having too little sleep, becoming immune to stress, and the loss of empathy that goes with it. Many of them do, it's true, take self-confidence to an extraordinary level. Malcolm bucks the trend: he's a good surgeon and a good guy. But I'm pretty sure most people think I'm one of the psychos: clever, but nasty. I let them think it. But it isn't true – at least not entirely.

I had to believe in myself, because nobody else did, during those long years of studying and training. My mother certainly didn't – the day I voiced my aim to be a heart surgeon, aged not quite fifteen, she laughed uproariously, as if it was the best joke she'd heard in years. Then, trying to specialize, to gain experience, I came up against that hoary old cliché – male prejudice – not to say sexual harassment and breathtakingly outrageous behaviour. Some bad things were said, and done: like the operation I undertook under supervision when the supervisor was an old goat of a professor, eminent and respected, who stood behind me and rubbed up against me, sighing, for the whole time I was cutting and stitching, determined to make me slip. What I wanted to do was stick my scalpel where it would hurt him most; but I didn't. I knew the only person to suffer the consequences would be me. My revenge then was completing a textbook bit of surgery, and continuing to work and study till I was the best in my field. I just needed to succeed. And that's what I did, and what I'm still doing. That old professor may be senile, or dead; I won't be weeping. Whatever; they can't come out with any claptrap about female cardiac surgeons when I'm around. Leaving out the unforeseen, I'm headed for a consultancy before I'm forty. Who cares what any of them – my mother, my superiors and colleagues, past and present – think? I've got no time for most of them, and they know it.

The day before Craig Rawlins' funeral I rooted around in my wardrobe and found a black skirt and jacket I'd used for innumerable interviews. I hung them on a hanger hoping the creases would drop out overnight.

I picked Malcolm up on time. He came out of the house swathed in a vast black overcoat, with his plastered arm clutched to his chest and one arm of the coat hanging limply.

"You look almost Napoleonic," I said as he squeezed into my car. "Just need the tricorn."

"Hm," he grunted. He slammed the car door shut and shuddered. "Horrible month for a funeral, February. More depressing than ever."

"Not much of a month for anything," I said as I swung out onto the main road.

"You still running?"

"When I can. But only if it's not too wet or icy. We don't need another surgeon with a broken bone." I glanced at him. "It can't be too long, can it, before they take your plaster off?"

"About ten days, probably."

As we left the bypass we came up against a long tailback of traffic. Malcolm groaned, peering out of the window. "Now what? We'll be late."

"Some idiot going too fast, I guess. Maybe skidded off the road. It's a bit of a blackspot." I turned off the engine. "Who told you when the funeral was going to be, anyway? Not Ms Rawlins herself, I imagine."

"No. It was her priest, Father Vincent. I've met him a couple of times. He seems to be the only person who knew the Rawlinses well, apart from a couple of women who used to be Eve's lodgers. I asked to be informed."

I cleared my throat. "Malcolm, if you don't mind me asking a personal question – are you a Christian?"

He pulled a face. "Funny you should ask that," he muttered. "To be honest with you, I've never quite made up my mind. I'm an eternal oscillator, really. Sometimes I swing towards belief, then I get cold feet and retreat. Bridget is – but you know that. Sometimes she enquires after my spiritual health, but mostly she keeps a diplomatic silence." He squirmed in his seat. My little car was restrictive for a bulky man in an even bulkier overcoat. "What about you, Rachel? I imagine you are, at the very least, a sceptic."

I smiled. "It's hard to say, really. My mother was, and is, quite scornful and dismissive, though she enjoys the colourful aspects, the pomp and show. But my dad was a staunch believer and he encouraged his children to follow on. Martin – my brother – abandoned any faith he might have had, but I hadn't, not quite, despite everything. Maybe because it was something my dad valued so much – who knows? I don't practise; I barely even think about it. It's well and truly on the back burner. But I think it's probably quite a deep part of me. Maybe one day I'll have the space in my life to revive it."

Malcolm was looking at me with raised eyebrows. "Well, you do surprise me." He thought for a moment. "It's odd, though. Something Bridget said a while back makes me think she might have suspected… Bridget's a bit uncanny that way. And you can never tell what's really going on in someone else's mind."

I was curious. "What did she say?"

But Malcolm was looking out of the window again. "Hold on, Rachel. I think there's movement ahead. Brake lights. They must have cleared whatever it was."

A few moments later the cars ahead of me started to move off. I restarted the engine and followed at a distance. As we came off the bypass and took the exit into the city centre we saw the problem: a jackknifed lorry, now on the hard shoulder surrounded by an ambulance, police cars, and breakdown vehicles.

I dropped Malcolm off outside the church and managed to find a parking space up a nearby cul-de-sac. An icy wind, spitting rain, whisked round my barely covered ankles as I ran up the church steps. I opened the tall wooden door as quietly as I could, and located Malcolm in a back pew. He beckoned me over and I slid in beside him. A few heads had turned as I entered; now everyone was looking forward again. I saw a sea of black: suits, coats, hats, armbands. The church itself was high and wide, a modern building of red brick, with tall plain windows. Around the altar there was more ornamentation, and on each side paintings whose rococo style jarred with the plainness of the rest: I noted a few bleeding hearts and punctured saints.

Before the altar, in the middle of the nave, the coffin rested on a wooden trestle. It was white with gilt handles, and seemed pitifully small. Facing the congregation, between coffin and altar, a tall, balding priest was speaking; his voice was soft, and from where I was standing I could hear almost nothing of what he said. It was no loss. All I wanted was to escape unnoticed, and soon. Malcolm frowned at me, and I realized I'd been restlessly shuffling my feet.

There followed, interminably, singing, prayers, an address. Then I realized that there was also to be a communion service – this was going to be a long job. The church was full, and everyone shuffled forward when their turn came. I stayed in my seat, head down. Finally the priest raised his arms in benediction and the organ pealed forth. I touched Malcolm's elbow and waved my hand, discreetly, towards the exit. He shook his head. I felt a sinking in my stomach as the black-coated pall-bearers marched down the nave, hoisted the coffin onto their brawny shoulders, swung it round, and paced slowly back towards the doors, their gloved hands respectfully folded. Directly behind them came Eve Rawlins. Her bowed head was covered with a square of black material. Two women accompanied her, one on each side, holding her by the elbows, both of them weeping. The congregation fell into line behind them and filed out. I felt terribly exposed; the last thing I wanted was for Eve to look up and see me.

She did not look up. Then it was our turn to follow the procession out.

Malcolm stopped me before the door, his face sombre. "I should speak to her, however briefly."

As we left the building I veered away from Malcolm and slipped in between other members of the congregation who were shifting uncertainly about, not knowing what to do or what should happen next. At the foot of the steps a hearse was waiting, and the pall-bearers were closing its rear doors. Inside, the white wood of the coffin seemed to shine in the gloom of the day: threatening black rain-clouds were already massing, cutting out what little light there was.

From the middle of the crowd my eyes sought out Malcolm's sturdy figure, and I saw him finally, on the other side of the flagged open space in front of the church doors, about twenty feet away. His head was bowed towards Eve, who stood already overshadowed by the tall priest – Father Vincent, presumably. I saw her raise her head, the blood-red birthmark stark against the pallor of her face, and I saw her hands come up like claws, and Malcolm backing away. Then, to my horror, she looked beyond Malcolm, her eyes wildly searching, and she saw me.

Until then there had been little sound – just the swoosh of the passing cars, the whistling of the wind, the muted talk of the mourners. But now there came from her stretched mouth the most horrible scream. Every head jerked up. Suddenly she broke away from Malcom and the priest and ran, her arms extended, towards me. Horrified, I backed away, but there was nowhere to go.

"Murderer! Bloody murderer!" she shrieked. "Butcher!" She slipped a little on the wet stone but regained her balance and hurtled forward until her outstretched hands were within inches of my face. I was unable to move, as if paralysed. People around me suddenly seemed to wake as if from a trance and on either side hands grabbed her. She struggled and writhed like a captive serpent, gasping and wailing. Then Father Vincent came lumbering up, panting, kilting up his cassock with one hand and taking hold of Eve with the other.

"Eve, Eve – no, don't do this!" he pleaded. "You're making things worse. Come now, come away; don't do this to yourself."

Suddenly she seemed to crumple, and the eldritch wail became heaving sobs, unbearably loud. People around me started to move away, their expressions baffled, horrified, or merely embarrassed, looking at me sideways as they went. Father Vincent put his arms round Eve's shoulders and turned her away from me. He looked back, over his shoulder, shaking his head. "I'm so sorry," he murmured. "Perhaps it's best if you leave now."

I nodded and started down the steps, uncaring if Malcolm was following me. People parted and drew away from me as I made for the street. But Eve Rawlins hadn't finished with me. As I hesitated at the kerb I heard her shout, "I'll hound you, butcher! I'll never let you rest! I'll make you suffer, as you made me suffer!" Then her voice was suddenly muffled, and the crowd closed in behind me, cutting her off from my sight. There was a surge towards the street, and Malcolm appeared, his normally ruddy face pale with shock.

"Oh, Rachel," he muttered. "I'm sorry, so sorry. I should never have asked you to come. I truly never thought –"

"Never mind," I said grimly. "Let's just get as far away from here as we can."

There was a village we knew, off the road back to Malcolm's, with a pub called the Flag and Whistle which had a huge log fire. I parked the car and we went in, saying nothing. Malcolm ordered at the bar and I found two deep armchairs where we sat in silence, staring into the flames.

Eventually Malcolm roused himself, shifted uncomfortably in his seat, and picked up his drink from a wobbly little table at his elbow. He took a deep draught. "I can't believe what we just witnessed," he said.

I chewed my lip, gathering my whirling thoughts. "In all the time you've had dealings with them – Eve and Craig – did you ever suspect she might be mentally ill?"

His head came up. "Is that what you think?" he said sharply.

"It's an explanation."

"It explains nothing," he shot back at me. "I always found Eve to be clear and logical. Yes, fiercely possessive and protective of her child, as any mother might be. But rational."

I sipped my drink, feeling its warmth and bite as I swallowed. "So, what do you think?"

"I don't know," he said. "I'm a surgeon, not a psychiatrist. Temporary insanity brought on by shock and grief?"

"So you imagine she'll recover."

He frowned. "Don't you?"

"I have no idea." I shook my head. "I hope she does come out of it, and soon. The look on her face... I was scared, Malcolm."

"Of course you were. Have you ever had adverse reactions before?"

"Yes, I think most of us have, haven't we? Irate or emotional patients and relatives taking out their feelings on us. But nothing like this. You have to admit – she was nothing short of deranged."

"Hm."

A large woman in a blue apron appeared. "Your meals are on the table in the alcove," she said with a beaming smile. "Let me know if there's anything else you need."

"Thank you," Malcom said. "Give me a hand-up, Rachel, can you? It's tricky getting out of this squashy chair with only one functioning arm."

We followed the heady aromas of soup and warm bread to our table and were soon chewing and swallowing. I'd been feeling cold, despite the fire – cold and threadbare and vulnerable, but the effect of hot food was heartening. I finished my drink and wiped my mouth with the paper napkin.

"Malcolm, if you call this thing a 'temporary insanity'... well, how temporary? Is she going to come after me? Some kind of bloody vendetta?"

Malcolm's eyebrows rose. "I hardly think so." He thought. "Perhaps I need to speak to Father Vincent. Obviously she needs some kind of psychological help – if she'll accept it."

"Meanwhile, where does that leave me?"

He leaned forward, pushing his empty plate aside. "Look, Rachel. You have to leave it behind. Behave as if nothing has happened. Otherwise you'll go off your head as well. You did nothing wrong – you tried to save the lad's life, and it didn't work out. If we let every patient's death floor us we'd be no use to the surviving ones."

"I know that," I said impatiently. "I'm sorry Craig died, of course. But I did my best, and my best is pretty good. I don't blame myself any more than I blame you, or Father Vincent, or the Man in the Moon. My conscience, such as it is, is clear. It's not Craig I'm worried about; it's his crazy mother."

***

I was busy, and time flew by. I had clinics and ward rounds and surgery, as well as reading and writing and teaching to do. Little by little the terror of Eve Rawlins flying at me like some clawed harpy faded into an uneasy background. Several days after the funeral Malcom rang me at home. "I spoke to Father Vincent," he said. "He's working on persuading Eve Rawlins to accept some kind of counselling. She hasn't agreed yet, but he thinks she seems calmer. Try to put it behind you, Rachel."

I went over to Beth and Jimmy's for dinner one Sunday evening. Jimmy excused himself after doing the washing up. "Got this tricky section to write up," he said. "You girls can do without me." He kissed the top of Beth's head and disappeared from the room, gathering up a pile of books as he went.

Beth and I sat opposite one another in her comfortably disordered lounge, mugs of coffee in our hands. Beth had commandeered the sofa, and half-lay with her legs tucked up beneath her, one hand unconsciously stroking her swollen belly.

"You're very quiet, Rach," she said. "Are you worried about something?"

I sighed. "Actually, I'm trying to put an incident out of my mind, because worrying won't solve anything. But I'll tell you, if you like." I recounted the saga of Malcolm's accident, Craig's operation, his sudden death, and the events at his funeral. I tried to describe Eve Rawlins fairly, but she still came out of it like a creature from hell.

Beth's eyes were round with horror. "Good grief, Rachel! That's horrific! How can you concentrate on work?"

I shrugged. "Because I have to. Otherwise nobody on my list would get their operations done. Someone else might die unnecessarily. People would be in pain. I have to work."

"Well, I get that…" Beth said. She grinned suddenly. "Surgeons have a reputation for being cool and focused to the point of inhuman, don't they? It's a caricature, but maybe not so far off the mark. You never cease to surprise me, Rachel."

"In a good way, I hope," I said.

"Maybe not always." She burst out laughing, and I laughed too.

The next day was Monday, not a day I normally operate. It proved fruitful, though, as I spent part of it with students. I always felt energized being around those in whom I detected – or thought I did – that same obsessive hunger to shine that I'd had at that age – and hoped I still had, in some measure.

It was an especially foul day, wet and windy, and I'd taken the car to work. Usually I'd walk or run; it set me up for the day. But I didn't want to arrive drenched and have to waste time changing my clothes. I left the hospital about six o'clock, and looked forward to a quiet evening in my warm (if rather bare) flat, with the chance to catch up on some paperwork. My car was parked against the wall of the Oncology Department, sheltered from the worst of the weather. As I approached, fishing my key out of my pocket, I frowned: something looked different, odd. There was something on the windscreen and over the bonnet, and the wing mirrors – something dark and clinging. I reached out and touched it. My hand came away sticky. Tentatively I sniffed it, and instantly recoiled. Blood. It took a second or two to process this, but when my brain caught up a wave of horror rippled through me, engulfing my body. I felt my face flush and my stomach sicken.

For a moment I stood there, swaying a little. I fought down the nausea and endured the hot sweat, and bit by bit I came back to myself. I let myself into the car and found a cloth in the glove compartment. I soaked it in a puddle and cleaned enough off to be able to see. Only then did it occur to me to look round the car park; but it was deserted, especially in this dark corner. I drove home, trying not to think, trying not to imagine a furtive figure with what? – a bowl of blood? a bag? – trying to persuade myself that it was some medical-student prank, knowing it was not. I parked outside my flat and let myself in, ran a washing-up bowl full of hot soapy water and scrubbed the sticky mess off my car. I was breathless when I'd finished, but although the car was clean I felt tainted, as if the blood was still clinging to my hands. Of course, I was used to blood: bright and fresh, gushing or oozing. But not like this – not used as a weapon.

Once the initial shock had passed a thought occurred to me: should I involve the police? But what are they going to say or do? I dismissed it, and a grim resolve that I would not be cowed rose up in me. I hadn't come so far in my career to be derailed by a vengeful maniac. Even so I found my every sense, that long evening, to be on high alert. Every sound had me sitting upright, listening. I wondered if I would sleep. Eventually I did; and nothing happened.

Nothing, that is, until about a week later, when that sense of alertness had dulled, when all my focus was back on my work. I'd just finished in the theatre for the day; in the morning I'd done an operation which should have been routine but which had developed complications, demanding fast thinking and a certain creativity on my part, and making it a much longer job. Eventually I sent the patient off to ICU in good shape, anticipating a full recovery. I was tired, feeling the day's efforts in the muscles of my shoulders and back, eager to get home and stand under a hot shower.

As I came down to the ground floor I was about to leave the building when a nurse at the desk called me over. "Ms Keyte! Someone left this for you." She indicated a square brown-paper-wrapped parcel. It was labelled simply "Ms R. Keyte" in black felt-tip and felt heavy when I picked it up. This was unusual, and I frowned. Then, as I started to wonder, a shudder ran through me. Surely not again…?

"Who delivered this?" I asked the nurse. "Did you see? Was it a woman? When was it?"

"About half an hour ago, I guess," she said, looking uncomfortable. "No, not a woman. It was a young lad, quite tall, wearing a grey jacket with a hood. Is something wrong?"

"No, no, it's OK." I forced myself to smile. "Thank you. Goodnight."

I drove home with the package on the passenger seat beside me. Once indoors I opened it, using a pair of sharp scissors to cut away the paper wrapping. As soon as I uncovered the white cardboard box inside I caught the smell – the unmistakable smell of rot and dead flesh. A tell-tale dark ooze was leaking from one corner of the box. Gingerly, trying not to gag, I cut away the lid. Inside, wrapped in a clear plastic bag, was a heart, sitting in a puddle of congealed blood, and it stank.

Of course I'd seen hearts before – hundreds of them. But it was not the heart, or the blood, or even the foul smell, that sent me flying to the bathroom to puke. It was the hate that came with it.

Later, when I had calmed down and poured myself a stiff reviving drink, I identified the offending thing as a pig's heart, easily sourced from any butcher in town. She – who else could it have been? – had left it to turn and rot before sending it to me. But there was no way I could trace it back to her. My enemy may have been crazy, but she was no fool.

I pondered what to do. I had to tell someone – this was unendurable. I rang Malcolm. I told him about the blood on my car, and now this repulsive parcel.

"It has to be her," I said. "No one else that I know hates me this much. I can't prove anything, of course. But what should I do?"

"Rachel, this is unbelievable," Malcolm said. "What did you say that time? Something about a 'bloody vendetta'? I brushed it off, didn't I? Dear heaven. Let me think." He was silent for a moment. "Look, the only thing I can think of at the moment is to contact Father Vincent. I know of no one else who can speak sense to Eve. I'll phone him, and I'll get back to you as soon as I have anything to report." He paused. "What about getting the police involved?"

"And say what? It's too flimsy. No, I don't want to go that route. Not till I absolutely have to."

He sighed. "It's your call."

As it happened it was a few days before Malcolm phoned me. In the interim I'd tried my best to carry on as if nothing was amiss, but it was far from easy. That smell seemed forever lodged in my nostrils, and there were times when, uncharacteristically, I lost my focus. One or two of my more perceptive colleagues may have noticed, but fortunately no patient suffered from my moments of inattention.

Eventually Malcolm phoned. "I spoke to Father Vincent. He was appalled, of course, but also cautious. Wanted to defend Eve, I suppose. Though how he could be in doubt I don't know, not after that display at the funeral. Anyway, he promised to speak to her. He's just got back to me, and even he is rattled. Apparently he went round to her house and she refused to let him in – unheard-of, according to him. She kept the door on the chain and only spoke to him through the opening. He couldn't see much, but he said the house was in darkness, and smelled airless and stale. Again, unheard-of – Eve Rawlins has always, to my knowledge, been very meticulous about hygiene, certainly while Craig was alive. They were both always spotlessly clean, if a little shabby. Anyway, she wouldn't open the door. She was reluctant even to speak to him. When he told her why he'd come, she became hostile. Said she'd been unwell, hadn't been out of the house since the funeral. He begged her to let him in, to let him help her. She said, 'No one can help me. Just go away and don't come back.' And she shut the door in his face."

I let my breath out. "What about those two friends of hers, the women who were with her at the funeral?"

"Ah, yes, I was coming to that. Father Vincent was at a loss, as you can imagine, and very worried. He went round to one of these ladies, and she said neither she nor her friend had seen Eve since the funeral. They'd tried to phone, but she'd never answered, and when one of them went to her house it seemed like there was no one in. They were on the point of contacting Father Vincent when he called."

"Is there anything we can do, then?"

"I don't know, Rachel. What if she's telling the truth? Is there anyone else you can think of that might have it in for you?"

"No," I said flatly. "It's her, Malcolm. It has to be."

I heard him sigh. "Let me think." After a moment he said, "Look, my plaster comes off in a day or two. I won't be able to be back at work just yet, but if I work hard at the physio it can't be too long, and Sefton's back now that his eyes are clear. Why don't you take a break, go on holiday, visit friends? We can cover your list."

I felt my old obstinacy rise then, and I was glad of it. Through the years of graft and struggle that tough core had served me well. "Not a chance," I growled. "Thanks for the thought, but some old harpy with a grudge and a sense of the dramatic isn't going to scare me away from my work with a repertoire of grisly parlour tricks. I'm staying."

I'd bought my flat about a year ago; I thought it was time I stopped renting, and it looked like I'd be staying at Porton West hospital for the time being. The flat was nothing special, just a springboard to jump off from: one bedroom, a sitting room, bathroom, and kitchen on the ground floor of a low-rise building with easy parking. It was convenient and warm, but I had no sentimental attachment to it: it was just a place to store my books and lay my head and a step on the property ladder. Even so, when I came home one evening and saw what had been done to it, I was sickened. And frightened, and horrified, and finally incensed. My front door had been white, the bricks beside it a sort of honey colour. No longer. Across the door and the wall had been sprayed, in huge red letters, "MURDERER!"

Swallowing down nausea, I let myself in. I packed a bag and left it in the hall for a moment. Then I crossed the patch of grass to the flat next door and rang the bell. I didn't really know my neighbours, but I knew a quiet, respectable elderly couple lived here. A small white-haired lady opened the door, still on a chain, and peered out cautiously.

"Hello," I said. "I'm Rachel Keyte from next door."

"Oh, yes, the doctor, from the hospital. Hello."

I hesitated. "I don't want to worry you, but I wondered if you'd seen any one hanging around, someone you didn't recognize."

She frowned. "No, I don't think so. We don't go out much. This weather… I'll ask George. Has something happened?"

"You could say that." I told her about my door, and she gasped. "Come and see if you like."

"Hold on a moment." She left me on the doorstep, and I heard muffled talk. A few minutes later she reappeared with her husband, a short, burly man. They'd both put on shoes and an overcoat.

They followed me the short distance to my flat and stood there shaking their heads, eyes wide.

"Look," I said, "there's nothing for you to worry about. This is directed at me alone. Someone with a grudge. The reason I've told you is that I'll be going away for a while and I'll need to organize someone to come and paint over it. I'll have to come back sometimes to get my post, or I might ask a friend to drop by. Just so you know."

The woman turned to me. "How terrible," she said. "There you are, trying to help people, save their lives, and this happens. We'll keep an eye open, won't we, George?"

"Thanks. I was going to ask you if you'd let me know if you see anything suspicious. I'll give you my mobile number." I gave them my card with my contact details. "I don't know how long I'll be away. Just as long as I need to sort out this mess." I indicated the door; but the mess was worse than that, of course. "Don't get cold," I said to them. "That wind's vicious." I smiled, I hoped comfortingly, and they trudged back into their flat, stopping at the door to wave.

I went back indoors and collected my bag. I closed the front door, and took several photos of the graffiti. Then I sat in my car and rang Beth. "Beth? Can I crash on your floor for a few days? I'll explain when I see you."

Beth had made up a bed for me in the room that was to be the nursery.

"You didn't need to go to all this trouble," I said. "The sofa would do."

She laid a hand on my arm. "Are you going to tell me what's going on?"

I showed her the photos of my front door, and she shrieked. "Oh, Rachel! This is horrible! Shouldn't you tell the police?"

"I haven't decided what to do yet. But she knows where I live – I had to get away. I need to find someone to paint the door, and I need to talk to Malcolm. I'm sorry I've had to involve you, but I didn't know where else to go."

"Don't be silly. You're welcome to stay – you know that. At least until the baby arrives. It might be a bit cramped then." She tried to smile, but her eyes were full of tears.

I took her arm. "Don't worry," I said. "We'll sort something out. Let's get a cup of tea – or coffee in my case – and talk about it calmly."

"Sorry." She wiped her face with her hands. "I'm a bit hormonal at the moment – can't think why." She laughed shakily.

We sat down with mugs and chocolate biscuits, and I rang Malcolm.

"Good grief, Rachel! I think it's time to involve the police, don't you? Where are you? You could have come here, you know."

"I thought of it, Malcolm, and thank you. But if she managed to find me, she can find you too. Where I am now I think she'll have a tough job."

He sighed. "All right. Look, I'll talk to Bridget. She'll know what's best; she always does. But Rachel, go to the police, please."

"Yes, I will. I'll call in tomorrow morning. I need to organize someone to paint over the door as well. But I've taken photos, so I've got evidence. I'll keep you posted."

The next day I visited the police station, a huge building with plate-glass everywhere. I thought it looked a bit like an aquarium. The entrance hall was vast, and completely deserted. Was there no crime in Porton? Inside a set of swing doors, a female in plain clothes looked up from an expansive desk. "Can I help you?"

"Yes. I need to talk to someone about my house being sprayed with an abusive slogan."

"Can I have your name?" she said to me.

"Rachel Keyte." I spelled it for her.

"Hold on, please." She picked up an internal phone and spoke into it.

She made a note. "Please take a seat. Someone will be down in a moment."

I waited for ten minutes or so, then a female officer in uniform trotted down an open staircase from the regions above. "Ms Keyte? Is that the correct pronunciation – to rhyme with 'feet'?" I said it was. "I'm PC Fellowes. Come with me, please."

She took me down a short corridor and into a small, bare room. "Sit down." I sat. "So what's this about your house?"

I explained about the graffiti, and showed her my photos. "I'm sure I know who did this," I said.

"Go on."

I told her about Craig, and about Eve Rawlins' wild threats at the funeral. "Since then, I've had my car daubed with blood, and I had a parcel delivered to the hospital containing a rotting pig's heart," I told her.

She made a face. "Nasty." She leaned forward across the desk. "Has anything like this happened before?"

"Never."

She was silent for a few minutes, her lips pursed. "Look, Ms Keyte, I understand this is very disturbing for you. But we have no proof that this woman is responsible, and until such time as this harassment goes beyond threats there's not a lot we can do."

I frowned. "She's defaced my property. And she knows where I live. I'm worried she'll do worse. I've had to leave my flat – I'm camping with a friend. I can't work like this." I saw her hesitate, and I ploughed on. "Are you telling me that she actually has to attack me before you'll do anything?"

"Let's hope it doesn't come to that. Look, I'll tell you what we'll do. I'll get someone to go round to her place – in uniform, in a police car. It might be enough to make her see sense. We can't accuse her of anything without concrete evidence, but we can ask her if she knows anything. Will that do?"

"I suppose it'll have to. I'll find out the address and let you know."

I made several phone calls from Beth's: first to someone Jimmy recommended to paint over the door, arranging to leave payment with the neighbours. It seemed a roundabout way of doing it, when I would normally just have made a bank transfer, but the painter was an older man who liked cash in hand, and I wasn't going to argue. Anyone else would probably not have been able to get it done so promptly. Then to Malcolm, to ask him to find out Eve Rawlins' address from Father Vincent. He got back to me within an hour, and I phoned the police station with the information. "Keep me posted, Rachel," Malcolm said. "We have an idea I want to run past you, but there are people we have to consult."

I went to work from Beth and Jimmy's. It wasn't ideal, but they lived close enough to the hospital for me to walk, so I could leave my car parked in their road. I hoped that with me gone, and my car absent from the hospital car park, Eve would give up the chase.

A few days later I asked Beth if she would go over to my flat to collect any post and ask the neighbours to see the painter was paid. I was expecting a package of some stuff I'd ordered from the internet and I didn't want it left outside. That day I decided to leave the hospital at lunchtime and work from Beth's. There was no need for me to stay at work, and somehow I felt safer hiding with Beth and Jimmy.

Beth opened the door to me. She seemed very pale.

"Are you all right?" I said.

"Yes." She answered automatically, then paused. "No, not really."

"What is it?"

"Take your coat off and I'll tell you." I followed her into the kitchen. She was making a batch of soup – vegetables were in the process of being chopped and peelings were littered all over the counter.

"Rach, I went over to yours," she said. "I called in on Mr and Mrs Chilton and asked them to pay the painter. I gave them the money and told them when to expect him. They asked after you. They seem nice people – offered me coffee, but I didn't want to stop. Then I let myself into your flat. Everything seemed OK, apart from the front door, of course. No gory messes on the doormat or anything. I checked everywhere."

"Thanks."

"But then, when I let myself out, I saw someone."

"What? Who was it?"

"I don't know. It was just for a moment. I didn't have time to get a good look. He or she – impossible to tell, but thin, and moved like a woman – I think – or it could have been someone quite young. He – or she – was just standing at the corner of the road, but it looked like they were watching the house. When I came out they scooted away, round the corner and out of sight. Like I said, it was just for a moment."

"You didn't get a look at their face? If it was her, you couldn't fail to notice the birthmark."

Beth seemed to sag. "No. They were wearing a kind of parka,

dark blue I think, with a hood. Fur round the edge, you know the kind of thing. The face was in deep shadow. I'm feeling a bit dodgy, Rach. Going to sit down."

I sat on the sofa beside her, holding her hand, till she felt a bit better. "I'm really sorry, Beth. I shouldn't have put you through that."

Beth shook her head. "You weren't to know. But if I tell Jimmy he'll say I'm not to go back. Not the way I am. I've only got five weeks to go. We don't want anything to happen."

"I don't want anything to happen either," I said softly. "Certainly not on my account. Jimmy is absolutely right. Don't let it get to you. I'll think of something."

Malcolm rang me the following evening. "Come and have a meal with us tomorrow, Rachel. Give Beth and Jimmy some space. Bridget has an idea."

The next day, when I got back from work, Beth said, "The police rang, Rach. PC Fellowes. Asked you to call her back." She glanced at the clock. "Ring her now, before she goes off duty." She gave me a scrap of paper with a number. "That's her direct line."

I lay on my makeshift bed in the nursery and rang the number. As I waited for an answer Beth tiptoed in with a cup of coffee. I mouthed my thanks. Then PC Fellowes answered. What she had to tell me chilled my blood, more than gruesome packages and inflammatory graffiti.

"We went to the address you gave us," she said. "Parked the car in full view of the neighbours. I went myself, with a brawny young constable for back-up. The lady you described answered the door. It was definitely her – no hiding that birthmark. She was charm itself – obliging, helpful. Invited us in, asked us if we'd like a cuppa. The house was immaculate and so was she."

"Good grief. Not what we thought."

"We asked her a few questions – did she know you? Yes, you were the surgeon who operated on her son. Did she remember her behaviour at her son's funeral? She became very solemn and said, yes, she'd behaved appallingly, she was very ashamed, but perhaps we could understand she wasn't in her right mind. She said she was going to write you a note of apology."

"I doubt that," I muttered.

"So then we asked her if she knew anything about the pig's heart, and the blood on your car, and the paint on your door, and she looked very shocked, and said she certainly didn't."

"She's some player. I almost admire her."

"You can see we can't really do anything. Perhaps it wasn't her. Even if it was, we have no evidence. She didn't deny what others had witnessed – her behaviour at the funeral. But as to everything else, she denied all knowledge. All I can say is, if anything happens to worry you, get back to us immediately. Until then…" she tailed off.

"Until then, I have to sprout an extra pair of eyes," I said sourly. "Capable of looking round corners."

"Just be extra careful," she said. "Don't go anywhere alone. You might think of getting one of those alarms some women carry."

"Maybe I will. Well – thanks." *For nothing*, I thought.

When I arrived at Malcolm and Bridget's it was clear that Bridget had made a special effort, far too much for an unimportant guest like me. I supposed it was Bridget's way of expressing solidarity. The table was immaculate with shining cutlery, linen napkins, and matching plates, in stark contrast to my usual custom of eating from a takeaway box with a book beside it.

"Whatever you're cooking smells amazing, Bridget," I said. "I hope you haven't gone to too much trouble."

Bridget was wearing a floral apron over her dress, and her hair, scraped back as always into a bun, was escaping in random tendrils round her face. She locked eyes with me, her expression serious. "Let me get this cooking finished," she said. "Then we'll talk."

An hour, three courses, and too many glasses of wine later, Bridget pushed back her chair with an air of ceremony. She turned to Malcolm. "Would you make the coffee, please, darling? Now that you've got the use of both arms. Rachel and I will sit in comfort in the lounge." She took my elbow and guided me in a quite determined manner to a large sofa, and she sat down opposite me.

I looked at her with a smile, my eyebrows raised. "So what's this idea of yours?"

She leaned forward, her hands on her knees. "I'm worried, Rachel. This Rawlins woman is clearly mad – perhaps not permanently so, but she obviously needs help, and it seems unlikely she'll accept it, not if she's denying all responsibility. And here you are, a senior surgeon at the hospital, having to sleep on your friend's floor!"

"It's not so bad," I said. "It reminds me a bit of camping with my dad and my brother when I was a kid."

"Well, it can't go on for ever, can it?" Bridget said firmly. "Your friend is about to have a baby, I hear. Rachel, you may be inclined to downplay all this nasty drama, but I think the chances of Eve Rawlins stopping all this of her own accord are very slim. I told a friend of mine the story – mentioning no names or specifics, of course – in fact I made out it was hypothetical. She's a psychologist at the university, and she said the incidents would almost certainly escalate. Eve Rawlins may be feeling almost invincible, triumphant even – it seems she's clever, so she'll know how far she can go without bringing retribution on herself." She shook her head. "Rachel, I really think you should get away from here, before she moves on to something far nastier than blood, a pig's heart, and a vandalized door."

Malcolm pushed open the lounge door with his foot and came in carrying a laden tray, which he set down carefully on the low table between me and Bridget. "And I agree," he said. "Get right away for a while – not necessarily for ever."

Bridget poured the coffee and handed me a cup.

"Such as where?" I said dubiously.

Malcolm sat in an armchair next to Bridget. "You're familiar with Brant Lyon Trust, aren't you?"

I frowned. "A bit. I did a stint there, six months or so, way back when I was a very humble house officer. Barely handled a scalpel in all that time. Is that where you want to exile me?"

Malcolm smiled. "It'd be a very nice exile, and you'd definitely get to handle a scalpel. My opposite number at Brant is a man called Peter Axton. You won't have met him; he wasn't in post when you did your six months there. He's a fine surgeon and a good friend, Rachel. And he's been after head-hunting you for quite a while."

"Really?" I was amazed. "You never said."

"I had no desire to lose you if I didn't have to. But now things are different. We have a full team here, given that I'll be back in harness soon, and Sefton's over his infection. There are one or two good people coming through the system too. And you, I believe, are under threat. I'd hate anything to happen to you just because we cravenly did nothing. You're an excellent surgeon, one of the best, with years of hard work and study behind you, and you should be working in a safe environment without unnecessary stress."

"You're our friend too," Bridget added. "We don't want to see you hurt."

"I don't know what to say," I said. "You guys seem to have it all worked out."

"Think about it, Rachel. It makes a lot of sense, practically as well as professionally."

"But…where would I live?" I struggled to get my head round the details. "Brant is quite a long way away. A hundred miles, isn't it? More? Give or take?"

"What is there here to keep you, in the circumstances?" Malcolm pressed on. "Your flat's just a place to sleep, as far as

I can gather. You could let it out. What friends do you have in Porton West, apart from us, and the friends you're staying with?"

"No one," I murmured. "There's my mother, but she won't miss me."

"And you've always said she's well cared for in that home she's in," Bridget said. "Look, Rachel, what Malcolm hasn't mentioned is that Peter and Angela Axton are very good friends of ours from way back. There was a time when we went on holiday together, when our children were young. We've always kept in touch. I spoke to Angela on the phone yesterday. She and Peter have a lovely place by the river, just walking distance from the hospital…"

"Which is a centre of excellence as far as cardiac surgery is concerned," Malcolm interrupted. "You knew that, I dare say. It's a research centre too, so some very nice equipment…"

"Hold on, Malcolm," Bridget said. "I need to tell Rachel about my conversation with Angela." She turned back to me. "Peter and Angela had some kind of an outbuilding converted into a little… well, a flat, I suppose – in the garden, just across from their own house, very close, for Peter's mother, who was elderly and disabled in some way, I'm not sure exactly how. She died last year. Their daughter sometimes uses it, but she's at university now, like our boys, and it stands empty. Angela said you could use it if you like, until you find yourself another place – or more permanently if you preferred – at a peppercorn rent. It's very convenient, and you'd be quite independent." She paused for breath.

"I'm dazed," I said slowly. "A few weeks ago I was pursuing my career in familiar surroundings. I had things sorted out the way I liked them. And now it seems I'm going to be some kind of refugee."

"Hardly that," Malcom said. "Think of it as an opportunity – it'll look good on your CV. A new set of colleagues to dazzle. I'll be sorry to let you go, but Peter will be crowing. And perhaps it won't be for ever. This nonsense might blow over, given time."

We were all silent for a moment, sipping our coffee.

"You're both very kind," I said, "to take such trouble."

"At least think about it," Bridget said. "Perhaps talk to your friends. See what they say."

"Yes." I paused; there was a lot for me to process. "Yes, I will. I'll think. And I'll let you know."

On Thursday, my day off, I had Beth and Jimmy's place to myself all morning. Beth had an antenatal appointment, and Jimmy was seeing his PhD supervisor. I made myself comfortable with a large cup of coffee and a slice of cake made by Beth, and settled down to clear a backlog of emails, mostly routine things.

Beth came back around midday and collapsed onto the sofa with a groan.

"I'm glad I'm not an elephant," she said. "Forty weeks is way too long." She patted her distended belly fondly. "You're getting big and heavy, my son or daughter. Nearly time to get born."

"Everything going OK?" I asked.

"Yeah, I think so." She struggled to get up. "I'll get us some lunch."

"No you won't," I said sternly. "I'll do the honours. Just let me finish this." I sent the last email and closed down my computer. "Done and dusted."

"You know, Rach, I've been wondering," Beth said thoughtfully. "This plan of the Harries' – how on earth is Malcolm going to swing it? Don't these things require paperwork and applications and interviews and what-not? I mean, normally people don't just up sticks and go and work elsewhere, do they? At short notice?"

"I don't know exactly what Malcolm has up his sleeve," I said. "I do know he's well connected with the powers-that-be at the hospital. He's on loads of boards and so on. He's probably in with the CEO. I've got a lot of annual leave left as well. But the two hospitals are partners, aren't they? Along with some clinics and specialist centres and dental practices, I think. So maybe that will make it easier. Perhaps there'll be some kind of job-swap – maybe one of Brant's cardiac team will come here. Whatever happens, I'm quite sure Malcolm will find a way."

"What it is to have influence, eh?"

"Indeed. Do you want lunch now? Should I do some for Jimmy?"

"In a minute, and yes, definitely. I don't know where Jimmy puts it all! He says he's eating for two."

I smiled. "He would. He's a good guy, Beth. You're lucky. But so is he!"

"Mm, very true." Beth looked at me, her head on one side. "Don't you ever feel you'd like to be with someone, Rachel?"

"No."

Beth burst out laughing. "Just like that – 'No'? Are you sure? I seem to remember a time when you might have thought differently."

"Ugh, that was ages ago. And I'm sure I made the right decision."

"You were on the point of getting married, weren't you?"

I shook my head. "That's a bit of an exaggeration," I said. "Fact is, he asked me if I would. I said 'yes', but then after a while I saw it couldn't possibly work, and I called it off, at which point he went off in a massive huff."

"I've forgotten his name."

"Howard. Howard Franks, and he was a budding obstetrician."

"So he was. And you broke his heart."

"I think it was more a case of deflated ego, actually."

"Didn't you feel even a bit tempted?" Beth asked.

I shrugged. "Possibly for about half an hour. But then I saw how it would be. Howard was not the guy for me. Maybe there is no such creature. But even if he was the world's most perfect partner, he'd still be a huge distraction. I knew that if I went along with his plans, my own would be in the bin."

"It doesn't have to be that way, you know."

"Maybe not for most people. But I want to be a consultant before I'm forty. I've come a long way, and it's been tough. I love my work. It's what makes me feel... I don't know, useful, fulfilled, whatever. And I've still got a way to go. A man in my life would just deflect me from that. And I never met anyone who'd be worth shelving my career for."

"Aren't you ever lonely, though?"

"Nope. Too knackered when I get back from hours of surgery."

"Work isn't everything, Rach."

"Mine is, for me."

"So what about after you're a consultant? Don't you ever want children? What about later, when you're retired? No family, no one to look after you in your dotage..."

I laughed. "I don't plan ever to *be* in my dotage. And you can have six kids and still be on your own. They have to live their own lives, don't they? If I ever retire I'll travel, I think. Anyway" – I jumped up from my chair – "you never know, once I get my consultancy and I've enjoyed it all for a year or two, maybe I'll have a couple of kids. Who knows? Time for lunch? Shall I warm up some soup?"

Beth heaved herself up and followed me into the tiny kitchen. "That's all very well, but presumably you need to find someone to have children with, and that doesn't happen overnight. And you'll be in your forties, Rach – menopausal, even."

I put my arm round her shoulders. "Don't you worry about me, mother hen," I said. "If I feel the lack of young company I'll come over and borrow your little treasure."

We'd had a similar conversation before, and I hadn't changed my mind. Perhaps the Howard fiasco had made me even more sceptical about the prospect of a permanent relationship than I might otherwise have been; but that my work was all-important to me was still very much the case, and I wasn't going to do anything to damage my upward journey. One thing I wouldn't say to Beth: it had been harder for me to succeed in cardiothoracic surgery because of my gender, not just because of entrenched prejudice but also because I'd had to fight my own tendency to be distracted – and that, I believed, was the experience of many women. I realized early on that I seemed hard-wired to think about several things at once. In some ways this is important for a surgeon, but total concentration and focus is also essential, and acquiring that has been one of my hardest won skills over the years. I couldn't afford to be thinking about what to cook for dinner or a child's illness or having to get the shopping or take my coat to the cleaner's. I had to keep my life simple and under control so that my ambition might flourish; and I was more than willing to make the personal sacrifices that this involved.

Beth, however, was clearly not finished with me. I moved my laptop and a pile of papers and we sat at the table in the corner of the lounge which also served as a dining room and ate warm crusty bread dipped in Beth's home-made soup. "We need people like me to fix hearts," I said between mouthfuls. "And people like you to make soup and cakes."

"Excuse me," Beth said sternly. "I can do a bit more than that. As you well know."

"Just kidding."

"Hm. Actually, though, while we're still vaguely talking about men and so on, Jimmy and I know someone who works at Brant Lyon."

"Oh?"

"Yeah, Jimmy shared a flat with him when they were students. He's not a medic – he's an IT genius, I think. Works in hospital admin. Nice guy, and very good-looking as I recall." She looked over at me and grinned.

"Honestly, Beth, you never give up, do you?"

"Well," she protested, "you might need a friend. You're starting a whole new chapter. Sometimes it's nice to know someone when you move to a new place."

I groaned. "And the name of this wonder-guy?"

"Rob. Rob Harker. Shall I give you his number?"

"You can, but I won't be ringing him."

"Can I give him yours, then?"

"I suppose so, if you really must. Now, can we change the subject?"

Our light-hearted mood evaporated with sobering suddenness when Jimmy arrived home an hour later. He came in quietly, put his bag on the table, and sat down with Beth on the sofa. There was none of his usual clattering entrances and loud hails.

"What's up?" Beth said. "Rough supervision?"

Jimmy put his arm round her shoulders and drew her close, all the while looking at me. "Rachel, not good news," he said.

I sat up. Something cold seemed to clench my stomach. "Tell me, Jim."

"Coming home just now, there was someone crouching by your car."

"What – not her?"

Jimmy shook his head. "A young guy in a grey hoody. When I challenged him, he scarpered. I didn't get to see his face clearly."

I blew out my breath. "The same kid that delivered the bloody heart, I guess. I wonder who he is."

"Who he is doesn't really matter, does it?" Jimmy said. "The point is, they know where you are – or at least where your car is."

"Oh, Rachel!" Beth wailed, her eyes round. "What are we going to do?"

I got up. "What I am going to do, my dear friend," I said, trying not to show the dread I felt, "is depart. I can't stay here and involve you and Jimmy in my troubles any more. I'm really grateful to the two of you for putting me up. But since I have nowhere else to go, I'll have to go along with Malcolm's plan. That's if he's managed to organize it."

"But where will you go now?" Beth said, her voice low and husky.

"Back to my flat. If my car's not here, there'll be no reason for anyone to bother you. I'll start putting a few things in the car ready to leave, once I've spoken to Malcolm. If it's all sorted I'll go tomorrow. Even if it isn't, I can't stay here."

Beth hauled herself up from the sofa, came over to me, and enveloped me in a hug. "Rach, I'm so sorry this had to happen to you. It's so unfair."

"Seems to me it's just bizarre," I said, hugging her back. "I'm convinced Eve Rawlins has tipped over the edge. Someone needs to help her." I disentangled myself, smiling down at Beth. "I'll go and get my stuff. Don't worry about me, Beth. I'll survive."

"I don't like you being in your flat on your own, even for one night," Beth said. "Jimmy will come and keep you company, won't you, love?"

I shook my head. "There's no need. I'll let you know I'm OK in the morning before I leave." A thought struck me. "One thing, though: Jim, could you send on any post? I'll let you know the address when I get there."

"Yeah, sure, Rachel. No problem. I'll keep an eye on your flat at the same time."

"Thanks – for everything. You two have been great." I paused in the doorway. "And of course I'll be wanting to know your news. Can't believe it's only just over a month, if the baby's on time."

As I drove across town that afternoon, I won't deny that I was apprehensive. But somehow all the long years of work and self-discipline helped. In the past, when something had gone wrong – when I had messed up, or when someone had behaved badly towards me, or at moments of disappointment, or when some perceived injustice had been perpetrated – I'd turned it all to work, to experience, to building myself up as a surgeon and as a person. Some would say, no doubt, that it had made me hard, and maybe they were right. Now I was glad of that core of stubbornness. I wasn't going to run away scared; I'd go because I saw the need and I'd go in my own time. Nevertheless, I admitted to myself that I'd be glad when the morning came and I could be on my way, as far from this mess as I could get.

Meanwhile I decided that a little theatre might help, as much to convince myself as anyone else. I parked outside the flat with no attempt at concealment, slamming my car door shut, even humming with apparent insouciance. I went directly next door and rang the Chiltons' doorbell. When George Chilton answered the door I spoke to him much more loudly than I would normally do, laughing and joking with him as if nothing whatever was amiss in my life. I told him – and his wife, who came to the door when she heard my voice – that I was taking some long overdue holiday. "If I don't hurry and use my leave, I'll lose it. Can't have that! So I just thought I'd let you know I won't be around for a while."

"That'll be nice for you," Mrs Chilton said. "After all the trouble you've been having."

"Oh," I said airily, "that's all over now, I think." I looked over at my flat, seeing the once-again white front door. "The painter's been, then. Good. I said I wanted it done as soon as possible. Thank you for handling that for me – I appreciate it."

"That's all right," Mrs Chilton said. "So where are you off to? Somewhere nice and warm?"

I'd thought I might be asked this and I allowed myself a small lie. "Not sure just yet. I'll be touring round in this country for a week or two, and then, as I've got so much time owing, I might go abroad. Perhaps I'll send you a postcard!" I laughed loudly, as if I had made a hilarious joke. "Anyway, if you see a well-built black guy coming round, don't worry. That's my friend Jimmy, who's going to send on any mail. He'll know how to get hold of me if there's any emergency, and he'll deal with any problems with the flat if something comes up – a broken gutter or something."

Mr Chilton frowned. "Sounds like you plan to be away for some time."

"Quite a few weeks, probably," I said. "It'll be nice to get away with the spring."

With that, and more thank yous and goodbyes, I let myself into my own flat. It smelled dusty and airless, and I threw open a few windows while daylight lasted. I took out my largest suitcase from the wardrobe, and a rucksack I hadn't used since student days, and filled them with everything I thought I might need – clothes, shoes, books. I owned very little, and when I'd finished the flat looked bare. As dusk was falling I took my bags out to the car and loaded them into the boot. I looked up and down the road as the streetlights came on. It had always been a quiet area, and there was no one about.

I went back indoors, washed my hands, and rang Malcolm. "I'm leaving tomorrow," I said without preamble. I told him about the boy lurking round my car. "That means I've got nowhere to go here. I don't want to cause any trouble for my friends, not when they've been so good to me. So what's the deal with Brant Lyon?"

"I'm working on it, Rachel," he said. "Got a meeting the day after tomorrow to thrash out the details. But that needn't worry you, even if we can't get you to work straight away. You can take that overdue holiday, get settled in with the Axtons, reacquaint yourself with Brant. One thing, though…" he hesitated.

"What?" I realized from my sharp response that despite my determination not to let this thing get to me, I was nevertheless on high alert. I unclenched my fists.

"What would help," Malcom said slowly, as if with reluctance, "is if you'd visit your GP before you go."

"What for?"

"In the circumstances, you could get signed off for stress. That would account for the need for haste."

It took me a few seconds to process this. "Absolutely not a chance, Malcolm. Sorry." But I wasn't. I was furious. Not with Malcolm, but with Eve Rawlins. I wasn't going to let her, or the fear of her, of what she might do next, take over my life any more than I absolutely had to. "I'm not having being signed off for stress on my medical records. It looks bad, weak, as if I can't cope. Sorry if that is no help to you, but I plan to protect my reputation. Eve Rawlins can go to hell, frankly."

"I understand you're angry, Rachel," Malcolm said quietly. "But hell is almost certainly where Eve Rawlins is right now." I said nothing, allowing the heat of my feelings to die down. Malcolm sighed. "All right; I'll do my best to sort things out this end. You just get away."

"Yes, I will. First thing. I've spoken to the neighbours, and Jimmy's going to send on my post and keep an eye on the flat. I'll make sure I keep in touch. And Malcolm – thank you. For everything."

If I'd had any doubt about the wisdom of my decision, that night dispelled it. I'd left my car parked brazenly under a streetlight for anyone to see; and I suppose somebody did, along with the lights on in the flat. Who, I didn't know, nor did I see a living soul.

I phoned out for a takeaway, and a van duly turned up and delivered it. Having eaten it and thrown away the wrappings, I reminded myself to put the rubbish out in the morning. Sleeping in cramped conditions at Beth and Jimmy's hadn't been ideal, and I was tired. I went to bed early, and despite the feverish workings of my thoughts I fell asleep quickly.

I was woken by the shrilling of my landline. This was a rarity in itself; I hardly ever used it. I surfaced from the fog of sleep, not understanding, for a moment, what the sound was. As I realized, it stopped. I looked at the clock on my bedside table: ten past four. Who would ring me on my landline in the small hours? If it wasn't a wrong number, there was only one answer to my question. I felt a chill creep up from stomach to throat. Then the ringing started again. I got out of bed, threw on a dressing-gown, and padded to the hallway where the phone was mounted on the wall. Swallowing my surge of dread, I picked the handset up. "Hello?"

For a moment there was silence, then a quiet click and the dialling tone. I put the handset back with a shaking hand. Immediately the phone started ringing again. I snatched it from the wall, killed the call, and left it off the hook. For a few minutes I stood there, trying to control my shuddering. I was cold, but at the same time sticky with sweat. I took a deep breath, then another, forcing myself to breathe naturally, trying to be calm.

Chilled, I decided to take a warm shower before going back to bed. At least no one could call me on my landline tonight. I stood under the warm, soothing water, feeling it flow down my body, imagining it taking my troubles with it down the drain. I was stepping out of the shower, reaching for a towel, when I heard a loud bang, unnervingly close. I felt my skin tingle with fright. Quickly I towelled myself down and put my bathrobe back on. Then I opened the bathroom door gingerly, holding my breath. I padded barefoot and silent into my bedroom and stood in the doorway, my stomach lurching sickeningly. My window was wide open, the curtains rippling in the night breeze. Was it possible I hadn't shut that window properly as darkness fell? My bedroom overlooked a grassy area at the back of the flats. I tiptoed over to the window and twitched the curtain back, standing so that I couldn't be seen. Here it was darker, the streetlights more widely spaced; but there was nothing, no lurking intruder, no threatening shadow. I closed and locked the window. I went into the lounge, which overlooked the street, and peered out. There was my car, under the streetlight. No menacing figures under the hedge. I checked the window and closed the curtains, letting out my breath – until that moment I hadn't known I was holding it in.

Obviously I hadn't shut the window properly. That was my thought – until I went back to the bathroom to get another towel for my hair. On the other side of the bathroom was another door, to an airing cupboard. On this, unnoticed before as I'd gone to the bedroom, in red spray paint, that one word again: MURDERER. The shock of it sent me lurching into the bathroom where I puked into the toilet.

Eventually I sat back on my heels, my brain reeling, my throat harsh from vomiting, a foul taste in my mouth, my heart pounding. Someone, while I was showering, had been in my flat – someone who wanted, at the very least, to terrify me.

The thought of going back to the police did cross my mind. Now they'd have to take it seriously, surely? Someone with evil intent had actually broken into my house. Anything might have happened. But nothing *had* happened. And at that moment all I wanted to do was get away from Eve Rawlins and put her behind me, once and for all.

I managed to get to my feet. I swilled my mouth out with water at the tap. Then I hunted through every room. My flat isn't big: bedroom, lounge, kitchen, bathroom. There was nobody, of course. They were long gone. I checked the door and the windows: all secure.

I made myself a cup of coffee and sat all the rest of that long night in an armchair in the lounge, dozing and twitching awake and dozing again, pursued by chaotic dreams, until at last the thin light of dawn shone into my weary eyes and woke me to the grim reality of my life.

It was still far too early to set out, because I knew there was somewhere I had to go before I could truly escape. Exhausted, barely caring if every lunatic and hooligan in the city were on my doorstep, I fell back into bed and slept. By the time I awoke it was after nine. I had another shower and forced down a piece of toast. Then I rang the Harries' number.

Bridget answered. "Hello, Rachel dear, how are you?"

"Fine, thanks, Bridget," I lied. "I'll be leaving soon, but I may not go straight to Brant today. I forgot to ask you for the Axtons' phone number. I might need to ring them."

"Of course." She reeled off the number and I stored it in my phone. "Good luck, Rachel. I do hope and pray this will be a good move for you. We'll miss you, of course."

"You've been more than kind, Bridget. I guess Malcolm's at work. Say goodbye for me, won't you?"

On Friday 16 March I left Porton for Brant. I took the A road as far as the turn-off that led to the sheltered flats where my mother lived. I had no idea how long my exile might last; and whatever happened I was unlikely to be keeping the next monthly appointment. I had no great desire to see my mother but thought I'd better tell her that I wouldn't be around for a while, even though I felt certain that she wouldn't welcome an unscheduled visit. True to lifelong habit, she still preferred to be well prepared – hair done, makeup immaculate, on top of her form. *Too bad*, I thought. *It's now or never.* I glanced at my reflection in the wing mirror as I parked outside the building and gave a bitter little smile. *At least she'll have something to comment on – I look a wreck.*

I made myself known to the concierge and went to the large lounge where I thought mother would be holding court over morning coffee. There she was, sitting at a round table with several of her permed and cardiganed cronies, playing cards. She had her back to me, and I heard her say in her usual plummy and ringing tones, "Doris, dear, it's your turn. Do keep up."

At this point the woman opposite looked up and saw me, and her jaw dropped. "Frances, it's Rachel, your dau –"

Mother cut her off. "I'm trying to concentrate here, Edna," she said severely.

I pulled up a chair and squeezed in between Mother and the woman beside her, who obligingly and with the sweetest smile moved sideways to accommodate me. "Morning, ladies. Morning, Mother."

To say she was surprised would be an understatement –

her expression was more horrified. "Good heavens!" she said, gathering herself. "What on earth are *you* doing here?"

"Sorry to intrude, Mother," I said with heavy sarcasm. "Sorry, ladies, to interrupt your game. I thought I'd better come and say goodbye. I'm going away."

My mother frowned, as only she can do. I remember, as a child, thinking of her frowns like black clouds massing on the horizon. "Oh. And what about your *work*?" How anyone could load that small word with so much disdain has always amazed me. I honestly believe she thinks me barely better than a butcher with a side of beef.

"I'm taking some leave," I said. "I haven't had a holiday in a long time, so I have a lot left."

"I see." She looked at me up and down. "You certainly do seem... well, a bit ragged. Exhausted, I dare say. In need of rest. Not to mention a good hairdresser. So where are you going? And how long will you be away?"

"I don't know yet, to both questions," I said. "So if you need to contact me you'll have to use my mobile number."

One of the ladies cut in. "Rachel, wouldn't you like some coffee? I'm sure there's some in the pot."

"Thank you, Doris, I'd love some."

Doris got up and bustled away to where the cups and saucers and coffee pot stood on a nearby table. My mother tutted under her breath. Her card game was not to be interrupted – especially as she was winning, judging by the small pile of coins by her elbow. And clearly she had no plans to be upstaged. As Doris returned and put a cup of coffee in front of me my mother said abruptly, and loudly, "You're not pregnant, are you?"

She never fails to wrong-foot me, even now when I am no longer a tongue-tied child. "What?"

Some of the other ladies gasped and tittered. Mother was wearing the blackest of disapproving frowns, but suddenly, like the sun after a spring shower, it cleared, and she laughed, her expression all sweetness and charm. "Oh but no, of course you aren't! You don't have time for such frivolities as men friends, do you? Silly me!"

Doris – braver than most – murmured, "Now, Frances, do behave! Rachel has come to say goodbye. Be nice."

"My dear! When am I not?" Mother turned to me and patted my hand. Her rings were heavy and scratchy. "Keep in touch, then, dear. Have a nice trip. We'll no doubt see you at some point."

"No doubt," I repeated. I shook my head. Truly, she was impossible. I downed my coffee. "Cheerio, then, ladies," I said, pushing my chair back. "Nice to see you all looking so well." They chorused goodbye. "Cheerio, Mother," I murmured, and bent and brushed her powdery cheek with my lips. "Keep up the good work."

I left, duty done.

I decided to leave the main highway for less frequented, and more rural, roads. Up till now I'd barely registered the arrival of spring; now as I drove at a steady pace I noted daffodils in gardens, and trees in bud. After an hour or so I felt my concentration slipping, and I realized just how tired I was. I had an idea that somewhere along this road was one of those cheap hotels where you don't need to book and which offer a clean, characterless room with coffee-making facilities and complete anonymity. At that moment the notion of fresh white sheets, coupled with the radical possibility of turning off my phone, was little short of heavenly. True enough, at the third roundabout the place I remembered appeared on the right-hand side. I indicated, slowed, and turned into the car park. For a while I simply sat, almost nodding off as I listened to the ticking of the engine as it cooled. With an effort I gathered up a few necessities in a supermarket carrier bag, locked the car, and went inside. There were plenty of rooms, and after a bit of form-filling I found myself in one of them, no doubt identical to hundreds more across the country. I made a cup of coffee and put it on the bedside table. Then I flopped down onto the bed, feeling the mattress give beneath me and mould to my weary limbs.

I awoke more than three hours later, and for a moment I had no idea where I was. When I remembered I also recalled what had driven me here. I was glad to be away from it, but at the same time I felt adrift: cut loose from my normal moorings of work and routine tasks, from everything that had given me purpose and a sense of who I was. It was a strange thought that nobody knew my whereabouts – stranger still, that even I didn't really know either.

Putting aside this disturbing and unproductive train of thought I heaved myself off the bed and went in search of food. There was a pub on the site and I bought a sandwich and a glass of juice and found a quiet corner. Apart from the large and rather sleepy barmaid the place seemed deserted, and it added to my sense of dislocation. It was almost as if I was a survivor of some global disaster which had left the world intact but robbed it of life.

Back in the room I keyed in the number that Bridget had given me. A bright, friendly voice answered after just a few rings. "The Pines, Angela Axton speaking."

I introduced myself and had a brief conversation with Angela Axton. We arranged that if she had to go out she would leave a key to the flat under a white flowerpot. I could arrive when I liked.

The sense of dislocation faded, and I began to feel free. It was an odd, unfamiliar feeling.

In the late afternoon I checked out of the hotel and drove on through the countryside. A bank of cloud blew in from the west, bringing squally rain and premature darkness. Wanting to take the journey slowly, I found another, similar hotel and checked in, this time taking my backpack with me. I showered and ate dinner in the hotel restaurant, content with my own company and looking forward to sleep, uninterrupted and peaceful. As I got back to my anodyne room my mobile rang, and I was reminded that the world was never very far away, however hard I strove to escape from it.

A familiar voice, as clear as if it were in the same room, standing beside me: "Hey, Lizzie! How're you doing?"

Only one person in this world calls me Lizzie: my brother Martin. Dad used to call me this too, a long time ago. He told me he wanted me to be named Elizabeth – he was a great supporter of the monarchy – but Mother wouldn't have it. She wanted Rachel after some thespian idol of hers, so Elizabeth was relegated to second place; but for me, Lizzie is the name of a loved and cherished child, and hearing it brought tears to my weary eyes.

"Hey, bro! Where are you?"

A brief pause, then a throaty chuckle: "New Zealand. About to get on a very small boat."

"What's the time there?"

"Whoa, I dunno… just after ten in the morning."

"So what's all this? Why the honour of a phone call?"

"Ha, well, I've been talking to our beloved parent. Says you've taken off somewhere."

"You make it sound like I've gone walkabout. Just taking some overdue holiday, that's all."

"OK, as long as you're all right."

"Of course I am." I spoke brightly, and hoped he didn't hear how false it was.

"Gotta go, sorry; the skipper is waving to me, looks a bit agitated. I'll call you again when I get settled."

"OK. Good to hear your voice! Bye."

I lay on the bed, propped up by pillows, and thumbed through the photos on my phone. I knew it was probably not a good idea, but I did it anyway. There weren't many, because I rarely took any; but there was one I'd kept, of Martin the last time I'd seen him, almost two years ago.

In the photo he was leaning up against a bollard, a bulging backpack slung over one shoulder, and at his back a sparkling sea. He'd come back to the UK for a short while, and we'd gone to the seaside for the day and pretended to be kids again. I zoomed in on his smiling face. His eyes were – are – bright blue, his wayward hair very fair, his stubble slightly ginger. Apart from being built on a slightly smaller scale, he is a dead ringer for our father, and that's my problem. I have no photos of our father himself. I am sure that if I asked my mother for one she would hoot with laughter and make me feel like an idiot, and I can't risk undoing my armour even one chink when she's around. She'd be in for the kill with whoops of glee.

I don't know why I sought that photo of Martin, when reminding myself of Dad is so uselessly painful. Just sometimes I feel, perhaps masochistically, impelled to bring Dad back, even though it's not him at all, and remember the laughing six-foot Viking who so dominated my childhood and then left me bereft. Perhaps this time it was because I felt so unreal; perhaps because in this anonymous wasteland between two lives I had little to lose and could be free, for a while, to be that naïve and vulnerable kid again. But these memories, though so old, were still raw, bringing up painful sobs that hurt my chest and stung my eyes to blindness.

Apart from my mother, nobody really knew how it had been when my dad finally gave up the struggle. Martin is five years older than me, and he was away at college for most of that time. I'm sure he was concerned, but his freedom was precious, and he wasn't going to risk losing it. I was not even fifteen, and had nowhere to go. Even now, Martin's chosen career – as a wildlife photographer – took him all over the world, and he was rarely at home – wherever that was. As far as I knew he had no partner, no settled roots, and no desire for any of the usual things people work for. We couldn't have been more different; and yet there was, despite everything, a bond of sibling solidarity between us, and perhaps he, like me, had decided to bury his memories of Dad very deep where no one could trample on them.

One day, I thought. Perhaps one day I'll take Dad out of that mental closet and say hello. Maybe one day I can empty all pain and anguish out of my thoughts of him, and survey them with calm. One day.

PART TWO

BRANT LYON

The first time I came to, in an unfamiliar room full of shadows, I was calm, no doubt drugged to the gills. From a distance I was aware that I had no idea where I was, but it didn't seem to matter. My eyes closed all by themselves, and my brain shut down with them.

The second time consciousness was sharper, and as I tried to focus my eyes a wave of panic shot through me. I heard a shout, and I wasn't sure if it came from me. Someone came into the room and spoke softly – a woman. "Hush, Rachel; don't worry, you're OK. Go back to sleep." I opened my mouth to answer, but nothing happened. She laid a hand gently on my shoulder. "Not time to wake up yet," she whispered. I obeyed, because I couldn't do anything else.

The third time I opened my eyes, I knew where I was, and my body prickled with fright. The skin of my face felt tight and stretched. Behind me thin curtains let in morning light, and I could see the room – a familiar room, complete with a familiar smell, recognizable anywhere, and for a medic, home from home. I was in hospital, but what hospital, and why? I seemed incapable of moving my head, but I swivelled my eyes and saw the dripstand and a monitor with blinking lights. This time I know I cried out, wordlessly, a moan of utter terror, fuelled by incomprehension.

The door opened, and a nurse came in, perhaps the same one that had soothed me hours – minutes? months? – before. Or had I dreamed that? "All right, Rachel, you're awake."

She looked at the monitor, checking, then back at me. Her eyes were light brown.

I tried to speak, but my voice was harsh and my throat hurt. "What – where? What happened?"

"You don't remember? Don't try to talk, Rachel. Best if you rest, try to sleep again. Mr Wells will be along later. I'll give you something for pain."

Pain? Yes, now I felt it: a stinging within the tightness in my face. I tried to lift my hand to touch my cheek, but it wouldn't move.

"Whoa, try to keep still," the nurse said. She put an arm behind my shoulders and gently raised me up. "Just drink this. It'll help." She put a small plastic cup to my lips and tipped a pink viscous liquid into my mouth. I choked a bit, and swallowed. She wiped a dribble from my chin. "There."

Before she let me down again I saw them – my hands, resting on the white sheet, immobilized by bandages and plaster splints. I looked up at the nurse, my eyes wide and frantic. "What –?"

"Try not to get upset, Rachel. Sleep now. Mr Wells will talk to you later. Try not to worry."

When she closed the door behind her, wild ungoverned thoughts raced through my mind. Why are my hands bandaged? Why can't I move them? What's wrong with my face? Am I in the grip of some horribly real nightmare? Have I lost my reason? And who the heck is Mr Wells?

***

I had a week, maybe ten days, when I first arrived at Brant before the authorization came through and I was allowed to start work. Malcolm had obviously been busy, but no doubt there were rules and protocols to be followed. I didn't bother even to think about them; I focused on preparing for the new life I had been forced to adopt. I was determined to make the best of it, to climb and shine and conquer. It was the only way I knew to be, and so far it had served me well enough.

The granny-flat which the Axtons had lent me was more homely than I was used to with its comfortable lounge, galley kitchen, bedroom, and bathroom. Their house, a sprawling building with two wings, was set in an acre of garden whose lush lawns sloped down towards the bank of the river that wound slowly round the city. On the other side, across water-meadows dotted with trees and ponds, stood the hospital – a huge futuristic edifice of glass and steel. I could walk to work, across one of a number of little bridges, some alarmingly rickety, and along footpaths frequented by cyclists and dog-walkers; the car was no longer a necessity and at the Axtons' invitation I parked it in one of their empty outbuildings.

From the beginning Peter and Angela Axton were perfect hosts: friendly, thoughtful, but never pushy. From Angela's comments I got the clear impression that I was regarded as some kind of visiting dignitary, which was both amusing and uncomfortable. It could only have been Malcolm's work, bumping up my reputation. It was evident also that they knew why I was there, but they were discreet. Early on Angela said something like, "Naturally, Bridget mentioned your trouble back at Porton. A shocking thing! But you needn't worry: Peter and I won't be spreading any gossip. As far as everyone else is concerned you've been headhunted for the department for an unspecified term." The vagueness of my appointment must have added to my mystique; there were to be moments when I felt like some kind of cardiothoracic celebrity.

I spent the first few days exploring the city, on foot and on Angela's bicycle. I hadn't been back since my brief stay there as a student, and quite a lot had changed. Here, further east, spring was later in coming, and it was still cool, but as the month wore on the grass grew greener and the spring flowers opened as a weak sun shone. For the first time in weeks I felt safe, and I knew that as soon as I was into the swing of work I would be focused and content.

Before this happened Angela phoned one morning – she was always polite and never called round uninvited – to ask me if I would like to go with her and Peter to a reception at the hospital to say goodbye to a team of visiting researchers from somewhere in Africa. "It'll give you a chance to meet some of the people here at Brant before you are far too busy with work," she said. "We can introduce you to some of them. But we'll quite understand if you'd rather not." I wasn't at all keen. Socializing with colleagues had never been my cup of tea, and here I knew no one. But I felt it would be rude to the Axtons to decline when they had been so kind, so I feigned an enthusiasm I didn't feel, and asked Angela's advice on what to wear and where I could find a reasonable hairdresser: my hair had grown, its wildness verging on unprofessional.

At five o'clock I emerged from the salon looking unusually tidy, clutching a bag containing a dress I had been persuaded to buy – something far more expensive than I would normally have contemplated. The young woman in the shop had enthused about the colours, so complementary to my skin tone (*really?*) and I hoped that my weakness in agreeing would not result in me feeling like an awkward over-floral eyesore in an assembly of critical strangers.

The shadows were lengthening as I walked back across the water-meadow to the Axtons'. I calculated that I probably just had time for a shower before Peter and Angela called for me. As I strolled up to my new front door my phone rang. I fished it out of my pocket, frowning: who could be calling? That irrational reaction, puzzlement tinged with a frisson of fear, made me realize that the events of the recent past were still hanging over me like some kind of threatening cloud.

"Hello?" I answered the phone, my tone guarded, and an unfamiliar voice replied.

"Rachel? Hi, I'm Rob Harker."

I very nearly said "Who?" stupidly and rudely, but then I remembered: Beth and Jimmy's friend. I'd forgotten all about him.

"Oh, yes. Hello."

"How are you? Have you settled in all right?" He sounded warm, friendly, almost breezy.

"Pretty much, thank you."

"Started work yet?"

"Not yet. In a few days."

He cleared his throat. "I was wondering… well, I know it's terribly short notice, but I wondered if you were free this evening. There's a reception at the hospital, and I thought it might be nice for you to meet a few people. I could pick you up –"

I interrupted. "That's very kind of you, Rob. But I'm already going, with the Axtons."

I heard him exhale. "Of course. I shouldn't leave things to the last minute, should I? I'd forgotten about it, to be honest. I probably wouldn't have bothered going, but then I thought of you, not knowing anyone, and I thought…" he tailed off.

"Well, thanks, for thinking of me. But if you are now going, I expect we'll see each other there."

"How will I know you?"

"Do you know the Axtons?"

"Mm, we've met."

"I'll get them to introduce us, then. Anyway, you could hardly miss me. A woman in a shop persuaded me to buy a dress this afternoon. I'll be the one looking like a tropical fruit bowl."

I heard him chuckle. "I look forward to it. See you later."

Beth had described Rob as good-looking. But she could be prone to exaggerate, and she always thought better of people than they deserved – even of me. However, when I met Rob Harker I had to agree with her: he was very handsome in a curly, boyish, artless kind of way that might have made a less cynical woman wobble. His brown hair, worn long to his collar, bounced with health; his blue eyes, fringed with improbable lashes, sparkled with good humour. His tenor voice was well modulated and pleasant, with no discernible accent. He was just under six feet tall, slim but not skinny; and he was extremely charming. Nothing about him rang false; the charm emanated from a kindly soul well content with himself and the world, or so it seemed. He had the unusual habit of listening intently, sometimes smiling and nodding, and keeping those eyes fixed on my face, as if my banal conversation was the most fascinating thing he'd heard in years. He was also funny, and I found myself grinning despite myself. He had a chuckle that came from somewhere deep inside his torso and travelled upwards to light up his face; and, I noted, a perfect set of teeth. I surprised myself (inwardly) by being quite taken with him, in a careless sort of way. That was also a surprise: I had rarely ever allowed my relationships, few as they were, to be careless. I had ended my engagement to Howard as soon as I'd squarely faced the fact that I couldn't stomach the idea of being with him for the rest of my days. (A year later he married someone else, and I truthfully wished them well and felt immense relief.) I had never put myself in the position of being dizzy, dependent – or dumped. Chatting to Rob, I had the vague thought that I might be letting myself in for something, but I deliberately ignored it. That was another surprise.

Angela Axton steered me away from Rob after a while, determined that I should meet as many hospital luminaries as I could that evening, but not before Rob had extracted from me a promise to find an evening free for him alone. I remembered few of the people to whom I was introduced. The only ones of real interest were the colleagues I might well be working alongside: heart people.

A few days later I plunged eagerly back into the world I loved, where I knew who I was and what I was for. Gowned and masked and gloved, something sharp in my hand, a draped chest waiting for an incision – that was where I fitted, in this hospital or any other. Surgery, clinics, rounds, lectures, study, more surgery. Complications dealt with, dramas overcome. It could well have been enough to banish the uneasy feelings that sometimes rose up in me, nameless and unwelcome.

Perhaps I was more fragile than I knew or would admit. Perhaps the events in Porton had made me vulnerable. Or maybe I was allowing myself, outside work, to be more human.

Whatever the reason, I let Rob Harker under my defences. For the first time in years I was unreservedly happy. Perhaps at some level I worried that I might be courting catastrophe – but I gave such thoughts no room, and before long they were simply engulfed and overwhelmed.

The weather turned unseasonably warm early in April. Daffodils flirted in the breeze, turning their faces up to the sun. Houseboats appeared on the river, colourful and slow. Behind a screening row of conifers at the bottom of the Axtons' garden I could sometimes hear the voices of walkers on the towpath.

As it happened Thursday was still my day off, and I started it early, almost as soon as it was light, with a run that took me along the river which flowed in a wide meandering circle round the city, a distance of probably seven or eight miles. I saw almost no one – just the occasional fellow-runner, whom I greeted with little more than a grunt or a perfunctory nod. The sun was high in the sky when I returned, and after a pounding shower I opened the windows and sat in the kitchen with coffee and toast and some learned reading matter. Rob was working, as he did every weekday. He had an office which functioned five days a week from nine to six, and his weekends were free. I regularly worked at weekends, for emergencies or on call, and my days were often long, but Thursdays were my own, and I was glad of the disparity in our schedules: I needed no excuse to have time to myself.

After lunch I decided that the day was too warm to be indoors, and I found a garden chair in the Axtons' shed and set it up on the lawn. There was little sound except for birdsong, the occasional burst of chatter from the river, and the distant rumble of traffic on the bypass. The spring sun was warm, the breeze gentle and laden with the wafting scent of spring flowers. I stretched out in the chair, my cotton trousers rolled up to just below the knee, a pair of sunglasses perched on my nose. I had a book to hand, but it stayed unopened on the ground.

It had been a tough week, with several long operations. I'd started the day early. Small wonder that in that peaceful garden I drifted off to sleep.

For the first time in many months I dreamed about my father: sweet, uncomplicated snatches and snippets of unconnected events, images that flitted past my mental vision with frustrating speed and insouciance. There he was, on the deck of a little dinghy we owned, standing barefoot with a rope in his hand, squinting in the sun and laughing; then a fleeting image of his denim-shirted back as he hunched over a camping stove, his hair flattened by the rain. I saw for a moment just his hands, capable and strong, holding a hammer, and I noticed the light glinting on his wedding ring. I knew Martin was there, but I didn't see him.

I wanted more – I always wanted more. But I was jerked suddenly and sickeningly awake by a snuffling wetness on my bare leg; then something jumped up on me, hot breath fanning my face, causing me to double up as I hurtled back to consciousness.

"What on earth – ?" I shoved the burden off my stomach, and my hands encountered fur. My eyes flew open and my brain re-engaged. Sitting decorously beside me, its paws now neatly side by side, its jaws open and panting in what looked like a knowing grin, was a dog: a middling-sized black and white border collie, one ear up, the other quirked sideways, and it was looking at me with its head cocked at a cheeky angle.

"Where did you come from?" I muttered. "You scared me, jumping on me like that. Horrible beast."

This was untruthful: I liked dogs. We never had one when I was growing up, because my mother wouldn't hear of it (*"nasty smelly things, always dropping hair"*), but my father, brother, and I would sometimes borrow the chocolate Labrador that belonged to our elderly neighbours when we went on camping trips. The neighbours were glad to have someone exercise their overweight dog, and old Bertie was amiability itself. This collie was a beauty, all taut muscles, glossy coat, and bright eyes, and I soon forgave it for its poor manners; but the shock of its arrival, and the lingering ache produced by the dream, had unsettled me and broken the peace of the afternoon. I gathered up my book. "Come on, dog. Let's go and see if Angela knows who you are." I slipped a finger under the dog's red collar and located a metal disc in which "Dulcie" was etched, along with a phone number.

"Right, then, Dulcie. Come with me."

Dulcie trotted along beside me without demur as I crossed the lawn; occasionally she looked up at me quizzically. I could see Angela in her big shiny kitchen, doing something at the counter, her back to me. I tapped gently on the window and she turned round, peering over the top of her glasses. She was wearing a blue striped apron, and held an open book in her hand. A knife lay beside a wooden chopping board on the worktop.

She smiled and beckoned me in. With my hand on Dulcie's collar I opened the door just wide enough to call through.

"Angela, sorry to bother you, but I seem to have found a dog. Thought you might know who she belongs to."

Angela opened the door wide. "I might have known! Hello, Dulcie, you little monster." She bent down and ruffled the dog's smooth head, and had her hand licked in exchange. "Come on in, both of you." She looked up at me. "Dulcie is very well behaved as a rule, indoors anyway."

I smiled back at Angela. "I found one of your garden chairs and I was dozing in the sun. She leapt on me and freaked me out."

"Sit down, Rachel," Angela said. "Now you're here I'll get the kettle on."

"Sure I'm not disturbing something important? It looks like you were doing some serious cooking."

"Oh, no; it can wait." She filled the kettle and switched it on, then rooted around in one of the cupboards for a bowl which she filled with water for the dog. Dulcie lapped noisily and we both watched her.

"So who does Dulcie belong to?" I asked. "Where's she come from?"

"Dulcie belongs to our neighbour a few houses down along the river," Angela said, waving a vague hand. "Mike Wells. He's at the hospital too, a plastic surgeon, very well thought-of. I wouldn't have thought he'd have left Dulcie in the garden while he's at work. I wonder how she got out." The kettle came to the boil and switched itself off. "Would you like tea, Rachel? Or coffee perhaps?"

"Coffee would be nice, thanks. Black, please."

Angela busied herself with cups and spoons and a few moments later set a steaming mug in front of me. "It's not the first time we've had a visit from Dulcie, is it, you mischief?" The dog flopped down beside her chair. "She's been known to dig a hole under the fence and get out, so as far as I know Michael was keeping her indoors more. She's a bright little lass and gets bored, I expect. Is your coffee all right?"

"It's perfect."

Angela shook her head. "I wonder..." I waited for her to enlighten me. "I suppose it must be the Easter holidays, mustn't it?"

I nodded. "Easter's next Sunday, so I guess so. And I've heard children's voices on the towpath the last few days."

"I wonder if Jasper is visiting. Perhaps he's supposed to be looking after the dog."

"Jasper?"

"Mike Wells' son. I'd better ring the house and see if he's there. Excuse me a moment."

She got up and padded through to the hall. I heard her speak, fall silent, and speak again.

"Yes, Jasper's there," she said as she came back into the kitchen. "Full of apologies. Said he was busy revising for his GCSEs and didn't notice the dog had sneaked out. He'll be round in a minute with Dulcie's lead." She sat down. "Oh, sorry, would you like a biscuit?"

"No, I'm fine, thanks."

There was a rather awkward silence as we sipped our drinks. Then Angela said, "I do hope you are settling in all right."

"Yes, I am. Work is very absorbing. And the flat is lovely. I'm really grateful to you and Peter for giving a home to this refugee."

"You're very welcome. I hear you've been making a new friend, too."

"What? Oh, you mean Rob. Yes, he's good company." I spoke casually and hoped she wouldn't pursue this line of talk.

"I don't really know him," Angela said, "but people say he's terribly clever at what he does."

"I don't doubt it," I said. "IT's not my area of expertise, though."

She smiled. "Nor mine, not at all."

We heard Dulcie whine then, and Angela and I both looked up and out of the wide kitchen window. A skinny lad was haring up the garden from the direction of the river.

"Jasper." Angela got up and opened the door. He was flushed and panting. "Sit down, Jasper. There was no need to rush."

The boy flopped into a chair. "I'm sorry, Mrs A. I only took my eyes off her for five minutes."

"It's all right," Angela said. "Dulcie likes to go visiting, don't you, Dulcie? It isn't the first time I've found her at my kitchen door."

"I know. But I was supposed to be looking after her. Dad would be so upset if I lost her."

"She knows her way home, I shouldn't wonder. Would you like a cup of tea now you're here?"

"Yes, please. That would be nice."

"Sorry, I'm forgetting myself. Rachel Keyte, Jasper Wells. Rachel's a cardiac surgeon, Jasper. Visiting us from another hospital for a while."

Jasper stretched out his hand, and I shook it. He had dark hair, almost black, straight and worn long, and dark grey eyes in a serious face. "Nice to meet you, Ms Keyte," he said. "How are you finding it here?"

I was amused by this courteous teenager. GCSEs? So he was sixteen at most. "I like it a lot, thanks," I told him. "Heart operations are similar wherever you are, but Brant has some wonderful equipment. And I'm very much looking forward to my first surgery with Professor Axton next week."

Angela came back to the table with a mug of tea for Jasper. "Oh, so is Peter! He's quite excited to have you in the team."

Jasper turned to me. "Are you a very high-up surgeon, then, Ms Keyte?" he asked, his eyes wide.

"Absolutely not at all," I said with a grin. "Mrs Axton is exaggerating."

"No, I'm not," Angela said. "Rachel has quite a reputation, Jasper."

I smiled slightly. "Don't ask for what." Inwardly I wasn't smiling. An image had flashed across my mental vision unbidden: Craig Rawlins' white lifeless body.

"Are you all right, Rachel?" Angela said. "You've gone a bit pale. I hope you're not overworking."

I forced out a laugh. "You're beginning to sound like your old friend Bridget Harries!" I said. "I'm quite all right, thank you." I turned to the boy opposite. "So are you at school here in Brant, Jasper?" Polite conversation! Did I care? No. But it was a way of deflecting interest away from me and my well-being.

"No," Jasper said. "I go to school in London. I'm just visiting for the holidays."

"Oh."

"I lived here till I was eleven, and I liked it," Jasper said, a rather sad little smile on his lean face. "There's a lot more countryside around here, and I prefer that. There's a lot to do in London though, and one good thing is that there's an Olympic-size swimming pool a couple of Tube stops away from where we live now."

"Jasper's a very accomplished swimmer," Angela said, "as is his father."

"I'm nowhere near as good a swimmer as Dad yet," Jasper said. "But I'm working on building up some muscle. Dad says he was skinny like me at my age."

"So will you be swimming much while you're here, then?" I asked.

"I hope so. There are a couple of good pools here. When Dad isn't working we'll go together. It'll make a nice change from revision, anyway." He finished his tea. "I'll take this escape artist home now, Mrs A. Thanks for keeping her for me." He stood up and turned to me. "It was nice to meet you, Ms Keyte."

"You too, Jasper." I smiled up at him. "You know, as we are neighbours, please call me Rachel. Otherwise I'll feel depressingly old. You may think I already am, but I'd rather not admit it."

"I don't think you're old!" Jasper said, and I noted the flush that spread momentarily across his cheekbones. *Ha, that's exactly what he thinks! I suppose I am just about old enough to be his mother. What a sobering thought.* Jasper muttered a word to the dog and bent down to clip the lead to her collar. As he straightened up he said, "Was that you I saw earlier, running on the towpath, Ms – er, Rachel?"

"Probably."

"Would you mind if I ran with you one day? I'm training for a triathlon and I've got no one to run with here. I could bring Dulcie. She needs lots of exercise." He hesitated. "Unless you prefer to run alone."

"I don't mind company once in a while," I said. "I go pretty early, though."

He smiled, and his dark eyes seemed to fill with light. "Early is OK." He turned to Angela. "Thanks for the tea, Mrs A. I'd better be getting back now. Dad will be in soon.'

"Don't worry, Jasper – we won't tell!" Angela said.

"Oh, no, it's OK; I'll tell Dad myself," Jasper said, quite serious again. "We tell each other most things. See you soon, I hope." He gave us both a little wave. "Come on, Dulcie."

Angela and I watched him and the dog trot across the lawn until he vanished through the conifers onto the towpath.

"Nice kid," I murmured.

"Yes, isn't he?" Angela said. "Clever, too. I often think he's a bit lonely, all alone in the house while Michael is working. But he always comes down for a good part of the school holidays, and as far as I know he spends at least a month in the summer with his father. They have a place in France somewhere."

"Nice."

"I think it is, though I haven't been there. Michael did show me a photo once. But don't ask me where it is!" Angela sighed. "I feel a bit sorry for Jasper. I get the impression he'd much rather live here, don't you?" I raised my eyebrows in polite enquiry – it was really none of my business – but Angela took it as evidence of my interest. "His parents split up when he was eleven, and his mother – Alison – took him off to London. I think she felt it was the right time – he'd be changing schools anyway then – but it must have been hard for the lad, separated from his friends and his father."

"I suppose so." Something more seemed to be expected from me so I said, as neutrally as I knew how, "Why London?"

"Oh, well, Alison remarried soon after. Obviously she had this new man in her life already, and he's based in London. I don't think it's the easiest relationship for Jasper, though he says very little. He's a funny chap, a bit old-fashioned, I always think. It's not every teenager who'd want to keep company with his elderly neighbours! Whatever else, Alison's brought him up well."

"How well did you know her?"

"Fairly. She's nice enough, not as bright as either her ex-husband or her son, I'd say, and perhaps a bit more materialistic, though I'm sure Michael isn't poor; consultant surgeons earn a fair salary, don't they? But who knows why marriages go wrong?

Sometimes I think I've just been very lucky."

I drained my mug and pushed my chair back. "Well, I'm certainly no expert! Thanks for the coffee, Angela. Now I should go and let you get on with your cooking."

"Feel free to drop by any time, Rachel. It's nice to chat."

Head down, I strode back across the lawn, put the garden chair back in the shed, pushed open my front door that still stood ajar, and closed it firmly behind me. *Chat? Not too often, if I can help it, nice as Angela is.*

***

Time slowed. I tried to move my head, to see if there was a clock anywhere, but the motion made me feel nauseated and dizzy. I tried to persuade myself that I was actually dreaming, but there was too much evidence for reality: the tickling of a wisp of stray hair on my unbandaged cheek; the rucks and wrinkles of the sheet under my buttocks; the muffled voices from outside. I tried not to panic, to force myself to calmness, but terror rose up in my throat so irresistibly that I thought I would scream the place down. Instead a weak, shuddering moan was all that escaped me. I felt a tear leak from my left eye. When I realized that my right eye was in darkness another fierce wave of panic hit me so that I shook and juddered and felt my stomach heave. This time I shouted, but not in words – more an animal shriek; and then the door opened and a nurse hurried across the room and looked down at me.

"All right, Rachel, let's sit you up." She stacked up the pillows and looked at me closely. "What's the matter?"

I swallowed, fixed her with my one eye. When my voice emerged it was a growl. I forced myself to speak slowly. "Why…" Deep breath. "What… am I doing here?"

"You don't remember what happened? All right, Rachel. I understand you're frightened. Mr Wells is here now. I'll ask him to come and talk to you."

She patted my hand and was gone in a rustle of cotton. I heard her speak outside the door, and a man's deep voice answered, a voice that resonated somewhere in my fractured memory. The door opened again, and with a wave of relief that brought new tears spilling from my eye I recognized the man who came to stand at my bedside: Michael Wells, Jasper's father. That momentary relief, at being able to remember something, was swiftly overtaken by a fresh spurt of panic. Why was he here? What was his connection to my captive state, to the dressings on my hands and face? Why couldn't I remember?

His dark grey eyes, reminiscent of Jasper's, rested on my face. "Rachel. It's Michael Wells. Do you remember me? Or my son, Jasper?" I nodded. "Anything else about how you came to be here?"

My voice had shrunk to a whisper. "No."

"All right. You must be very frightened. You've suffered a trauma that's blanked out a lot of your short-term memory. But don't worry – it will come back – probably quite slowly though, as it's a kind of defence mechanism. Let me ask you something to test your long-term memory: we had a conversation about dogs – do you remember that?" I shook my head and winced: the movement had sent a shot of pain across my face. I was sure he noticed it, but he said nothing. "You told me about a neighbour's dog you used to play with as a child. Can you remember his name?"

Immediately a mental picture leapt to my mind: a brown overweight dog lumbering along beside me through a summer meadow. I managed to mumble, "Bertie."

"Good." He paused, searching my face. Then he took my unresisting hands, turned them over so that they were palm up, and gazed down at them. "Rachel, you were attacked, yesterday afternoon. I was here, and we got to you very quickly. Thankfully your facial injury missed your right eye, and just nicked the top of your lip. I've put your hands back together as well as I know how, but we won't know the exact outcome yet – it's too soon. When you feel up to it there are people who want to speak to you – including a rather impatient police officer. I've told him you can't be seen yet. It'll be up to you to say when you feel strong enough, and when your memory starts to return. Meanwhile you'll stay here. I'll come and see you as often as I can, and I want you to know you are safe."

***

I was in the kitchen of my garden flat, throwing together a semblance of an evening meal. I wondered if it was a bit weird that a sixteen-year-old boy wanted to hang out with me. Maybe Angela was right – he was just lonely. The light was beginning to dim on a fine spring day, and I was thinking about something I'd been reading. A light rapping on my front door startled me. I wiped my hands down the side of my trousers – I'd been slicing onions – and opened the door. I had never met the man who stood there, but he held a lead in his hand, and an innocent-looking Dulcie sat at his side. Even if he had been alone I would have known him as Jasper's father. He had the same almost-black hair, though wavier and streaked with grey, and the same dark, intent gaze. He was taller and broader than his son, but there was an unmistakable family resemblance that gave him away.

I smiled. "Mr Wells."

"Ms Keyte." He held out his free hand, and I shook it. "I've come to apologize for my dog, and to thank you for looking after her."

"I didn't do much, but you're welcome." I remembered my manners. "Would you like to come in?"

"Thank you, but I see you are busy cooking, and so I should be too. It was lucky for me that you seem to like dogs."

"I do. And Dulcie is a very lovely girl, despite her wicked ways." I bent down and stroked Dulcie's smooth head.

Michael Wells hesitated for a moment. "I gather my son has invited himself to run with you. I hope that's all right."

I straightened up. "It's fine with me, if it is with you. Unless you feel it's not appropriate."

His eyebrows shot up. "That's not what I meant. I just wouldn't want him intruding on you."

"I'll let him know when I'm next going out and feel like company. But you shouldn't worry about Jasper. He was very polite."

He smiled for the first time, and the likeness to Jasper intensified as his eyes brightened. "That's good to hear. Well, I'll wish you a good evening, Ms Keyte. We'll probably meet again, if only in the hospital."

As he turned to leave, I said, "In which case, please call me Rachel."

"Rachel. And I'm Michael. Or Mike. But not Mickey."

I suppressed a grin. "No, I guessed not Mickey."

That weekend, lounging on Rob's sofa, a large glass of wine in my hand, watching Rob busying himself in his tiny kitchen as he prepared a meal for us, I idly mentioned I'd met the Wells family: father, son, and dog. "Do you know them?" I asked. I wondered how well thought-of Michael was as a surgeon.

"Wells senior, yes, vaguely," Rob said. "A rather serious chap, I seem to remember."

"Yes, he gives that impression. Maybe it's something to do with his work."

Rob bent and put a dish in the oven, closing its door with a clang. "Don't plastic surgeons do boob jobs and facelifts? What's gloomy about that?"

"I don't think that's all they do, ignoramus. They do all sorts of very serious stuff, like fixing people who've been injured or burned, or have terrible deformities." For a fleeting moment I remembered Eve Rawlins and her birthmark, and suddenly felt cold.

Rob peeled off his floral apron – a joke present, he'd told me, from his older sister – and slid down beside me on the sofa. He put his arm round my shoulders and pulled me towards him.

"Hey! Careful, you'll spill my wine!"

He took the glass from my hand and put it on the floor. He stroked my hair away from my face and kissed my eyes and mouth and neck.

I closed my eyes and sighed. "Mm. I like that."

"Shall we go somewhere more… comfortable?" he whispered against my skin.

"I thought we were going to eat."

"We are, but it won't be ready for, oh, at least an hour. I thought perhaps a little exercise might sharpen our appetites." His hands were straying in all sorts of places, gently unbuttoning, and I began to feel warm and languid.

"Exercise?" I murmured. "What, something vigorous? Tennis?"

"Vigorous, very likely. But not tennis."

He stood up, took my hand and pulled me to my feet so that I was held close up against him, his hands on my back. "Come with me." His voice was low, inviting, full of laughter and promise, and I went with him like a lamb.

Some time later, as the shadows outside grew long and the curtains billowed gently in the early evening breeze, Rob yawned, stretched, and rubbed his eyes. He gently removed my arm which was draped around his waist and put his feet on the bedroom floor.

"I guess," he said, "I'd better go and sort out this meal."

"Mm. I am very hungry. And there are some delicious smells wafting in from the kitchen."

He did not move for a moment, and then suddenly turned to me and took my hand. "Rachel, I've been thinking. About you and me."

"This is a fine time to dump me, Rob. Can I have dinner first?"

"Be quiet, will you? Actually, I've been thinking about getting down on one naked knee and proposing."

I opened one eye. "Ha, ha."

"No. I'm a bit embarrassed to admit it, but I'm serious."

Now both my eyes flew open, and I sat up. "We've only known each other for a few weeks – and carnally only for one of them."

He had turned away from me for a moment; now he faced me, and his expression was endearingly solemn. He looked about fourteen. "I know. But I feel…"

"Better stop there, Rob," I said, as kindly as I could. "I like you a lot too. But it's a bit soon for cohabiting and commitment."

He stood up and started pulling on his clothes, managing to button up his shirt all wrong. "All right," he said. "But I'm not letting you get away. I shall ask you again. And next time," he said with a knowing grin, "I shall ask you *before* we go to bed, when you are mad with lust."

Over the next weeks Rob proposed marriage at least a dozen times, in all sorts of embarrassing places, so that at times I was speechless with laughter. But every time I turned him down – of course I did. I felt I was beginning to know him, but I was sure he barely knew me.

"All right," he said, one Sunday afternoon as we idled by the river. I sat on a park bench, eyes closed, my skin warmed by the sun, and he sprawled on the grass at my feet. There were plenty of people about, enjoying the weather, but he took no notice of them. "Tell me: have you never thought it might be nice to be with someone all the time? Set up home and all that?"

I pulled a face, remembering Howard. "I did get engaged once, actually."

He sat up. There was grass all down one side of his sleeve. "Well? What happened?"

"I decided against it."

"Just like that? Poor bloke."

"I don't think he was heartbroken. He married someone else a year later. As far as I know he's happily domestic."

Rob looked up at me, his expression all sympathy. "Do you mind?"

"Not at all. I'm happy for him – and for me. Lucky escape."

"Does that mean just an escape from him, or marriage in general?"

"Certainly from him. He's a good chap, but not for me. As to the rest, the jury's out."

I heard him give a disgusted grunt as he flopped back down on the grass. "But Rachel" – now he sounded imploring – "don't you think it might be time? I mean – how old are you?"

"You know perfectly well how old I am."

"Yes – thirty-seven. And I'm thirty-four. I didn't think I would feel this way, but I do. I've had loads of girlfriends, but you –"

"Why don't you tell me about those 'loads of girlfriends'? I'm fascinated."

He scrambled up and planted himself on the bench beside me. "There are far too many," he said smugly, "so many I can't remember all of them."

"All right," I said, "just the most recent."

He sighed. "Oh, dear. Yes. That would be Sammy. I finished with her a few weeks before you came here. But she was a bit different – we'd been together two years, give or take."

"So what went wrong?"

"Ah." He suddenly looked pained. "That was me. I cheated on her. I'd been out with some friends, had a skinful. No excuse. She found out, we had a huge row, I accused her of being over-possessive, said I'd had enough."

"Do you regret it?"

He turned to look at me. "Not now," he said, taking my hand. "Not now I've met you. Rachel, you're –"

I shook my head. "Rob, you don't know me."

"I adore you," he interrupted.

I ploughed on. "You don't know me, and you'd almost certainly dislike me after a month."

"How can you say that?" he moaned.

"With absolute conviction."

The next working week began with a long meeting with Peter Axton, preparing for the major operation which we were to undertake jointly the following day. The rest of the team were also there: people known to Peter, of course, people with whom he'd worked on innumerable occasions, but either unknown to me or only superficially acquainted. Some of them, I thought, seemed to eye me with scepticism, others with a grudging respect, or at least curiosity, but one with downright resentful hostility. This was no surprise. I'd breezed in, or so it must have seemed, all untested reputation and professional hype. This man probably thought the role of Peter's protégé should be his; I was a usurper of unknown quality. I had everything to prove.

That evening Rob rang, wanting me to go with him to see a film he fancied. I declined, despite his protests that I worked too hard.

"There's no such thing as putting in too many hours in my job," I told him. "What we do tomorrow potentially means life or death for the patient. I'm going to spend the evening studying, and then go to bed early. I need to be fresh first thing tomorrow. Not tonight, sunshine." He rang off, grumpily muttering.

I'd only assisted at myxoma surgery on two occasions, some years before. I trawled all the internet sites I knew, read, and took notes. Finally, around ten o'clock that evening, I stretched and walked around a bit, flexing my muscles, made myself a cup of coffee, and thought about the patient: a forty-one-year-old woman, overweight but otherwise in reasonable health until the accidental discovery of a left atrial myxoma three years before, when she had visited her GP with chest pain and incidences of fainting. Transoesophageal Echocardiography had provided a definitive diagnosis, and she had the myxoma excised without unnecessary delay. Myxomas, while benign, were potentially lethal, because of the possibility of their preventing normal blood flow, and because of their fragility. If a fragment broke off it could wind up in your brain or your eye – anywhere, really – and kill you.

Unfortunately for our patient, that first surgery failed to remove every bit of the tumour, and it had recurred close to the original site, so now we at Brant had the job of opening her up again. Peter had been at pains to remind us that re-operation was often trickier, and this patient's health had declined. "I didn't do this surgery, and it wasn't done at this hospital," he said. "Mrs Gooch has moved house in the last year. She's in a more vulnerable condition than she was: that's our challenge. This time we have to be sure we get all of it."

"Is the mitral valve affected?" I asked.

"Not as far as we know. But if we get in there and find it is in fact regurgitating, we'll have to do a repair at the same time."

I fell silent for a moment, thinking, and was aware that Peter and the others were listening, not saying a word. More and more I got the distinct impression of being tested. "It might be as well to take a look at the valve even if it appears to be normal," I said.

"Go on."

"I read somewhere in the historic literature that a myxoma was successfully excised, but when the valve leaflets were prised open, another, tiny tumour was found there. It would have been impossible to detect with the technology available at the time, but even with what we have now it wouldn't be easy to see."

Peter nodded. "Good point. This time we have to get it right."

Soon afterwards he closed the meeting and people left, leaving just him and me in the room. "How do you feel about leading this surgery, Rachel? Obviously, I'll be on hand, but the decisions will be yours."

I nodded. "I welcome the challenge, and I feel confident," I said. "It'll be good to have someone of your experience there, of course, in case of the unforeseen."

"So – anything else you need to bring up?"

"Not to do with this particular operation," I said. "But I'm sure you're aware of what's going on elsewhere, in America and China and other places, with minimally invasive techniques. Atrial myxomas have been removed with robotic assistance on numerous occasions."

He sighed. "Just not here at Brant – not yet. And I doubt that it'll be common practice while I'm still working. It's a different story for you, though." He looked at me keenly. "Is it something you're particularly interested in?"

I nodded. "I would very much like to do the specialist training. Surgery for all kinds of cardiac conditions will one day be done this way, don't you think? With less pain and quicker recovery times." In some ways I was finding that as far as innovation was concerned, contrary to expectations, Brant was a bit of a backwater.

"I'm sure you're right." He put a casual arm round my shoulder. "But for now, it'll be crack open the chest as usual." He dropped his arm and tapped his chin thoughtfully. "Rachel, I wonder…" I waited, and he turned to look at me. "I get the impression, and please correct me if I'm talking nonsense here, that you're not the sort of surgeon who's in a hurry to get to the pub with your friends after a ten-hour op."

I smiled. "You're quite right. I'm more likely to slip away, ditch the scrubs, and walk the long way home."

"I thought so."

"I hope it doesn't come over as unfriendly, or even arrogant," I said – not that I really cared what most people thought of me. "I just prefer to unwind on my own."

"Fair enough. If you have a few minutes, there's something I'd like to show you."

I nodded.

"Come with me." He led me out of the room and turned right down a long corridor. At the end a door led to a sharp bend to the right. He pushed through a set of swing doors, revealing a staircase that clearly belonged to a different era. "As you know," he said, "much of this hospital was rebuilt in the last decade. Huge portions of it were actually pulled down. But some parts of the old Victorian building – parts that weren't required for strictly medical purposes – were retained, especially as it was felt by some that they were of architectural interest." He was leading us down a rather dilapidated staircase, and he looked back at me and smiled. "I hope you're taking note of the route! Nearly there."

Another set of doors took us into a deserted corridor, and at the end of it Peter pushed open a heavy wooden door on our left. "We're at the far end of the hospital here," he said. "Only a few people know about this place – I think it was used for some administrative purpose way back when." He showed me into the room. It was long but quite narrow, with a huge table in the middle, and at one end a window that stretched from floor to ceiling, with elegant cream-coloured curtains. I walked up to the window and looked out. We were on the ground floor now, and the window gave onto a flower bed planted with roses – well pruned and not yet flowering – a few feet below. Beyond the rose bed was a wide paved path, and people were walking in both directions, some in white coats, some carrying armfuls of files, others simply chatting in groups.

"This end is very near some of the university buildings and research units," Peter said as he came up behind me. "At this time of day there are a few students about, as you can see."

"Do you come here often?" I asked.

He smiled. "Once in a while. I'm not a pub-goer either. And –" he waved a hand towards a table which stood against the right-hand wall – "as you see, coffee-making facilities are always available. If you wanted to, this is a nice place to make yourself a drink, and you'll most likely have it all to yourself. Feel free to come here whenever you like."

"Thank you. It's kind of you to share your hideaway."

"Anything to help," he said. "Getting pitched in to work somewhere different, especially when it was not your choice, isn't always easy."

"You've already helped me enormously," I said, "you and Angela. I'm really grateful." Oddly, I meant it.

At my old hospital I was known for being a fast cutter – bold and decisive, but never hasty or careless. From the reading I had done through the years I'd come to the conclusion that a dithering uncertain surgeon is a danger to his or her helpless patients. Preparation is vital, and so is a speedy gathering of information once the chest is open and the heart exposed. As it turned out, Mrs Gooch's operation was straightforward. The myxoma was what we thought (and hoped) it would be, not a myxosarcoma, malignant and perilous; and where I expected it to be, having studied the most recent scans – adjacent to the fossa ovalis, a favourite spot. Once I had checked that there were no unforeseen complicating issues I excised the golfball-sized lump of jelly without hesitation and dropped it in a dish for the pathologist. I heard a barely suppressed gasp from someone round the table and looked up over my mask, fixing the culprit with a hard, challenging stare. Then I focused once more on my patient, carefully removing a circle of tissue round the spot where the tumour had been connected to the atrial wall. Once this was done I slowed my pace a little, checking meticulously for any sign of small myxomas or breakaway fragments. Satisfied, I left the clean-up and closure to others.

The surgery had gone well, I thought. I peeled off mask and gown and gloves as Peter joined me in the room adjacent to the theatre. "Excellent work, Rachel," he said, and shook my hand. "Most impressive."

"Thank you."

"What's on your agenda now?" He stripped off his own gloves and dropped them in the bin.

"Oh, I think a gentle stroll across the fields and home," I said. "It's a beautiful afternoon, but it's April and everything could change tomorrow. I'll drop by ICU in the morning and see how Mrs Gooch is doing."

"Yes, that would be good. It's my day off tomorrow, so I'll happily leave that to you."

As I crossed the meadow, the sun warming my bare head, I heard my phone bleep. I paused, found a handy bench, sat, and opened the text. "Amelia Maria," I read, "born this morning, 3.5 kg. Baby perfect, Beth recovering, photo to follow. All well at yours, Jimmy x." Smiling, I sent a reply. "Congratulations, look forward to photo, love to Beth x." They wouldn't have expected anything more gushing. I didn't envy them, but I was pleased that my friends had their baby safe and sound.

I pulled myself to my feet and walked on. As I approached the river I heard someone yelling from behind. "Rachel! Wait!" I turned and saw a skinny figure loping towards me, a black and white bullet streaking along in front. Jasper caught up, flushed and panting, and Dulcie frolicked all round me as if we had been unbearably parted for weeks.

"Hello, Jasper. Hello, Dulcie." I bent and stroked the dog's gleaming coat.

"I gave her a good brushing this morning," Jasper said. "Doesn't she look shiny?"

"Sure does."

"Can we walk with you?"

"OK. I'm heading for home."

"Yeah, me too. We've just been for a really long walk, and even Dulcie needs a rest. Not for long, though. She'd be up for ten walks a day if they were on offer." He smiled. "Have you been operating?"

"Yep. A re-operation, as it happens. Left atrial myxoma. Nice and uncomplicated."

Jasper nodded slowly, his face serious. "You have a lot of responsibility in your job, I think. As does my dad."

"Any idea what you want to do for a living, Jasper? Something in medicine, maybe?"

"I don't know yet. It's a lot of effort, isn't it? You need to be super-dedicated."

"I suppose you do." I thought of the years of work and study, the long hours, the many discouragements, the necessary sacrifices. It was almost twenty years since I'd left school. Two decades of keeping on top of everything. Had it been worth it? Without a doubt.

Jasper broke into my thoughts. "Rachel, can I run with you on Thursday if you're going?"

"I guess so. Yes, OK, I'll be at your back gate at seven. That's morning. Do teenagers recognize morning?"

Jasper grinned. "Not if they can help it. But I am not typical."

"See you at seven, then. If you're not there I won't wait, OK?"

"Done."

We crossed the river and went our separate ways, and Jasper turned and waved as he rounded a corner and the trees hid him from view. I wondered again, fleetingly, if this was OK. Why would a sixteen-year-old lad, even one that was considered atypical by himself and others, want to hang out with someone like me? Perhaps, as Angela had said, he was lonely. But although I had little interest in other people's opinions of me, I didn't want anyone making unsavoury assumptions about my friendship with Jasper. Perhaps I would sound out Angela. Discreetly.

***

I could hear myself screaming. The sound filled my head, jangled in my ears, blotting out all other sounds. And yet – was I perhaps dreaming? Was this some illusion? Were my lips not tightly shut?

Where was this screaming coming from, if not from me? It was as if a peal of bells was being rung inside my skull, relentless and wild. Among all this noise I saw him, my father, through the terrified eyes of a child not yet fifteen. He lay flat in his bed, silent and still. For months he had been propped on several pillows: it was the only way he could breathe, and even then his chest crackled with every breath. I stretched out a tentative hand and touched his inert hand. His blue-grey skin was cold and moist. Did I begin to understand? The bedroom door opened, and I saw my mother. Her face showed anger, and her mouth was moving, but I heard nothing but the screaming, on and on, unbearably harsh.

"Rachel! Rachel, wake up!" I felt myself gently shaken.

I began to see light through screwed up eyes, and felt hands behind my back raising me up and organizing pillows behind me. My lips were shut tight, but I could hear myself moan: the thin, anguished sound of an implacable grief.

"Wake up, Rachel. Open your eyes." The voice was soft, urgent but kind. I allowed my eyes to open a little, and I saw a fuzzy image: a pair of light brown eyes, a blue uniform. My lips peeled back from my teeth as I sucked in breath; my throat felt dry and cracked. The owner of the eyes seemed to understand: a moment later a beaker was held against my mouth and cool water slid down my throat. I choked a little and then drank greedily.

"Steady!" A cloth wiped my mouth. I dared to open my eyes wide, and saw the nurse I recognized.

"I'm still here," I heard myself croak.

I saw her smile. "Still here, yes. You were dreaming. Moaning and crying. I had a job to wake you. I think you were dreaming about your father. You were calling out, 'Daddy!' Do you remember?"

Before I could answer I heard the door open, and she turned towards the sound. "Oh, Mr Wells. Rachel's awake. Been having a bit of a nightmare, I think."

He came to stand on the other side of the bed. "Hello, Rachel." He had a deep voice, but he spoke quietly. I didn't feel threatened; instead my tight shoulder muscles began to relax as I sank back against the pillows, and I felt helpless tears dribble down my cheeks.

"Do you feel able to talk to me now?" he said. I nodded. "All right, that's good. I don't want you to be frightened, but we need to know what you can remember. If you can tell me, maybe you can talk to the policeman as well. Think of it as a dry run."

"OK." My voice felt dry and hoarse. The nurse offered the beaker of water, and I drank again. She put the beaker down on the bedside table and left the room.

Michael drew up a chair and sat next to me. "All right, Rachel. Tell me what you can remember."

The tears welled hot from my eyes. I remembered everything.

***

Jasper was sitting on his garden gate, swinging his feet, when I rounded the corner. Dulcie raced up to greet me and Jasper jumped lightly down.

"You're early," I said, surprised.

He jogged up and down on the spot. "I didn't want you to go without me. So, are we ready?"

"You're very keen," I commented as we started off side by side. Dulcie ran ahead and dived into the bushes at the side of the path.

"I've been up for a while," Jasper said. "My curtains aren't very thick. The sunshine comes in and I'm wide awake!"

I smiled. "All right, let's run." I glanced around. "Where's your crazy dog?"

"Don't worry; she'll catch up. Dulcie knows her way around here, and everybody knows her anyway. She's probably off looking for rabbits." He grinned. "Or something dead."

I pulled a face and put on a spurt. Jasper kept up easily, arms and legs pumping in rhythm, and a few minutes later Dulcie reappeared, racing round us in circles till we almost tripped over her.

"Dulcie, calm down and give us some room!" Jasper said.

"You know what, Jasper?" I said. "That dog of yours could do with proper training. She's very bright, but it's going to waste.'

"I know," Jasper agreed. "I've tried, but I'm not really here long enough for it to work. And Dad's so busy. It's a shame. We love her, but she's a bit of a headache sometimes."

Forty minutes later I called a halt by a wooden bench. "Time for a breather – I'm in a sweat. That sun's warm for April." I flopped down, breathing hard.

Jasper too was flushed and panting. "Did you bring any water?"

"'Fraid not." I glanced at my watch. "Ten minutes, OK? Then I thought we'd cross the river by that little bridge and head over the meadow to the next one, cross back and turn for home. Suit you?"

"Fine." He leaned against the back of the seat, lifted his face to the sun, and closed his eyes.

"I hear you have a place in France," I said. Now that we weren't running I thought I should probably make conversation, and he seemed a nice enough kid, after all. "Do you get down there a lot?"

He opened his eyes and shook his head. "Not really. I go for a few weeks, maybe a month, in the summer every year. My dad goes down more, though. When he can."

"What's it like?"

Jasper shrugged. "It's just outside a little town – or maybe a big village; I don't know. Called Roqueville. We have one neighbour, then there are some fields before the town starts. So we're a bit of a way out, but you can still walk in if you want, to buy bread or whatever."

"Is there much to do there for someone your age?"

"No, not much at all," he said. "But I told you I'm not typical!" He smiled. "I like it. And it's a chance to hang out with my dad. If I come down here, like now in the school holidays, he's usually working. And most of the time I'm in London. I miss him."

"So what do you get up to for a whole month?"

Jasper thought. "Well, we see friends. Dad's friends, mainly, but they're mine too. Our neighbours are nice – Monsieur and Madame Boutin – he's a retired policeman and he has a huge moustache. Bit of a cliché, isn't it, but he's proud of it. We do a fair bit of swimming – there's a good pool in the nearest big town. I read, fool around with Dulcie, go for walks. Dad does the garden… sometimes we invite people over for a barbecue. It's just part of my life, I suppose. We've been going there since I was four."

"It sounds peaceful."

"Yeah, it is. Sometimes all you can hear is the wind in the trees and the birds singing. Or maybe a tractor. It's a farming area, so there's loads of cows. Maybe it sounds boring, but it's a nice change from London."

"How's your French?"

"Hm, not great. Do you speak any languages?"

"No, I'm hopeless. We did French and Spanish at school, but by the time I was your age I knew what I wanted to do so I was heavily into the sciences."

"You 're lucky. I still don't really know what I want to do."

"Not everyone's like me." I sat up and flexed my shoulders. "Shall we move on?"

We made our way back and parted at Jasper's gate. "Thanks; that was good," he said. "Can I come again some time?"

"Sure. Bye for now, Jasper."

***

I have been known to forget my birthday. Filling in a form I sometimes hesitate and frown, or if someone asks me when it is I look blank for a moment. Remembering other people's birthdays is even less likely. But there's one date I will never forget: 28 May 2012.

The day started unremarkably. I had no particular commitments in the morning, but I went in to the hospital at ten thirty to check on a patient in ICU. I had replaced this man's diseased aortic valve the previous Friday; the surgery had gone well and I had no reason to expect any complications, but I liked to make sure there was nothing I needed to know about the patient's recovery over the weekend. As it happened he was doing "as well as could be expected in the circumstances" – such a useful catch-all bland bit of medical speak, designed to give away nothing and yet provide encouragement for the patient's family.

Leaving ICU I went up to Peter's office and booted up his computer. He was not there: he was in theatre that morning and I was free to use the room. There were a few things I needed to look up. An hour later I looked at my watch; it was almost noon, I had been up for many hours, and my stomach was rumbling. If I went to the hospital restaurant early there'd be few people there. I bought a sandwich and a bowl of salad and took them outside to a seat that overlooked a grassy area in front of the building. The afternoon was taken up with clinics and a session with a PhD student, and at four o'clock I was free.

For some reason I felt restless, unwilling to go home just yet. I decided to make a cup of coffee in the little-used room that Peter Axton had shown me some weeks previously. I'd used it on a couple of occasions and found it tranquil, conducive to uninterrupted thought. I was due to operate the following day, and I needed to think about the research I'd just done, in case of unforeseen complications. I strolled along the corridors and through the sets of doors slowly, deep in thought. I saw no one.

In the room I made a cup of coffee and stood by the long open window, looking out but seeing little. I suppose there were people walking up and down, some ambling, some purposeful, because there always were people there; but I couldn't remember afterwards. As I stood there, cup in hand, my phone bleeped and I dug in my pocket and pulled it out. It was another photo of baby Amelia, now almost six weeks old, posted by her adoring father. I smiled to myself as I thumbed an appropriate message before putting it back in my pocket.

I registered a tiny sound, and then was aware of the door clicking shut. I felt a spurt of annoyance: other people used this room very occasionally, but I had come to regard it – quite unjustifiably – as my own quiet hideaway. I turned, a false smile plastered onto my face.

And then, in a flash of horrible recognition, I felt every moment of the past few months at Brant come hurtling towards me like a gale-force wind, so that I staggered and swayed. In the face of what I saw before me everything fell away, as if it had been sheer illusion. She stood there by the door – tall, thin, bent slightly forward, her eyes wide and fixed, the birthmark furious red against her pallor. Then she uttered a strangled cry and came flying towards me down the long space beside the table, her arms raised high and wide. In her right hand I saw the flash of a blade as it caught the light from the window. In the paralysis of my shock I had no time to react. She was on me, shrieking wordlessly. The coffee cup was jerked out of my hand and I registered hot scalding liquid as it fell. Instinctively I raised my arms in front of my face and chest but I was too late: I felt a stinging slash down from my temple, skirting my eyebrow and slicing across my cheek. I heard a kind of moan, but I had no idea if it was mine or hers. I backed away towards the window, but she came on, unstoppable, and I felt sudden and agonizing pain in my hands, first the left, then the right, as I raised them in useless defence. I think it was then that I screamed, because my heel had found the shallow sill of the long window that stood open, and I felt myself fall backwards, arms flailing, half blind from the blood masking my face. The last thing my blood-free eye registered was her: Eve Rawlins, standing above me, eyes bulging, looking barely human. I think I saw her throw the knife down. But then there were sharp needles in my thinly clad back and a thump that robbed me of breath, and I blacked out.

This is what I told Michael Wells as he sat silently beside my bed. I faltered and stumbled and finally dried up, but he waited patiently until I had finished. Then he took the beaker of water and held it to my mouth, and I drank.

"All right, Rachel," he said softly. "What's behind this attack? It's not random, is it? She followed you. She must have been tracking your movements."

I nodded. "I'll tell you, if you like." My voice sounded rough. "But shouldn't you be at home? What about Jasper?"

"Jasper isn't a baby. He can cope."

"Did you tell him what happened?"

'Yes, I had to. I was preparing to go home when they paged me. When I heard it was you I scrubbed up again while they prepared the theatre."

"Thank you." I felt tears well up and leak down my face. "Sorry."

He made an impatient sound. "Tell me the story, Rachel. Think of it as a rehearsal. That policeman I told you about, Brightwell I think his name is, will be back. He'll want to hear it all."

I swallowed as a cold thought struck me. "What about her? Eve Rawlins?"

"Your attacker? Oh, they caught her. She didn't need much catching: they found her wandering about in the corridor, covered in blood – yours, of course."

I shuddered, remembering. "She came at me like some kind of demon."

He shook his head. "Well, that had all gone when they found her. She was like a crumpled rag, apparently. Forget her for a moment, if you can. Tell me what's been going on."

Slowly I told him about Craig, the operation that went like clockwork but ended so badly; Eve's reaction, the funeral, my car daubed with blood, the pig's heart, the painted door, and finally the intruder. "That was what drove me here," I said. "I couldn't stay after that. I went to the police, but they said they couldn't do anything with the lack of evidence against her. She's very clever."

He frowned. "Are you saying she sent you a pig's heart, painted your front door, broke into your flat – and there was no evidence?"

"No, I don't think she did it all herself. She probably bought the heart and parcelled it up, but I don't think she did the other things. There was a boy in a grey hoody. I don't know who he was, but I think she was behind it."

"And you came here to be safe. My goodness."

"I thought it was over," I said. My voice shook. "But nobody knew how deranged she was – is. She must have been nursing that hatred all these weeks. But now what?" I gulped back a sob. "What about these injuries?"

Michael reached over to the bedside table, pulled a tissue from a box, and gently wiped my tear-streaked face and dribbling nose. "Believe it or not," he said as he threw the tissue into a paper bag that served as a bin, "you have been lucky. The facial laceration was superficial. You should only have a thin scar."

"Huh! I'm not worried about how I look."

He shook his head. "It's not about that. The knife missed some vital structures – not only your eye but facial nerves. If they'd been cut my work would have been much more difficult. You might have been left with permanent damage."

"But –"

He interrupted. "You're worried about your hands? I understand, Rachel, believe me. I'd be worried if it was me. Your hands are your work. You sustained flexor tendon injuries in both hands as you tried to defend yourself. I have repaired them, but I can't tell you yet what the end result will be. I'm not going to lie to you, Rachel: recovery won't come easily or quickly. It will be in large part up to you. You'll need weeks of physiotherapy. Endless exercises. I'll keep track of how things are going. We'll know more later."

I lowered my head; my neck seemed stiff. I looked at my hands, bandaged and plastered, lying on the sheet palm up, my fingers exposed, bent like claws; and I felt hollow. "I guess I was lucky you were there," I whispered. "Word is you're one of the best."

He smiled faintly. "People say all sorts of nonsense. I did what I would do for any patient in your position, and it was a tidy job. I hope my best was good enough. Don't think I wasn't aware of what was at stake."

There came a quiet tap on the door, and the nurse put her head round. "Mr Wells, Inspector Brightwell is back."

Michael turned to me. "Are you strong enough for this?"

I sighed heavily. "I suppose so. Might as well get it over with."

"All right. I'll ask the nurse to come back and sit with you while he asks his questions. I'll go home now, Rachel. See what that boy of mine's up to. I'll come by again tomorrow."

He pushed his chair back and stood up.

"Why you?" I said dully. "Why are you taking all this trouble?"

He shrugged. "Because I am the plastic surgeon who stitched you up. Because we know one another. Because you're a colleague." He smiled slightly. "Because you seemed unwilling to talk to anyone else."

"Oh. I don't remember that. Sorry."

"It's fine. People who've suffered a trauma need gentle handling. Let's hope Inspector Brightwell knows that." He smiled down at me, his serious dark eyes warm and sympathetic. "See you tomorrow, Rachel."

I did my best with Inspector Brightwell, but I knew that there were still gaping holes in my memory. My account of what had happened before I came to Brant was jumbled and out of sequence, and there were moments when he sighed and crossed out the notes he'd taken. When I told him about my visit to the police station he made a harrumphing noise and muttered something which I didn't quite catch, but assumed to be uncomplimentary to his colleagues at Porton.

"They went round to Eve Rawlins' house," I told him. "But of course she denied everything – except her behaviour at her son's funeral, which people saw. And, of course, that was easily put down to her grief and momentary loss of control. As to the rest, they said they simply didn't have enough evidence to pursue her any further."

He closed his notebook with a snap. "Well, we do now," he said. "Anyway, she confessed. She seems a sad sort of character to me, not like someone who could attempt murder."

My undamaged eye widened. "Is that what she'll be charged with? Was she really trying to kill me?"

The inspector shrugged. "She says not. Says she was just trying to hurt you. So you could 'feel her pain'. Anyway, for the moment she's out of my hands. Been referred to a psychiatrist."

I felt this like a physical blow. "What are you saying? That she might get off because she's insane? Where's the justice in that?"

He shook his head. "Look, I don't know. We'll all just have to wait and see what happens." He handed me a card. "My number, in case you think of something you haven't told me." He stood up. "Thank you, Ms Keyte. I'm sorry you've been through this. I hope you heal up all right."

When he'd gone the nurse – Jenny – said, "Could you use a cup of tea, Rachel? I'll have to get you one of those old-people beakers with a spout."

"Lovely," I said sourly. "I'd rather have coffee, if possible. Black, no sugar."

She came back a few minutes later with a tray. "Hold on a sec; let me put this down." She bustled out of the room again and then opened the door and stood in the doorway, in her arms an enormous bouquet of roses: pink, yellow, and white. "Gosh, these must have cost someone a fair bit," she said. "Just delivered – but I can't put these in your room; it's not allowed. Risk of infection. I thought you'd like to see them, though. Seems you have an admirer." She sounded dubious, as if this was improbable for someone like me.

"Is there a card?" I asked.

She pulled off a small envelope and extracted a card from inside. She put it on the bed, open, where I could see it. "There you go. I'll just put these in water. Lovely, aren't they? But why don't shop roses smell? It seems a waste, roses that don't smell."

The writing was scrawled, and my unbandaged eye watered with the effort of deciphering it: "Darling Rachel, I am appalled at what has happened. I'll come in and see you very soon. Love, hugs and kisses galore. Rob."

Over the days that followed I endured visitors – some expected, some surprising. Jasper was the first, followed by Peter and Angela. They were all equally horrified and concerned and asked the same questions. Eventually Nurse Jenny noted my pallor and shooed them out. "You can come back another day," she said firmly, "but now Rachel needs to rest."

Did I? Or did I just need to hide away? That's what I thought I wanted, anyway; but word of something so dramatic and scandalous as an attack on a surgeon going about her business in a major hospital was sure to cause a ripple of interest, including, so I was told, in the local papers. Happily there were few details – nothing about what had happened in Porton – and I was thankful for that.

On the Wednesday following the attack I had the first of many visits from the physiotherapist, a small but (as I found out) formidable young woman called Josie, who removed my plaster splints and replaced them with lighter, plastic ones.

"These should be more comfortable," she said. "I'm going to tell you what's going to happen over the next few weeks, so pin back your ears."

She talked at length about the need to protect the tendon repair. "Mr Wells will have done a proper job," she said. "We have to make sure it keeps that way. You'll need an orthosis, like a sort of tailor-made glove, for each hand. They let your wrist and fingers move within a restricted range but make sure the repair isn't stressed."

"Just tell me how long," I said. I know I sounded surly.

Josie was unperturbed. "Rehabilitation normally takes six to eight weeks after surgery," she said calmly. "Of course, a lot depends on the wound itself, the skill of the surgeon, and the cooperation of the patient. It could be less, it could be more."

"I can't believe... two months?" I whispered, appalled. I think in that moment I couldn't have loathed Eve Rawlins more.

"The sooner we get started, the better," Josie said with matron-like briskness. "We have to talk about an exercise regime, swelling management, wound care, minimizing scar tissue formation – among other things. We all want you to get your hands back, don't we? You're a surgeon too, I hear. All the more reason to work hard and persevere."

She made me feel like a mutinous adolescent. But I had to admit she was right.

Michael came to see me every day, even when he was off duty. He made sure I was keeping up with Josie's orders, and my frowning sulks made his mouth twitch with barely hidden amusement. He, though, was a welcome visitor: unthreatening, calm, empathetic, and he absorbed my grousing without complaint. The day after I met Josie he announced that the next day he would be removing my facial sutures.

I shuddered. "So I'm to prepare myself for a new level of hideousness."

"Nonsense. That long, thin scar will serve only to make your face more interesting. You can dine out on it."

"Thanks. But I think my dining-out days are over."

"Not at all," he said. "I'm afraid you'll just have to exercise patience."

The following morning he appeared – masked, gloved, and white-coated – accompanied by a demure young nurse I didn't recognize. He looked at me keenly over the edge of the mask. "You don't seem too well."

"I had a rough night," I mumbled. "Too much dreaming, none of it pleasant."

He shook his head. "Let's get these stitches out and see what's happening." Gently he peeled away the dressing, starting at the top by my temple, easing it over the cheek, and pulling it away from under my jaw. "That looks all right, don't you think, Gemma?" he said to the nurse.

"Very neat and clean, Mr Wells."

"Pass me those small scissors, please."

A moment later it was done. He took a swab and wiped it carefully down the scar line. "Want to look?" he asked me. "I promise there's no resemblance to Frankenstein." I heard Gemma giggle.

"Go on, then. Pleased you find my disfigurement so funny."

"We don't," Michael said. "And you aren't disfigured. Find me a mirror, please, Gemma."

The nurse produced a mirror and held it in front of my face. Michael stood by, arms folded, silent. The side of my face was a mess of bruising: purple, red, yellow. But I could see it was already fading. The suture line was thin, likely to disappear to almost nothing. There was a notch inside my eyebrow, and another at the corner of my upper lip. It was a mess, but I knew it could have been much worse.

"OK. I'm still a radiant beauty queen," I said. To my horror I felt an ache in my chest and throat and tears flooding my eyes.

Michael turned to the nurse. "Thanks, Gemma," he said. "You might as well go now."

When she had gone he turned back to me. I was flopped back against my pillow, eyes closed, tears dribbling. "I feel so feeble," I muttered.

He mopped my face with a tissue. It was getting to be a habit. "You're still suffering from shock," he said. "So far you've scornfully refused any psychiatric input. Perhaps you should rethink that. Counselling isn't feeble – it's potentially restorative. I assume that's what you want – to be restored. Isn't it? That's what we all want for you."

"Maybe one day. Not now," I said fiercely. "I'll just talk to you." My eyes flew open. "That's if you don't mind."

"No, I don't mind," he said, "but I'm a plastic surgeon, not a counsellor. I can listen to you as a friend, that's all."

"Perfect." I closed my eyes again, feeling suddenly exhausted.

"Do you want to tell me about these dreams of yours?"

"Boringly predictable, I'm sure. Even for an amateur shrink like you."

"Try me."

"No, they're mostly about my dad. Of no interest to anyone except me."

"All right, Rachel. You look as if you need to get some sleep. I'll come by again tomorrow and check on your face. And maybe we could have a chat about your dad. Sounds like he could be at the bottom of your problems."

"I don't have any problems," I said sleepily. "Apart from murderous maniacs with birthmarks." *And my dad did nothing wrong, apart from die too soon.*

On Saturday morning Josie arrived, brisk and bustling. She eyed me with professional scrutiny. "I have to say," she announced, "you don't look that good, Rachel. Are you eating?"

"I have to be fed," I said. Even to my own ears I sounded

peevish. "Obviously, since I can't use my hands. The nurses make sure I take in some form of nutritious slop. They don't want me to starve on their watch. But I am not keen."

"You have to eat to build up your strength. You are too pale."

I glowered at her. If my black looks were designed to frighten her away, they were not working. "You may have noticed," I said with elaborate sarcasm, "that when it comes to digestion, what goes in must also come out. I am not in any hurry to be wheeled to the bathroom and attended to like an infant."

She sighed loudly and shook her head. "Well, I don't see any way round that, I'm afraid. I just popped by to let you know your orthoses will be ready some time next week. Unfortunately for you there's a long Bank Holiday coming up – with the extra day on Tuesday."

"Oh, is there?" I said vaguely.

"It's the Queen's Jubilee," Josie said, her eyes wide at my ignorance.

"So it is."

"Anyway, once we've got you used to them you'll be able to do a bit more for yourself."

"Thank you," I said grudgingly.

I was left alone with my thoughts, and they were hard to bear, because they were impossible to ignore. Where was Rob? I tried not to feel hurt, but apart from the flowers I'd had no word from him.

After lunch I must have dozed, because I was awoken by a tap on the door. The little dark-haired nurse called Stella put her head round. "Visitor for you, Rachel. Are you decent?"

"Very funny," I said sleepily. "As if there's any chance I might be dancing round the room naked. Yes, send him in."

But it wasn't Rob that came cautiously into the room. At first I didn't recognize him: the last time I'd seen him he'd been in priestly garb – cassock, surplice, and something round his neck

116

that I didn't know the term for. Now he wore a crumpled and dusty blue suit over a black clerical shirt complete with dog collar. He paused in the doorway, a tall, stooped figure leaning on a stick.

"Oh!"

"May I come in?" he said.

"Father Vincent, isn't it? I didn't expect to see *you*." I didn't try to mask my surprise. He said nothing. "Well, since you're here, pull up a chair." I heard the sound of my own voice – hard, mutinous, as if I were a sulky child again.

He lumbered across the room, picked up the chair that had been left by the window, and pulled it closer to my bedside. He lowered himself into it with a grimace of pain. "Of course you're surprised," he said, "and I have no expectation of welcome. But I come as a messenger."

"From her?"

"From Eve, yes. She begged me to come."

"Why? What can she possibly have to say to me that I would want to hear? According to the policeman who interviewed me, she didn't actually plan to murder me – just damage me. As you can see, she has succeeded in that." I could feel my fury rise, threatening to choke my voice.

"I know; I see what she has done," Father Vincent said. "I am appalled – anyone would be. But the fact is, so is she. Now she sees the result of her actions, and she's absolutely horrified."

"Oh, really?" I grated. "How does that help me?" I lifted my pink-splinted hands a few inches off the sheet, wincing. "See these? I might never work again. How does that help anybody?"

He shook his head. "It doesn't, I know. But she asked me to come, and so I have, even though it's a long way and these days I don't travel well. She knows it's totally inadequate, but she wants you to know she is sorry."

"Ha! Sorry? She's sorry? What about the weeks of planning, the stalking, that must have gone into this? Not to mention the things she did, or got someone to do, before I left Porton! The blood, the pig's heart, the graffiti on my door? And she's *sorry*?"

"Please, Ms Keyte, I beg you; hear me out. As I said, I've come a long way. She said she lost her reason when she lost Craig. She saw you as a callous murdering monster that failed to care for her son. Of course everyone knows that's crazy. You did your best, I have no doubt of that. She said she seemed to be in another universe, where you had to be hurt – you had to share her pain. But then as soon as she saw your blood it was as if she suddenly woke up and saw the reality of what she'd done." I said nothing. "You know she's been referred for psychiatric tests?" I nodded. "Now she seems absolutely normal. Just as she always was, except that she is anguished, racked with guilt. When I went to see her, she said, 'I want to be found fit to plead. I should be punished. I should go to prison. It's what I deserve.' She is in another hell, Ms Keyte – one of her own making."

"Do you expect *me* to feel sorry for *her*?"

He sighed. "I expect nothing at all. I came only to deliver her message – of sorrow and contrition. I know her, Ms Keyte. I believe she is honest in this. I don't suppose you are interested in my opinion. But if you could, one day, forgive her, it would be better for you as well."

"Oh, please!" I said. "Spare me the saintly truisms. She's ruined my life and hers. Why should I care?" He did not answer, simply sat with head bowed. "I guess you're going to tell me she had a deprived childhood, or something. Or could it be that horrible birthmark that's messed up her life?"

He spoke quietly. "I don't think there was much wrong with her childhood, as you suggest. But yes, in many ways her life has been hard, and the birthmark hasn't helped. But all that is beside the point. For months she thought of you as a kind of demon. Now she knows how wrong, how mad, she has been, and she doesn't want you to think of her in that way, even after what she has done." He struggled to his feet. "I won't bother you any more,

Ms Keyte. I understand your anger and bitterness, of course I do. But please, think. If you let it, it will burn you up. That, more than anything, will be what ruins your life, even if your wounds heal – as I truly hope they will." He inclined his head. "I'll go now. We're praying for you at St Joseph's, as well as for her. Goodbye, Ms Keyte."

My thoughts were in disarray, and I had no time to process them. Father Vincent had been gone no more than ten minutes when with the merest of knocks my door flew open. Fleetingly I registered the hum of voices from the main ward where visiting was still going on, and then at last Rob came flying across the room and flung himself into the chair that Father Vincent had vacated. He was all motion and colour, and I felt a wave of sheer joy, as if he had brought the sun with him.

He looked at me aghast, his mouth agape. "Oh, Rachel, darling! What has that madwoman done to you? You poor thing!" Unable to grab onto any part of me that was visible and not likely to hurt, he leaned over and planted a kiss on my forehead, very gently.

"Hello, Rob," I murmured. "Where have you been?"

"I'm so sorry; I wanted to come sooner, really I did, but it's been… well, it's been a difficult week."

"You're here now. Thanks for the flowers – they were beautiful, even though I only got to see them for a moment: hospital rules, fear of infection, etcetera."

"Yes, I think I saw them in a vase on a table in the corridor," Rob said. "They're fully out now." He fell silent, gazing at me with those wide blue eyes, and to my dismay I detected the shine of unshed tears.

"Rob, are you all right? Is something wrong?"

"No – yes – something is, and I don't know how to tell you." He gulped. "Oh, Rachel! I'm sorry, so sorry; it's all gone to pieces! All I wanted was you, and I would have gone on asking till you said yes just to shut me up, but now I can't have you, and it's such lousy timing, just when you need me, I feel such an utter –"

"Hey, slow down! What are you talking about?" I spoke lightly, but there was something in his manner, something wild and unlike the Rob I knew, that was sending a cold wash down my spine.

He took a deep breath and wiped his face with his palms. "You remember I told you about Sammy – the girl I was with before you came to Brant? She called me, said we needed to talk. Said it was important." He swallowed and looked away. "Rachel, she's… Sammy's pregnant."

I swore under my breath – I, who rarely swear. My heart seemed to be lurching out of rhythm, though I knew this was hardly likely. "So," I said coolly, "it's yours, is it, this child?"

He looked at me then, startled. "Of course! Why would she tell me if it was someone else's?"

"Because you're a bit soft?"

"No, no, that's not right," Rob said, his voice rising. "Sammy's not a liar; she's a good person. It's definitely mine, and anyway the dates fit. She's waited this long, wondering what to do, but now she's fifteen weeks and you can see the bump. Rachel, don't you see? Whatever my plans were, I can't just abandon her and the baby. I have to do what's right. I have to go back to her. You do understand, don't you? It's not what I would have chosen, but it's my responsibility."

"So what did this Sammy actually want?" I spoke coldly.

"She didn't want anything. She wasn't asking for anything from me. She just thought I should know – that I had a right to know."

I felt a vast weariness descend on me. What could I say? I had turned him down a dozen times, and I had seen it all as play. I sighed deeply. "Of course I understand," I said dully. "You have to follow your conscience. I'm sure you'll make a good dad. I wish you well, all three of you."

He stood up and stared down at me, chewing his lip. "It would almost be better if you screamed at me," he said softly. "I know I've let you down, Rachel, and I can't begin to tell you how sorry I am – for me as well as you." He tried to smile. "I'll come back tomorrow, see how you are."

I lifted my hand from the sheet, winced at the pain, and let it fall. "No, Rob. Please don't. I'll be out of here next week, and there's really no point, is there? Clean break time."

"Are you sure?" A tear leaked from his eye, and for a moment I did feel pity.

"Yes, it's better. You haven't really done anything wrong, if I'm honest. Except be a bit careless."

He nodded and heaved a sigh. "Yeah. Well, I'm getting my comeuppance." He gazed at me earnestly. "I hope you get better quickly. I'll see you around the place."

"Sure. Good luck, Rob."

I asked the nurse on the night shift to open the curtains at my window. I couldn't see out – my bed was the wrong way round – but the light of a moon almost at the full washed into the room, and I could imagine it sailing in a cloudless inky sky, casting its enigmatic borrowed light across the face of the earth. Often, when our father took us camping as children, if the night was fine we would sleep out under such a sky and wake damp with dew. I remembered those nights, and on this night I wished – foolishly, for what use are wishes? – that the intervening years might disappear and take me back to an unchanging past. Until his illness and death I had never dreamed of disaster.

That long night I lay awake, thinking about him, and asking those questions that are both useless and dangerous: What am I for? Who cares? My damaged hands lay on the sheet, throbbing and sore and stiff in their splints, a testimony to my vanished hope. I knew I was being melodramatic, but the circumstances of my life seemed to warrant it. Would I ever be able to operate again? Maybe, but at what level of risk? Would I ever recover that dexterity and confident dash I was known for? Probably not. And without the work to which I had wholeheartedly given myself for almost twenty years, who was I? What could I offer? I had nothing, or so it seemed – no work, no future, a reputation that could not be maintained, ambition that could bear no fruit, no realistic goals to strive for. I had no husband, no lover, no child. I had nothing. I was nobody.

I felt myself slipping and sliding down something like a mineshaft – the walls of which were glassy-smooth, without handhold or traction – towards a depth that was dark, fathomless, warm, comfortable, a cosy form of death; and I offered no resistance. Coolly I thought of the opportunities for self-destruction available to someone with medical training and plenty of leisure, and this thought kept me going. It bore at least some resemblance to control.

Towards morning I must have slept, because I remembered a dream of drowning. I had been bound hand and foot and thrown – who by, I had no idea – into a swimming pool, and the only time I could breathe was when, briefly, I bobbed to the surface, and in that all-too-short moment before sinking again I had to choose whether to breathe or to scream. I woke abruptly to a thin early light and a cool wind ruffling my curtains, and to the sound of a rattling trolley in the corridor. I was sweating and sick with dread.

A smiling black face appeared round my door. "You ready for a cuppa, my love?" she whispered. "It's a bit early, but I thought you might be awake."

"Thanks," I croaked. "Black coffee, please." As she turned back to her trolley, I smiled to myself, a hollow, bleak little smile. In the midst of tragedy there's often farce, as now – my suicidal thoughts interrupted by a bustling tea-maker; and I recognized my dream for what it was, a loud-hail from a more robust part of myself, a part that would never have countenanced drowning in self-pity.

Nevertheless, I needed to think: what could the future hold for me? Even if I worked relentlessly at my exercises, even if my scars faded and my hands could be used, what then? My life, without the work I loved, was purposeless and empty; I had allowed it to become so and I had no means of knowing if I'd get it back.

That Sunday morning had its high points. A nurse took me to the bathroom, and with my arms wrapped up in plastic to the elbows I stood under water that many would have found too hot, and wallowed till my skin turned pink. Then I allowed my hair to be washed. Normally a shower is just something you do every day for the sake of basic hygiene, but this, after days in bed, was a slice of heaven, even if I got back into bed exhausted.

The same nurse brushed my hair into a semblance of order. "Does that feel better?" she said kindly.

"Infinitely," I replied. "I feel like a regular member of society, not something rescued from the jungle after forty years."

"You're funny," the nurse said as she stood up, pulling my hairs from the brush. "Not too long now till lunch time." She gave a wry grin. "Something else to look forward to."

"Now who's funny?" I said.

I wasn't at all interested in lunch, or any other meal, but at least it broke up the day, and I was beginning, reluctantly, to get used to someone spooning food into my mouth. Sunday lunch might once have conjured up visions of roasted meat and crisp potatoes, but not here, not now. Maybe one day. However that Sunday lunchtime dished up a surprise.

I heard the trolley, and voices, back and forth, and I frowned: one of the voices was familiar and didn't belong to any of my known nurses. I heard a burst of laughter, and the door opened a crack.

"Hey, Rachel. Can I come in?"

"Jasper! Of course, yes. I didn't know you were still here."

"I'm almost not." He came in carefully, and I saw he was

123

carrying a tray. "But I asked if I could be your slave – do you mind?"

"What – *you're* going to feed me?"

"I won't if you hate the idea."

"I hate the idea of being fed, but you can do it if you like." I couldn't be bothered to argue, and I knew he was trying to be kind. "How did you persuade the powers-that-be?"

He sat in the chair by my bedside. "That's not difficult. Relatives help with meals all the time. And the nurses know me, because of Dad." He lifted the lid from my plate. "Hm, this looks… interesting. You ready?"

"I suppose. But why are you still here?"

He loaded the spoon and put it into my open mouth. "How's that?"

"Oh, absolutely first class," I said sarcastically. "Go on, tell me all your latest."

"We're on our way back to London," Jasper said, loading and reloading the spoon and feeding me with surprising delicacy and skill. "Half term is over, and I have to say it wasn't much fun – more or less all revision. We only went swimming once, and Dad even took Dulcie out so I could work. I guess I have to, though." He sighed and wiped gravy off my chin. "I'm even going to have to work on a Bank Holiday when the entire nation is off work and having fun."

"When's your first exam?"

"Thursday. History."

"That's something you like, isn't it?"

He scraped the plate. "I like history generally. I don't like what we've been doing the last couple of years. Unbelievably boring."

"Please, Jasper, no more."

"You've hardly eaten anything."

"I'll have that tub of yogurt. Protein and vitamins. Have you thought any more about your A-level subjects?"

"Yes," Jasper said, peeling the lid off the yogurt. "Dad and I had a long chat about it last night. He said if I still had no idea what I wanted to do I should choose subjects I liked, and if I ended up stacking shelves in the supermarket at least I'd be an educated shelf-stacker."

"He said that? I haven't seen much evidence of his sense of humour."

Jasper looked up in surprise. "Oh, he definitely has one! I guess," he added, sobering, "what happened to you isn't something he'd find funny. So he'd hardly be visiting you and cracking jokes. Open up, please."

I obeyed, and the yogurt was dispatched with merciful speed. "So, what have you decided?"

"History, psychology, biology, statistics. I can ditch statistics next year."

"Not the most obvious combination."

He grinned. "I keep telling you: I'm not the most obvious person!" He took the tray and put it on the windowsill. "Now," he said, planting himself back in the chair and folding his arms, "enough of all that boring stuff – what about you? I want to hear everything."

"What, the grisly details of my trip to the shower this morning?"

"OK – no, not that," Jasper said, and I was amused to see him blush. "What I mean is, I want to know how you really are."

I sighed. "Well, my face you can see for yourself. Your father tells me it will be very thin and discreet, with time. I've been put under the care of a fearsome physiotherapist called Josie, and at some point she's bringing me some orthoses. Know what those are?"

"Yes, I've heard of them." He hesitated. "But Dad's told me how the operation went, and how you seem to be healing up OK. I guess he'll take a look at your hands tomorrow, won't he, when the splints and bandages come off. I'm sure he's done a brilliant job, because he always does. People say that, so it's not just me being a loyal son!" He bit his lip. "I meant more, how are you doing, like, in your head? I'm worried you might be getting post-traumatic shock, or depression, or something."

I was surprised, not for the first time, and touched by his concern. I hadn't thought anyone might be worried about me. Nevertheless I frowned. "So you and your dad have been discussing my mental state?"

"Oh no; not at all," Jasper said. "I've just been thinking about it. Dad doesn't actually discuss his patients with me, but you're a friend, and he knows I'm worried."

"Well…" I took a deep breath. "I don't know what to say, Jasper." I thought, and he watched me. "Yesterday I had a really unexpected visit, from a priest. One of his congregation is my attacker, Eve Rawlins. He wanted me to forgive her."

Jasper's eyes widened. "Really? What did you say?"

"What do you think?"

He blew out his breath. "I don't know, Rachel. Maybe one day? That's hard."

"And then," I said, "I had another visitor. Someone you might have described as my boyfriend. But he isn't any more."

"What?" Jasper said, his dark eyebrows shooting into his hairline. "He dumped you *yesterday*?"

I shook my head. "It's not as bad as it sounds. He had very good reason. And I don't think we'd have made much of a couple, not for long."

"But Rachel," Jasper's voice rose, "how can you be philosophical? That's awful! How could he do that, I mean, now of all times? I feel like I want to go find him and whack him."

"Just as well you don't know where he lives then, isn't it?" I said, smiling. "Anyway, I don't think whacking is really your style. Look, Jasper, please don't worry. I'll be OK, especially when I get out of here and don't feel like a helpless, useless invalid. Put me out of your mind – I don't want you to be at all distracted from your exams because of me."

"I can't believe someone could do that to you, Rachel. It's terrible."

I heard a light rapping on the frame of the door, which Jasper had left ajar, and Michael appeared in the doorway. He smiled. "Hello, Rachel." He turned to his son. "JB, sorry, but we have to go. Otherwise the traffic will pile up."

Jasper stood up and put the chair back. For a moment he just looked at me, his eyes searching my face. I said nothing, but looked back at him enquiringly. Then he said, in a jumbled rush, "Look, Rachel – I have to get back to London. But I'll pray for you."

"You'll –?"

"Sorry, got to go." He leaned over me and brushed my cheek with his lips. "Bye. Get well."

I had a few lonely hours to ponder Jasper's surprising offer. He was a decent boy, I knew that, and in his own words "not typical". But I hadn't seen him as someone who might pray, and that gave me a lot to think about. Was it just him, a maverick convert, or were one or both of his parents Christians – or someone else in his circle? It was a puzzle.

But surprises weren't over for me that strange Sunday. I had just managed to drink a cup of tea – a drink I normally avoid, but that's all that was on offer that afternoon, and I was parched. Not only was the weather outside warm, but the hospital was kept at what I felt was a wholly unhealthy temperature. Tea makes me bilious, and today was no exception. I'm sure I looked as bad as I felt.

At about five thirty a knock came at my door. "I suppose you can come in," I said ungraciously. I couldn't think of anyone I really wanted to see – except perhaps my brother Martin, and he was on the other side of the world. Michael appeared in the doorway. "Permission to visit?" he said. "I'm just back from taking Jasper to London."

"Seems to me you already are visiting," I said. I couldn't be bothered to crank out the charm, but he obviously didn't mind, because I saw him smother a wry smile.

He pulled up the chair and sat down. "Am I allowed to ask how you are, or is that too tedious?"

"It's very tedious. Most people who ask that question want to hear some gallant little lie, like, 'Oh, not so bad, getting there; many people worse off, etc.'"

"Perhaps I am not 'most people', though," he said.

"That's almost what Jasper says about himself."

"With reason."

"So," I eyed him suspiciously, "are you here in a professional capacity, or just as a friendly visitor?"

"Just a visitor," he said. "I'm not on duty. I will be tomorrow, when I come by and observe the removal of your splints and dressings, and see what your hands are looking like – despite the fact that it's a national holiday. But for now, I *would* like to know how you are, and I don't need defending from the truth."

I heaved a deep sigh. "Then you're braver than most." I turned my head, avoiding his steady gaze. "I feel rubbish. Sore, useless, humiliated, angry. I would scream, but it would upset the other patients, and I'm sure many of them are in a worse state than me."

"Yes, some of them are." He fell silent for a moment. "Rachel, I need to ask you something." His tone had altered, and I felt compelled to turn back and look at him, but I said nothing. The silence lengthened. "Tell me to get lost if I am overstepping any boundaries," he said, "but I've been talking to a psychiatrist friend, and I feel bound to ask. Do you feel, have you felt, at any point…"

"Suicidal?" I said bluntly. "Sure I have. Not at this moment, perhaps. If you were in my shoes, wouldn't it occur to you?"

"Of course not," he said, and I blinked at the sharpness of his tone. "Life is precious. And people would be hurt."

"Maybe in your case they would," I countered. "I would soon be forgotten; nothing but a vaguely uncomfortable memory." To my horror, despite my every effort and my proud look, I felt my eyes well up. "Bother, damn, and many stronger words," I muttered.

His voice softened. "Look, I empathize with your situation. To lose the use of my hands would be a disaster. But I'm hopeful that you won't lose the use of yours, provided you do as you're told by the physiotherapy team – and me." He smiled. "That's going to be tough, I know."

"Even if what you say is true," I said, "can you guarantee I'll be able to work at the same level?"

"No, I can't. Obviously. There are too many factors, too many unknowns." He pursed his lips, thinking. "Let me ask you something else. Before it ever occurred to you to be a surgeon, what were you good at? What did you like to do?"

"Whoa! You're talking a long time ago. I was just a kid."

"So what did the child Rachel like doing?"

I managed a faint smile. "For a start, only my mother and my teachers ever called me Rachel. I spent most of my spare time with my dad and my brother, and they always called me Lizzie. Martin still does."

"So what do you think of when you remember being Lizzie?" he said softly.

I raised my eyebrows. I thought I knew where this was going. "Oh, you know," I said with patently false lightness, "nice things: innocence, safety, acceptance, fun. Love – yes, that too. All in the past." He was looking at me gravely. "Your psychiatrist friend would be digging away by now, wouldn't he? Unearthing all my secrets."

"Maybe he would, but since you refuse to talk to him it's academic. And you haven't answered my question."

"What, the things I liked doing?" He nodded. "I liked doing things with my dad. He taught me and my brother a lot of things

– useful, practical things, as well as the stuff parents normally teach their kids."

"Such as?"

"How to swim. Ride a bike. Make a pie. Rattle off our multiplication tables." I paused, summoning up a time long buried. "He made us do our piano practice. Martin resisted; I never did. But less obvious things too. By the time I went to secondary school I knew how to wire a plug, change a wheel, grow simple vegetables. I could tell a flower from a weed. He taught us how to cook. Catch a fish. Pitch a tent in the rain." I glanced Michael's way. "Not bored yet with my reminiscences?"

"They're hardly that," he murmured. "Anything else?"

"Plenty. He taught us to love music. Even Bach and opera, not things ten-year-olds normally appreciate. And he shared his love of nature, animals, birds, forests, mountains, as well as human achievements – artistic endeavours, scientific discoveries. Museums, castles, churches, history."

"Tell me something you remember."

"Hm… camping out, lying on our backs in the grass at night, naming the stars." Suddenly I felt this had all gone far enough. "And," I said with some asperity, "I learned how to train a dog. I practised on the amiable Bertie, who was none too bright. Compared to him your Dulcie is a canine genius. She could definitely do with training."

Michael chuckled. "I don't dispute that. Feel free, any time."

I gave him what I hoped was a stern look. "Why do you have a dog like Dulcie, when you can't spare the time to train her properly? It's a terrible waste, letting a collie run wild. Aren't they one of the cleverest breeds?"

"I agree," Michael said. "I am a failure as a dog owner. But as to why I have her, she was a present – one I couldn't refuse, in the circumstances." I raised an eyebrow. Michael cleared his throat. "Jasper gave her to me, the Christmas after he and Alison left Brant for London. Jasper had just turned twelve. He was worried I'd be lonely."

"It was his idea? He didn't consult?"

Michael smiled. "Not that I know of. I'm pretty sure his mother would have put a damper on it – sensibly, of course."

"How did a twelve-year-old boy, in London, acquire a collie puppy?"

"Ah, well, he organized it even before they left. The family of a friend of his from his primary school here had a pregnant bitch. Jasper earmarked one for me, and because the family knew us they didn't object. But he said nothing to anyone. Came down here one weekend, went 'for a walk' and came back with a black and white bundle of fluff in his arms. She was nine weeks old. Absolutely irresistible: tiny and defenceless, but brave and sturdy with that knowing look collies often have, that dash of sheer delightful wickedness."

I was silent for a moment, thinking about a lonely boy worrying about his father. "Resourceful Jasper," I murmured. "Perhaps a little misguided, but very kind."

"So," Michael said, "in your opinion, have I done better as a parent?" I had challenged him, and he was amused.

"Yes," I said, "of course. Jasper is both clever and good, from what I have seen of him. But for all I know that could be his mother's influence." Michael raised his eyebrows and did not comment. But there was something I wanted to know, and if he thought it was OK to grill me, then I felt I could ask him personal questions too. "You know, I was intrigued by what he said when he left."

"What was that?"

"He said he would pray for me. You must have heard him."

"Oh. Well, that's not a surprise, except that he actually said it. He is bolder than his father." He paused. "We have both prayed for you."

"That answers my question." I didn't really know what to say, and Michael wasn't helping. Memories were intruding; I wasn't certain that they were welcome, but they were insistent. "Actually, my dad was a believer. He wasn't much of a churchgoer, but he delighted in creation, as he put it. It filled him with gratitude, he said."

"Did he communicate that to his children as well?"

Suddenly I felt I was stepping out onto quicksand, and I shivered. "Yes. As a child I took it all on board. But I'm not a child any more, and the things he taught us are all very much in the past." I pulled a face. "I'd probably struggle with tent-pitching these days."

He was silent for several moments. "Is your mother still alive? You barely mention her."

I smiled sourly. "Very much so. But she wasn't much of a parent. Never wanted to be one."

"Should we have informed her what has happened to you?"

"Please, don't bother. It will make no difference."

A wave of weariness washed over me, and Michael saw it. "I'm sorry. You're looking tired. I'll leave you in peace." He stood up, looking down at me. "I'll see you in the morning. In my professional role, white coat and all." I nodded. "Hope you get some sleep. But I'd like to carry on talking about this, if you feel up to it."

I closed my eyes. "Whatever."

He paused at the door. "Bye for now."

I lifted one splinted hand off the bed. Then he was gone.

"*Rehab?* What am I, a drunk, a drug addict?" I knew I was being cantankerous and obtuse.

"No," Michael said. "Just someone who needs rehabilitating, as you are well aware."

"I thought I was going home. Or what serves as home these days – my little granny flat."

"And how are you going to look after yourself?" he reasoned.

"Wash, cook, dress, and so on? With those on?" He waved a hand at my hands, wrapped in webbing orthoses, just the top joints of my fingers showing. "You want Angela Axton popping in every time you need the toilet?"

I shuddered. "I don't want anyone."

"Two weeks," he said. "That's all. Then if things are going well you can go home. You'll have to do as you're told and work hard." Did I see a gleam in his eye? Was he enjoying the thought of my having to learn meek obedience? I said nothing, my lips in a tight line. "Rachel," he said, "it's only two weeks, but they may be the most important weeks of your life to date. Think of it as the first step to getting back to where you want to be. You can do that much, I know."

"Really?" My eyes narrowed.

"Think about all the years of graft you've put in. All the pompous fools you've suffered. All the old goats who've leered at you at the same time as putting you down for being young and female in a male-dominated specialism."

I was startled. "How do you know about them?"

He shrugged. "It's part of the culture."

"It's true," I said. "Years ago an eminent senior surgeon had huge fun rubbing up against me when I was actually operating. If I had slipped and severed something vital it would have been my fault, wouldn't it?"

"How did you handle that?"

"What could I do? I ignored him."

"You got on with the job in hand. And that's what you have to do now –the job is to recover what you've lost, by whatever means are on offer. Two weeks with the rehab team, physiotherapy till you're sick of it. With any luck, when it's over you'll be able to attend to your own physical needs and keep your dignity intact."

I sighed. "OK. When do I start?"

He smiled. "Just as soon as we can get it organized – probably in the next few days. From what I saw of your hands when we took the splints and bandages off they're healing well."

I turned to look at him. I was lounging on the bed in my pyjamas; he was sitting in the chair, leaning back. I thought he looked tired. "I must have had a pretty decent surgeon, then," I said. "Wouldn't you say?"

"Oh, I don't know. Might have been that butcher they employ in this hospital. Just a fluke he didn't carve you up well and truly."

"Very funny. Honestly, Michael, I know I owe you one."

"Nonsense. It's my job." He stood up suddenly. "This won't do. I'm going to set the wheels in motion, get you discharged and a room ready for you in rehab. Better pack a bag."

"Even with these on my hands," I lifted them up, "I can pack two pairs of PJs and a toothbrush."

He shook his head. "You'll need more than that. You'll be in your own clothes. I'll call round at the Axtons' and ask Angela to gather a few of your things. Is there anything you specially want?"

I shrugged. "T-shirts and jeans, I guess. I suppose I won't be needing the sequinned dress for a while. Or the tiara. But I'd like my phone."

"Right. I'll see what I can do." He paused in the doorway, noting my expression. "Something else on your mind?"

"Hm. I suppose the rehab team are a lot like Josie, aren't they? Fiendishly bossy."

"Of course. It's part of their training to deal with awkward patients like you. They probably have to practise martial arts as well. Just grit your teeth – it's only two weeks."

"Will you come and see me? I might get very, very bored."

He shook his head. "You won't have time to be bored. When they're not making you work you'll be only too glad to sleep. And it wouldn't be a good idea for me to visit, even if I had time. You know what hospitals are like – hotbeds of gossip. It's different now, when you're still in the hospital, when I have every reason to check how things are going. But if I were to visit you there, when I don't do it for other patients, there'll be whispering and gossips will put two and two together and make fifty."

"I guess so."

He heard my gloom and relented. "I'll ring you from time to time, if you like."

"That would be nice. I want to know how Jasper's exams are going." He nodded and made as if to go. "Michael –" He raised his eyebrows enquiringly. "Thank you for being so kind. I don't know why you are when I am so feeble and difficult, but thanks anyway."

"You're welcome. I particularly like feeble and difficult people."

"Go away! If I could I'd throw a pillow at you!"

Those two weeks – a bit less, as it turned out – were among the most gruelling I could remember. Michael was wrong – I was horribly bored – but not because I had too little to do; on the contrary, I was kept at it without mercy. The rehab team were not bullies at all: they were patient, professional, unruffled. But they were also determined. I spent many hours squeezing a tennis ball, pounding dough, rolling out pastry. As time went on and my strength and flexibility improved, the orthoses came off for longer and longer each day, until I was wearing them only at night. Finally I was allowed in the shower by myself – such a small thing, so taken for granted by the able-bodied, but such a relief. I knew that by their standards I was doing well. They told me, *go on like this and you'll soon be home.* But it was never enough: I didn't just want to be independent in ordinary life, though that was of course hugely desirable – I wanted to be back where I was, in the operating theatre, and I knew that was still far out of reach.

"I *am* bored," I said to Michael one evening when he phoned. "I don't care for idiot television. I don't need things to do – I have plenty of that all day – I need things to think about. Can you get someone to bring me some of my books? My laptop? I need to keep up with what's going on."

He sighed. "Send me a list."

I was relatively young, and in good health; I worked hard at the prescribed exercises; I tried to keep fit, using the gym next door as far as I was permitted with my injuries. Physically I healed. Mentally, emotionally, though I hid it well, I was a mess. I could feel the fear, the doubt, the anguish, welling up inside me, threatening to engulf my rational self, and it took all my willpower to thrust it down. *No one must notice, no one must feel concern, interfere, suggest counselling – make me feel even weaker.* All I wanted was to go home, lock the door, and fall apart unseen.

They sent me home, full of praise for my attitude and my progress, apparently not noticing the weak and sickly smile with which I greeted these effusions. If they had seen what was really going on inside my head, what would they have done? Flapped about like elderly chickens trying to escape the fox? Reported me to the psychiatric wing?

I came back to my flat, which I found clean and gleaming – no doubt the work of Angela Axton, that kind and efficient woman. I shut the door, and did nothing, because it seemed there was nothing to do. It was June, and warm, but I closed every window except one, which I left open just a crack. I didn't want to hear the sound of revellers on the river, or the thwack of cricket balls, or the song of the birds. I wanted to be in the dark: to embrace a sense of nowhere and nothing. Such thoughts as I had were chaotic and senseless. I didn't even have the energy or determination to wash down a bunch of pills with a bottle of vodka. The Rachel of rehab, false construct that she was, quickly turned into Rachel the nonentity, who was at best a sopping dishrag of self-pity, wallowing in a glutinous emotional soup. I went to bed and pulled the quilt over my head. I thought I would find a safe, grey place in sleep, but sleep was populated by hideous images: staring eyes and bloody knives and open-chested corpses that crawled off operating tables and danced around, exposed organs spattering the walls with sticky red. I had no tears, but screams welled up, and I covered my face with my pillow to stifle them lest anyone should hear.

I'd been home less than two days when a hammering came at my door. I ignored it, but it became more and more insistent, and then someone was shouting, and this alarmed me so much I dragged myself off the bed and up the hall, and pulled the door open just to shut it up. I stumbled back and half-hid behind the door.

"Rachel, what in heaven's name is going on? Why is it so dark in here?" Michael stood in the doorway, in his hand a dog's leash, with Dulcie on the end of it, straining to be free. "Can we come in?"

I said nothing. He came in and shut the door, then bent and unclipped Dulcie's leash. Free, she leapt up on me, almost knocking me over, then proceeded to race around the flat like a missile.

Michael snapped on the light. He looked suntanned, and in need of a haircut. He stared at me, his eyes wide. "How long have you been home?" he asked softly.

My voice came out in a croak. "Two days, maybe. Two months. I don't know. What day is it, anyway?"

"Saturday. I've been away. I didn't know they were discharging you, or I'd have come back sooner."

"It doesn't matter," I mumbled.

"Clearly it does," he said, his tone harsh. "Has anyone been in to see you since you got back?" I shook my head. "Good heavens, Rachel – what a mess. It smells stale in here." He shook his head, looking around at the flat. "Have you eaten today?"

"No. I don't want anything."

"Come with me." He took my hand, led me into the sitting room, and sat me down on the sofa. He sat down beside me. "Look at me, Rachel." Reluctantly I faced him. "This can't go on." He spoke softly, but there was steel in his tone, and I felt myself shudder. He still had hold of my hand. "If you are feeling this bad, you will *have* to see my friend the shrink." I shook my head violently. "All right. But you said you'd speak to me, and I'm going to insist you do. Agreed?" I just stared at him. "Agreed, Rachel?" I made myself nod. "OK. First you go and take a shower, and put on some clean clothes. I'm going to open the windows. Even Dulcie can't stand it, and she loves things that stink. Then I'm going to make you some strong coffee and something to eat. If I know Angela there'll be ingredients in the fridge. After that you're going to talk to me. I won't go away until you have."

I didn't move. "Why?" I muttered.

"Because I'm not going to let you fall apart. Not when you have come this far. Now please, do us all a kindness: go and wash."

I did as he said, and it took me a long time. I used to go for a run, shower, and be back at my books in an hour. Now I seemed to go into a brainless dream, waking to find that I was still standing under the pounding water, soaking, soap in hand, motionless. At last I managed to step out, dripping everywhere, towel myself down, and rub my hair into damp clumps. Despite everything it felt better to be clean. I wrapped the towel round myself and scuttled into the bedroom, pulled on jeans and a T-shirt at random, brushed my hair into a semblance of order, then doubled back to the bathroom to clean my teeth. As I emerged Dulcie was sitting outside the door, head on one side, a canine smile on her knowing face.

I bent and ran my hand over her flanks. "Hello, girl."

Michael came out of the kitchen. "Come and sit down." The harshness was gone from his voice; he spoke so gently I felt unwelcome tears well up. *No! No crying*, I told myself savagely.

But it was no use. From somewhere a tap had been opened, a fountain switched on, and I felt my chest heave and tears brim over. Michael took me by the elbow, guided me into the kitchen, and pulled out a stool. "It's perfectly all right to cry," he said. "Tears are not a sign of weakness; they're an outlet for something that can't be held back any more – grief, shock, depression, trauma, loss, whatever. And you're suffering from all of those, Rachel. If you won't be kind to yourself you'll have to let others do it." He tore off a sheet of kitchen paper and handed it to me. Then he poured a mug of coffee from a steaming cafetière and put it in front of me. "Drink." I picked it up with a shaky hand and sipped. It was scalding and strong. "I just made you some toast. For now. Proper food later, when you feel like it. But I'm not moving from here till I see you've eaten something." Surprising myself, I found I had no wish that he should leave. I took a bite and chewed. Butter ran down my chin. It tasted amazing. How had I forgotten the taste of food and the restorative effects of caffeine? Michael leaned up against the kitchen counter, arms folded, nodding his approval. He said nothing till he saw me finish the toast and take several gulps of coffee. "Right. Let's go and sit somewhere comfortable and you can tell me what the heck's been going on."

He followed me into the sitting room. Dulcie, who until now had been lurking under the kitchen table in case I dropped a morsel of food, came with him, looking up at him in hopeful enquiry. "Lie down, girl," he said, stroking her ears. "I'll take you for a walk later." I curled up in the corner of the sofa, put the coffee on a small table beside it, and wrapped my arms around my body. He planted himself in a chair opposite and sat silent, just looking at me, waiting for me to say something.

"Nothing's been going on." My voice was a croak from lack of use. "I've been here. That's all."

He drew a deep breath and let it out in a sigh. "OK. What's been going on inside your head?"

I closed my eyes. "Why would you want to see that crazy stuff when I don't want to see it myself?"

He shook his head. "I don't want to know your secrets, Rachel. I'm not trying to be nosy. Maybe I should come clean – you said you wouldn't talk to my friend John Sutcliffe, the psychiatrist. So I asked him about you, what I should do, because I'm all at sea."

My eyes flew open. "You've been talking about me?"

He shrugged. "What else could I do? I told you before – I'm a plastic surgeon, not a trained psychiatrist. John just gave me a few general suggestions, because he agreed with me that you need to open up the closet and let your skeletons out – for the sake of your mental health."

"Huh. My skeletons are probably the sort that'd dance round the room, out of the door and down the High Street, playing the bagpipes. Are you telling me I'm crazy?"

"You admitted to suicidal feelings."

"OK, OK. What do you want to talk about?"

"Your mother, maybe?"

I sat up. "My *mother*?"

"All right, here's something more specific. Did your parents divorce?"

"No." I unfolded my arms, picked at a loose thread in the sofa fabric, staring at it till the weave went out of focus. "They stayed married, more or less, until the end."

"Were they happy?"

I pulled a face. "Maybe once. I don't know. Their relationship was a mystery to me, still is when I think about it – which is hardly ever." I looked up at him and scowled. Why was he asking all these questions? Though of course I thought I knew.

"How did they meet?"

I sighed. "All right. I'll tell you the sad story of the dysfunctional Keytes, if that's what you're after." I looked at him sideways. "Maybe I'll ask you some questions, seeing as you're not my psychiatrist."

He smiled, his eyes crinkling. "Feel free."

A thought struck me. "Where have you been? You said you'd been away."

"Oh, just down to Roqueville, our little place in France. It's a while since I went, and it's June, so the garden needed attention. I only went for a few days – it's all I could spare."

"What did you do with Dulcie?"

"Normally she'd have come with me, but it wasn't worth it for such a short time. The Axtons had her for me."

"And what about Jasper? Are his exams over?"

"Not quite. But even when they are, he'll be starting on his A-level courses. The school likes to keep its students busy." He paused. "So... your parents. John tells me it all starts with them. What was so mysterious?"

"What they saw in each other," I said. I felt the past creeping up behind me, like a cold draught, and I squirmed deeper into the sofa. "Apart from a pretty intense sexual attraction, which children don't normally want to contemplate, even if they have any notion of what it's all about." I saw him frown. "My mother was very beautiful in her day – you can still see traces of it, even though she's in her seventies now. And very vain, too – nothing's changed there. She's always perfectly made-up and immaculately turned out. Her shoes always match her outfit. She's very disparaging about women who *let themselves go*, *don't take the trouble* – I'm a complete failure in her eyes." I tried to smile, but it was more of a sneer. "Anyway, there she was, in her twenties, an up-and-coming actress, stage and screen, considered to be talented. You might even have heard of her – Frances Chester. It's been a while, of course."

"Mm. You know, I think I might have seen something she was in," Michael said, surprised. "The name's familiar."

"She was best known in her twenties and early thirties, but she went on working for quite some years till the parts dwindled and finally ran out. Then she did some radio work. She had – still has – a very striking voice."

"Were you proud of her achievements when you were young?"

"No. All I knew was she was never there. She never wanted us, especially me. All she cared about was her career. And there were some nasty rows." I shivered.

Michael frowned. "Are you cold?"

"No. But I'm not really having a lot of fun."

"It's therapy, not pleasure."

"Oh. I thought we were having a conversation." I knew I sounded like a sulky child.

"Rachel, don't be difficult."

"Ha. That's like saying, 'don't breathe'. I know you're trying to help, but did I ask for it?"

"You agreed: me or the psychiatrist. OK, what about your father?"

I gathered up my thoughts, let the memories coalesce. "Henry Keyte, always known as Harry – or even Hal, sometimes. He was a carpenter, got involved in making stage sets. That's how they met." I hesitated, thinking. "I think my mother would have been quite happy to have had a torrid affair with my father and then moved on when she was bored. But she never did get bored, not with him – just with the tedium of family life. Anyway, he wouldn't hear of it. It was marriage or nothing. So she gave in. She told me once it was a big mistake, that she was blinded by lust." I saw Michael blink. "It was an odd thing to say to a nine-year-old. I asked my dad what it meant. He was not amused. Sparked one of their rows. But that was later."

"What was he like?" Michael said softly.

"Six foot three. Blond and bearded, bright blue eyes, always laughing. He looked like a Viking. All he needed was the horned helmet and the longboat. For me the mystery's not what she saw in him but what he wanted from her. They were a pretty ill-matched pair."

"He wouldn't have been content with a fling, then?"

I looked up. "No, I told you," I said sharply, "he was a believer in his way, a man of stern principle. He wanted a family, and a proper base for his children, as he saw it. How he thought he'd have what he wanted with her beats me. He wasn't at all stupid. Maybe he was 'blinded by lust' too." I heaved a sigh. "Anyway, he wanted children, she resisted, but eventually she gave in and said she'd have just one. That was Martin, and she was affectionate to him when she remembered. Then the crunch came – Dad wanted another child; she refused quite fiercely, said it would wreck her career which was doing well at that point, and her career was her focus, what she cared about most. Even today remembering her past glories is what keeps her going. Martin was looked after mostly by my father and paid carers, and when he went to school she thought she'd be free – not that she really ever let being a mother get in her way. Still, accidents happen. I was that accident: an unwanted, unlovable, puking little accident. She wanted to abort me, but my father went crazy and wouldn't hear of it."

Michael's eyes widened. "How do you know that?"

"She told me herself. She was in a rage; she'd lost the chance of some audition because I was ill with some childish ailment and my dad was working away."

"Maybe she didn't mean it."

I shook my head. "No, she meant it." I picked up my coffee cup. "Ugh, this has gone cold."

"I can make some more if you like."

"Haven't you got anything more important to do, Michael? You must be bored witless."

"On the contrary. And I have no particular plans, except that later I'd like to make you something to eat and stand over you till it's all gone."

"I thought you were a nice man, not a bully."

"Just shows how wrong you can be, doesn't it?" He smiled that crinkly smile. "Right – coffee. Don't run away."

Five minutes later he returned with a fresh cup. "What a

blessing you had one kind parent," he said thoughtfully. "All the worse to have lost him. How old were you?"

I grimaced. "Not quite fifteen. But I don't think I'm strong enough to talk about him dying. It wasn't just that he died; it was the way it happened. Let's leave that for another day."

He got up from the chair and flexed his shoulders. "I need to give this dog a walk," he said. "Do you want to come?"

I shook my head. "No, thanks; not today." I frowned. "You don't seem so careful of the gossipmongers now – why not?"

"Because we're not in the hospital. You're discharged and no longer my patient."

"I see."

"I'll be twenty minutes, no more. Look in the fridge and see if anything takes your fancy."

"I doubt that."

He stared down at me sternly. "I insist you eat."

"Ha. But I am not your patient. I can tell you to…"

"Stop right there."

When he had gone I sat and sipped my coffee, thinking. Why was this man being so kind? How had we, rather suddenly it seemed, become friends? I strongly suspected that Jasper may have had something to do with it. Or perhaps I was seen as a bit of a sad case, a friendless victim who needed support and cosseting. I bristled at this thought. Could Eve Rawlins have known just how much she was to take from me? Potentially, my whole career, worked for through long years; but also my self-respect, my independence, my peace. Or had these always been mere chimeras? Was this rock-bottom existence reality after all?

It seemed that Eve Rawlins was also on Michael's mind. He was gone for much longer than twenty minutes, and when he came back he was on his own. "Sorry, my wretched dog rolled in something disgusting down by the riverbank. I had to take her home and give her a bath. I left her looking damp and very sorry for herself." He looked at the kitchen table. "What's this? I thought I was cooking."

I shrugged. "You were ages. I made myself get up and do something. It's only a bit of salad, but it's all I want."

"Fine. Could you drink a glass of wine with it?"

"I might just manage. There's some white in the fridge, courtesy of the generous Axtons."

Michael pulled the bottle out. "Looks like one I brought them back from France. I'll find a corkscrew."

He poured the wine into two large glasses and we sat down at the table. "What have you been doing in my absence? Apart from washing lettuce?"

"Nothing," I said between mouthfuls. "Washing lettuce was unnervingly wearisome."

He chuckled. "I'm imagining you leaning on the sink exhausted, a limp lettuce leaf in an even limper hand."

"I'm glad you find my pathetic state amusing. I wish I could say the same."

He speared a tomato. "Seriously, though. I have been thinking about your attacker."

"So have I," I said. "It's not pleasant."

He looked at me with a curious considering gaze, as if I had turned green or developed a hideous rash. "How angry are you with her?"

"You have no idea. If my anger were blazing instead of smouldering this place would be hot ash in minutes."

He frowned. "It's not good for you, harbouring such feelings. It's not the house that'll burn, it's you – from the inside out."

I threw down my fork with a rude clatter, and he paused, eyebrows raised. "For heaven's sake, not you as well!"

"What? What do you mean?"

"I had a visitor while I was in the hospital. The first of two I received the Saturday after the attack. A priest."

"Father Vincent Cornish?"

My jaw dropped. Slowly I picked up my napkin and wiped my mouth. "How do you know about him?" I whispered. "I don't think I mentioned him. Or did I talk to Jasper? I don't remember." Miserably I dropped the napkin onto the table. "What's wrong with me? My brain has turned to mush." I gripped the wine glass with a trembling hand.

"Let me tell you what happened," Michael said gently. "That Saturday I was coming to see you, but I was overtaken in the corridor by a young man in a hurry – brown hair, wearing jeans and a pink T-shirt."

"Yeah. Rob. Well, you did know about him, I imagine."

"I saw him knock on your door and decided to leave you to it. I turned round and headed back to my office – there were a few things I needed to check. But on the way I noticed an elderly man in a blue suit, leaning on a stick, wearing a clerical collar. He looked worn out."

"He'd come all the way from Porton on the train. For a frosty five-minute interview."

Michael nodded. "I know. I asked him if he was all right. He said he was, but then he seemed to sag. I persuaded him to come with me to the cafeteria and I bought him a cup of tea and a slice of cake."

"You're full of good works," I said sourly.

Michael ignored this and went on. "He told me why he had come, and the reception he'd got. But I was interested: he obviously knew your attacker – Eve, isn't it? – quite well. I asked him a few questions, and he told me a bit about her background."

I pushed my chair back with a loud scrape and stood up. I found I was shaking, and I clenched my fists at my sides. "I don't want to hear it. What's this, anyway? Some kind of do-gooder ploy to make me feel sorry for her? For *her* – a madwoman bent on smashing my life to pieces? I suppose you want me to forgive her, just like that priest. I wouldn't know where to begin, and I don't intend to make any effort to find out."

I saw him bite his lip. "Forgiveness isn't forgetting," he said. "No one can ask you to forget. And it isn't something you do and then it's all over. It's a process, sometimes a long one."

I felt my fury bubble up, and I swallowed hard. "Why should I even try?" My voice grated.

"Because it would be better for you if you did," he said simply. "You could even include your parents while you're at it."

"What?" I said wildly. "My mother, yes, for being a lousy parent, for making me feel like a piece of rubbish, but why do I need to forgive my father?"

"For deserting you." He held up his hands as I opened my mouth to protest. "I know it wasn't his fault. Even so."

For a moment I stood and stared at him, my mouth open, my eyes narrowed. "You know what? I'm sick of people foisting their homespun psychology on me." I felt my breathing become laboured, my throat choking. "Look, I'm grateful for all your kindness. I'm sure you mean well. But I'd like to be on my own now, if you don't mind. I'm very tired."

He got to his feet. "I'm sorry, Rachel. I had no intention of upsetting you or making things worse. Please believe that. I'll go." He took his plate to the sink and put it on the draining board. He turned to me, a frown wrinkling his brow. "There's so much more I wanted to talk to you about. But perhaps you'd rather not. I just –" I waited. "I can't help worrying about you. I'm sorry, but there it is. I won't bother you, of course. But please don't think you are all alone. There are people who care."

"I don't see why they should."

"No, I know you don't. Well, I'll say goodnight."

"Yes. Goodnight."

I watched him walk to the front door, open it, and walk out. I caught a glimpse of the evening sky, studded with early stars, and smelled the fragrance of cut grass and roses. As the door closed behind him I broke into a torrent of crying. I leaned on the wall, shaking and sobbing, until my legs buckled under me and I sank to the floor. I had weathered so much over the last almost twenty years, but it was the scent of roses that threatened my undoing.

The next morning, to my surprise, I awoke clear-headed, and I remembered recorking the bottle and putting it resolutely back in the fridge. There may have been times when I was tempted to kill pain with alcohol, but I knew enough to recognize it as an extra problem, not any kind of solution to current ones. But a clear head and a crisp memory have their disadvantages. I felt bad that I had sent a kind friend away with the proverbial flea in his ear. At best I had been ungrateful.

I looked at the clock: it was after nine. I found my phone under a pile of cushions in the sitting room and keyed in Michael's number, but after several rings it went to voicemail. I had no message to leave. I padded into the kitchen barefoot and made coffee. Sipping, I looked around the flat. My occupation had tarnished Angela's efforts: here was someone else whose kindness I had abused. It was time, as my mother frequently told me in acidic tones when I was a child, to "pull my socks up".

I finished my coffee. Galvanized by caffeine, I tidied stuff away, put my bedsheets – grisly from intense use – in the washing machine, and vacuumed the carpets. It wasn't much, but I was soon exhausted. With a last burst of determination I opened the windows at the front, letting in the scent of flowers which had done for me the night before, and with it the sound of church bells, several competing at once, a joyous jangle which sent me back a quarter of a century to another life: not forgotten – never that – but deeply buried, until Michael came along innocently with his spade and started digging.

When I was nine years old my father, in a fit of enthusiasm, decided we should learn to be bell-ringers. "They don't just call the faithful to prayer," he said. "They remind all those who don't believe there's something else out there." I had only the vaguest idea what he meant but as always I did whatever he wanted, not in a spirit of subservience but simply because I loved him and he had the best ideas. Martin, now fourteen and sceptical, could not be persuaded, so my father and I went along by ourselves. I never amounted to much – really I was too young and skinny and weak, and as often as not sat out in the pew, watching and listening – but he threw himself into it, and for a few months we were in our local church tower every Tuesday for practice and many Sundays. I don't know why we stopped going in the end, but that time stayed with me: the glorious cacophony of the bells, the smell of polish on the pews, the teetering piles of hymn books, the dull brassy glow of the lectern, and the height of the barrel-vaulted roof, drawing my child's eyes upwards to another plane.

I was brought back to the reality of the present by the sound of a powerful car engine outside, and I opened the front door. Michael's dark blue estate car was passing where the towpath met the lane, and I saw him glance towards my door. Seeing me standing there he waved and smiled. I returned the wave, realizing that he was going to church this fine summer morning. My momentary sense of well-being evaporated, swallowed by a cold sense of my own isolation. Family, friends, even God – these were things other people had, things from which I had cut myself off so resolutely, depending only on my work for fulfilment – work which I could no longer do. I closed the door, and the clangour of the bells diminished.

How odd it was that for the second time I heard my mother's voice, remembering the sharp tones I had so resented as a teenager. *Do stop wallowing, Rachel. Self-pity is nauseating. Nobody wants to listen to your gripes.* The worst of it was, she was right. I drifted over to the Axtons' bookshelves, stocked by Angela with a number of titles I had barely registered – novels I would never read, biographies of people in whom I had no interest. I'd added my own well-thumbed reference works to the lowest shelf. But on the top was a Bible. I hadn't really noticed it till now. I took it down, planted myself on the sofa, and looked up "anger" and "forgiveness".

There was so much I had forgotten (or perhaps I had simply sent it down to the dusty archives of my memory where only rats scuttled and beetles ate the mouldering pages). My father, though he was only an irregular church attender, had great reverence for Scripture. He made sure I knew all the usual dramatic stories, but he also read me bits of it, even though a lot was incomprehensible to a child. Now I found passages which resonated from that far-off time: plenty about the anger of God but also about his mercy and restraint. Then I came across two short verses in Ephesians which made my skin prickle. "Get rid of all bitterness, passion, and anger. No more shouting or insults, no more hateful feelings of any sort. Instead, be kind and tender-hearted to one another, and forgive one another, as God has forgiven you through Christ." But wasn't there something else, about the forgiveness of God being conditional? I hunted it down; there it was, in Matthew 6: "If you forgive others the wrong they have done to you, your Father in heaven will also forgive you. But if you do not forgive others, then your Father will not forgive the wrongs you have done." And, I realized, these were not the words of any old prophet, however wise – they were the words of Christ himself. It came to me that Michael, Jasper, Bridget Harries, even Father Vincent, had tried to be "kind and tender-hearted" to me, and I had rudely repudiated their efforts. I took a deep breath, and blew it out again. I had a long way to go, but I had to begin.

I made another cup of coffee and munched on some chocolate biscuits I found in the cupboard. Tentatively I picked up my phone again, and dialled. It went to voicemail. "Michael, I owe you an apology. You've been very kind, and I was ungrateful. I'm sorry." I put the phone on the table, and waited.

I thought he'd ring back before long, and maybe we could make some kind of peace. But he didn't ring, and the day wore on, with nothing to do except, listlessly, my physiotherapy exercises, which were very dull and soon palled. Bit by bit my fragile little spurt of confidence, my tiny gleam of hope, evaporated in a welter of cynicism and self-blame. Why would anyone want to befriend me, of all people, when I was so rude and ungrateful, when I barely knew how to be a friend, let alone have any? I supposed that all those who'd tried to be kind to me lately were doing it out of some kind of charity, and in my scarred pride I found the thought humiliating: they didn't want me as their friend because I was witty or good company, or for any reason to do with my worthiness; it was simply because I was in need. This notion stuck in my throat like a fishbone. All my adult life, apart from a few transient and half-baked relationships – even the engagement to Howard fell in this category, I realized, with a small shock – I had relied on one person alone: myself. If I fell apart, who was there? Through that long, lonely day I gathered up the loose threads of my vulnerability, and resolutely ignored the metaphorical clang of closing doors: doors which had so recently let in the scent of roses.

But two things happened that day which were to turn me upside down once again. I'd listlessly eaten up some of the leftover salad from the previous day, and fallen asleep on the sofa over a heavy tome on congenital heart defects, something which would never have happened before the attack. I was jerked awake by the shrilling of my phone, and the book fell with a thud to the floor, painfully catching my bare foot on the way. I hobbled to where I had left the phone on the table, trying to douse a shaming spark of hope that it might be Michael, and he wasn't offended. But it wasn't Michael; for the second time in six months – something else that was almost unheard-of – I heard my brother's warm and lazy tones: "Hey, Lizzie."

"Martin! What's this? It's not my birthday, is it?"

I heard him chuckle. "I know, I'm a rubbish brother, but there's no need for sarcasm." He cleared his throat. "Just checking in to see if you're OK. Heard you've been in the wars."

"What?"

"Someone carved you up."

I blinked, astonished. "How on earth did you find that out?"

"I read a little item in an old newspaper. We do get them, you know – newspapers – even here in the Antipodes. It was just a few column inches, but the headline caught my eye: 'Female surgeon in deadly assault' – or something like that. And your name appeared. So I did a bit of digging on the internet and got a bit more of the story."

"Good grief!"

"Hm," Martin said. "Didn't think to let your relatives know, then?"

"Well, in your case it seemed a bit pointless. You're many thousands of miles away. What are you going to do except worry? And they did ask me if I wanted to inform our mother, but again, what's the point if it's going to cause her concern, which I doubt."

"Hey, come on, Liz, be fair. Of course she's going to be a bit concerned at least. And if I heard about it in New Zealand, she's going to hear about it when you're just a couple of counties away."

"But hang on, bro," I protested. "I didn't even know there was anything in the press, not till now – apart from very local papers that have a circulation of ten."

"What, no reporters snooping around the hospital?"

"Not that I knew of. I was interviewed by the police, that's all. Didn't think it was worthy of note."

"You're kidding! Look at it from their point of view. Nice scandalous story: eminent lady surgeon, crazy parent, family tragedy, deadly knife attack. Bread and butter to the press. So if you know nothing about it, I guess the hospital sent the reporters packing. Someone was defending you, for sure."

I thought for a moment, chewing my lip. "Are you telling me Mother knows?"

"Yep, someone saw the item in your local rag, a fair bit after the event. She rang me, which has *never* happened before. So what do I tell her?"

"No, you're right," I conceded. "I'll ring her myself. Sometime soon. Anyway, all that aside, how're you doing?"

"I'm OK, but more to the point, what about you? Were you badly hurt?"

"I was lucky, bro. Slashed across the face, but eyes and major structures escaped. Just a thin red line now, and I was never going to be Miss World, was I? Worse was the damage to both hands, but they've been expertly repaired, and I'm doing lots of tedious exercises."

I spoke lightly, but Martin was not fooled. "*No*, Liz! Not your hands! Will you be able to work again?"

"Not sure. Jury's out. Maybe."

I heard him swear softly, and loved him for it. But before either of us could speak again, there was a tapping on my front door. "Mart? I'd better go; someone's knocking. Look, thanks for ringing, OK? Don't leave it so long next time! And I'll ring Mother."

"Yeah. Might be coming home soonish. But I'll let you know when I know more myself. Bye, Liz. Take care, you crazy fool."

I rang off. The tapping had stopped, but I went to the door and opened it, and saw a skinny figure loping away across the grass towards the river, a black and white dog at his heels. I surprised myself by the little dart of delight that leapt up in me. "Jasper!"

He stopped, turned, waved, and ran back. There was a big grin on his face as he came level, Dulcie frolicking round his feet, both of them panting. The day was warm. "Hi, Rachel!"

"Hello, Jasper. Hello, Dulcie. Sorry, I was on the phone – to my big brother in New Zealand."

"Oh. I didn't know you had a brother."

"I don't see him very often. He's a wildlife photographer, travels all over."

"Awesome!"

"So what are you doing down here? Not slaving away at your A levels, then?"

He jogged from foot to foot. "Exams are over, hooray! And we've been given a week's so-called study leave before we get going again. So I thought I'd come down and see Dad. He came to collect me – we just got back. Dulcie needs a walk and I thought I'd see if you wanted to come."

I was going to decline, but I saw his hopeful face and thought better of it. "OK, yes, why not? Give me a minute and I'll get something on my feet."

We walked along the towpath in the late afternoon sunshine, away from the city. Others had the same idea: there were families and pushchairs and other dogs, and we occasionally lost sight of Dulcie as she met a friend and capered off in a canine game. The farther we got from the city the fewer people we met. Down on the marshy ground which in places flanked the river, lone fishermen sat by salty creeks on tiny folding seats, dozing over their rods as the sun declined. "Can't be catching much down there," I commented.

"Eels, maybe," Jasper said. "What I know about fishing wouldn't cover a pinhead."

"Me too, now, though a hundred years ago my father taught me to fish. Look, Jasper, do you mind if we sit for a while? You and Dulcie are young and sprightly, but I've only been out of rehab a couple of days."

"Oh, yes, of course. Sorry, Rachel, I wasn't thinking."

We found a bench by the side of the towpath, and Dulcie was content with scampering after a ball that Jasper produced from his pocket and bringing it back to drop hopefully at his feet. "She's been cooped up all day," he said. "Needs to use some of that energy." He looked sideways at me. "How've you been since I saw you last?"

"OK, more or less. I was in rehab for about two weeks. It was a huge bore, but I guess it had the desired effect. No more dressings, and I'm getting to do a lot of things with my hands these days."

"Do you have follow-up appointments?"

"Yes, once a week at the clinic. Going tomorrow morning, actually. They like to make sure I am doing all the exercises. Big yawn."

Jasper looked at the ground, tossing the ball gently from hand to hand as the dog lay flat on her stomach, nose between her paws, following his every movement with her eyes. "You've healed up really well," he said. "Quicker than I thought you would." He looked up at me, his face serious. "Maybe that's because I was praying for you."

"Maybe indeed." I paused, looking at him sideways. "So, Jasper, on that subject – how do you get on at school? Don't they bully you because of your beliefs? As I understand it teenagers can be pretty horrible."

He nodded. "Some can, of course. You get that anywhere. My school's pretty serious about bullying, but there're ways to get at someone without breaking the rules, without anyone noticing except the victim. Anyone who's a bit different is a potential target."

"So do you keep quiet, play it down?"

"No, I'll say stuff if it arises and people know, but I don't go ramming it down their throats. Everyone's entitled to their own views. Anyway, I have a secret weapon." He smiled, and his eyes lit up.

"What's that?" I thought he'd say something about being divinely defended, but he didn't.

"In a boys' school like mine, you get respect if you're good at sport," he said. "Not so much for being clever, because some people think that makes you a geek. My swimming trophies are my defence."

"You're really good, then, are you?"

"Not bad," he said modestly. "I'm hoping to get some swimming in this week, maybe with Dad on his day off."

"If I'm not being too nosy, how come you're a Christian? Was it because that was how you were brought up?"

"Partly," he said. "My parents made sure I knew what I was getting into." He smiled. "But it was my own decision."

"When was that?"

"Oh, um, about three, maybe four years ago. I was having a bit of a rough time at school: there was one particular boy who seemed to have it in for me." To my surprise, I heard him chuckle. "You might not believe this, but I was a bit fat in those days."

"Really? You amaze me. There's nothing to you now."

"Mum and I moved to London when I was eleven, nearly twelve. I had a lot of adjusting to do, I guess, and I wasn't handling it well – new house, new school, different friends." He stared down at his hands, draped across his knees. "And I missed my dad, and worried about him being here all on his own. I stopped swimming for a while, and ate too much chocolate! Eventually I started swimming regularly again and doing other sports as well, and weirdly the boy that teased me and I became quite good mates in the end, even if he had been pretty horrible about my flab."

"So what caused you to make up your mind?"

"It's hard to say. I knew my dad was praying for me when things were tough at school, and so were the people in the church where we all used to go to and he still does, and that had a good effect I reckon. Then a speaker came to our school and what he said just started me off thinking, and that was it."

"Never looked back?"

"No, not really. Though I still have moments… everybody does."

"Do you go to church in London?"

"Yes."

"With your mum?"

"Sometimes. But she doesn't go that much these days, so I go on my own."

"Brave man."

He laughed softly. "You think so?" He sighed. "I wish my mum did come with me, but she's always thinking about what Jack would like."

"Jack's your stepfather?"

"Yes. Don't get me wrong – he wouldn't stop her or anything. She can do what she likes, whatever makes her happy, as far as he's concerned. He sees it as a sort of harmless hobby, I think. Nothing to get worried about because it doesn't connect with the real world – not his reality, anyway."

"D'you get on with Jack OK? If you don't mind me asking."

"No, I don't mind. Yeah, Jack's all right. We just don't really inhabit the same universe, that's all. As long as he treats my mum OK that's fine with me. I won't be living at home for ever, anyway, will I?" Dulcie started to fidget, butting his knees with her head. He glanced at his watch. "I'd better get this dog home. She's telling me she wants her dinner. So do I, and Dad's cooking." He got up, stretched out a hand and took mine, pulling me to my feet. "Come on, grandma."

I pretended to box his ears. "Cheeky whippersnapper," I growled.

We ambled back along the towpath, and even Dulcie seemed content to slow down. I parted from them at their back gate.

"Don't you want to come in for a cup of tea?" Jasper said.

"No, thanks. For one thing, it's time for dinner, rather than tea. Plus I never drink tea. It makes me feel ill."

"What? Are you even British?"

"Who knows? Also, I may not be too popular with your dad right now."

Jasper's eyes widened. "Why?"

"You'd better ask him. Anyway, I have a phone call to make which may be a bit sticky – to my mother. And don't say, 'I didn't know you had a mother', or you'll be in trouble."

Jasper grinned broadly. "Well, you don't ever say much about your family."

I grunted. "It's not much of one, to be honest." I bent and ruffled Dulcie's fur. "Be seeing you, Jasper."

The shadows were gathering when I went back indoors. It smelled too lived-in, and I opened the windows and let in the scents of evening. The perfume of the Axtons' roses was a sharp, unsettling reminder of how easily I seemed to crumple at the moment; I suspected, though I hated to admit it, that my physical healing was far outstripping the healing of my spirit. I warmed up some soup and ate without appetite, dumping the bowl in the sink when I'd finished. Darkness was now absolute, and I closed the curtains. Looking at the wall clock I guessed that it was time to ring my mother, before she settled down to watch her favourite Sunday evening dramas (which she usually found lacking in some way – refinement, clarity of dialogue, characterization, credibility of plot). In her own eyes at least she was still an expert.

The phone rang several times before she answered. "Frances Chester," she purred.

"Hello, Mother. It's Rachel."

Her tone altered instantly. "Rachel? Oh, so you're still alive, then?"

"Yes."

She sniffed. "I suppose one must be thankful. It's a shame you didn't think to inform me what had happened."

"Frankly, Mother, I didn't think you'd ever hear about it, and what could you do, anyway?"

"Not hear about it? It was in most of the papers. And what a garbled story it was! I didn't know what to believe. So what's made you call now?"

"Martin rang me earlier today, asking how I was. That's the first I knew there was anything in the papers beyond the local news, or that you knew." I hesitated. "I'm sorry if you've been worried." The emphasis I laid on this word would not be lost on her; it was clear I didn't believe she'd be worried at all.

"Of course I was worried!" she remonstrated. "I am your mother. That's what mothers do." *Some of them, maybe. Possibly most of them. But not this one; not about me, at any rate.* "Well, now," she continued, "are you recovered?"

"Not completely. I'm visiting the physiotherapy people once a week, and doing exercises."

"What happened to the woman who attacked you?"

"As far as I know, in custody awaiting trial."

"So you could come home – here, to Porton. Move back to your flat." Unspoken, I heard her meaning: *Nearer to me.*

This had not occurred to me, oddly. It filled me with dread, though I barely knew why. Eve Rawlins was there, yes, but not at liberty. What was there to fear?

I swallowed. "Yes, perhaps. I'm not sure what I'll do next. I'm signed off work, obviously. I may go away; I have a lot of leave owing. But I'll try to stay in touch a bit more."

I heard her sniff again. "So I should hope."

"Are you well, Mother?" I asked, hearing the stiffness in my voice.

"As well as can be expected, I suppose. I'll ring off now, Rachel. It's almost time for something I'm following on television. Not that dramas are much to write home about these days. Try to stay out of harm's way, won't you? Goodbye."

There was something I wanted – no, needed – to try, though I was deeply apprehensive. The next morning I set out early and walked slowly across the river-flats to the city. It was a long way round, but I had nothing else to do, and the day was fine: a summer morning of pearly light and high white clouds. My appointment with the physiotherapy team was for ten o'clock, and they were pleased with my progress. At my request I was given more exercises, designed to improve fine fingertip control. As I left Josie had the last word: "Don't try to do too much at once." I smiled and nodded compliantly, but I guess nobody was fooled.

I went on into the city, noisy and bustling, searching for a small shop whose location I had looked up on the internet. I found it eventually, tucked away in an arcade away from the huge department stores and cut-price outlets: a narrow frontage bright with knitting wools and craft paraphernalia. An old-fashioned bell jangled as I went in. I soon had the pleasant woman there hunting in dusty boxes for items she rarely had call for – so she said: threads of different thicknesses and needles of varying gauges. They were just ordinary sewing needles, of course, but it was something to start on.

I hurried back to the flat as fast as I could and laid my treasures on the table, then made some coffee and tried to calm myself as I drank it. I washed my hands and dried them thoroughly. I took one of the thickest spools of thread and began to tie the tiny knots that I had learned long ago as a student. They told me then that if I could tie knots with one hand, using my elbows and the back of a chair, I might have the makings of a surgeon. I remembered the hours of practice, sometimes late into the night, my eyes crossed and my fingers numb, until I could tie knots not only one-handed but with my eyes shut. Now, however, I was once again as awkward as the average person. My fingers felt thick and uncoordinated and the thread slipped out of their control. I found both hands were clumsy, the right one worse than the left, because it had taken the brunt of Eve Rawlins' knife. In the end I was shaking with the effort and had to stop. I told myself crossly that it would take time and practice to get back to where I had been – what did I expect? However good a job Michael Wells had done, however assiduously I worked on my exercises, it was too soon to expect fine-motor improvement. I told myself these things, as if I were someone else trying to offer encouragement; but it didn't really work.

I decided to leave further attempts until after lunch when I would be rested. I gathered up my courage and found a ratty old T-shirt fit only for decorating and then throwing away. It took a very long time to thread even the biggest needle, and of course these needles were nothing like the ones I would use in theatre on a live body; but it seemed better than nothing. It turned out that I could still sew, but the stitches were huge and uneven. If I had sutured a blood vessel like that my patient wouldn't have survived.

To say I was disappointed and frustrated would have been a gross understatement. However hard I tried to reason with myself, I had hoped for better things, and it took all my self-control not to wail in despair. Would I ever get back to what I was? And if I couldn't, what sort of a life was there for me? It was all I knew and all I cared about. If I couldn't apply my long experience and fine-honed skills to saving the lives of heart-compromised patients, what could I do?

Later that afternoon a knock came at my front door. I heaved myself off the sofa and ambled down the hallway. I was half-expecting Jasper again, perhaps with some new notion, but it wasn't Jasper: it was Michael.

"Oh! Hello." I found myself drained of words, and his serious expression didn't help.

"Can I come in?"

"Sure, of course." I stood back to let him pass me. "I'm just in the sitting room. Can I get you something? There may be tea – I haven't looked."

He smiled, rather stiffly I thought. "No, thanks. I don't need anything." I saw his gaze sweep the room. I'd left my sewing lying around; he couldn't have failed to see it, and he would know why there were lengths of yarn knotted round the kitchen chairs. I didn't doubt he'd have gone through the same tortuous rigmarole many years before.

"Please, have a seat," I said.

He took the one armchair and I sat on the sofa opposite him. The atmosphere seemed awkward and curiously charged.

"I got your message," he said, "but not till we got back from London. There was no need to apologize. I do understand how difficult this must be for you."

"There was every need, however difficult things may be," I said. "Am I forgiven?"

"Of course." Now he smiled more naturally, and a kind of cloud lifted.

Once again he looked around the room. "You've been practising," he said.

"More like testing," I said. "To see if I could still do it."

Now he looked at me. "How did you get on?"

I sighed. "It wasn't a great success. I tried for quite a while, till I was exhausted. My fingers felt like uncooked sausages. Maybe it was too soon, but I needed to try." I bit my lip. "Do you think –" I found I couldn't say what I wanted to.

"Do I think you'll get it back – the use of your hands?" I nodded. "Yes, I do. You will. But I don't know, nobody knows, just how far you'll be able to reclaim what you had, that fast dexterity. All you can do is keep on with the physio and don't give up. Never that."

"It's hard."

"Of course it is. Look, if you like, if you want to go on practising stitching and tying knots and suchlike, I can at least get you some proper materials. I can ask Peter too – he can get you the things you'd normally use. But, Rachel –" he leaned forward, his hands on his knees – "go at it slowly. Be wise. It's not going to happen overnight. Besides –" he hesitated.

"Besides what?"

"Well, there are other things you can do – not just exercises specifically to improve your fine control – general things, spread your wings a bit."

I frowned. "What do you mean exactly?"

"I realize I'll have difficulty persuading you, but you could see this time, these weeks of relative inactivity, as an opportunity, not just as a regrettable hiatus in your career." I opened my mouth to protest, but he held up his hand. "Hear me out before you go off at the deep end, OK? Jasper had an idea, and he wanted to race round and put it to you, but I said no, it has to be me – she'll just smile indulgently at you and say thanks, but no thanks. I left him supposedly reading a psychology textbook and looking cross." He smiled.

"I have no idea what you're talking about."

"Sorry. Jasper – we – thought it might help if you spent some time at our place in France."

"Oh!" I was utterly flabbergasted.

He stood up suddenly, put his hands in his pockets, and started to pace around the small space between us. "I, we, just feel it's not only your body that needs to heal. I'm sorry if that sounds patronizing."

I shook my head. "No... I was beginning to think the same myself, even though I didn't want to acknowledge it. I guess I have to process the shock as well as the injury."

He stopped and looked at me intently. "Yes, but it's not just that. Please forgive me if you think I am being presumptuous, because I don't really know very much about you, but I imagine you have had to sacrifice a great deal to get where you are."

"Where I was, you mean."

"No, where you are – where you will be again. That's what I meant when I suggested this might be a period of opportunity. To do other things, not just activities connected with heart surgery or advancing your career. Things that you might have enjoyed once but haven't done for a long time. Things that go together with rest and healing, looking after yourself."

I frowned. "Go on."

"I'm thinking of somewhere peaceful, different, away from here, where you don't see the hospital every time you open your front door – the hospital that means work and ambition and struggle, but also the hospital where you were attacked." He sat down again suddenly, facing me. "Perhaps somewhere where the pace is slow. Where you have the space to walk, rest, listen to music, even pull up a few weeds if you were feeling energetic. You could read – something other than heavy tomes with anatomical diagrams." He looked sideways at the bookshelf and smiled. "Like those. I'm guessing they're all you've been reading, ignoring Angela's helpful choice of books."

"I haven't read a novel in years," I said. "Never had the time."

He nodded. "But stories carry their own truths – truths which perhaps can't be mediated any other way, because they have to be viewed through the reader's own perception, understood in the light of individual experience. Not all truths are facts."

"Now there's a revolutionary thought," I murmured with a sly grin. "So this was Jasper's idea?"

"Yes. And when I really thought about it, I saw he had a point."

I took a deep breath. "Well, I don't know what to say. I don't know why you guys are so kind. Why would you want an awkward house guest?"

"As far as Jasper is concerned, you are his friend, and that's reason enough."

I wanted to ask, *And what about you? Am I your friend too?* but I sensed it was sensitive ground, and I was suddenly, inexplicably, afraid.

"The thing is," Michael said, "Jasper and I can't travel over until August. There's a swimming event he wants to be part of, a few days into the holidays. Not to mention that the Olympics are on and he'll be glued to the TV at every opportunity. I wondered if you would like to drive down there by yourself initially, and then we'd come and join you as soon as we could." He looked at the floor. "The reason I thought that, and this is why it needs an adult head, is that if you had your own car with you, you wouldn't have to stay on if you didn't want to. You might prefer to come back rather than be with us. At least you would have the choice."

"You've thought of everything." My voice was faint.

He grinned suddenly. "I'm not totally without self-interest. I just came back from there, as you know, but it wasn't for long, and I couldn't do much. Our farmer neighbour keeps the orchard grass down with his sheep, but the garden otherwise will be getting very out of hand."

"I could do the weeding, I suppose," I said. "But my French is very rusty, and never was much more than schoolgirl level."

"I thought of that," he said, and now his eyes lit up with enthusiasm as he sensed I was not entirely opposed. "And also we have to be sure your hands are up to a longish drive. You'd need to get your car out and practise, build up the miles gradually. Meanwhile you could brush up your French, make sure you have enough to get by. You wouldn't be too alone, if that would worry you – we have some delightful neighbours just a garden away. They don't speak much English but they would help you if necessary." He paused. "It's a very quiet place with a low crime rate. But I had another thought. You could take Dulcie."

"What?" I felt my eyebrows shoot through my hairline. "Take Dulcie? You'd trust me with your dog?"

"Of course I trust you." Michael frowned, as if the idea that he might not was truly preposterous. "It'd be company for you, and nice for her. She loves it there. I have so little time for her when I'm working." His smile broadened. "You've been saying she needs training. You'd have plenty of time for that, just the two of you, during the long summer days."

"When I'm not gardening, chatting to the neighbours, reading all the books I've neglected." I smiled back.

He stood up. "Look, Rachel, I'm going to leave you to think about it. I realize I've kind of dropped it on you from a great height. But it might be preferable to staying here, working single-mindedly to get your hands back, facing the inevitable disappointments alone. You can do all that when you get back – it's only for a few weeks, after all." He paused, scuffing the rug with his toe. He looked down at me, his face once again serious, and he spoke softly. "You've had to adapt and compromise many times over the years, I imagine. Perhaps with a bit of distant perspective you might come to see the current situation as yet another twist in that winding path."

Just another twist. Not, then, wholly and necessarily, a life-destroying disaster? Were Michael and Jasper offering me a rickety ladder out of my black hole? Or was it all just a putting-off of the inevitable reckoning? Whatever the case, at some point I had to face the reality of my future, and it looked bleak and impenetrable. Could I take time out of it, though, time to rest, recover as far as I could, remember, ponder, do things I had almost forgotten? I thought of sitting in the sunshine with no company but a friendly dog, and it was a most strange thought, unsettling, alien, almost fearful; but what was my alternative? Right now, I was running short of choices.

That night once again I dreamed of my father, but this time there was no remembered horror. In it I was a small child, lying against his chest as he propped himself up on my pillows, reading out of some simple book, while I sucked my thumb and drifted sleepily off. When I awoke to the real world and the sound of busy birds outside my window, I was aware of a strange combination of comfort and sadness. I took no pleasure in either; it seemed to me then, sitting on the edge of my bed, my bare feet on the floor as I contemplated getting up and making a pot of coffee, that I had let the past have its way for far too long. Even while I gave it no conscious room, it was there, unresolved, dragging me back. I told myself the only way was forward, although I was afraid of what the unseen future might deliver; afraid, too, that I would be unequal to it, whatever it was. I would take up Michael's invitation, even though it felt reckless. What did I have to lose that I had not already lost? I had, it seemed to me, already lost control of my life. What else remained?

Later that morning I decided to visit Angela. It was time I thanked her for all her kindness, not only in supplying all manner of things she thought I might need, but also in tactfully leaving me alone. It was time to act like a reasonable human being. I made some breakfast, washed and dried the dishes, and put them away. I showered and dressed in fresh clothes. Then, feeling like someone who had been taken apart and put back together slightly out of true, I shut my front door and walked slowly across the lawn to the Axtons'.

I rang the doorbell and waited, but no one came, though Angela's car was parked on the drive. Then I thought I heard a shout from behind the house. I crossed in front of their bay window and walked down the path at the side, my canvas shoes crunching on the gravel surface. There was a wooden gate, which opened when I tried it.

"Hello?" I called. There was no answer, but now I could hear voices. Rounding the far side of the house I came upon Angela, stretched out on a sun-lounger, and beside her, cross-legged on the neatly mown grass, Jasper, with Dulcie milling round him, trying to draw his attention away. It was Dulcie who first became aware of me as I stood at the corner of the building, feeling a bit of an interloper. She bounded up to me, her ball in her mouth, a picture of hope.

Jasper looked up. "Dulcie – oh, Rachel!" He scrambled to his feet and came trotting over, as Angela turned her head towards us, taking off her sunglasses. She swung her feet to the ground.

"Come in, Rachel!" I walked towards her with Jasper and Dulcie like sentries at my side. "How lovely to see you out and about! How are you?"

"I'm getting better all the time, Angela," I said. "I've just come to thank you for everything you've done for me. You've been very kind."

"Nonsense, it's the least we could do. Can I get you some coffee?"

"No, thanks," I said. "I've only just had some. I didn't realize you had company. Am I interrupting?"

Jasper laughed and put his arm round my shoulders in a gesture of easy familiarity. "I don't think I really count as 'company', seeing as I pop in and annoy Mrs A most days," he said. "It's hard to concentrate on school work when it's sunny and Dulcie keeps distracting me because she wants to go out and play."

"Jasper, make yourself useful, please," Angela said. "Get Rachel a chair from the shed."

"OK." He loped off and returned a few minutes later with a folding seat which he set down for me with a flourish. "Madame."

"I won't stay long," I said. "I'm sure you're busy." I sat down, and Jasper again curled up on the grass.

Angela smiled. "There are a dozen things I should be doing, but when the weather's good I don't feel like doing any of them. I was lying here reading when Jasper and Dulcie arrived."

After a pause Jasper said, with an air of innocence, "So, Rachel, did my dad come round to see you yesterday?"

"I think you know very well he did," I said, looking at him with a mock-severe frown. I was amused to see him blush.

Angela looked from me to Jasper and back again. "Am I missing something?"

"Sorry," Jasper mumbled. "Dad said I wasn't to say anything till Rachel had decided."

Angela looked puzzled. "Decided what?"

I suppressed a laugh. "It's OK, Jasper. I have decided to take your father up on his kind invitation. Which I think I have you to thank for."

Jasper leapt up, copied at once by Dulcie, who had been lying quietly at Angela's feet. "That's great news, Rachel! I'm so glad!"

"I don't know why," I demurred.

"No, really, it'll be fun. Just as long," he said, sobering, "as you won't be too lonely while you're on your own."

"Is anyone going to enlighten me?" Angela asked. "You are both being most mysterious."

"Sorry, Mrs A," Jasper said. "I said to Dad Rachel should come down to France with us this summer. Get away somewhere different."

Angela clapped her hands. "What a marvellous idea! And you've decided to go, Rachel? I'm sure it will do you good – a change of scene, fresh air, lovely French bread and cheese –"

"And wine," Jasper interjected. "Dad's got a nice selection, if we didn't drink it all last time. And we can have some barbecues, and read, and play with Dulcie and go for walks and –"

I held up my hands. "Steady on, Jasper! I'm exhausted already!" I turned to Angela. "The idea is for me to go down by myself for a couple of weeks, and take Dulcie with me," I said. "Then Michael and Jasper will join me later."

"Will you be all right driving all that way?" Angela said, her forehead furrowed.

I shook my head. "I don't know. I'll have to practise – get the car out and do a bit of driving each day, see how I get on. It'll be a few weeks yet, so I'll have a chance to polish up my French too." I cleared my throat. "No, I must be honest. My French doesn't need brushing up; it needs resurrecting." A thought struck me. "Have you got all week off, Jasper?"

He nodded. "But I have to go back to London on Saturday."

"I was thinking about getting one of those courses on tape. You could help me with a bit of French conversation. As long as you don't forget to do your school work."

Jasper beamed. "Yes, I'd love to. But I'm warning you – I'm not that good."

"Then we'll stumble along together," I said.

I decided to set out on Monday, 23 July. It gave me four weeks to work on my driving and improving my rudimentary French. It wasn't long; but I figured if I found driving hard after four weeks of practice then the plan was a non-starter, and four weeks would be enough to reacquire basic French if I worked at it every day. After I left Angela and Jasper I went back to the flat just to collect my handbag, and walked briskly into the city, determined to act before my resolve faltered. In a bookshop I found something that would do: a French course for beginners, complete with a book and a CD.

Jasper came by on most days during his study week, and spent an hour talking with me in French. I was hopeless, and he wasn't a great deal better, so it had its humorous moments, but there was only one way to go and I slowly improved. I reasoned that I would only be on my own for a fortnight – Michael and Jasper were due to arrive on 6 August after the swimming event on the previous Saturday.

Driving was a different matter. The trip down would take five hours or so from the French ferry port. Once he knew I would go, many things occurred to Michael that I absolutely should know. "You should stop at least twice," he told me. "Dulcie travels well, but she'll need to get out for comfort breaks and to stretch her legs. So will you, plus regular infusions of coffee. You mustn't think of driving for longer than, say, an hour and a half at a stretch. French motorways are empty compared to UK ones, so it shouldn't be too stressful, but we have to take care of your hands. Try to remember not to grip the wheel too tightly."

"OK, OK. I'll get the car out today."

He frowned. "Is your car all right?"

I was surprised. "It's fine. Four years old, regularly serviced."

"Hm. France requires you carry certain items in the car to be legal to drive there. I'll get them. And a dog guard. Can't have Dulcie leaping about all over."

The driving was tough at first, and I worried about the effect on my hands. But bit by bit I learned to alter my normal habits, relaxing my grip, and as the days went by my confidence grew.

It was good to have these two projects to focus on, as well

as continuing with physiotherapy appointments and exercises. I thought of my list of "Things to do in France" while I was alone there: training Dulcie, walking, hand exercises, resting, reading. Perhaps I would do a bit of garden tidying – it was the least I could do to repay Michael's kindness, even though any heavier gardening was probably not a good idea. I might be able to do something with the neglected kitchen garden he'd mentioned; at the very least I could do a bit of digging if the ground wasn't too hard. I didn't mention my list to anyone, but I knew it to be utterly necessary. To all who watched or enquired, I made a good show of gaining in confidence, but a show was all it was, and the list was the only thing, as I saw it then, that stood between me and despair.

PART THREE

ROQUEVILLE

Where did it all begin?
Was it on the ferry, as I thought at the time, watching the tide of travelling humanity, anonymous yet somehow intimate? Or must I go further back, to the moment of Craig Rawlins' untimely and unanticipated death, a moment that jarred my life out of its smooth rut? Or perhaps even further, to the moment when I realized that my father was gone forever, taking with him my comfort, my protection, my warm cave of acceptance? Was it even more distant than that, when I came howling into the world, despite my mother's murderous plan?

I couldn't say, and it was useless to conjecture. In another time I wouldn't have given such thoughts houseroom. But there they were, intractable.

Michael prepared me well – too well, I thought irritably. Perhaps he regretted his invitation, his idea that I should travel down alone as an advance party with no company but a dog. Perhaps he began to see all that might go wrong. He invited me to dinner one evening with the express purpose of telling me as much as he could about the journey to Roqueville and how I should manage when I got there. He insisted that we look at a road map together, and he drew a pencil circle round the service areas that had somewhere to walk the dog, or sold good coffee.

He told me about motorway tolls and French road signs and speed limits. We rehearsed the French for various motoring instructions – even though I told him that there was a chapter in my French course that dealt with such things.

"I have driven in Europe before, you know," I said.

"A long time ago, I imagine."

"Mm, maybe ten years."

"That's what I thought." He ploughed on, suggesting what I should do if I got lost, or the car broke down.

"I'll get European breakdown cover," I said. By this time I was taking in little of what he was telling me. He had fed me a fine French meal: a fishy terrine, a Provencal chicken dish, and a lemon tart. He was an excellent cook. I had also drunk more wine than I was used to; somehow my glass kept filling up.

He looked at me keenly, as if taking in my enfeebled state for the first time. "Maybe I should make some coffee," he murmured.

The coffee sharpened me up in time for the next round of instructions. "Make sure you text me when you arrive. I'll be at work, but I'll keep my phone handy."

"For goodness' sake, don't worry!" I said with a drunken smile. "I'll be fine. I'm a grown-up. I'll call for help in my schoolgirl French. Some Gaston or Guillaume will come riding to my rescue."

"Or spin you a line and steal your car," he said sternly. "OK, I'll assume you've arrived in Roqueville without mishap and have found the house. It's not difficult: 22, Rue des Hauts Vents, turn left at the church and keep going. There are two gates, one on the road, the other nearer to the house. It's my way of keeping Dulcie from getting onto the road. The garden is well fenced. The only way she can get out is over the stile that leads to our neighbours the Boutins: I think Jasper told you about them."

"The retired policeman with the splendid moustache."

Michael smiled. "He sometimes tries to persuade me to grow one."

I shook my head. "I don't think it would suit you. And think of the upkeep!"

"Perhaps I should give it a go. I can always shave it off at the end of the summer." He caught my frown and chuckled.

"Not that it's anything to do with me," I said stiffly. "You can grow your hair down to your knees if you like, I suppose."

"Dulcie will probably go visiting," Michael went on. "Don't worry – the Boutins love her and their garden is secure as well. There are only the two houses on that stretch of road: beyond mine there are just fields, owned by our French neighbour Bertrand. I'll ring him before you leave and he'll take his sheep away."

"Would Dulcie worry them?" I asked.

"I hope not; but I'd rather not find out. I've tried quite hard to be on good terms with the neighbours."

"So is it just sheep?"

"No, the fields to my side, to the front on the other side of the road, and at the back are growing maize – winter feed for the animals. On the other side of Gérard and Marie-Claude is a stretch of fields with not much growing at the moment. I'm not sure who they belong to. Sometimes there are a couple of horses grazing there. Then you get to the edge of Roqueville itself. So we're not cut off, but we're very quiet. Two tractors and a car make a traffic jam." He smiled.

"What's the house like?"

"Old, maybe about three hundred years. Stone with a slate roof, typical of the region. It was a farmhouse at one time, but the Boutins have a modern bungalow. I guess at some point whoever owned the farm sold off some of the land for building. I'm not sure who had Gérard and Marie-Claude's before them – they've been there for about fifteen years, I think. They're very good neighbours, and you'll probably find a box of eggs on the doorstep when you arrive – maybe even some vegetables from their kitchen garden."

"Do they speak any English?" I wanted to know. "I'm getting on OK with the French course, but I am far from fluent."

"Marie-Claude doesn't, but Gérard can get by. Between you you'll be all right, I expect."

"That's no problem," I said sarcastically. "I'll just ring you for advice when you're in the middle of a tricky bit of surgery."

He refilled my coffee cup. "No you won't."

A thought struck me. "Who do they think I am? What have you told them?"

He shrugged. "All I said was that you were a colleague, recovering from an operation – which is true."

"Do you think they believed you?"

He frowned. "Why should they not?"

"I don't know. People can put… constructions on things."

"There's nothing you or I can do about that, is there?"

"I suppose not." I squirmed in my chair. "I'd better get home. It must be late."

He looked at his watch. "It's eleven thirty. Drink your coffee and I'll walk you back."

I frowned. "There's no need. It's only a quarter of a mile."

"Dulcie would appreciate a stroll. And that's another thing – it might be a good idea, before you go, to take her out for a few walks, so she gets used to you being in charge."

I got up. "I was going to suggest that myself. Not," I added, "that Dulcie admits to anyone being in charge, I reckon."

This made him laugh. "But you're going to set that right, aren't you?"

He dropped me off at my front door. "There's more you need to know," he said. "Where the sheets are, where the washing machine is, how to turn the water and electricity on – things like that."

"Oh, not a well, then, or candles for lighting?"

"Mm, no. We are more or less in the twenty-first century. Except for manners – there we are proud to be old-fashioned."

I remembered mine. "Thank you for a delicious meal," I said. "I am impressed. My cookery skills are not up to much, I'm afraid." I thought for a moment. "Are you free tomorrow? Why don't you come by for coffee – I can manage that. Then you can tell me all the other stuff. Maybe I'll be sober and receptive by then."

"Not tomorrow – I'm in theatre. Make it Wednesday."

When he had gone I thought about his house – not the French one, which of course I had never seen, but the one I had just left. I'd not been there until this evening, and I remembered thinking how big it was, far too big for one man and a dog. I'd only seen a bit of it: the downstairs loo, the kitchen, and the dining room, where the French doors gave a view of lawns sloping down to the river; but there were doors all over, and a staircase. Obviously at one time this had been a family home, with a wife and son in residence, and perhaps then all of the rooms had been used. I wondered why Michael had never downsized. But it was none of my business, after all. Maybe he kept it as it was for Jasper; maybe it was simply convenient for work.

The weeks that followed were filled with useful distractions: walking Dulcie, and in a small way starting her training, was one. She was puzzled for a while, but very soon caught on, and being the clever creature she was she delighted in getting things right. The weather continued fair, I was out for much of the day, and my pallid skin began to catch a singe of the sun; I looked almost healthy. I practised my French; I wrote down Michael's many instructions and pieces of advice, quietly keeping my own counsel. I began to pack a few things. And then it was the weekend before my departure, and I surprised myself by the febrile mixture of elation and fear that I felt. It was as if something other than my own will was behind me, driving me on without a hint of mercy.

The journey to the port took about two hours, maybe a little more. The boat was due to leave at nine forty-five, and I started early. "You want to take the drive down nice and easy," Michael said. "But you don't want to arrive at the house in the dark." On the ferry I parked the car in a row of other vehicles, said a temporary goodbye to the dog, who was curled up in the boot on her favourite rug, and tramped up the stairs to the seating area. I found the cafeteria and bought coffee and a croissant. It was chewy, and I hoped the French ones were better.

The ferry was busy. Although most of the schools hadn't yet broken up, there were families with younger children on board, and a school party of excited teenagers crowding the shop and milling around the public areas while their teachers clustered at tables in the bar, clearly in holiday mood. I found a small space with my back to a wall and sipped my coffee.

Not so long ago, on the rare occasions that I found myself more or less idle in a gathering – at a work party, for instance – I would have been observing the people and looking for signs of heart disease. I would imagine that I saw symptoms, and saved myself from small talk and boredom by imagining incipient cardiac issues beneath well-ironed shirts and dresses. Now I watched my fellow-travellers. About half an hour into the crossing I realized with a small shock that I had not once thought about illness. Was it because I hadn't worked for almost two months? Or was there some other reason I couldn't fathom? I found myself observing parents and small children, noticing their chatter and laughter, the manner of their interaction, their unthinking care for one another. There were several elderly couples within my range, and I thought they were probably seasoned travellers; perhaps they had caravans or campers, and were getting on the road before the school holidays. It came to me that these people seemed well, and relatively happy. Was this how ordinary people acted? I had not known, shut away in my own rarefied world. Covertly, I listened to conversations while pretending to read, and I marvelled at the sheer banality of people's talk, the apparent lack of consequence, the breezy trotting out of clichés, the snatches of chat about the weather, and camp sites, and the price of petrol. Foolish as it was, it seemed a revelation to me, and I wondered if my life as a surgeon, dedicated so completely to work that every other aspect of my existence fed into my obsession, had somehow made me less than human. It was an uncomfortable thought. It was true that I had minimized everything that had no bearing on my chief focus. I ran, but that was to keep fit and deal with inevitable stress. My friends were few, my hobbies non-existent. Yes, I had let myself go a bit with Rob; but somehow now it all seemed a bit flimsy, just a careless fling and I saw with the benefit of distance that it would never have worked, and that I would probably, in the end, have treated Rob with the same cavalier casualness as I had Howard, my one-time fiancé. I shivered, wondering if – secretly – people thought of me as a bit of a monster.

My mind tracked back to something Michael had said. He'd decided to deliver Dulcie to me just before I left for the port, and at half past six that luminous summer morning he arrived, walking at a leisurely pace, as Dulcie scampered behind and in front, pausing only to sniff in the verges. When she saw me beside my tightly packed car, waiting, she came racing up and did several circuits round my feet, tongue lolling, bright-eyed. I poured some water from a plastic bottle into a bowl and she lapped it.

"Good thinking," Michael said with a smile. My boot was open. "Up you go, old girl." Dulcie leapt in. He bent and stroked her silky ears. "You be good, dog," he murmured. "I'll see you in a couple of weeks." He dropped a kiss on her smooth head, and closed the boot lid. I'd opened the window at the back to keep the car cool.

He looked at the ground, scuffing the gravel with his smart black shoe. He was already dressed for work: dark trousers, white shirt. He cleared his throat, and looked up at me. "All set? Nothing forgotten?"

"If I've left something vital, you can bring it." I squinted at the strengthening sun. "Any last words of advice?"

He smiled wryly. "I suspect you'd ignore it. No, not really. Except… well, I'm not really into fanciful things, but I'm hoping you'll find something – I don't know, something like peace and healing at Roqueville. I've found being there very calming to the soul, especially when things have been difficult, and other people have said the same."

I wondered if he was referring to the time his wife had left, taking Jasper with her. "You think my soul needs healing?"

"Doesn't everybody's, at one time or another? I don't know,

there's something about the atmosphere of a country town in rural France, something of a lost age, of neighbourliness and civility, a relaxed pace, the rhythm of the seasons in an agricultural area... it's something we tend to forget in a big noisy city, with high-pressure jobs like ours. Anyway, I hope it does you good, whatever you need."

"Thank you. Well, I'd better be off. Don't worry about Dulcie, will you? I'll take good care of her."

"I know."

"I'll speak to you this evening."

"Yes."

I hesitated. Was there something else I should say or do? He too seemed awkward. "Right, then. Bye, Michael. See you in two weeks." I got into the car and started the engine. As I rolled down the drive he still stood there, watching. I saw him wave, then I turned onto the road and he was lost to sight.

Michael's description of the house at Roqueville, and the one or two photos on his phone, had not really prepared me for the real thing. The only testing part of the journey came when I left the motorway and had to take several crucial turnings, but Michael's directions were explicit, and I rolled into town at a leisurely speed at about six o'clock that evening. Dulcie, asleep in the back until I slowed down, suddenly became alert, looking out of the rear window and giving the occasional soft whine.

"Nearly there," I called back to her. "You'll be free soon."

The church, dedicated to St Nicolas, was a huge grey barn of a place with a tower, topped by a shallow spire. I turned left as instructed, passed the town cemetery with its ornate funerary monuments, and was soon in open country. Fields stretched away into the distance, many of them green with closely planted maize at head height. Trees in summer foliage stood along the borders, marking boundaries. The land rose and fell gently, until I saw a higher range of hills on the horizon, with more trees on their tops, and incongruously a line of pylons marching away into the distance. The evening sun bathed everything in gold, low enough to dazzle my eyes. Then I came upon two houses on the right, and recognized the Boutins' bungalow from Michael's description, set back some distance from the road. Beyond it stood a weathered stone house, low and four-square, with glimpses of outbuildings. I indicated, left the engine running, and climbed out of the car, a bit stiff from sitting. There was no one else on the road. I stretched my arms, legs and back, and undid the padlock which secured the galvanized farm gate leading to Michael's drive. I drove in, stopped again and shut the gate, then rolled slowly forward to the second, a stout wooden one this time. A few moments later I parked on a gravelled courtyard, with both gates secured behind me. I lifted the boot lid up and Dulcie bounded out, sniffed, wagged her tail and was off, racing round the house and back again, clearly a happy dog.

While she checked out her domain, smelling everything of note and marking it with her proprietary scent, I stood and looked, turning in all directions. I took in the orchard of cider apple trees, in full leaf with small fruit visible, in neat rows running from the courtyard back towards the road. The grass under the trees had been neatly cropped by Bertrand's sheep. Beyond the orchard a thick hedge ran the length of the boundary, disappearing behind the house. Another hedge divided the property from that of the Boutins. For some minutes I took in the sun-washed building in front of me. What Michael had not said – perhaps because it was so familiar to him – was how beautiful it was: the soft irregular grey stone, the sun glancing off the roof-slates, the heavy weathered front door, the windows covered with wooden shutters. It looked as if it belonged in the landscape with all its subtle tones of green and grey and brown.

Dulcie had disappeared round the back, and I followed her. Here there was a big garden laid to lawn, if lawn was the right word for a rough area of grass in need of cutting. There were some leafy shrubs and a few desiccated pots and planters, and over to the left, against the hedge, a weedy tilled area which had been a kitchen garden at one time but was now overgrown. At the end of the garden was a row of tall trees, and beyond them a stout fence. The hedge began again at the border with the Boutins and I saw the stile that Michael had mentioned. There was no sign of Dulcie, and I was glad he'd told me she was likely to visit the neighbours so that I didn't have to worry she'd escaped.

I came back to the front and opened the main door, leaving it ajar while I took things out of the car. Once it was empty and my stuff piled up inside, I moved the car to a ramshackle building to the right of the house which served as an open garage with room for two cars, and parked it in some welcome shade. Then I went indoors, weaving a path between my various bags. It was dark and dusty, and smelled unlived-in. I undid the shutters in the room I was in, and went outside again to fasten them. Now light poured in, catching the dust in sparkling streams. I stood in a large open area, clearly serving as a dining room, because there was a long wooden table and eight chairs, currently covered in plastic sheeting. To one side was a vast fireplace, big enough to sit in, with a cast-iron wood-burner at its centre. At the back of this room another door led to a well-appointed kitchen, modern but in keeping, with a wide window overlooking the back garden, and next to it, sharing a back door, a scullery, with a deep porcelain sink and a flagged floor: probably left as it had been when it was a working farmhouse. A small and rather grimy window gave the same view as the kitchen. I doubled back, past the fireplace and through another door to a high, wide lounge area with a window to the front and double doors to the back. I opened the shutters here too, disturbing a scuttling spider. The furniture was shrouded in sheeting, and I took it off and folded it up, revealing a sofa and two easy chairs as well as several small tables. As I took the dustsheet off a flat object in one corner I exclaimed quietly: there stood a large electronic keyboard, black and dusty, its lead lying on the floor next to a socket. Neither Michael not Jasper had mentioned they played, but it came to me that perhaps I might tinker with it, since I was going to be alone for two weeks with no one to hear my fumblings. If nothing else it would be exercise for my hands. There was a small cupboard next to it, and in it I saw piled up books of piano music. Thinking about playing again gave a tight twinge to my chest as I remembered my father encouraging me in my childish efforts, applauding even when not only my notes but also my rhythms completely obscured the sense of the piece. I sighed deeply, wishing that these memories would just sink down somewhere and keep out of the way.

Between the fireplace and the door to the kitchen a wooden stair zigzagged up to the first floor. The space at the top was a cross between a landing and a mezzanine, with a tall old-fashioned wardrobe. The stairs continued up to the main upper floor, with two good-sized bedrooms and a spacious bathroom. One of the bedrooms overlooked the back; the other had double aspect windows, with one at the side over the garage roof. The bathroom faced the front. The staircase now narrowed and climbed again. Set into the roofspace was another small bedroom, again with a view of the back garden, and a tiny en-suite bathroom under the eaves. This was to be my private lair. There was room for a single bed, a chest of drawers, and a clothes-rail. The wooden floor had been sanded and left bare, except for a small cotton rug beside the bed, colourful once but faded with use.

I hauled my things into this little room and piled them up on the floor. The window sloped backwards; I tilted it open, and at once the smell of the country blew in, sweet and fresh with more than a hint of manure. If I craned my neck sideways I could see the fields stretching away beyond the hedge. In the distance, shimmering in the heat, a small herd of brown and white cows munched and shambled. I looked in the other bedrooms, their furniture covered in dustsheets, and noticed flyscreens at all the windows: necessary, I supposed, with farm animals all about.

I went downstairs and through the kitchen to the back, where there was a house-wide paved patio. To the left, before the kitchen garden, a small outbuilding stood, clearly once a bread oven. The oven part of it had long since crumbled and been roughly bricked up, but the roof, covered with heavy orange tiles, was still good. I ducked under the low wooden lintel and saw that this little place was stacked floor-to-ceiling with logs for the woodburner. Did Michael and Jasper come here during the winter? I supposed they must. Thinking about them made me remember that I had promised to text Michael when I arrived. I leaned on the warm wall of the bread oven and took my phone out of my pocket. "Arrived. No adventures. Didn't see Gaston or Guillaume. This place is amazing, even if it needs a duster and a mower. Talk later. R."

I sent the text and pocketed the phone, and then I noticed someone leaning in over the stile: a large, florid, white-haired man with a massive moustache, and beside him, her paws on the stile, a panting, prick-eared black and white dog. Gérard Boutin waved a meaty hand, and I walked over the tussocky grass towards him. Michael had warned me to expect a welcome effusive by British standards: "Gérard may be restrained when he first meets you, and shake your hand. After that expect kisses on both cheeks. Three – maybe even four. Marie-Claude will dispense with the handshake."

"Monsieur Boutin," I said carefully as I came up. I extended my hand, and he shook it vigorously. "Enchantée de faire…" I had no chance to finish my rehearsed greeting.

"Non, non, Gérard, s'il vous plaît!" he boomed. Then, still gripping my hand, he turned his head and yelled something totally incomprehensible over his shoulder, presumably to his wife, who after a moment or two came trotting over, wiping her hands down her apron. Of their subsequent talk I understood not a word. Finally he turned back to me, ruddy face split into a grin which revealed several blackened and missing teeth. "You are vairy welcome, Madame."

"Rachel," I said politely, then pronounced it the French way: "Rachelle."

"Bien sur," he said, still beaming. "Ma femme, ah, my wife and me we hope you will, mm, come and have some dinner with us. Tonight, yes?"

My French wasn't up to excuses so I gave in – gracefully, I hoped. "Merci, Gérard. Merci, Madame. Tres gentil."

He shrugged expansively. "Er, vers vingt heures, oui? Eight of clock?"

I nodded and smiled, and at last he let my hand go. "Oui, merci beaucoup. A bientot. Come, Dulcie."

"D'accord. A bientot, Rachelle." Still nodding and beaming, the pair of them watched me walk Dulcie indoors.

It was an extraordinary evening. How we managed to communicate remains a marvel. Gérard plied me with aperitifs and wine in vast quantities, a different wine with every course, and as my French deteriorated so did his English. It didn't seem to matter; they were hospitable, the atmosphere convivial, and all three of us were more than a little tipsy. Marie-Claude served up numerous courses: tiny hors d'oeuvres, squares of bread with eggs and anchovies and olives, then grilled pork and beef with a huge bowl of potatoes, followed by a palate-cleansing dish of simple dressed leaves, grown in their garden. Out of the window, between courses, I noted their immaculate lawn and kitchen garden, the chicken coop, the rose bushes, the clipped hedges. Then a platter of several cheeses with bread, and a fruity dessert with cream, and coffee and liqueurs. I hoped they didn't eat like this every night, but both of them were well built and rotund, so maybe they did. However little we understood the finer details of each other's conversation, we managed to laugh immoderately.

At last I made my excuses. I didn't have to feign weariness –

a huge meal with such a river of alcohol, plus a long drive on a warm day, had left me with a headache and wobbly knees. Dulcie had come with me to the Boutins' – they looked surprised when I'd left her indoors and insisted I fetch her – and apart from gobbling up titbits that accidentally or otherwise fell from the table had spent most of the evening curled up in front of their fireplace. As I departed Marie-Claude gave me a carrier-bag stuffed with salad and eggs. "De nos propres poules," she said proudly. "Un peu sale, mais bon." I thanked her with a smile – I had no problem with slightly dirty home-laid eggs.

I had had little time before dinner to do anything except feed Dulcie, throw a ball for her in the garden, find some sheets for my bed, and send Michael a second text: "Dining with neighbours. Talk tomorrow." Now home, I drank a long draught of cool water, washed my face, and cleaned my teeth. I knew nothing that night of hunting owl or marauding wildlife, nor did any dreams haunt me.

The sun woke me the next morning: I had forgotten to pull down the blind, and light poured through the angled window onto my disordered bed. I heaved myself up and put my feet on the floor, holding my aching head tenderly in both hands. I stumbled downstairs, feeling wavery and half-dead, but a cafetière of strong coffee did its work. I sat on the back patio on a rickety canvas chair and drank several cups. Dulcie, hearing me stagger about, had met me at the top of the first flight of stairs, and now lay beside me in the sunshine, her nose on her paws, her eyes on my face. I threw a ball feebly for her a few times. "Sorry, pal," I mumbled. "I need to take a shower. Then I might feel a bit more human." Unfortunately I had forgotten to switch on the water heater the night before, so my shower was bracingly cool. I made myself eat some of Marie-Claude's eggs, and started to feel better. It was still early – no more than eight thirty – but I heard the Boutins' car start up and roll away down their drive onto the road. We were alone, the dog and I. For a moment I felt myself wobble and sway inwardly, but then I told myself sternly that I had a list, and it must be followed. I was on holiday, wasn't I? People on holiday didn't think about work, and neither would I. I would do the things other people did on holiday – seek out new things, read, relax, sleep. I decided that today I would start Dulcie's training in earnest, and then when I had worn her out both physically and mentally I would go to the supermarket.

By the time I got into the garden with Dulcie the heat was already building. For ten minutes or so I threw a ball for the dog to take the edge off her energy; then it was time for work. I clipped on her lead, and she looked at me with an eager, enquiring look. "Nope, we aren't going for a walk," I told her. "It's lesson time."

For half an hour we practised walking to heel. Every time she strained at the lead I pulled her back, and when she walked as I wanted I slackened off the lead and praised her. Praise made her delirious and undid some of the training as she frolicked and jumped about and got the lead hopelessly tangled. I thought I probably needed some healthy dog treats and would look for them when I went shopping. It occurred to me that I knew nothing of what a provincial supermarket might stock. We persevered, and after a while she began to get it. I loosened the lead, told her firmly to "Watch me!" and walked quite slowly the length of the garden, saying nothing to her until we came to the trees on the border. "Now sit," I said. She sat. I unclipped the lead and looked her in the eyes. "You did very well," I told her, my voice soft and flat. "Good girl. Now off you go." She continued to sit, looking at me uncertainly. I raised my voice. "Well done, Dulcie!" I threw the ball, and she leapt after it, tail high. It was clear to me that this dog had the brain and the will to learn fast.

I threw the ball for her till she was panting and hot. The sun was well up, and I too was beginning to roast. "Right, in we go, Dulcie," I said. "More lessons and more play time later, but now you need a drink and some breakfast, and I need to wash and get to the shops." As we went towards the house I took a closer look at Michael's vegetable patch, which the day before I had dismissed as nothing but a weedy overgrown eyesore. Now, on closer inspection, I saw that he had planted things. There were a couple of sprawling courgette plants, with small fruits forming – one green, one yellow. There were half a dozen tomato plants, badly in need of staking and watering. There were two rows of leeks, about as fat as a man's thumb, and a patch of strawberries with reddening fruit. But the buttercups and dandelions had got a hold, and the whole area needed urgent attention. Perhaps I could do something about it, clear the weeds, give the plants a chance. If I could find the mower, I might even cut the grass. It was, it seemed to me, the least I could do, and it would be nice for Michael and Jasper to arrive and find they had some flourishing fresh vegetables.

I left Dulcie snoozing in her basket in the dining room, then locked up and got the car out. A night parked in the shade of the garage had left it pleasantly cool. I'd found some shopping bags in a cupboard in the scullery, and I put them in the boot. With the dog firmly shut indoors, I closed the inner gate for safety but left the outer one open for my return.

The journey to the town took all of five minutes, and I found the supermarket with no trouble. The first thing that struck me as I entered the shop was the smell – one so overpoweringly pungent I stopped for a moment to take it in. Clearly the whole area was immaculate. The floors had been mopped, the lights were bright, piped music twittered in the background. Then it dawned on me. What else could it be but cheese? With an inward smile I made my way to the cheese counter. The array of choice was vast. I picked some that were familiar – a soft wedge of Brie, a Tomme de Savoie. Then I paused and branched out: a bright orange Mimolette and a whole mini-cheese with a picture of a monk on the wrapping, called Pere Matthieu.

I was a long time in the shop, not only because I had no idea where everything was, but because it was fascinating. I'd never loved shopping – it was a necessary chore, to be got over with as quickly as possible. But this was different. Around me people were choosing their goods, and if they caught my eye, they smiled and said "Bonjour, Madame." It was a far cry from shopping in England where people rarely spoke. And the shop seemed to stock an enormous variety of things – books, garden tools, children's toys, clothes for all ages, wellington boots, fishing tackle, watches and jewellery, as well as having a large wine section, fresh produce, a fish counter, a butcher's, and a bakery. I bought bread and croissants, butter, yogurt, milk, a big bag of tomatoes, apples, wine, and in a moment of rashness a huge steak which I thought would last at least two meals. I passed a delicatessen counter and bought a selection of fat, oozy olives. Then I backtracked to the fruit and vegetables and bought avocados, an aubergine, onions, peppers, and garlic. *I can make ratatouille. A big pot to last several meals, perhaps even some for the freezer.* With a small shock I realized how unusual this was: that I was not only thinking about food with anticipation, but also planning to cook, even if it was something simple. I shrugged. *Isn't this too what people do on holiday?* I glanced at my watch; it was almost noon. I hunted around in the pet department and found some treats for Dulcie, as well as a stock of canned dog food. It was time to go to the checkout. I was a little apprehensive, but Michael had assured me that all I needed to do was smile, say "Bonjour" and "Merci", and present my credit card. On the way I passed through the women's clothing, and it struck me that I had no swimming costume with me. Jasper had said he hoped to swim while they were in France. Should I be prepared to go too? I used to swim, once, though almost certainly not to the level that the Wells men did – but should this deter me? I looked at the selection of swimming costumes with a jaundiced eye. The sizing was different from that of the UK, but I found one eventually that had both British and European sizes listed, in a not too horrible shade of red. I held it up against me, wondering if it would stretch if necessary. An elderly man in a flat cap passed me, raised a bushy eyebrow, and winked. "Très jolie," I heard him murmur, and felt my face heat up.

I passed through the checkout without a problem and felt that I had somehow triumphed. With my purchases stowed in the boot, I drove back to the house. It was hot, and I rolled the windows down, enjoying the breeze ruffling my hair and the smells: dusty tarmac, floral scents on the air, hay and hot grass.

With the gates secured and the car back in the garage, I unloaded my shopping and let Dulcie out. I packed everything away and made myself some lunch: Marie-Claude's leaves, olives and tomatoes, bread and cheese. I opened a bottle of wine, put it all on a tray and took it onto the patio. It was far too hot for exertion. Dulcie followed me and flopped down on the paving with a sigh. There was a lean-to at the back of the scullery, and I found a garden umbrella there which I set up to shade my lunch table.

The red wine I had opened was almost warm and slithered smoothly down my gullet. The bread was fresh and crusty with a feathery middle, the butter cool, inviting me to slather it on far too thickly, and I tasted every one of the cheeses and found them excellent. Tomato juice ran down my chin – but who was watching? I couldn't remember a meal, however elegant, I had enjoyed so much as this simple one, with the sun beating down, the smells of the countryside wafting in on the tiny breeze, the sleepy chattering of birds, and bees rumbling in the blue-flowering rosemary that grew in a pot at the edge of the lawn. I munched on an apple, stretched out my legs, and closed my eyes.

After a while I realized that if I nodded off the sun would move round and scorch me. I heaved myself up, gathered the remains of my lunch, and went indoors, struck by how pleasantly cool it was, defended by thick stone walls. I put the food away and stacked the dishes by the sink. I called Dulcie in. "It's too hot," I said. "We'll go out again later, when the sun starts to go down." She seemed quite happy to lie on the floor and stretch out, closing her eyes and giving a throaty sigh.

My new swimming costume lay on the dining-room table where I'd thrown it as I came in. There was a full-length mirror by the front door, presumably there to check if you were presentable before going out. I peeled off my T-shirt, shorts, and underwear, knowing that no one could see me from the road. Standing in front of the mirror, I saw where the sun had caught me: my face and neck, arms and legs were a pinkish-brown, but my torso was deadly white. I picked up the swimming costume with a pang of doubt. I am not at all a standard size and shape: tall, and people say I am thin, but I am not so much thin as narrow, especially my shoulders, chest, and hips. I admit to having thin arms, with long-fingered hands, but my legs are well muscled and strong from all the running. Oddly, despite the narrowness of my ribcage, I am not flat-chested – I have soft, squashy breasts which refuse to fit into clothes with any elegance or neatness. Physically, I am a bit of an oddity, I suppose. *As well as in other ways.*

I struggled into the swimming costume and after some adjustment of straps was pleasantly surprised: it moulded its fabric to my shape, even somehow giving an illusion of curves. Now I needed to even up my skin tone – the contrast between tanned and white was hideously stark. I peeled the swimming costume off my hot body, and seeing myself in the mirror a thought struck me: my hair – dark, wiry, unruly – was too long, especially for this weather. Perhaps Marie-Claude could recommend a hairdresser in town. I smiled wryly. How bold I was becoming!

I climbed the stairs – hot, weary, a little fuddled from afternoon drinking – pulled down the window-blind, and collapsed onto my little bed. For a moment I felt a sweet surge of memory, of stretching out just like this with Rob, excited, then sated, mindless, relaxed. *No chance of any of that*, I told myself, and slipped down into sleep.

I awoke confused: the room was dark. Was it so late? I groped on the bedside table and looked at my watch – ten to five; it shouldn't be dark. I shivered – it seemed chilly as well. I got up, raised the blind, and looked out. Dark thunder-clouds were massed above the trees at the end of the garden, and as I looked there came a soft grumble of thunder. I heard Dulcie whine downstairs. Was she afraid of storms? I didn't know; the subject hadn't arisen. I pulled on my dressing gown and padded downstairs.

"You OK, girl?" I said to Dulcie as she greeted me, and bent to stroke her. "Scared of thunder and lightning? Don't worry. I'll keep you company."

It turned out that Dulcie was more or less OK with storms if someone was with her, except for the flashes of lightning, which made her jump and yelp. I liked watching storms but for the dog I closed curtains and blinds. Still in my dressing-gown, I made a pot of coffee and set to preparing the vegetables for the ratatouille. Beyond the kitchen window the rain fell in noisy cascades and the rising wind whipped the trees into a frenzy. It seemed impossible that the branches should remain attached to their trunks, but somehow they did, despite their wild dance in the roaring wind.

My phone rang as I piled the vegetables into a large pan and set it on the hob to simmer. I added a spoonful of oil, licked my fingers, and answered it.

It was Michael, his deep voice a distant comfort against the background of lashing rain and thunder.

"Don't pass out with amazement," I said after explaining about the storm, "but I am actually cooking. Just some ratatouille – to be eaten later with half of an enormous steak. And wine too, of course."

I heard him chuckle. "You've been gone a day and a half and you're turning into a French person." He paused. "Too bad I'm not there to eat it with you; I hope you're not too lonely?"

I laughed. "You're forgetting I've lived on my own for a long time. And anyway, I've already met the neighbours; they invited me to dinner. It was absolutely vast, not to mention the quantities of alcohol we put away. And I got sent home with eggs and salad. They were very kind."

"Did you manage to talk to each other?"

"Kind of. I wanted to pop over today to thank them, but they went out in the car very early."

"It's Tuesday; they've probably gone to visit Pascale, their daughter. She doesn't live locally – it's about a 150-mile round trip for them." He paused. "Pascale is a bit, I don't know, vulnerable."

"How do you mean?"

He seemed to hesitate. "I don't know the details, but she has a husband, or partner, who's not at all what Gérard and Marie-Claude would want for their daughter. Apparently he gambles, hardly ever has work, drinks, possibly even knocks Pascale about. They've tried to persuade her to come home with them, but she refuses. There's a child too – a little boy about three years old, I think."

"Must be really worrying for them."

"Yes. So they go down there every Tuesday, and take food and money and clothes for their grandson. Marie-Claude cooks, does the laundry, and cleans the flat."

"Do they have other kids?"

"Yes, a son, younger than Pascale – Stephane. He's in the army."

I paused, taking it all in. "It seems quite a lottery, being a parent." Then another thought struck me. "Do you think I should invite the Boutins over here? I'm not sure my cooking skills are up to a five-course dinner, but maybe I could offer some distraction?"

"That's a nice idea. You could ask them in for drinks – keep it simple. But I'd give them a day or two. They're often quite depressed when they get back from visiting Pascale."

"No wonder. Why won't she leave?"

"I've no idea. What do any of us know about other people's lives, or their private thoughts?"

"Hm." I digested this for a moment.

There was a long pause, as if we'd run out of things to say.

"Oh, one thing," Michael said. "It's market day in Roqueville tomorrow. I thought that might be worth a visit. You could take Dulcie. It's a meeting place for dogs as well as people. If the weather improves it'll probably be bustling."

"Mm, maybe I will. Thanks."

After he'd rung off the house seemed particularly quiet; I hadn't noticed it before, but now I felt a pang of loneliness that was quite unlike the old Rachel. Even the dog seemed subdued, but that might have been because of the storm. When I lowered the blind and turned away I saw that Dulcie was skulking against the wall, shivering. "Sorry, hound," I said. I squatted down and put my arms round her neck. She smelled of clean, healthy dog. "It'll blow itself out before long." She licked my hand and hid under the dining-room table.

While the ratatouille simmered I picked a novel from Michael's bookshelf at random and sat at the table to read, my bare feet against Dulcie's warm furry side. It was a fanciful story, based on some fictitious planet in the distant future, but well-enough composed, and I read it at speed, letting the writer take me along with him for the ride without undue criticism. When I looked up I smelled the ratatouille wafting in from the kitchen. It was well and truly done; I'd been reading for an hour, oblivious. The storm seemed to have abated, so I opened the back door and went out. Dulcie appeared at my side with a little anxious whine. "It's OK, old girl," I whispered. "It's all gone. No more bangs, no more flashes. Peace." She looked up at me, then trotted down the garden to relieve herself, and raced back indoors. Clearly she was not convinced.

The patio was awash, the grass flattened, and the chair I had used earlier and chosen not to put away was sodden and dripping. In the sky the clouds were drifting off, and one or two stars were blearily visible. I stood there in just my dressing-gown, the cool wet flags of the patio under my bare feet, inhaling the scents of soaked vegetation, hearing nothing but the drip of water. I shivered, suddenly chilled, and went indoors to finish cooking my dinner.

I awoke the following morning to a grey, misty day. Looking down the garden, a cup of coffee in my hand, watching Dulcie ferreting about under the trees, I could sense a faint warmth from the sun, but it was struggling to be seen. I showered and dressed, and threw a ball for Dulcie. She came in wet and I had to towel her down, which she tolerated amiably. I fed her and made myself breakfast from Marie-Claude's eggs and the dry stump of yesterday's bread.

The sky was beginning to clear when I reversed the car out of the garage, opened the boot, and let Dulcie out of the house. "In you get," I said and she leapt in eagerly. As we rolled into town the sun came out in strength, and the wet fields began to steam as it warmed them. When we got to the edge of town I realized I should have left the car at home; stalls were set not only in the market square itself but also up all the little roads radiating from it, and there was little parking to be had. I thought I might park at the supermarket, but the car park there was full, and I drove round and round, getting more frustrated as I tried to avoid shoppers standing in the middle of the road in clusters, chatting and taking no notice of cars trying foolishly to get through.

In the end I saw a car leave a tiny space between two white vans opposite the church, and dived into it triumphantly before anyone else could snaffle it. I got Dulcie out of the car and snapped on her lead. "Remember your lessons," I said to her. "I want you to walk to heel. There are lots of people about, and I don't want you jumping on anybody, or getting the lead tangled, or any of that nonsense." A woman passed me, a basket over arm, and gave me a strange look; but Dulcie looked up at me as if she understood every word.

The sun was now blazing from a blue sky, drying up the pavements, and people were taking off raincoats and collapsing umbrellas. With Dulcie on a short lead I strolled among the stalls, intrigued by their variety. There was a mobile barbecue with huge sausages sizzling on a griddle and mountains of part-cooked chips steaming; there were vans with awnings selling raw chickens and eggs, cheeses and butter, pork products, and fish. I watched the people at the fish stall queuing for crab and mussels and an array of fish, many of which I didn't recognize. With the aid of pointing and smiling I managed to buy a handful of prawns. Dulcie sniffed at the bag appreciatively. "Not for dogs," I said. The man behind the counter, wrapped in a vast apron slimed with fish-blood, smiled and nodded.

There were stalls selling plants and flowers in dazzling colours, fruit and vegetables, handbags, shoes, hats, garden equipment, mattresses and chairs, trinkets and toys. One stall was selling nothing but enormous bunches and ropes of pink garlic; another had a huge pan of paella steaming; a third had honey and beeswax soap. The aromas of onions, cheese, fish, frying and flowers battled for supremacy, and there was a constant rumble of talk. People stopped to gossip in groups and I had to weave my way around them. I stood for a moment and watched two women buying a red azalea. The older lady was stout, her ankles grossly swollen, her puffy feet crammed into open-toed shoes. Her waterproof was clearly too hot, and she was red-faced and flustered as she tried with difficulty to stuff the pot into her carrier bag. The younger woman, middle-aged, almost certainly her daughter, was patiently helping her, murmuring a soothing running commentary. Plant finally stowed, they walked away slowly, the mother holding on to her daughter's arm. I remembered the families on the ferry, and wondered at myself, because I wasn't criticizing them or revving up with impatience; I was watching them with interest, as if I was an invisible visitor from a distant planet.

I put the prawns into a string bag that I had in my pocket. I bought a melon, apricots, nectarines, eggs, and bread. On the outskirts I found a stall selling tiny vegetable plants, and I bought a dozen mixed lettuces – some green, some reddish-brown, which the hand-written label told me were called "feuilles de chêne". I decided, once I had cleared the weeds, I would plant a row of lettuces to go with Michael's tomatoes.

After half an hour I'd had enough, and walked slowly back to the car. I put Dulcie and my purchases inside. On an impulse, feeling like a tourist, I thought I would look inside the church; I was curious to see what a provincial Catholic church might be like. I knew it was open because I'd seen a woman go in carrying an armful of flowers. I opened the car window an inch or two so that Dulcie had air. "Shan't be long," I told her.

Tentatively I pushed open the tall wooden door and slipped inside. It was pleasantly cool. In contrast to the severely plain exterior, the interior was ornate and full of colour: light poured in through the high windows, one or two of which had stained glass, and there were many large pictures and painted statues. The woman I had seen with the flowers appeared near the altar and looked at me curiously. I had no wish to converse even if I'd been able to, so I slid into a pew in a side aisle and bent my head; I didn't quite have the gall to kneel. I heard the heels of her shoes clack away as she went about her business. It came to me that I had no right to be there – I was no sort of believer, and certainly not a Catholic, and I felt a surge of embarrassment, almost shame, at my own hypocrisy. Here I was, pretending to pray, treating with contemptuous frivolity something which had been sustaining people for two thousand years. I told myself I should either pray honestly, or leave at once. Guiltily I mouthed, "Sorry" to a God I wasn't sure existed, and got up to go.

As I crept back down the nave to the door I had entered by, trying to make no sound with my shoes, I stopped in front of a large painting. There was the conventional, stylized Jesus, a beautiful young man with long smooth hair, beard, and unlikely blue eyes. In the middle of his chest, his heart stood exposed: nothing, of course, like a real human heart, as I well knew. One hand pointed inwards to the heart; the other was raised in blessing. The heart itself was pierced, drops of blood gently dripping from the wound. A circlet of thorns surrounded it, a cross within a flame stood on its top, and a weird light radiated from it. In the past I had mocked such images, looking at them as a scornful medic might, but that day, for some unfathomable reason, I knew I had missed the point. I didn't care much for this kind of over-the-top devout imagery, but I was intrigued, almost uneasy. Where had it come from? What did it mean? What, if anything, was I missing? I thought of the Christians I knew, or had known: my father, perhaps, was one. Certainly so were Bridget, Father Vincent, Michael, and Jasper – all good people who had been more than kind to me. More, perhaps, than they needed to, certainly more than I deserved. Perhaps I might have countered, "Yes, but what about Eve Rawlins? What kind of Christian was she, attacking me with vengeful hatred, in an attempt to destroy my reason for being?" But I would have to have answered, in honesty, "A bereaved mother maddened by grief, now bitterly repentant and paying the price of her actions."

I had a sudden desperate need to leave the building, to get away from the disturbing thoughts which seemed to have come from nowhere; but as I approached the door with a sense of relief I stopped again. A statue I hadn't seen as I entered stood beside the door: improbably beautiful and calm, a blue-robed Mary, a gold crown on her head, holding in her lap a flaxen-haired child, his blue eyes looking just a bit blank, his pudgy infant hand raised over a suffering world in blessing. Seeing this mother and child, almost immediately after thinking about Eve Rawlins, gave me a sudden insight that pierced me, so that I almost gasped. I thought what I had not allowed myself to think until now: what must it have been like for Eve to lose her son? What must it have been like for the real Mary to watch her son die by crucifixion? Images crowded into my mind of the crucifixion scenes I had seen elsewhere which showed the sheer brutality of this death – the back scourged bloody, the slow suffocation. I thought of Michael too, and imagined what it would be like for him if he lost Jasper; and I felt physically sick. I ran to the door, pulled it open, and stumbled out into the sunshine of the busy market town. For a moment I leaned against the sun-warmed wall, swallowing down my nausea. Even in my confusion I knew I had experienced some kind of unwelcome epiphany, and I sensed that my world was spinning out of control, something to which I had been deliberately blind, but which was now manifesting itself in a way I could no longer ignore. *I'm sorry, I didn't understand. I still don't, not really. Someone has to help me.* Who was I talking to, in the silence of my mind? Maybe the God I had denied for most of my life.

I heard a sound behind me, and the woman with the flowers came out of the church, closing the door behind her, and locking it with a large key. She looked at me curiously, and said something I didn't understand. I smiled feebly and waved my hand, as if waving her away; then I crossed over to my car, got in, and started the engine. In the rear-view mirror I saw the woman as I drove erratically away. She was frowning and seemed to be shouting. I felt myself smile with a dark humour – maybe she thought I had come into the church to steal the coppers that worshippers had left for candles. I drove slowly home. If I couldn't explain to myself, what chance had I of explaining to her? Or to anyone?

When Michael rang that evening he seemed distracted, as if, unusually, he was only half listening to my tales of market and dog-training and lettuce-planting. He told me he had an important meeting the following morning and had been busy preparing for it, but he didn't say what it was about, and I didn't ask. I had absolutely no right to feel wounded by his apparent lack of attention, but it niggled me, and I wanted to shake him.

"Michael."

"Hm?"

I had the distinct feeling he was looking for a reason to ring off. "I realize you don't know me all that well, but would you say I lacked empathy?"

I was unprepared for his reply; perhaps he really had been listening all along.

"I'd say so," he said calmly. "I don't know all the circumstances, obviously, but I imagine any native empathy you might once have had was probably killed off by your will to succeed."

"Oh."

"That's not intended as a criticism," he added. *But what else could it be?* "Sacrifices have to be made. You chose a gruelling line of work, and some things are inevitably lost. We can't be everything."

"Can something like that be regained?" I said, trying not to let my voice show the disturbance I was feeling. If he had said, "Rachel, you are a most unlikeable person", his opinion couldn't have been clearer.

"Maybe, but at a cost. Empathy is painful. Standing in someone else's shoes can be distressing. Most of us shield ourselves to some extent."

"What about you? Do you consider yourself empathetic? How does that pan out in your work?"

I could almost hear him shrug. "I try to keep some kind of balance. More of an oscillation, really. Look, Rachel –"

"Yes, I know. You need to get on with your preparations. Everything's OK here. I'll ring off now."

"I didn't mean –"

"It's fine, I understand. Perhaps we'll talk again tomorrow. Bye for now." I replaced the receiver before he could answer. I knew the game I was playing, and no doubt so did he, but although I was not proud of my words I couldn't seem to help myself. I threw down my phone and stood chewing at my thumbnail.

I brooded on the notion of empathy causing pain, and perhaps inevitably an image of the crucified Christ flashed across my mental vision. He, so they said, had borne the world's sin. I couldn't even cope with what I knew of mine.

In the days that followed I worked myself to weariness, all ideas of rest abandoned. I kept up with Dulcie's training; I weeded the vegetable patch, staked the tomatoes, planted the lettuces. In an outbuilding attached to the garage I found a ride-on mower, and with a little help from Gérard I checked the oil, filled the tank with petrol, and started on the grass at the back. But distraction doesn't always work as thoroughly as one might wish. The awkward questions multiplied, and the answers weren't keeping up.

Michael rang again on Thursday evening. I was determined to try to hide any trace of annoyance or hurt in my voice. But exchanging pleasantries seemed only to irritate me even more. I tried to steer the conversation towards neutral subjects.

"How is Jasper? Has the school broken up yet?"

"Just. He finishes today."

Thinking of Jasper, I couldn't help but smile. "I'm looking forward to seeing him."

"He's looking forward to seeing you too. Tomorrow you can talk to him instead of me if you like."

"Oh!" I said. "Fed up with me already?" There was a pause, and I wanted to say goodbye and leave him wondering if I was offended, but then I relented. *Grow up, Rachel.*

"Look, Rachel –" He hesitated. "Did I annoy you the other day? Hurt your feelings? Behave like a lout?"

"No, of course not," I began, falsely bright, then changed my mind. "Yes, maybe a bit. But I have no right to expect unduly tender treatment anyway. Forget it."

"I won't. And I apologize unreservedly."

"Apology accepted. But you are not a lout."

I heard him chuckle. "Let me know if I am becoming loutish."

"Let *me* know if I am being self-righteous and prickly."

After that the air cleared a little. I told him about my attempts at gardening, and artfully avoided a direct answer to his questioning about my exercises. In my mind my hands were getting plenty of use, in a much more productive way than squeezing a ball and flexing fingers endlessly. But there were two things I hadn't mentioned. One of them I wanted to be a surprise: I had dusted off the keyboard and begun to tinker with it, stumbling through some of the simpler music. Fortunately there was no one to hear because I made heavy weather of it. It had been so many years since I'd played, and I was as clumsy as a drunken rhino. Even if it came to nothing, at least it was more exercise for the fingers.

The other thing I didn't tell him, and had no intention of telling him, was my decision to go to the service at St Nicolas on Sunday. I didn't want him to read too much into it. It was curiosity, I told myself. Nothing but that. I'd arrive late, conceal myself in a back pew, and slip out discreetly when I'd had enough. I suspected the church, big as it was, would be quite full; it was summer and there were tourists passing through. No one, I hoped, would even notice me.

As it turned out, Sunday had the quality of farce, the result of my ignorance and poor decisions. It didn't seem funny at the time, of course – except to others, when they found out.

For a start, I wavered about the protocol of appropriate dress, and decided my knees and shoulders should be modestly covered, which meant I sweltered. I put a scarf in my bag in case head-covering was also a requirement, but when I got there – at three minutes to eleven – nobody else was dressed in this peculiar way, not even the much older ladies. I chose a pew three from the back door and parked myself resolutely at the aisle end for a swift exit. But, later even than me, a cluster of people came in with irreverent clatter and loud voices, greeting their friends as books were handed out. A small woman of indeterminate age, wearing a flamboyant orange cardigan, decided my pew would do and shoved me up the length of it in a friendly manner, nodding and smiling, followed by several other women, clearly friends and neighbours. So one pillar of my plan was knocked sideways from the outset, because I found myself up against the stone wall, unable to get out, unless I disturbed the service. Despite what I had observed to be acceptable behaviour from the natives, I realized I was far too British to contemplate making a fuss or drawing attention to myself, two activities sternly disapproved of by my mother, which considering her own tendency to drama was a bit rich.

The service was not long – less than an hour – but for me it seemed interminable. I had a hymn book, but the hymn numbers were announced so quickly that I couldn't understand them. Another small woman, this time in a blue cardigan with flowery embroidery, took pity on me and leaned over from the pew behind, pointing to the right page. I smiled weakly, muttering "Merci, Madame." She asked me a question I didn't catch, and waited for an answer with raised eyebrows. I swallowed hard and whispered, "Anglaise", a response that forced her back with an expression of horror on her face, as if I had told her I had plague. After that I had no more help, but I heard her muttering darkly to her friend all through the sermon. Her apparent antipathy to the British was not general, however: many of the women in my pew smiled encouragingly, as if they thought I was a bit simple.

I understood the odd phrase or two of the sermon, but for the most part it was all lost on me. The singing was a hearty drone, led by someone at the front. Seeing who this was brought a fine sweat to my face: it was the woman I had seen come in with flowers on market day. I should have been relieved that I was too far away for her to recognize me. I wouldn't have been at all surprised if she had marched down the aisle and revealed me to all as a hypocritical impostor, as I'd clearly broken some protocol on my last visit, if not an actual thief.

Finally, after a great deal of sitting, standing, and kneeling, came the mass for which the assembled worshippers were waiting. Several of the congregation, once they had received the wafer, to my surprise simply left; they'd had what they'd come for. One last hymn was announced, full of references to the Virgin Mary. Some sang, others shuffled, preparing to depart, and it was then that I saw the distinctive head of Gérard Boutin on the other side of the church towards the front. Beside him, round and diminutive, stood Marie-Claude. They must have come in by a side door. I cursed myself for not thinking that they might be here. How was I ever going to preserve any kind of anonymity now? As the blessing was pronounced and the congregation began to leave, chatting all the while, I waited for my pew to empty so that I could scuttle out. But then Gérard raised his massive head and a huge smile broke out under his signature moustache. "Rachelle!" he boomed, and several heads turned. If ever I had wished to be a church mouse racing unobserved for her hole, this was that moment.

Embarrassed though I was, I decided to behave as if all was normal. Grinning like a demented monkey, I waved to Gérard and forced my way up the aisle against the flow: several others were doing just this and nobody took any notice. Gérard clasped me to his chest in a rib-cracking hug, kissing me on both cheeks at least four times, and Marie-Claude followed suit, clucking and trilling incomprehensibly. Gérard took me by the elbow, bellowing over the noise of the crowd something about having refreshments at the local bar, and I was propelled out of the building and diagonally across the road to where several tables had been set out on the pavement. I was pressed into a chair, several people shook my hand, and I began to feel that my smile was cemented on. A tiny espresso appeared at my elbow, then a glass of brandy. I drank both down, grateful for the instant relief they offered. I had no idea who was buying, but a few minutes later another brandy appeared. At this point I thought I had better be careful; I didn't want to make a *complete* drunken spectacle of myself.

Eventually, after a great deal of talking, shouting, hand-shaking, kissing, and laughter, the party broke up. Gérard discovered I had walked to church and insisted on driving me home. It was only a five-minute drive, but it took fifteen: he drove slowly, meandering across the central line, and singing in a fruity baritone. Happily we encountered no tractors – of course not: it was Sunday. The local farmers were indoors, well scrubbed, knocking back their Sunday lunch of half a dozen courses and enough wine to sink the entire British Navy.

I thanked my kind neighbours and got over my embarrassment. After all, nobody else seemed to think anything was out of the ordinary. Very carefully, I asked the Boutins if they would like to come round for aperitifs the following evening. I felt quite humbled by the enthusiasm of their acceptance. What had Michael told them? It was as if they had me down as some celestial visiting dignitary, rather than an inept foreigner getting everything wrong.

When Michael rang that evening he'd obviously already heard the story of my visit to St Nicolas, Roqueville. I hadn't realized till now that he and the Boutins were also regularly in touch. From the bubble of merriment in his voice I concluded that he was making an almighty effort not to laugh.

"Go ahead, laugh," I said bitterly. "I'm glad I'm such a hilarious spectacle. I dare say the whole of northern France is in on the joke. Perhaps it'll be in tomorrow's *Gazette*."

"I'm sorry, Rachel," Michael said, obviously not sorry at all.

"I've only heard what Gérard told me, and there was nothing funny about that. It's what my imagination has added – you trying to be anonymous, stuck up against the church wall by a bunch of French ladies."

"Well, I suppose you've got to laugh," I said grudgingly. "And to be fair I think I was the only person who felt uncomfortable. Nobody else thought anything of it."

"People round here are used to odd Britons," Michael said. "Mostly they regard us as harmless eccentrics, so you've probably confirmed them in that view. But Rachel, if you have a yen to go to church, there's no need to attend the Catholic one and struggle with the language. When Jasper and I are in France we go to an Anglican church called St Luke's. It's about a forty-five minute drive, but you'll be welcome, and you could take Dulcie – they like dogs there. Also," he added slyly, "they often have lunch after the service. If you're interested they have a website, with directions."

I took note of the address.

"I'll tell them to look out for you," Michael added.

"No, please don't," I said hastily. "Because I may not go. Anyway…"

"Anyway what?"

"No, it doesn't matter." I had been about to say, "I don't want anyone to notice me." But even if I did go, it wasn't any kind of commitment, was it?

The evening with the Boutins went off reasonably well. I'd gone out and bought an array of what were whimsically called "gâteaux aperitifs" – the English equivalent of "nibbles". I'd inspected the cupboard in which Michael kept his stock of drinks and realized I didn't have to buy any more. Gérard had smoothed down his unruly thatch with water; during the course of the evening tufts of it sprang to life as they dried. Despite the heat he'd put on a tie, and was far too hot as a result. As each glass emptied his face grew more and more flushed, and I began to be anxious for his health. Marie-Claude had taken off her apron and put on a dress that was pretty but rather too long for her height. Clearly they felt it was an occasion of some significance, demanding a certain formality. Between Gérard's interesting English and my inadequate French we managed somehow to talk to one another, but it was a struggle on both sides, and Marie-Claude simply twittered, talked to her husband, and smiled at me.

There was something I'd been thinking about, and I felt she was the person to help me, so I addressed her directly rather than through Gérard, which made her flustered and nervous. "Marie-Claude," I said, "Peut-être vous pouvez m'aider?"

"Bien sur," she squeaked, her voice disappearing into a distant upper register.

"Pouvez-vous me conseiller? Mes cheveux sont trop longs; j'ai besoin d'une coiffeuse. Vous pouvez recommander quelqu'un?"

She looked at me blankly; I hadn't thought my accent quite so difficult to understand. Gérard interpreted, and a heated interchange took place between them, as I looked from one to the other like a spectator at a tennis match. I caught one or two words of the stream, including a name: Nathalie.

At last Gérard turned to me. "You wish to cut your 'air? My wife – " he gestured to Marie-Claude as if I didn't know who she was "– she like to go to a, what do you say? Hair-cutter?"

"Hairdresser," I murmured.

"Yes, young lady in Roqueville, Nathalie. Good cutter, cheap. Vous voulez faire un rendezvous?"

"Oui, yes, um, I think so."

"OK, demain, tomorrow, yes? Marie-Claude telephone for a rendezvous."

Marie-Claude said something to her husband and he turned back to me. "She sayed, you want her to come with you? Help you talk French?"

"Oh, yes, please! Oui, merci!"

Marie-Claude turned to me, her dimpled cheeks pink, her eyes sparkling. "I 'elp you," she said simply. "I telephone, demain." She seemed energized by her task: this was something she knew about, her field of expertise.

Nathalie was a petite blonde in her mid-twenties. Her salon, in a side street off the market square, was tiny: obviously just a front room in her house, but neat and well-equipped. I was grateful that I'd taken up Gérard's offer of a lift, as I'm not sure I would have found the place on my own. She had one other customer when we arrived, an elderly lady under a drier, who looked at me suspiciously but then saw Marie-Claude and smiled, revealing an almost complete lack of teeth. Marie-Claude greeted her and explained who I was – so I gathered from the glances in my direction. There was a great deal of sage nodding. In the corner stood a pram, with Nathalie's sleeping baby in it. Nathalie gestured to me, inviting me to sit, and gave me a pile of magazines devoted entirely to hairstyles. I obediently turned a few pages but found nothing sufficiently simple. All I wanted was a short, neat cut.

I called over to Marie-Claude, and tried to explain. Unfortunately, although I'd looked up the appropriate vocabulary before coming out, Marie-Claude found my French accent incomprehensible, and we had to call in the cavalry: Gérard, who arrived in response to his wife's call and pushed open the door almost furtively. Clearly this was not a place where a man, and an ex-policeman into the bargain, felt comfortable. After checking with me a rapid discussion followed, and eventually Nathalie seemed to understand what was required and Gérard was able to retire to his seat in the bar opposite and bury himself in the *Gazette*.

Half an hour later the job was done, and Nathalie showed me the back of my head in her hand-mirror. She'd done a neat job. My unruly, wiry hair was tamed, for now, trimmed into tidy layers and shaped into my neck. I looked different: younger, perhaps.

It was only after Gérard dropped me off at home that I remembered what day it was. I was aghast – had my haircut stopped them from visiting their daughter? I couldn't have protested, even if I had remembered; as far as they were aware I didn't know about their Tuesday visits. I could only hope they'd be able to go and see her, and their grandson, another day.

I wanted to ask Michael about it, but when the phone rang that evening it was Jasper on the line. "Dad's gone to some function at the hospital," he told me. "You'll have to make do with me." We chatted inconsequentially about what I'd been doing and how he was practising for the swimming event. He wanted to know how Dulcie's training was going, and I told him about her progress. "Can't wait to get down to France," he said. "I hope it stays sunny for when we get there. It'll be good to see you, Rachel."

After he'd rung off the house felt empty and echoing. Cheerful and charming as Jasper was, I found I missed my nightly talk with Michael. I thought I would go to St Luke's on Sunday – not, I told myself, because I really had much interest in church, but I was beginning to feel lonely and adrift. It would be good to be with people, and talk in my native tongue. I opened up my laptop and found the church website. It had a paragraph or two about the church's history, and I read that it had been founded some twenty years before by a couple of expat Britons and had grown. One of them had been a doctor, hence St Luke's. They'd had a priest but he'd retired and now the congregation kept it going by themselves, just calling in retired clergymen to deliver communion. I looked at a map which showed the area that the church covered: it was vast.

I started to prepare for Michael and Jasper's arrival, laying in food for the fridge and freezer, finishing the mowing and the weeding, making up Jasper's bed. Michael had told me not to bother with his, as he'd only used it for a few days on his last visit. I was looking forward to seeing them, and wondered if they'd notice any change in me. I was eating well and sleeping longer, working outside in the sunshine or sitting at the patio table, reading, relaxing. In the mirror I saw a different Rachel: skinniness filled out a little, skin tanned from being outside, hair short – but also a different look, something quieter and calmer. I looked down at my hands, black in places from ingrained soil. Michael would want to know how they were coping with the garden jobs I was doing. In anyone else's eyes they were perfectly adequate; whether or not they could wield surgical instruments with any speed, dexterity or accuracy none of us knew.

On Sunday morning I started early. I took Dulcie for a walk up the lane, giving her a chance to explore new smells, but also to put some of her training into practice. For a few moments I let her look at some black-faced sheep in a field, and she stood, stiff and keen, her ears twitching. "No, pal. Not for you," I told her sternly.

Back at the house I took a cup of coffee into the garden and surveyed my work. The grass was short and neat, the vegetable patch was flourishing, and the weeds were in retreat. I decided to leave it till later to clean the house so that it would be at its best when Michael and Jasper arrived. I felt I had gone some little way to say thank you.

I put Dulcie in the car and started the forty-five minute journey to church. The D514, while a main road, was almost empty, and I bowled along with the radio on. It was a French programme and I understood little of the patter but the music was familiar and at one point I began to sing along – something I hardly ever did. It made me think of my father, who was always singing – at his work, when we were out in the car, camping, or simply fooling around in the garden – and I realized that this was something else I had lost. What else would be on that list, if I were really to think about it? I put the thought firmly aside;

many things perhaps had been sacrificed, but in an honourable cause: the saving of life. I clung on to that, not wishing to dim this cloudless day.

We arrived without getting lost and with time to spare. The church was situated in a tiny hamlet of half a dozen houses. No longer needed by the local community, so the website had told me, it had been given over to the Anglicans by the local bishop. It was a typical, modest stone building with a long nave and a short tower, and in a niche above the main door stood a small statue of the Virgin, weathered by the elements. The churchyard was beautifully kept with gravelled walkways between the ornate headstones, the graves decorated with pots of artificial flowers and metal plaques – some with hands folded in prayer, others with an inscription: "Nos regrets"; "A mon oncle". The headstones themselves bore the names of families, and just a brief glance told how interconnected the local families were.

Dulcie and I had a look at the churchyard, then I took her for a brief stroll round the hamlet before putting her back in the car. She was having a drink when another car rolled into the car park. A woman got out, smiled at me, and took a wheelchair from the boot. She opened the passenger door and helped another woman, younger, out of the car and into the wheelchair. At once the woman in the wheelchair bowled over to where I stood guard over Dulcie.

"Hello!" she said. I suppose she was about twenty-five; her brown hair was held back with a clip; her round face was freckly. "Haven't seen you before." She held out her hand and I shook it. "I'm Letty Wetherly."

I smiled back. "Rachel Keyte."

Dulcie was wagging her tail – she obviously knew Letty.

"Your dog looks just like Dulcie," Letty said. "Doesn't she, Mum?" She called to the older woman, who came over and joined us.

"It is Dulcie," I said.

Letty looked up at me, her brown eyes wide. "So where's Michael? And Jasper?"

"Letty, don't be so nosy," her mother said gently.

"It's OK," I said. I smiled down at Letty. "They're not here yet. They're coming tomorrow. I'm staying at their house and looking after Dulcie. Or possibly she's looking after me."

"It's nice to meet you," Mrs Wetherly said. "Welcome to St Luke's."

That hour, I felt welcome. Nobody bothered me; nobody, thankfully, asked me if I was saved. But people smiled and said hello, and the service was an eye-opener. Maybe it was ordinary enough if you were used to such things, but my experience was limited, and not at all inspiring. It was a relief to listen and respond and understand every word, and though I didn't remember everything, bits of it came back to me later. The sermon was preached by a woman – she was robed, so not, I supposed, just a member of the congregation. She spoke of God being love itself, how his love radiated out into every part of creation, how it was love that underpinned everything: every leaf on every tree, every note of every hymn, every unconscious breath we breathed. All we had to do was hold out our hands. It was simple, perhaps even simplistic. Once I would have sneered and countered, "So why murder? Why destruction? Why infants blown apart by random bombs? Why cancer? Why abuse, greed, hunger?" And so on, and on. But now I wondered if it was our corrupt and damaged race that was responsible for so much that was evil. Maybe God had made the world good.

These thoughts raced through my mind as we sang: some of the hymns were familiar, others far more modern and unknown to me, but they were sung with such conviction and joy that I could ignore the slowing and the wavering pitch. There was no organist; a keyboard stood in a corner, draped in a green cloth, so perhaps they had one sometimes, but today it was all unaccompanied and perhaps predictably only just the right side of chaotic, despite the efforts of a tall black woman I took to be the choir mistress, who tried to keep in order a small group of singers to one side of the altar. It didn't seem to matter. Joy and delight were clearly the keynote here.

Afterwards I stopped for a cup of coffee in a small hall on the other side of the car park. I was instantly mobbed by Letty Wetherly, who bombarded me with questions. Her mother kept a watchful eye on her from where she chatted to another group, and she must have heard Letty ask, "What's that scar on your face?" because she came over and scolded her daughter. "That's personal, Colette," she said severely. "And aren't you rather monopolizing Ms Keyte?"

"It's all right," I said. "And please call me Rachel."

Now Mrs Wetherly shook my hand. "I'm Janet. I'm afraid Letty likes to know everything about everyone, especially if they are new to us. Are you here for long?"

"I'm not sure," I said. "A few weeks, probably."

"Oh, good! So will you be coming back next Sunday with Michael and Jasper?"

"I think I probably will. They seem to be very well known here at St Luke's."

"Oh yes, dear! They are. Jasper plays keyboard for the service when they're here. It's so much better than tapes, or unaccompanied. Do you play?"

I shook my head. "I used to, but not any more."

A tall, burly man in a brown corduroy jacket joined us and introduced himself. "Colin Wetherly, churchwarden." He had a gruff voice, the voice of a smoker, I suspected. "So you're staying with Michael. How are you enjoying it, here in France? On holiday, perhaps?"

"Yes, in a way," I said. "And I like it a lot." I told them the story of my foray into the local church last Sunday and they roared with laughter. "That sounds typical!" Colin Wetherly said. "Hemmed in by determined local ladies. Marvellous."

I looked at my watch. "I must get back," I said. "Lots to do. I'm hoping to give the house a good clean before Michael and Jasper arrive."

"You will come back next Sunday, won't you?" Letty said. "It'll be tons better with Jasper playing. I really like Jasper – he's kind."

"Yes, he is."

Janet Wetherly laid her hand on my arm. "Yes, do come again," she said. "If it's any temptation, there's a barbecue at the Bowmans' after the service."

"And we must introduce you to a few more of our little fellowship," her husband said. "Completely mad, all of them."

I smiled. "I'll look forward to that. Nice to have met you." And I meant it.

Something, I barely knew what, was knitting itself together in the dark recesses of my mind. Things I had read, and only vaguely remembered; things people had said to me, things I had overheard, snippets on the radio. Things my father had said, long ago. I didn't worry; I felt sure that they would float to the surface at some point. For now, driving back to Roqueville under the July sun, the road peeling away before me like a shiny black ribbon, devoid of traffic, sometimes bowered over by trees in full leaf, I was unreservedly happy. I was healthy, well fed, well rested. I had been with good people, and would be again. My wounds were healing; the prospect of getting back to work, though dim, was a real possibility; and Michael and Jasper would come tomorrow. Once I might have been unwilling to admit it, but I could recognize I had begun to feel lonely.

I had my usual lunch under the sunshade outside: bread and ham, tomatoes and fruit. I left Dulcie scratching about happily in the borders and set to work on the house, sweeping, polishing, scrubbing. By four o'clock I was done, and the old place gleamed. I'd gone at the work with great vim and was now hot and sweaty, so I stood under a tepid shower for a few minutes, then put on fresh clothes. It was time for Dulcie's afternoon training session, and her dinner.

Dulcie was nowhere in the garden. I called her, but she didn't appear; even rattling a box of dog biscuits elicited no response. I thought she may have got bored and slipped next door to the Boutins'; no one would hear me calling, because they usually had their TV on at full blast. I hopped over the stile, crossed their immaculate lawn, and knocked on the back door, which was open.

"Entrez, entrez, Rachelle!" Gérard's voice boomed from the front room. I could hear something noisy on his TV – motor racing, I thought. Marie-Claude appeared from the kitchen, flour up to her elbows.

"Bonjour, Gérard; bonjour Marie-Claude. Ça va?"

"Oui, oui, tout va bien, merci. Et vous aussi?"

"Oui, merci. Je cherche Dulcie. Est-elle avec vous?" Though I could see she wasn't.

Gérard frowned. No, Dulcie wasn't there. She'd come over earlier – perhaps about two o'clock, because they were still eating their lunch. But then she'd disappeared, and naturally they thought she'd just gone back home. I began to feel nauseated, but I thrust anxiety aside. She would be close, wouldn't she? Michael had said both gardens were secure. With the Boutins in my wake I went out again into their garden and called. And called. We went all around the perimeter, calling. When we got to the end of their garden Marie-Claude let out a little shriek. Hidden by two enormous hydrangeas was a break in the fence. Four or five lengths of timber had loosened and fallen forwards from the panel, probably as a result of the storm the previous week. It wouldn't have been possible to see from the house because of the shrubs thick with greenery, but it was easily wide enough for a lithe collie to follow her nose. We looked at each other in horror.

"We must go and look," Gérard said. He handed his newspaper to Marie-Claude, who said something to him rapidly. He nodded. "My wife, she says look again in your house. She may be there – sleeping."

I shook my head. I told him I had been indoors, cleaning. I'd been in every room. And Dulcie's hearing was acute: she'd never be sleeping if I'd been calling her for so long, especially as her stomach would be telling her it was close to dinnertime.

From the euphoria of a few hours ago, this was a shocking plummet into a cold bath of dread. Swallowing hard, I tried to be calm while I told Gérard of my particular fears: that Dulcie would find her way onto a road and be run over; or worse, that she'd find her way into a sheep field and be shot. Somehow I managed to make him understand, though by then I was almost faint with the effort. Gérard barked a string of orders to Marie-Claude, who flew into the house, her eyes full of tears. Then he turned to me and spoke gently. "My wife, she telephone our friends. Voisins, neighbours. Bertrand. Other farmers. They watch out for Dulcie. Now we go and look. Maybe she, ah, somewhere, hurt. Can't get home." He patted my arm clumsily. "We find her."

But we didn't find her. We searched every field, every copse, every ditch within a mile or so, calling till we were hoarse. Could she have gone further? I didn't know what else to do. All I knew at that terrible moment was that I had lost Michael's beloved dog. She was my responsibility, and I had failed. How could I tell him – and Jasper? I couldn't. I wanted to howl.

The light began to fade. In an hour it would be dusk, and then dark. The summer evenings were long, but night would come. Gérard must have been thinking the same. "I will go back, get, um, torch," he said. "You look." I nodded, watching him lumber away.

He was gone almost an hour, and for some of that time I guess he'd been looking for me. He told me that Marie-Claude had alerted everyone she could think of in Roqueville and its outskirts. We went on looking until the shadows lengthened, but we heard and saw nothing. There was no other course but to turn for home; in the dark, even with a torch, we could trip or turn an ankle, and I worried about Gérard – he looked exhausted, his normally ruddy face grey. "My fault," he muttered. "My fence broke."

"No, not your fault; you didn't know," I said hollowly. "I should have kept a more watchful eye on her. We all know she can be a bit of an escape artist." He looked puzzled. "Elle aime s'échapper."

He nodded. I thought there might be tears in his eyes.

When we got back to their bungalow Marie-Claude was standing on the patio, light streaming from the room behind her. She shook her head, put her arms round her husband's ample waist, and ushered him indoors. I declined their invitation to go in, and went back next door.

I could not remember a time when I had felt so wretched: fearful, guilty, appalled. Maybe it was only then that I realized how I had grown to love that amiable creature who had been my companion for two weeks. The phone was ringing; I let it ring. It would be Michael, or Jasper, and I couldn't face telling them I had lost their dog.

A thought slipped unobtrusively into my head. I remembered being fourteen, my impassioned prayers for my father: *Please, don't let him die. Let him get better.* At one level I'd known he wouldn't, but I'd felt utterly helpless. As now. Would the God I had sidelined and ignored for so long listen to me now – on behalf of a dog? Did dogs matter, in his great scheme? *Of course they did.* I closed my eyes, and tears dribbled down to my chin. I gritted my teeth. I felt that I might be sick.

God, if you are there, please don't think about what a complete failure I have been. Not just losing Dulcie, but in so many other ways. Please, bring Dulcie home. Let her be alive. Not for me, not for my conscience; for her own sake, and for Michael and Jasper. And Gérard and Marie-Claude. They feel bad, and Gérard looked sick. Please, let no harm have come to her. She's just a dog, but we all love her. I ran dry. I had no more words, only tears, and I sobbed.

I couldn't go indoors, not to the endlessly ringing phone. What must Michael and Jasper be thinking? They'd be worried about *me*, I guessed. I stayed on the patio, in the canvas chair, as the darkness deepened and the stars came out.

It must have been after ten o'clock when I came to from a doze and thought I heard something. I frowned, listening, just registering that I was cold. I heard it again – from next door: the whine of a dog. It was the sweetest sound I had heard in a long time. I jumped up, sending the chair crashing to the ground, raced barefoot across the lawn, and leapt across the stile in one bound. "Dulcie!"

In the light of the Boutins' back room, dimmed by their curtains, a shadow lay on their patio. I reached her. I could see that she was damaged: one of her front paws was held at an odd angle, and her face looked sticky, but it was hard to be sure because of her black fur. She was filthy with mud and vegetation, but she was alive, and she was back. I knelt down and gently stroked her head. I didn't want to hurt her. "Oh, Dulcie, thank God. Am I glad to see you!"

I hammered on the Boutins' back door, and after an age heard Gérard's lumbering tread. He pulled the door open. "It's Dulcie; she's back." To say Gérard bellowed would not have done it justice. He called Marie-Claude and a long incomprehensible conversation followed – almost an altercation, except that I knew that was just the way they talked to each other. Marie-Claude gave me a hug, dabbing at her eyes, then trotted indoors. Gérard stooped, grunting, and very carefully lifted Dulcie up in his arms, as if she weighed nothing. She whined, but her tail was slowly wagging. He carried her indoors, and I followed. He laid her on the kitchen table, and she licked his hand. Now I could see that one side of her face was bloody.

Marie-Claude came in and spoke to Gérard, who nodded and said nothing. He turned to me. His colour was back to ruddy, I was glad to see. "We take my car in town – the, ah, vétérinaire will meet us there." He spoke again to his wife, who went out and came back with a blanket. Between us we wrapped Dulcie up. I carried her, and Gérard went to get his car. Once it was in the drive we laid her on the back seat, and Marie-Claude got in beside her. Gérard went to lock his house, and that reminded me to do the same. It was bad enough that we had let his dog get hurt; I didn't want Michael to arrive and find his house burgled as well because I had left all the doors open.

The vet's surgery was in a side street just off the market square, on the opposite side to Nathalie the hairdresser. At this time of night there was no one about; even the bars were in darkness. The only light came from the square where a take-away pizza restaurant remained open. We sat and waited until the lights came on in the surgery, and then saw the vet appear in the doorway and beckon us inside. Gérard turned to me with a wry smile. "We OK now. Vet speaks English good."

The vet was a small woman, her light brown hair tied up in a ponytail. She ushered us into her surgery. I thought she looked tired, but she smiled at us encouragingly. Gérard carried Dulcie and laid her on the table. We unwound the blanket. The vet examined her in silence, sometimes muttering under her breath.

"OK," she said, raising her head. "Do you know what happened?"

I shook my head and explained how she went missing and reappeared at the Boutins' house.

The vet's eyes narrowed. "This is Mr Wells' dog, isn't it?" I noticed she couldn't pronounce W, as many French people can't. It came out as "Ouells".

"Yes, but Mr Wells isn't here yet. He's coming tomorrow, with his son. I was looking after Dulcie."

"OK. Well, she's been in a fight, probably with another dog."

"Oh! Poor Dulcie! She's no fighter."

"The other dog has bitten her – see? Here." She indicated Dulcie's blood-matted cheek. "But also she has broken at least one bone in her foot – probably trying to get away. Maybe she caught it in a root or a hole."

"Will she be all right?"

The vet nodded. 'I will give her a tetanus shot now. When my nurse gets here I'll do the surgery – sew up her face and set the foot-bone. One of us will stay with her tonight. She'll have an anaesthetic so she won't know anything for hours. You don't need to stay. I will ring you in the morning."

My relief was beyond description. Michael's dog was back, alive and likely to recover. *Thank you, God.*

The vet said as we left, each of us giving Dulcie a soothing pat, "This is expensive treatment. I need to warn you."

"It's not a problem," I said, "Thank you for seeing us so late. I'll bring my credit card when I collect her, if that's OK." At that moment I would cheerfully have sold my flat and emptied my bank account to cover the cost of Dulcie's recovery.

We drove home in sober and exhausted silence. As Gérard parked Marie-Claude leaned forward and tapped me on the shoulder. "J'ai beaucoup prié," she said, putting her hands together in case I hadn't understood. But I had. "Merci, Marie-Claude. Moi aussi."

I let myself into the darkened house. As I switched on the light the phone rang again, and this time I picked up the receiver.

"Rachel! Are you all right?" It was Michael, and he sounded worried. "Where have you been? We've been calling you since six."

"I know. Michael, I'm sorry; I couldn't speak to you earlier."

"What are you saying?"

Slowly, brokenly, I explained what had happened. He didn't

interrupt, but I could hear exclamations. "I'm so sorry – I should have kept a better watch on her. These have been among the longest hours of my life, I think."

"*How* long did you say you and Gérard were out looking for her?"

"Oh, I don't know – four hours maybe."

"You must be exhausted."

"Yes, but please don't be too kind! Between us, we lost her, and she came home hurt."

"For goodness' sake." Michael's voice was a growl. "These things happen. Dulcie likes to wander. It's not your fault, or Gérard's. You need to get to bed. You probably haven't eaten, have you? Have something, however little. Then sleep. We'll see you some time tomorrow afternoon. You can fill me in with all the details then."

I slept like a corpse and awoke with the light to loud birdsong. My head was thumping and I was sweating. I threw off the covers which had wound themselves into a tangle, trapping my legs and feet. I stumbled downstairs to the kitchen and made a pot of coffee. It was oddly quiet; no canine yawns and morning greetings. I realized what good company Dulcie had been; perhaps it was because her conversation was limited. She was just a friendly, uncomplaining presence. Again, remembering, I felt a wash of warm relief. I took my coffee onto the patio and slumped in what was becoming my favourite perch.

Just after nine the vet rang. "Dulcie is awake," she said. "You can come and get her when you like."

"I'll come now."

I put on some jeans, shoes and a T-shirt, got the car out, and drove into town. People were already about their business; Roqueville had an air of quiet purpose. I parked outside the vet's and went in. A young woman with fair hair and glasses looked up from behind the desk.

"Bonjour. Je viens chercher Dulcie," I said.

She smiled – obviously Dulcie was no stranger. "Bien. Attendez un moment, s'il vous plaît."

A moment later the vet herself appeared, with Dulcie attached to a long red and white lead. Her paw was encased in plaster, giving her a comical gait. The side of her face had been shaved, cleaned, and stitched, so that she looked lopsided. Someone had combed out the mud and burrs from her coat; the ragged wreck of the night before was gone. She greeted me with sleepy enthusiasm, licking my hands as I tried to take the lead from the vet.

"I'll put her in the car and come back to settle up," I said.

The vet nodded. "Ariane will see to you."

"Thank you," I said, "for being there for Dulcie so quickly. For all you've done. I'm very grateful."

She shrugged. "De rien. Bonne journée, Madame."

I put Dulcie in the car and returned the lead. The bill was eye-watering, but I didn't care. We drove home through the summer morning. All was well.

Dulcie and I had a quiet day. I'd been given instructions by the receptionist: what Dulcie should eat, how much she might be allowed to walk, as well as some antibiotics. We were both content to lounge in the shade and recover.

Later that morning Gérard appeared at the gap in the hedge. I called him over, and he climbed the stile awkwardly, landing with a thump. Moments later Marie-Claude followed, and they both made a fuss of the dog, who clearly enjoyed the attention. "Today," Gérard said solemnly, "I mend my fence."

I ate my lunch outside, and read my book. Dulcie lay at my feet, her nose resting on her plastered foot. The wind ruffled the tops of the trees and set them swaying hypnotically. I closed my eyes.

The next thing I knew was a high-pitched yip from Dulcie. I came to, my book slithering off my lap to the ground. Dulcie was sitting up, her paw hanging oddly with the weight of the plaster, her ears pricked. I heard the sound of a powerful engine, suddenly stilled, and the clang of a gate shutting, and a familiar voice. Could they be here already? Had I been asleep? What time was it? I had time to answer none of these questions, because with a wild whoop Jasper came racing round the end of the house and bounded towards us. Dulcie gave a loud, joyful bark, and I grabbed her collar just in time to save her from rushing to meet him and damaging her foot. Jasper flung himself to the ground, wrapped his arms round Dulcie's sun-warmed neck, and submitted to being copiously licked.

"Hi Rachel," he gasped. "Are you OK?"

"I am now," I said. "Now we've got your daft dog back and patched up." I looked down at him; he lay sprawled on the warm stones, Dulcie at his side. "Hey. You've had a haircut."

He squinted up at me and grinned. "So have you. I like it. So has Dad. We're all tidy."

Michael appeared round the side of the house, carrying a bag in each hand. I struggled out of the chair. As he came towards me, smiling, taking off his sunglasses, I saw how tired his eyes looked. He dropped the bags, squatted down beside Dulcie, and ran his hand over her furry flank. "Hello, fool of a dog," he muttered. "I hope you've learned your lesson." He straightened up, put his hands on my shoulders, and kissed me on both cheeks. He smelled of soap. "We're in France now," he said. "Traditional greeting, as I'm sure you've found out." He stood back and looked at me critically. "I like the new look."

"I went to Nathalie's salon," I said. "What about you?"

Michael laughed. "Nothing so sophisticated for us. We went to the barber's in Archer Street. Six quid."

"You both look very different," I said. "Jasper looks like a proper sixth form student – tidy and studious. Michael, you look… kind of tougher. Like a gangster." They laughed at this. "How did you get here so quickly? I didn't arrive till six o'clock when I came down."

"Don't forget, we didn't have to stop for the dog, and we know the way," Jasper said from the ground. "And Dad drove like a demon. Couldn't wait to get here."

"What would you know about it?" Michael said. "You were asleep most of the time."

"We athletes need our rest," Jasper said.

"Oh! Yes, how did the swimming go?" I asked him.

"Not bad," Jasper said modestly.

"Actually," Michael cut in, "he took second place out of fifty and came home with a silver medal."

"Wow! Well done you." I poked Jasper gently with my foot and he sat up, his arms round his knees.

"Any chance of a cup of tea?" he said plaintively. "I'm parched."

"Go and make it yourself," Michael said. "Rachel isn't your slave, and I should go into town and settle up with the vet before I do anything else."

I was prepared. "It's all taken care of."

"Then I will reimburse you," Michael said.

My chin came up, and I stared at him. "Not a chance."

He folded his arms and scowled. "Dulcie is my dog."

I drew myself up so that my eyes were level with his nose. "Yes, she is. But these past two weeks she has been my responsibility. This happened on my watch. It's a done deal."

"I can't accept –"

"Excuse me," came a small voice from beneath us. "Instead of arguing, shouldn't we just be thankful that Dulcie is OK? And that we're all here safely? Even with Dad's demon driving?"

Michael and I both laughed. "You win, JB. Now go and make yourself useful and put the kettle on."

Jasper groaned but went, calling out as he vanished into the house by the scullery door, "Come and get it in five, OK? Coffee for you, Rachel?"

"Perfect, thanks."

Michael got another chair from the lean-to, unfolded it, and set it down next to mine. Dulcie, without putting any weight on her injured foot, shuffled closer so that he could lean down and stroke her. "The garden looks amazing," he said, looking around at the lawn, the shrubs, the borders. "Are those real vegetables I see in my so-called kitchen garden?"

"No, they're plastic ones from the market, bought for effect," I said.

He looked at me and shook his head. "You've had too much sun, apparently. But you certainly look well: fresh air agrees with you. I think you might even have put on a little weight."

I raised an eyebrow. "First you say I am crazy. Now you think I am fat. But actually I *am* well, thank you."

"Let me see your hands."

I held them out, palm up. He took them in his own hands – brown from the sun, and warm – and inspected them silently, gently pulling and turning each finger, spreading them out, palpating the palms. "You've healed remarkably well," he murmured. He looked up at me, his face serious and doctor-like. "No discomfort at all?"

I shook my head. "Your handiwork, no doubt."

"Partly that, partly your own robust immune system. I have only one reservation."

"What's that?"

"They're filthy."

I threw back my head and laughed, in a rare moment of uninhibited joy.

"No, I have washed them, many times. That's ingrained from grubbing up your magnificent weeds."

"Garden gloves might have been a good idea," he said sternly.

"Do you really think there's much chance of infection now?"

"Hm, probably not. But…" He dropped my hands and traced the scar on my face with one finger. "Just a thin white line now," he said. "Do you mind?"

"Not in the least." I was suddenly aware how much things had changed. In the hospital, newly maimed and mended, his hands were simply those of a surgeon. Now it was different. I had a moment of discomfort that wasn't at all unpleasant – just a little alarming.

The moment was broken by Jasper's tetchy voice from the kitchen window. "Hey! This is a very long five minutes!"

After a pleasant few hours spent enjoying the garden and each other's company, Michael drove into town to pick up some pizzas for dinner.

Greasy cardboard boxes littering the table, Michael and I sat opposite one another, finishing a bottle of red wine he'd taken from a well-stocked rack. Jasper had gone off to his room with his laptop, taking Dulcie with him. Michael leaned back in his chair and closed his eyes. He flexed his shoulders. "I can't tell you how good it is to be here."

"You look tired."

"Mm. The last few weeks have been hectic in the department. I've had to reorganize things – one of my staff is ill. And then I had a one-day conference in London, the day before Jasper's swimming thing, so it was all a bit stressful trying to get ready to come here. Plus the drive on top of that. But I will unwind – to the point of becoming a jelly." He leaned forward, resting his arms on the table, looking at me with those watchful eyes. "Have you been all right? Really?"

I nodded. "Yes. What you said about this place is true – it's calm and somehow healing. I've had time to think – in between all the chores, of course." I flashed him a little grin, then said more soberly, "It's not something I've allowed myself much – thinking time, that is, except work-related stuff. It's been a bit unsettling. I told you about my visit to St Nicolas' in the town, didn't I? Well, admittedly it had its humorous side, but that wasn't all there was to it."

His dark brows contracted. "Do you want to tell me about it?"

"Yes… but not tonight. Tomorrow maybe, when you're rested."

Michael gave a weary nod. "OK; I will be much more use after I've had a good night's sleep."

"Look, why don't you get off to bed? I'll tidy up here, what there is of it. If you can find Dulcie I'll let her out. I'm not at all sure the vet would approve of her tackling the stairs anyway."

"I'll have a word with that errant son of mine," Michael said with a smile. "Strictly speaking Dulcie isn't allowed upstairs, but Jasper indulges her."

"And you indulge him."

"Guilty. It's one of the common pitfalls of being a part-time parent."

"And Jasper is an easy son to be kind to."

"Yes. He's a good lad, on the whole. Well. Goodnight, Rachel." He glanced around. "You've cleaned the old place as well, I see. It's never looked this gleaming."

"Just once; that's my limit!" I said. "Night, Michael. I'm glad you and Jasper are here." I was about to admit to feeling lonely, but thought better of it. "It's a shame, though, that Dulcie is out of action. She was doing really well with her training."

"That too! You've been busy. But now maybe it's time for you to relax as well."

I smiled wryly. "When you arrived I was dozing in the garden, pretending to read one of your books. No need to worry about me."

"I'd like you to tell me about Eve Rawlins," I said. "What you know; anything Father Vincent told you." We'd finished washing up the breakfast dishes; a second pot of coffee was brewing. Jasper was still asleep.

Michael's eyebrows shot up, perhaps at my lack of preamble. "How come the change of heart?"

I took a deep breath. "Before I went to the service at St Nicolas' that Sunday," I said slowly, gathering my thoughts, "I visited the church on Wednesday – market day. I put the lettuce plants and Dulcie into the car, and went inside. I was curious. No, maybe more than that; whatever impelled me to go inside is still a bit mysterious, even to me."

"Especially to you," Michael murmured.

I shrugged. "I'd seen a woman go in, carrying an armful of flowers, which is how I knew the church was open. It felt like an impulse, but maybe it wasn't." I looked at him but he stayed silent. "I found myself looking at the paintings. Horrible things, really; at least, definitely not to my taste. The Bleeding Heart, for instance. From my point of view, it's completely over the top, not to mention anatomically impossible." I smiled slightly. "But it was odd – not so long ago I'd have scoffed at all that, but then I understood it was probably someone's idea of expressing devotion, even in a highly conventional way, and maybe it inspired devotion in the onlookers as well. I was on my way out when I saw a statue, a stylized Madonna and Child, not at all realistic, serene and improbably beautiful – a baby young enough to sit on his mother's lap and yet old enough to have a full head of unlikely golden hair and be raising chubby fingers in blessing. So that made me start thinking about mothers and children, and as you know my own experience isn't without its shadows. Then on the other side was a crucifixion scene, and there's Mary at the foot of the cross, pale and fainting. So I couldn't not think about what it must be like to lose a child. I don't know that many people with children, but I thought what it would be like for you to lose Jasper, and I felt… well, it was awful, unbearable. It wasn't such a big leap to go from there to thinking about Eve Rawlins losing her son. I know I wasn't responsible. I know I did my best. But she had a child she loved, and he's dead." I took a deep breath. "Until then I hadn't allowed myself to think about it in that way. It was too hard. I was afraid – I was right to be, I think, because, as you said, empathy can be distressing. I just feel somehow, now, it's time to gather up my courage. To think of her not as a mad woman who wounded me but as a parent who will always be bereaved. And I thought, *You know what, Rachel, you should know something about her.* I wouldn't let you tell me before, but now I would like to hear."

I fell silent, and he said nothing for a long moment, just looking at me with that dark stare of his, unconsciously tapping the table with one forefinger. "Are you sure?"

"Yes."

"OK." He took a deep breath. "I only know what Father Vincent told me, of course," he cautioned, "and I may not remember every detail, but I have to say her story made quite an impression on me." He frowned slightly, obviously thinking. "It sounds like Eve had a tough childhood. Between being bullied about her birthmark and having to look after her ailing parents, life wasn't easy for her. After her parents died she sold her family home and bought a place in Porton. She found work in a library, and for the first time in her life, even made a couple of friends. They persuaded her to come out with them on occasion, even giving her tips about clothes and makeup which would to some degree camouflage what she saw as a hideous deformity. By this time they'd all been friends for some time and she trusted them. Father Vincent believed them to be nice enough girls, certainly not wishing any harm to come to Eve."

"I think I saw them," I said. "There were two women at Craig's funeral, more or less holding Eve upright, and they were crying."

"Yes, could be. From what Father Vincent said, they were her only real friends, apart from Father Vincent himself. And she was a regular at St Joseph's, so perhaps there were friends there too." He sighed. "Anyway, one night everything went wrong. The three of them were at some club or other, and the two friends were drunk and foolish and rather oblivious. Eve didn't drink much, but the friends thought someone must have spiked her drink because they saw her with some unknown man, at first talking and laughing, and then they lost sight of her. It was some time before they started getting worried and began searching for her. They didn't really know where to look; in the end they went home, but they were secretly worried, knowing that she was rather naïve.

"She turned up the next day, bedraggled and in a state of shock, with barely any memory of what had happened. She said she'd met someone, a man from one of the ships that was in port, and he seemed very nice and interested in her, but then everything went blank until she came to and found herself in some seedy bedsit she didn't recognize, with no clothes on and covered in just a grubby sheet. When she didn't leave straight away the man got rough and practically threw her out. She felt the whole horrible episode was her own fault for being a fool. Her friends of course were mortified, especially later when Eve found she was pregnant."

I shook my head, appalled. "And that was Craig."

"Yes. At first her friends tried to persuade Eve to terminate, but her faith meant she wouldn't hear of it. She resigned her job at the library and supported herself by renting out rooms. Later, when Craig was at nursery, she took a number of low-paid jobs, but only ones that allowed her to be there when he came home. From everything I have heard it sounds as if she was a most devoted mother – rather possessive, perhaps, but well intentioned. But it all got more intense, maybe even obsessive, after he became ill."

"Kawasaki's disease at age four," I said, remembering what Malcolm Harries had told me. "Originally misdiagnosed by some half-awake GP. By the time they'd got it right it was too late; the poor boy's heart was damaged." I could hear the bitterness in my own voice.

"Well, Kawasaki's is an unusual disease," Michael said gently. "Not many GPs would have instantly recognized it."

"The symptoms are clear."

"Mm, I suppose so. Anyway, for some while Craig seemed to

be all right, but then he started to show unmistakable symptoms of heart disease, and the rest you know, more or less.

"For Eve, though, it meant that her son became her only focus, his treatment an obsession. Maybe she was a little crazy. Maybe that escalated when she became fixated on you after Craig's death. But according to Father Vincent she is as sane now as you and me." He fell silent for a moment, and then he said thoughtfully, "Like the man in the Bible with the demons."

"What?"

"Oh, there was a man, chained up among the burial caves because everyone was afraid of him. Afflicted by a whole bunch of demons, calling themselves 'Mob' – do you know the story?"

"It rings a bell."

"When the villagers came they saw him sitting at Jesus' feet, 'clothed and in his right mind'. I don't know why exactly, but it reminds me of Eve Rawlins. From what Father Vincent said, it seems that the shock of what she did to you, seeing you frightened and bleeding, brought her back to her senses."

"In her right mind," I echoed. "I only knew her as a madwoman, of course. One who'd daubed my car with blood and sent me a pig's stinking heart in a box, etcetera."

"Perhaps," Michael said thoughtfully, "it's only now, now that you are healing, that you can afford to think of her with any compassion. Do you?"

"Do I what?"

"Think of her with compassion. No need to pretend to be obtuse."

"Hm, maybe. Well, yes. Who wouldn't? It's a horrible story – a sad and difficult life, and the only thing that brought her any happiness taken away too. Of course I'm sorry for her. I just wish she'd found some other way to express her grief."

We were silent for a moment, thinking our own thoughts. Then I said, "I've been thinking about the trial, whether they'll call me as a witness."

Michael shook his head. "I'm not sure, but I'd imagine they would. The police took a statement from you at the time of the attack, didn't they?" I nodded. "Well, from the little I know, the wheels of the law grind slowly. The trial probably won't happen for months yet."

"I guess so."

Those first few days flowed by, relaxed and easy. It rained a little, but soon cleared. For the moment the garden needed no attention, and the vegetables thrived. Michael and Jasper seemed tired and inclined to do little but eat and sleep, chat to the Boutins, and hang around the house. Jasper spent many hours in his room, mostly, I suspected, asleep. Michael got up and went to bed at regular hours, but more than once I found him sleeping in a garden chair, under a sunshade, a cold cup of coffee on the table. Asleep, he looked younger and less harassed, the furrows between his eyes smoothed out. But, I thought with an inward grin, he still looked like a gangster: he only bothered to shave when we were going out, and his jaw was dark with stubble. Because he had been to the barber more strands of silver were visible in his dark, almost black, hair.

On Thursday the phone rang just before lunchtime and Michael answered it. There followed an animated conversation – in English – with much laughter. When he had hung up I heard him mutter, "That'll please Jasper."

"What will?" I asked. I was washing salad stuff at the sink.

"Oh, that was a friend from church," Michael said. "Jill Bowman. Inviting us to a barbecue at their house after the service on Sunday. She and her husband Roy have a big house with a couple of acres of garden about fifteen minutes' drive from St Luke's. Plus, they have a good-sized pool which we can use."

"No wonder Jasper will be pleased," I said. I dried my hands on a small towel and opened a cupboard to find a bowl.

"That's not the only reason," Michael said, and when I turned to look at him I saw he was grinning. I raised my eyebrows enquiringly. "The Bowmans have five children, ranging from nineteen to seven. They've lived in France for years – Roy works here, and Jill has a business. Somewhere in the middle is a very fetching daughter called Genevieve. I suppose she must be fourteen now, and Jasper likes her a lot."

"She's fifteen, Dad, and thanks for giving away my secrets." Jasper appeared at the foot of the stairs, rubbing his hair with a towel.

"Oh, sorry, JB. I didn't know it *was* a secret." Michael didn't look sorry at all, nor did Jasper look really annoyed.

"Changing the subject," I said, "why do you call Jasper JB?"

"Family tradition," Jasper said dismissively. "All the Wells oldest sons get called Something Ballantine. Dad has it too. Someone told me why – maybe Grandma – but I've forgotten." He crouched down to greet Dulcie, who'd limped to him from her spot under the table. He stroked her velvet ears. "Morning, dog. No girl's as beautiful as you, so don't be jealous."

"Poor Genevieve," I murmured.

Jasper straightened up. "She hates that name," he said. "Last time I saw her she was calling herself Gen."

"When was that?" I asked idly.

"When we were here last summer," Jasper said.

"Oh, so it's a long-distance romance, then?"

Jasper wrapped the damp towel round his shoulders and looked at us both impassively. "Hardly that. Anyway, she's a temperamental girl who likes to change her mind every five minutes, so I might be either her best mate or just an annoying nobody. Also, my school is admitting girls to the sixth form, as of next term." He rubbed his hands together in self-parodying glee. "*Much* more interesting, and in the right country. Now if you've quite finished dissecting my love life, can we please change the subject? I'm starving."

The weather continued fine, and the temperature rose. Michael decided to mow the lawn again, and rode round the grass wearing only shorts, sandals, and a grubby old hat. Jasper lay in the sun, turning pink then brown, sometimes reading, sometimes snoozing, a flash pair of sunglasses shielding his eyes.

"Do I look like a gangster too?" he asked me hopefully.

"Not half as much as your dad does," I told him. "Bad luck."

"I suppose that must be Mum's genes, then," he said. "She's very blonde. If she was out in this heat she'd be red and crisp."

"What a horrible description."

I began to wonder if all this could continue. We were at ease and content, the weather was reminiscent of more southerly latitudes, and I, for once in my life, was simply happy. It was as if I had neither brain nor memory, and no shadows.

Nothing lasts for ever. On Saturday morning I emerged from my shower and heard music from downstairs. Jasper had spent a few moments here and there fooling around on the keyboard, but not for long; and this, as I crept down the stairs in my bathrobe to listen, was different, something I knew, something out of a past I wanted to forget. I stood in the doorway of the living room and watched him play. He was concentrating too hard to have heard my bare footfall, and I was unprepared for the huge upwelling of feeling that engulfed me, a fountain of rawness spreading from gut to face, so that I felt a flush of heat. My mouth opened, I heard a moan of pain, and realized that it was my own voice.

Jasper stopped playing and turned towards me. "Oh, Rachel! What's the matter?" He pushed the seat back and stood up. By this time I was sobbing uncontrollably, and he loped across the room. Before he reached me my nose started to drip blood, and mixed with my tears washed down my face in a red tide. I must have looked horrifying, but Jasper didn't flinch. He took my hand and led me to the sink, grabbed some kitchen paper and held it against my face. "Pinch the bridge of your nose," he said.

Michael came down the stairs, humming quietly, and strolled into the kitchen. He saw me leaning over the sink, Jasper bending over me. I found I could hardly breathe; I was gulping air in strangled gasps and the paper wad was soaked in blood. Michael was at our side in seconds. "What happened?" he said to Jasper.

"I don't really know," Jasper said. "I was playing the piano, and suddenly Rachel was there, looking at me, I don't know, as if she'd seen a ghost or something, and then she started crying, and I got up to help, and she had a nosebleed. It doesn't seem to want to stop."

"OK, throw this paper in the bin, JB, and we'll see what's going on." He'd slipped into doctor mode, brisk and authoritative, and both Jasper and I were comforted. "Look at me, Rachel."

I was reluctant, because I knew I looked a sight, but I complied. "Bleeding's more or less stopped. JB, can you get a clean flannel from the linen cupboard, please. And a small towel."

Jasper scampered away and returned moments later. He handed the flannel to his father, and Michael ran it under the cold tap, wrung it out and gently cleaned my face, avoiding setting the nosebleed off again. He took my hands, which were smeared with blood, and held them under the water, then took the towel from Jasper and dried them. "Make some coffee, please, son." He pulled up a chair. "Sit down, Rachel." I sat. My face was burning, and I felt horrible. The sobs had calmed, but now I was hiccupping as my diaphragm spasmed. Michael found a glass, filled it with water, and handed it to me. I sipped until the spasms subsided. He looked at me for a few moments, his face radiating concern. "What happened?" he asked softly.

I shook my head. "It was the music," I croaked. "It was, it was… from *West Side Story*. 'Somewhere' – one of my father's absolute favourites. He loved Bernstein. I haven't heard it in years. It just brought everything back in a huge flood. I'm sorry."

"There's nothing to be sorry for." He turned to Jasper, who was hovering anxiously. "How's that coffee, JB?"

"Just coming."

A moment later he set a steaming cup on the table in front of me. "Are you all right, Rachel? I'm sorry – we did *West Side Story* at school last year, and I got the piano version afterwards. I didn't know it would upset you."

"Of course you didn't, Jasper. It's not your fault. I feel like an idiot for being such a drama queen." I bit my lip. "Am I still bloody?"

Michael smiled. "Only a few streaks. Don't worry."

I took a sip of coffee. It was very strong. "I'm OK now," I said. "Thank you."

Jasper and Michael sat down with me at the table.

"Would now be a good moment," Michael said, "to talk to us about your dad?"

Jasper stood up. "I'll go if you'd rather."

"No need," I said. "But I understand if you don't want to be involved."

Jasper sat down again, leaned over the table and took my hand in his. "Rachel, you're silly. I thought we were friends. I want you to be OK, right? I'll go or stay – it's up to you."

I heaved a sigh. "You might as well hear it, then." I took a big gulp of coffee and began to feel more human. "I'm not sure where to start." Michael and Jasper were silent, waiting for me to collect my thoughts. They both looked at me, that same dark intent gaze, full of kindness. "That music… I remember being very small, before I went to school, maybe only three or four. I wandered into my father's workshop – I wasn't supposed to be there, because it was full of sharp tools. He was sawing something very vigorously – I remember the pencil behind his ear – and he was singing that song: 'Somewhere'. Very sentimental, I suppose. He had a loud, tuneful voice but he couldn't hold the key. He noticed me standing there, sucking my thumb. He stopped what he was doing, put the saw down, and picked me up, whirling me above his head, still singing at the top of his voice, and I was squealing with laughter." I looked up at them: they were both listening. "Perhaps that's why I flipped just now. Memory's a powerful thing, and we don't always know what's going to come and batter us over the head." I paused, but they said nothing. "Well, I'll tell you what happened in 1990. I would have been fifteen that November. You weren't even born, Jasper..." I paused. "That was the year I lost my father."

"What was wrong with him, Rachel?" Jasper asked quietly.

"It started a few years before that, when we'd all thought he'd just caught the flu. I was eleven at the time, just started at senior school. But he was really ill with it, took ages to get over it. It turned out his heart was inflamed, and he developed something called dilated cardiomyopathy, where the heart muscle becomes stretched and thin, unable to pump blood efficiently. At first we hoped he would get over it by himself, because he was a strong man – I couldn't remember his ever being ill before – so strong it took him three years to die. In the end what he needed was a transplant, but it wasn't available at that time, in that place, and anyway he was too ill to withstand such a major operation. Not only that, but with his kidneys beginning to fail he couldn't have coped with all the immunosuppressive drugs. I didn't know this at the time – I researched it all later. And now, of course, I've seen what a heart in failure looks like. When I first started to operate it was hard for me, working with patients in that condition, but I just had to set all thoughts of my dad aside and get on with the job. At the same time I thought, I hoped, perhaps I could save someone else's father." I swallowed, feeling a tear dribble down my cheek. "If we'd lived in the USA, or even if he'd been ill a few years later, he might have survived; by then he might have been given a VAD – that's a Ventricular Assist Device – giving his heart time to recover. The heart is an amazing organ."

Jasper squeezed my hand. "You should know."

I sighed deeply. "Well, he got slowly, steadily worse. He saw numerous doctors, but the reality then was that there simply wasn't the technology available in the UK. Someone in end-stage heart failure has a travesty of a life – they can't do anything. My dad looked grey. His pupils were dilated, his skin was damp, he had a crackly cough, his jugular vein was distended, his stomach was swollen. He complained of nausea. Worst of all, this strong, vibrant man started to suffer from anxiety and confusion, like someone much older. He told me what the problem was, and he told me he wouldn't make it. Of course, I refused to believe it, and I prayed – oh, boy, how I prayed! – that he'd get better." I shook my head. "Even with all this going on I did all right at school; I suppose it was a way of keeping myself distracted from him and his illness. But I couldn't ignore it when I got home."

"Who looked after him?" Jasper asked.

"My mother did, or if she was working, we sometimes had paid carers. That was in the beginning, before the funds started to run out. After that, if my mother had work, I looked after him, when I wasn't at school. My brother wasn't around much – he was away at college. So I saw a lot. At the end, nurses came, but I wasn't always there when they were." I paused, thinking. "Well, fast-forward to 1990. I told you my dad was a fan of Leonard Bernstein. He loved music and had plenty of favourites but Bernstein was special, and of course then he was still alive, still working, still in the public eye. In my father's view he was a great man, a musical polymath, and my dad was fond of quoting some of the things he said. 'Music can name the unnameable and communicate the unknowable.' Yes, that was one, or something like it. In August that year Bernstein conducted his last concert. My dad and I listened to it on the radio – Beethoven's 7th. It was magnificent. Bernstein was already a very sick man – he had a lung condition. That made my dad very sad.

"Dad hung on for several more weeks. Then he heard that Bernstein had died; it was a Sunday, October 14th. I was sitting with him as he lay propped up in bed – he couldn't breathe otherwise. I was doing some homework. He said, 'Oh, Lizzie – he's gone!' I instantly knew who he meant. Then he said, 'You know, Lizzie darling, I might as well go too. Follow the great man into the dark. Or maybe it's the light – I'd rather it was the light. I can't get better – you know that, don't you? There's no sense in hanging on in this half-life.' I cried and denied it. He held my hand, and he said, 'I'm counting on you, Lizzie. You're a clever girl: you'll do great things, just like him. Perhaps not in music, but in some other field. You'll make your mark, and wherever I am I'll be proud.' A few days later he did die, and it was me that found him, when I got home from school that afternoon. I went straight up to his room, and I've never been able to forget what I found. He was lying on the floor, on his side, but with his head twisted round so I could see part of his face. This was a man who could barely move, and yet he'd managed to fall out of bed; I imagined him panicking, desperate to breathe, flailing, and falling in some final burst of failing strength, and all this time alone. He looked dreadful: his eyes were staring, his mouth open, and his skin was no longer grey, but blue. I remember I screamed the house down, as if my noise could somehow undo what had happened."

I couldn't say any more; my voice had become a croak, and the memory of it in the telling was too stark. His dead face was before my eyes, and I cried, my whole body seeming to convulse. I heard Michael's chair scrape as he pulled it closer, and then his arms were round me and I felt his warmth and heard his heartbeat, strong and steady, as he held me close. I heard Jasper whisper, "What a story, Dad. Poor Rachel." Michael hadn't uttered a word.

After a while, with a great effort, I stopped crying and pulled away. Someone handed me a tissue and I blew my nose and wiped my eyes. I tried to smile, but it was probably more like a grimace. "When I think about the impact of Dad's death, it's as though all the colour, all the meaning in my own life had gone with him; nothing seemed to matter any more."

Michael locked eyes with me, his voice low: "Ichabod."

"Sorry, I don't know what that means," I said.

"It's from 1 Samuel. Maybe you've heard the story?" I shook my head. Jasper looked equally puzzled. "The people of Israel have been defeated by their old enemies, the Philistines. The daughter-in-law of Eli the priest is in labour, and she's dying. She knows that Eli and her husband Phinehas are dead and that the Covenant Box has been captured – the most sacred object the Israelites had, the symbol of God's presence with his chosen people. She gives birth to a son, and before she dies she names him Ichabod. It means 'No glory'. She meant that with the loss of the Covenant Box to pagan enemies God's glory had left Israel."

He spoke so gently that I almost started crying again, but I swallowed it down. "Yes, that's what it was like when Dad died." For a while I said nothing, and they didn't interrupt or urge or question me. "So you see," I said finally, "it's my father that set me on this path. I decided soon after his death that I would study and train to be a heart surgeon, however hard it turned out to be, and maybe spare some other family that pain. When I told my mother my plans – just after his funeral, it was – she laughed. 'Over-dramatizing as usual, Rachel,' she said. 'A heart surgeon? Ha! Well, I suppose you can try.' Her attitude was unfathomable, when you think about it – you'd have thought she'd appreciate a bit of over-dramatization. But maybe she felt that drama was her province alone."

"But you did it, Rachel," Jasper said.

"Mm. I did some research, took the right A levels, went to medical school. And so on. Any chance of some more coffee, Jasper?"

"Sure, I'll make it."

I looked at Michael. "I'm sorry. I guess this wasn't what you had in mind when you invited me here."

He shook his head. "It's exactly what I had in mind."

My brows contracted. "What?"

"Healing can sometimes be painful; you know that. And that's what I wanted for you: healing, or at least a beginning."

"You're both very kind," I said, hearing my voice break. "That's healing in itself. Look, if you don't mind, I'm going to go upstairs and wash my face. And then I'll come down and have that coffee."

"And some breakfast," Jasper said. "I don't know about you, but I'm a growing boy. Dad, I'll do some eggs and you can drive into town and get the bread. Oh, yeah, and some croissants."

Somewhere between two and three o'clock in the morning I woke suddenly. The first thing I heard was Dulcie, alternately growling and whining, and a moment later heard the reason: the harsh high bark of a night-prowling fox. I'd been struck by how few I'd seen or heard in France, and Michael told me that the local farmers were ruthless when dealing with such predators. I slipped out of bed and pulled back the curtains a few inches. Under a sailing moon a shadow passed boldly across the grass, a big dog fox with a fine brush. He quested among the shrubs and nosed around the dustbin at the corner of the scullery. Then, hearing or sensing something inaudible to me, he tensed and his head came up. In a moment he was away, loping silently across the garden and disappearing in the shadow of the trees. I let the curtain fall.

Lying sleepless my mind ranged over all the teeming life of the planet, from the scurrying ant to the indefatigable elephant and the deep-diving whale. I thought about our populous and hugely successful race, and wondered if, as some said, one day we would simply self-destruct. Would our earth be better off without humanity? Sometimes it seemed that way. And yet, weren't we, humans, supposed to be the pinnacle of creation, the apple of God's eye, of all his creatures most like him? What a mystery it was, certainly not to be fathomed in the middle of the night. The greatest wonder was that I was thinking these thoughts at all; after a lifetime of training myself in a ruthless pragmatism, I was finally allowing my mind to contemplate things I would have previously considered irrelevant.

I knew that something I could not name had shifted within me, and that a soft, vulnerable inside had been exposed – and yet no harm had come to me. This was puzzling, at once alarming and liberating. Alone, I felt safe. I felt fairly safe with just Michael, Jasper, and Dulcie, who all, it seemed, wished only my good. I could account for this by reminding myself that it was part of their creed. But what of others, the world at large? Surely some self-defence was necessary? I wondered about the day ahead, at St Luke's, and the socializing afterwards. Was I brave enough for this without my usual armour? Even if I'd wanted to, I wasn't at all sure that I could buckle it back on, so unwieldy and cumbersome it seemed to me now.

This openness, this feeling of lightness, persisted when I awoke to daylight on Sunday morning, and heard, as every morning, a joyous muddle of competing birdsong outside my window. I felt like a bone washed up on a lonely shore, bleached by the sun, white and clean and without feeling. I shook my head and told myself I was drivelling.

The warm weather was still with us but there was a heavy, humid feeling to it, as if we were due for another storm. Soon after nine thirty we piled into Michael's car, with Dulcie in the boot, and took the country road to church. I sat in the back and listened to Michael and Jasper talking about some of the hymns they'd sung over the years, laughing at the odd choices made, and both of them bursting into song as they recalled some of the odder ones – dirges, infantile choruses, some with eight verses and a refrain. They were both melodious: Jasper's breaking tenor and Michael's baritone blending harmoniously. Some things I faintly remembered from my childhood, but most were unfamiliar, and I felt a twinge of panic and a sense of being left out which I ruthlessly quashed. I didn't know if I belonged, or even if I wanted to.

When we arrived Michael took Dulcie for a short walk through the hamlet before giving her a drink and putting her back in the car in a shady spot. As soon as people started to arrive Jasper was monopolized by Letty Wetherly, who demanded that he push her wheelchair inside. I heard him say, "I'm playing today, Letty, and the singers need a little run-through before the service, but you can sit by the keyboard if you're quiet." Letty cackled at this and I understood that being quiet was probably not in her repertoire.

Michael shut the car boot and came over to join me as I hovered by the door. "What's the matter with Letty?" I asked him, my voice low.

He scratched his chin. "Not completely sure," he said. "I know she was born with a physical disability – I suspect some kind of cerebral palsy. She can walk, but it's awkward and painful and she's prone to falling. In the pool she's fine – wriggles around like a minnow." He smiled. "As I'm sure you've noticed there's some cognitive impairment too, which makes her a bit socially unaware, like a clumsy child. People understand and accept her for herself, and she can be very funny – as well as causing her mother considerable embarrassment at times. She loves Jasper."

"Yes, she told me, when I was here last Sunday. She said he was very kind." I looked up at him and smiled. "Like his father."

Michael shook his head. "Not always, I'm sure. Perhaps we'd better go in."

What happened during that service? I can recall and recount the facts, but there was something else, something almost numinous that lay across the ordinary events like gauze, or moonlight. I thought about the story Michael had told me about Ichabod, wondering if the glory could return. Of course my father could never come back, but could there be other sources of so-called glory? After all, he had been dead more than twenty years, and people do manage to cope with the death of a beloved parent, however traumatic. Simple thoughts, but not, until now, for me. For me that day they were nothing short of revelation.

The sermon was preached by a retired clergyman, a tall, balding man with a goatee beard. He spoke of Joseph, quoting from the very end of Genesis, where Joseph said to his brothers, "You intended to harm me, but God intended it for good to accomplish what is now being done, the saving of many lives." As he read these words from his Bible I felt a wave of heat wash over me, and my scalp prickled. It was almost as if they spoke directly into my mind. Harm intended for good? Was that possible? Could something bad be reversed, redeemed? Apparently it could, if you had faith. I had a long way to go before anything like that could be said of me; but the bit about saving lives was true enough. If my father had lived, what would I have done with my life? Becoming a cardiothoracic surgeon, with all its striving against the odds, would probably not have been high on my list of career choices. The idea that God, whom I had ignored and discounted for so long, might have intended good – for other people through me – was enough of a shock. To think he might have good intentions for me alone was a step too far.

Jasper played with competence and panache, singing along. There was, I had to recognize, immense joy there that morning, and the music affected me profoundly. Letty Wetherly sat in her wheelchair beside the keyboard and sometimes, in a quiet moment, cheekily struck a note or two. I saw her mother close her eyes and wince, but Jasper just took Letty's hand and removed it, shaking his head at her. When the singing started again she was the loudest, even if she wavered off the note and sang words that were totally random. I caught Michael's eye and saw his amusement.

After the service I was quiet, feeling almost dazed. Michael joined me in the hall and handed me a cup of coffee. "It's probably not very hot," he murmured. I nodded my thanks. "Are you all right?"

"I think so." I wondered what to tell him, if anything. "There's, mm, a lot going on in my head. Not easy to process. But yes, I guess I'm OK." I glanced to the other end of the hall, where Jasper was sitting at a table surrounded by a number of children. One little lad was talking to him almost vehemently, and an older girl, wearing, I thought, rather a startling amount of eye makeup, leaned on the table across from him, plucking at the tablecloth, a sullen expression on her face. "Genevieve?" I asked Michael.

He rolled his eyes. "The very same."

"Eeeuucch. Fifteen. Horrible age."

"Yes, for some." He looked at his watch. "You done? I think it might be time to depart for the Bowmans'. They've probably had time to fire up the barbecue by now, and it looks as though Jasper needs rescuing."

He strolled down the hall, speaking to people as he went, and bent over Jasper, muttering something in his ear. I saw him nod. Then Michael came back to me, and we walked out to the car. "We get to swim first," he said, "while Roy and his boys are cooking." A sudden thought struck him. "You do have a swimming costume, don't you? I completely forgot to ask."

"I thought one might be needed, so I bought one at the supermarket. It's red."

Michael laughed. "Why did I ever doubt? You are a woman of forethought." He looked over his shoulder. "Here's Jasper – a man released. Let's go."

The Bowmans' house was enormous, built on a vast gravelled courtyard with several outbuildings, at least one of which was more than habitable. Perhaps they rented it out, or kept it for visitors. The garden too was huge, well over an acre I guessed, with a croquet lawn as well as the swimming pool. This sported a bright blue cover, now rolled back, and was set behind a white-painted picket fence with a lockable gate. "Newish rules," Michael said. "In case someone gets in when they're not here and falls in,

I suppose. Might be EU rules, for all I know; France tends to be a lot less nannyish than many other countries. I took Jasper to a castle when he was younger and there were precipitous staircases and no handrails, not to mention unfenced holes and pits!"

People were beginning to arrive, parking their cars behind the house and in the lane that led to it. There were coolboxes dotted about on tables, filled with beer, wine, and soft drinks. I couldn't see the barbecue, but there was a rich smell of grilling meat and a plume of blue smoke rising from behind a shed at the edge of the lawn.

"Can I get you something?" Michael asked.

"I think I'll swim first," I said. "I don't want to drown while drunk."

Michael laughed. "We'd rather you didn't too."

"Yes," Jasper said. "Think of the inconvenience!"

I pulled a face at him. "So what about Dulcie?"

"Well, she can't run around as she normally does," Michael said, "but she can mooch and hang out with the Bowmans' dogs. And if she tries to overdo things we can probably ask one of the more sedentary guests to look after her while we're swimming."

"Mrs Crooke likes Dulcie," Jasper said. "I'll ask her."

"So where do we change?" I said.

Michael waved a hand in the direction of a wooden chalet at one side of the pool. "It might be a good idea to swim now, if we're going to. There are some clouds about, and it's getting hot and sticky."

I made my way to the chalet, carrying my bag with swimming costume and towel. There were four cubicles, and outside one of them was Letty Wetherly's wheelchair. I heard Janet inside talking to Letty, and from the tone of her voice I gathered that getting her daughter ready to swim was proving a problem. I tapped on the door. "Need any help?"

The door opened a crack. "Oh, Rachel, thank you. We're OK, I think, but what would be good is if you could keep an eye on

Letty while she's in the pool. She's very impatient and doesn't want to wait for me to change. Colin's supposed to be ready but he's talking to someone."

"Of course," I said. "Give me a minute and I'll be all yours."

I slipped into the remaining cubicle and shucked off my cotton trousers, T-shirt, and underwear. I could hear Letty's escalating protests and smiled. When I came out she was back in her wheelchair, punching the air vigorously and singing at the top of her lungs. Her mother, red-faced, passed her over to me. "One of the men will help you get her into the water," she said. "Once she's in she'll be OK: she swims like a fish. You'll just need to watch over her in case. Anyway, I won't be a moment."

"Don't worry," I said. "We'll manage, won't we, Letty?"

"Thank you, Rachel," Janet said and disappeared back into the changing-room.

I wheeled Letty to the side of the pool. She was strapped into her chair but started to unbuckle as soon as we approached, and I held her shoulder, anxious in case she fell out and hurt herself. A curly auburn head, dripping wet, appeared out of the water, followed by a grinning face and two outstretched arms.

"It's Danny!" Letty crowed, and before I could intervene she undid her restraints and pitched forward without another thought. The young man caught her as she plunged, and slipped back into the water with his arms round her waist. I watched, shaking my head in amazement, as her skinny twisted legs unwound themselves and floated out behind her. Her arms were strong, and she had no fear, sinking and rising, howling with laughter, thrashing and splashing, clearly utterly delighted to be free.

I saw Michael and Jasper at the other end of the pool, and suddenly I felt unaccountably self-conscious. I wasn't fat, and I wasn't lily-white. The costume fitted well. I had nothing to be ashamed of, logically; but I was overcome with a desire not to be seen, and promptly executed a neat-enough dive and came up spluttering: the water was bracing.

"Rachel, Rachel!" Letty bubbled. "Come on, let's race!" She was off, and I followed as she floundered and flapped her way up the pool, turning turtle and lying on her back as she tired.

I kept up and swam alongside. "This water's cold, Letty."

"I like it," she said. "Too hot outside."

Once her energy began to flag we turned and swam more sedately back to the shallower end. Janet was waiting, her well-rounded figure swathed in a floral swimming costume. "Mum looks like a garden," Letty said.

"Everything all right?" Janet asked.

"Yes, fine," I said. "You OK, Letty?"

"I'm puffed out," Letty said. "I'll stay with Mum for a bit."

"Right, I'll do some lengths." I turned to Janet. "If you want to swim I'll come and be with Letty."

"Yes, yes!" Letty said. "Come back, Rachel!" She lowered her voice. "Mum can go and swim. Because, because," she added breathlessly, "there's something I want to tell you."

I swam four lengths, avoiding others bobbing about. One of the teenagers had found an inflatable ball and was hurling it to his friends. As I came back to Letty and Janet it hit me on the side of the head. I heard laughter and "Oops, sorry!"

I trod water, smoothing my hair back from my face and wiping water from my eyes. "That was great. I'm warming up. Off you go, Janet."

"Letty, do you want to get out?" Janet asked.

"Not yet," Letty said. "I want to watch. Go on, Mum."

Janet shook her head. "Right, I know when I'm not wanted. You and your secrets, Letty!" She pushed off from the side and swam sedately away.

"So, what is it you want to tell me, Letty?" I said, smiling down at her freckly face.

For once she didn't yell. "For starters you have to promise not to tell," she said solemnly. "Cross your heart?"

"Cross my heart."

She edged closer and muttered in my ear. "I've decided," she said, "I'm going to marry Jasper – not Danny. He's nice, but not as nice as Jasper. And anyway, he's got a girlfriend."

"Oh." I was at a loss. "Well, you're right, Letty. Jasper is nice. But… isn't he a bit young? He's just a boy, still at school. How old are you?"

"Twenty-four." She frowned. "But I like him. I could wait till he's a bit older."

"I suppose you could," I said helplessly. "Have you told him your plan?"

"No!" she hissed. "And you mustn't either. You promised."

"I won't, of course, if you don't want me to. You know, Letty… things don't always work out just how we'd like them to."

Letty's eyes were narrow slits. "What do you mean?"

"Well, er, once, a long time ago," I invented hastily, "I liked someone, but he didn't like me – not as much."

"Oh, well, that's all right," Letty said, her face breaking out into a grin. "I know Jasper likes me."

"I'm sure he does, Letty," I said. "He likes you a lot, as a friend. But he's still very young – too young to get married."

I was saved by Janet coming back to us, puffing, her hair plastered to her forehead.

"I want to get out now, Mum," Letty said abruptly. She turned to me. "Don't forget, Rachel," she hissed. "No telling."

I shook my head. Had I said the right thing? What *was* the right thing?

Janet called to her husband, who by this time had changed and was hovering by the steps. He lifted Letty out, and she clung to him with her arms round his neck. A few moments later she was strapped back into her wheelchair, swathed in a large green towel. She waved to me as she was wheeled away, but her face was solemn. I hoped I hadn't upset her. I didn't want to encourage false hope, but at the same time I didn't want to bring her down – nor did I want to treat her like an imbecile.

I'd had enough of cold water, and after a couple more lengths I climbed out, found my towel, and stretched out on a sun-lounger. The swimming had given me an appetite, and the smell of the barbecue was wafting my way. Most people were now out of the pool and hurrying to change, or towelling themselves down on the edge of the pool, chatting in clusters. Only Michael and Jasper, serious swimmers, were still in the water, and I watched them. Jasper, long and skinny, swam like a silver eel, fast with an elegant stroke, cleaving the water with barely a splash or bubble. Michael, brown from the sun, broad-shouldered and powerfully built, kept up with him easily. His stroke was slower but stronger, his dark head rising as he took each breath. I watched the smooth long muscles of his back as he swam away from me, and I shivered. I thought about Letty and her longings – perfectly understandable, as she was in many ways a normal young woman, but surely doomed to disappointment – and I watched Michael and Jasper pause at the other end of the pool, holding onto the side with one hand, talking and laughing; and then the sun came out from behind a cloud and for a moment they looked gilded. Pieces of my fractured thinking, like a jigsaw puzzle suddenly clicking together under an unseen hand, were sliding inexorably into place, and I felt a wave of something almost like terror. I scrambled out of the sun-lounger and headed for the changing room, towel in hand. The need to be alone, to be invisible, even if only for a few minutes, was back in force.

I put my dry clothes back on, then sat on the wooden bench that ran the length of the cubicle and slowly towelled my hair. I could not stay long, with others needing to use the space, but I had to think.

I thought of the men I had known at close quarters, and there were a fair few. I could not say "men I had known and loved", because if I was completely honest I probably had loved no one since my father's death. I was very fond of my brother, of course, but that was different, and for most of the time he was just a distant reality: kindly, but not a part of my universe. Inevitably I thought of Howard, whom I had actually agreed to marry – why had I? I hadn't loved him – it had barely entered into my thinking. Poor Howard! He was a good man and deserved better than cold, uncaring Rachel. I truly hoped he was happy. Now that I was being ruthlessly honest with myself, I realized that, then at least, I needed a man in my life, if only for sex – which I liked very much. What an idiot! To have thought even for a moment that I could found a lifetime's partnership on the need to service my libido.

Something similar had happened with Rob, hadn't it? Good-looking, charming, and infatuated with me, easy to get into bed, easy to dismiss. Yes, I had liked Rob. And maybe I was lonely and a bit disorientated then. But there was no depth of feeling on my part. Sitting damp and alone in a wooden changing hut, I asked myself whether I was capable of anything other than superficiality. In some ways I had been like a typical young guy sowing wild oats: healthy, careless, out for everything he – or in this case she – could get.

But it wouldn't do. I couldn't, in all conscience, seduce Michael Wells – much as I might like to. Momentarily I closed my eyes, thinking about the warmth of his body as he held me close, the clean smell of his skin, the strong muscles of his legs and back as he swam. With a great effort of will I shut off my train of thought right there. Knowing what I knew of him, he probably wasn't as malleable and easily conquered as some of the men I'd known, but he was a man nevertheless, and – assuming he found me at all attractive, which he might not – most fall in the end.

Whatever else, he was my friend. He had been immensely kind to me, and trusted me not to abuse that kindness. And he had already been hurt and damaged by the failure of his marriage. I smiled to myself, a little bleakly. Here was a fine thing – perhaps cold, uncaring Rachel was not so cold and uncaring. Perhaps she was developing empathy. Whatever the case, this Rachel could not cut a swathe of pain through someone else's life. It wouldn't do.

Another thought struck me, and it was far, far worse. I looked at that old Rachel, self-obsessed (how otherwise could I have described my intense focus on my career, to the exclusion of all else?), vain, and hard, and the comparison with my mother was utterly horrifying. Why had I never seen it before? Sure, I could rein in my feelings for Michael Wells; I could behave as if nothing had happened – and nothing had, except in my head. I could carry on as usual, never betraying my desire. It wouldn't be easy, but one day we would go back to England, and then no doubt I would at some point return to Porton and resume my life and work as best I could, away from those kind dark eyes, those strong brown hands. But from my mother there was no escape: she was locked into my genes.

I made a point of mingling when we were all eating, sitting at a garden table with people I hadn't spoken to before, introducing myself as if I did it every day, even though my instinct was to hide. What I was doing, of course, was hiding in plain sight. It wasn't these people I wanted to avoid, but the people I was currently living with. I guess they noticed. Jasper would, I suspected, have thought nothing of it; Michael must have wondered.

As the day waned people began to disperse and say their goodbyes, and we collected Dulcie from Mrs Crooke and put her in the car. I was quiet on the way home, and so were the men. After a while Jasper dozed.

Michael looked at me in the rear-view mirror. "You OK, Rachel?"

"Yes, thanks. A bit tired, that's all. Too much sun, maybe. But it was a nice afternoon. They are good folk here at St Luke's. And it didn't rain."

"No." He glanced out of the window. "But it might, maybe even before we get home."

He was right. We'd been on the road about twenty minutes when we heard the first rumble of thunder, and Dulcie gave a little whine. Jasper woke up with a start. "Was that thunder?" he slurred. He pulled himself up from where he'd slumped in his seat. "That's one very black sky."

A flash of lightning bisected the cloud with sudden brilliance and I felt the hairs rise on the back of my neck. Dulcie growled and whined. "Don't worry, old girl," I soothed. I reached back into the boot and stroked her sleek fur. "We'll soon be home, and you can hide under the table."

For the next few minutes the lightning and the thunder alternated with breathless speed, and then the rain came, thudding down vertically onto the hot roadway, bouncing and hissing. The windscreen wipers were going at maximum, but visibility was dangerously poor.

"I'm going to pull over till it eases up a bit," Michael said calmly. He slowed and eased the car off the road onto a gravelled verge. There were no other cars in sight. "It'll blow itself out before long."

We sat and watched the storm. My eyes were dazzled by the sudden flashes, my ears assaulted by the accompanying cracks and rumbles. Little by little the time between light and sound stretched out. The noise and fury abated, the rain became just rain rather than a torrent, and the heavy cloud moved towards the horizon, shifted by a following wind.

I'd been trying to console Dulcie all the while. "There you go, girl," I murmured. "All over." I could feel her tremble under my hand.

Michael started the engine and pulled out onto the road. The surface was awash, and the car's tyres whooshed through standing water, but by the time we arrived back at the house the rain was reduced to drizzle, and the sky was beginning to clear. Dusk was falling, and the first hesitant stars were beginning to appear.

"I've just thought," Jasper said. "It's August 12th – shouldn't we be seeing some meteors later?" He turned to me. "We always watch the sky in mid-August. I think it's the Perseid shower tonight." He frowned. "I wonder if it will be clear enough."

Michael was unlocking the front door. "It should be. We've got several hours yet before it's fully dark – there's time for this cloud to disperse. We'll have to put something down, though – the grass will be saturated."

"Would you like to see some meteors, Rachel?" Jasper said, standing back to let me go indoors.

"I'm not sure."

I saw Michael flash a signal to Jasper and no more mention was made of meteors. As we drew curtains and closed blinds against the night, Michael said, "I'm thinking it's time we invited the Boutins to dinner. You two up for that?"

"Sure, why not?" Jasper said. "I could make an interesting starter and dessert."

"Not too interesting, please, JB," Michael said, smiling.

"I'm no cook," I said, "but I can clean the house before they come and wash up afterwards."

"Good, OK, then. I'll go round in the morning and see what evening would suit them."

No one seemed inclined for talking that evening, and as soon as I could I made an excuse and went upstairs, taking with me some of the books on Michael's bookshelf. I had a lot to think about.

I lolled on my bed fully clothed. I must have fallen asleep reading, because some hours later I awoke with a jolt. I could hear muted voices under my window. I got up and pulled the curtains back a few inches, and saw below me Michael and Jasper, shadowed by Dulcie, walking out onto the back lawn. They unrolled what looked like a groundsheet on the grass and both lay down on their backs. I looked at my watch – it was after two. Looking up, I could see that the sky had indeed cleared. I saw Jasper go back into the house and the kitchen light went out.

I put on my shoes and a sweater and padded down the stairs, feeling my way through the darkened house, through the kitchen, and out of the back door. I'd crept so quietly that neither of them was aware of me until I lay down beside them.

"Hi, Rachel," Jasper whispered. "You're not asleep after all. I hope we didn't wake you."

"If you did, I'm glad," I said. "I want to see a meteor. It's been a long time since I lay outside on a summer night to watch the stars." I spoke more bravely than I felt, but I told myself that the past was to be embraced, not shunned. Those were, after all, happy times, even if they were now lost. I remembered my brother, with all the self-importance of being five years my senior, telling me the names of the constellations.

We had to wait some forty minutes before anything happened. After the storm the night was cool and I was glad of my sweater. Then Jasper exclaimed, "There goes one!"

"Where?" It had gone so quickly I hadn't seen it. But then I did see one, streaking across the sky and quickly doused like a glowing cigarette butt suddenly plunged into water. We waited, the night grew darker, and I began to feel cold. Then several meteors came at once, flashing across the blue-black sky.

I could hardly see Michael and Jasper, and Dulcie was just a dark mass among the shadows as she lay on the edge of the groundsheet, her nose on her paws. I started, very softly, to name the stars we could see, and then as I lay looking up I felt a warm hand clasp mine. Not for the first time it was kindness that caused a sharp stab of pain across my chest, rather than any memories of the past. We watched for a little longer, and at one point we saw six or seven meteors all at once, like a celestial firework display. Then Michael sat up and groaned, flexing his shoulders. "Time for bed, I think," he said. "I'm getting cold. If you're staying, JB, roll up the sheet, can you, and put it in the scullery. Dulcie, you come with me."

I scrambled to my feet. "I think I'll come in too."

In the house, with the light back on, I saw how tired Michael looked. He saw me looking, and he muttered, "Still catching up. Can't cope with being up in the dead of night, not these days. Must be getting old. I'm going to make some tea. Would you like some?" He slapped his forehead lightly. "Oh, no, I forgot, you don't like tea." He filled the kettle and set it to boil. "Can I get you something else?"

"No, thanks."

"You seem pretty lively for three in the morning."

"Ah, well, I went to sleep reading," I said. "I don't suppose you did."

"No," Michael said. He put a teabag into a mug. "Jasper and I stayed up talking. Mostly about what he wanted to do with his life, what universities he was thinking of applying to, things like that." The kettle boiled and snapped off, and he poured water onto the teabag and stirred it. He leaned back against the kitchen counter, his hands braced on its edge. "You seemed very quiet this evening. Is everything OK?"

I shrugged. "So much has happened; so much has changed. Inside my head, I mean. Just telling you about my dad has stirred things up. I feel... I don't know, vulnerable, exposed. I'm not used to that. And being at St Luke's, and watching the people, talking to Letty, hearing Jasper play... such a lot to process for me, though I guess it's all quite normal for you." He said nothing, and I struggled on. "I don't want to keep you up; it's very late. But there are things I wanted to ask you. Tomorrow, maybe."

He took the teabag out of his mug and added milk. "Go on. You might as well hit me with it," he said, smiling wryly, "just while I drink this tea." He sat down at the kitchen table and I sat opposite.

I remembered my thoughts from earlier that day and felt hot blood rise in my face. "Well, actually, I wanted to know how you became a Christian in the first place."

His eyes widened. "Oh, OK. I suppose I could give you the

short answer. It's a bit late for anything else." I said nothing, and he cleared his throat and sipped his tea. "It was my ex-wife, as it happens – Alison," he said abruptly. "She brought me back, which is ironic, because now, as I hear, she's drifting away."

I felt that I might be on perilous ground. "Perhaps it's the influence of her new husband," I said, "if he's not a believer himself."

Michael sighed and shifted in his seat. "He isn't, and you're most likely right. He, as far as I can gather, is interested in everything that I am not. Acquisition. Being noticed. Making money. Socialising. Fun." He laughed derisively, and I waited. "Fun indeed. That's what she accused me of, when it all went belly-up. Of being too serious, no *fun*."

"Oh," I said. "That seems a bit of a flimsy reason to end a whole life."

He shook his head and took a gulp of his tea. "I guess," he said quietly, "Jack was already on the scene."

"I'm sorry," I said. "That must have been tough."

"Well, it happens. It doesn't matter much now, except that I no longer see my son every day. I miss that." He sighed. "Sorry, you asked me a question and I didn't answer it at all."

"It can wait."

"The short answer is, I was raised as a Christian, fell away in my teens and early twenties – too busy building a career – and when I met Alison she persuaded me to go back to church, and the rest of that mysterious process was without a doubt the work of the Holy Spirit."

"Thank you," I said softly. "I'll let you get to bed now."

He finished his tea and got to his feet. "Are you asking me because it's something you want to reclaim for yourself?" he asked. "Because I suspect you once had a hold of it, and you let it go."

"Yes, maybe," I said. "Being here, thinking about everything that's happened, seeing the people at St Luke's, has changed something, but I'm not sure I can say what exactly. Not yet."

"I'll keep on praying for you," he said. "Jasper will too, I'm sure."

"Thank you."

"Right, I'm going to bed. Goodnight, Rachel." His smile was weary, but warm. "See you in the morning. Probably not too early."

The next morning after breakfast Michael went over the stile to invite the Boutins to dinner. He was gone a long time. I sat in the garden, reading, Dulcie at my feet. When I came in to make some coffee I heard Jasper tinkering on the keyboard. I took my coffee into the living room. He heard me come in and stopped.

"It's OK," I said. "I promise not to go to pieces. I've just made coffee. Do you want some?"

"No, thanks." He looked at me for a moment, pondering. "You used to play, didn't you, Rachel?"

"Oh, that was years ago, when I was a child. I didn't play at all after my teens."

"Reckon you can still read music?" he asked. "I've got a duet book here, really simple. Why not have a go? There's nobody here to listen but us."

I hesitated. "Your simple and my simple may be two different things."

"Have a look," he urged. "Duets are fun." I crossed the room and sat beside him on the long bench. "The top part really isn't hard," he said. "Play it up the octave so we don't get in a tangle. The left hand's just one chord to a bar."

To my own ears I sounded like an elephant in ballet shoes – inclined to fall over. But Jasper drove me on with much encouragement and we laughed at my blunders.

"You're supposed to count," he said. "Otherwise you'll finish before me."

"Too much to think about," I groused. But we battled on with

259

much hilarity and after a while produced an almost passable tune, finishing together with a whoop of triumph.

"See?" Jasper said. "I thought you'd remember."

I didn't mention the few times I'd spent, before he and his father arrived, reacquainting myself with music. But he was right; it was fun. Was it just my fancy, or could I feel another tiny knot loosen inside me?

Michael came back as we were giving the piece one last go "for luck". He stood in the doorway and applauded as we came to the end, *fortissimo.* "That sounds almost OK," he said.

Jasper and I both laughed. "Talk about damning with faint praise!" I murmured and Jasper giggled. "Yeah, Dad's not known for being over the top," he said. "Not one for gushing." He got up and stretched. "You were a long time at the Boutins', Dad."

"You know what they're like," Michael said. "Coffee was offered, and a generous slug of Calvados added. And we had to discuss the world's problems, plus football, motor racing, and the weather. Anyway, they have accepted our invitation for Wednesday."

"We'd better think about what to have," Jasper said.

"I'm quite happy to wash lettuce," I said, "or peel a carrot. Wash up afterwards. Make the coffee. But you two can concoct the menu."

"We can get stuff from the market," Jasper said. "Shall we have loads of courses, Dad? Like they always do?"

I left them to their culinary discussion and took my book back outside.

The weather broke on Tuesday evening, and we heard the Boutins' car rolling through puddles as they returned from their weekly visit to their daughter. I watched the rain from the kitchen window sluicing down in great sweeps with a westerly wind behind it. Dulcie was beginning to be restless without her usual exercise, and Michael talked about taking her back to the vet to see how her foot was healing. "We could do it at the same time as shopping," he said.

On Wednesday morning the rain had stopped, leaving the garden saturated and the temperature considerably lower. Michael rang the vet before we left and she agreed to take a look at Dulcie's foot, so we piled into the car at ten o'clock and drove the short distance to town. While Michael and Dulcie were with the vet Jasper and I were deputized to acquire fish, shellfish, cheese, vegetables, and fruit.

"We won't be able to get everything here," Jasper said knowledgeably. "We'll have to go to the supermarket as well once Dad gets back with Dulcie."

Michael joined us, with Dulcie limping beside him on a long lead, as we were filling our bag with produce. "The vet was pleased with her," he reported, "but she has to keep the plaster on for a while yet. I said she was getting bored and the vet suggested we make up some brain exercise for her – games that don't involve running."

"What, doing the crossword in French?" Jasper suggested.

"*You* can't do the crossword in French," Michael said, "but I'm sure you can think of something. Right – what have you got?"

The rest of that day was devoted to food preparation, and I kept out of the way. I made myself useful sweeping, dusting, and pulling up a few weeds. The Boutins were expected at seven, and by then the house was fragrant with appetite-whetting cooking smells. Jasper had made a starter involving shellfish and home-made mayonnaise, and a simple strawberry mousse. Michael was responsible for the main course, a mix of fish, plus wild rice and roasted peppers, green beans, and a sauce which obviously contained a lot of garlic. An array of aperitifs and appetizers stood ready on a tray, the table was laid, and wine was cooling.

At six o'clock I went upstairs for a shower. I was in my bedroom, more or less dry, my hair standing up in spikes where I'd towelled it, when I heard the phone ring. My door was open, and I heard Michael answer it. Almost immediately the tone of his voice changed. I heard him say something to Jasper; it was clear that something was wrong. I threw on a T-shirt and a pair of jeans and ran downstairs, to be met by a white-faced Jasper. Michael was still on the phone, listening, interjecting tensely in French.

"Oh, Rachel!" Jasper said, his eyes wide as saucers. "It's really bad – it's Gérard – he's –"

I didn't wait for him to finish. Some instinct took over, and I ran for the back door, stopping only to pick up a pair of Jasper's dirty trainers which he'd left lying there. I hared across the still-wet grass, hopping from foot to foot as I stuffed my feet into the shoes, which luckily were far too big and easy to put on. I cleared the stile, ran across the Boutins' lawn, and shoved open their back door. The door to their dining room was ajar, and I could hear wailing from Marie-Claude. Following the sound I came to a shocking tableau: Marie-Claude gabbling into the phone, gesticulating with her free hand while tears ran down her chubby face, and on the floor, face down, his legs tangled up in the legs of their dining chairs, Gérard, unmoving.

I pushed two chairs out of the way, and with a grunt of effort managed to grab handfuls of blue cotton shirt and roll Gérard onto his back. His eyes were closed, his chest still, and his lips under the great white moustache were blue. I had no conscious thought in my mind, just instinct and training and memory from a long time ago: the first months of medical school. I knelt beside his barrel chest and started CPR, twice per second, counting.

When I reached thirty I stopped, leaned forward, pinched his fleshy nose, and sealed my mouth around his, breathing out into his inert lungs. Releasing him, I took another deep breath and repeated. His chest rose and fell. Then I resumed the CPR, steady and strong, willing his heart to revive. As I worked I visualized his stilled heart, imagining it responding. I barely noticed the arrival of Michael and Jasper, hearing but not hearing Michael's barked orders to Jasper, then Michael's voice on the phone speaking in rapid French. I focused all my will on Gérard's great chest, pumping, breathing. Pumping, breathing. I heard the phone go down, and then Michael's voice, quietly, urgently praying. In my mind I echoed him: *Amen*.

I kept on going: pumping, breathing. My arms were stiff and aching, my chest raw. Sweat was running down my face and back. I don't know how long I worked; time seemed immaterial. I heard Michael moving to the window and heard him call out, but as if from a great distance: "The ambulance is here." And at that moment I felt a shudder pass through Gérard. Something stirred under my relentless hands, and to my unbounded relief he gave a huge cough as his lungs filled. His eyes were still closed, but he was breathing unaided. I leaned down, putting my ear to his chest, and heard the sweetest sound I could have wished for: a stone heart once more become flesh.

I sat back on my heels, wiping my face with my forearm. "He's back."

Michael squatted down beside me and squeezed my shoulder. "Thank God." He turned to Marie-Claude, hovering hysterically behind us. "It's OK," he said, and got up to embrace her, gently ushering her into the kitchen to make way for the medics.

After some minutes the paramedics manhandled Gérard onto a trolley and wheeled him to the ambulance.

"I'll go in the ambulance with Marie-Claude, but I'll need you, Rachel, to bring us home at some point. The best thing you two can do is stay put and eat some dinner – it's going to be a long night for all of us. I'll call when I know more." He frowned slightly, obviously thinking. "We could do with your cardiac expertise," he said quietly, "but I don't want to leave Jasper on his own, and it's best if a French speaker goes to the hospital. Most of the doctors there will speak English, but we can't count on it."

He spoke to Marie-Claude then, and she nodded, heaved herself up, and left the room, returning with her jacket and handbag and with shoes on her feet.

"We'll go out to the ambulance, and I'll speak to the paramedics," Michael said.

I got up and staggered slightly, suddenly aware that my head was pounding and I was feeling dazed.

Michael took hold of my arm as I passed him. "Whatever else happens," he said softly, "you saved a man's life tonight."

"Maybe it was your prayers that did it," I said.

"Maybe it was both."

I nodded and smiled weakly, then let Jasper take me home.

It was a long night. Jasper put together platefuls of food and insisted I ate. I didn't want it, but felt better afterwards. I was shivering with cold, and Jasper sat me down on the sofa and wrapped a blanket round my shoulders.

"What do you think happened to Gérard?" he asked, plumping himself down beside me.

"Cardiac arrest."

"Could you tell that as soon as you saw him?"

"Yes. He wasn't breathing. He was a bit blue. He wasn't conscious."

"You've seen it before."

"Well, yeah. But usually I get to deal with the aftermath."

He blew out his breath. "What causes it?"

"It's to do with the heart's electrical system." I yawned. "Sorry. It's when there's an abnormal rhythm. If you don't get to the patient very quickly they'll die. Heard of VF? Ventricular Fibrillation?"

"Sort of."

"The electrical activity becomes so all over the place that the heart can't pump. It quivers – fibrillates – instead. No blood's pumped, so the brain and organs are starved of oxygen."

"And then they die?"

"Unless help comes very fast, yes."

"Did Gérard have a heart attack?"

I shrugged. "Something caused him to arrest – I don't know exactly what. It could have been a heart attack, but not necessarily. We won't know till the hospital's run some tests."

He hunched forward. "Will he be OK?"

"He's alive, Jasper. That's a good start. The hospital gets to look after him from now on."

"When can he come home?"

"So many questions! When they think he's well enough. But he'll be in hospital for a week or two."

Jasper settled himself more comfortably. "You know what, Rachel," he said sleepily, "we were a good team tonight: you, me, and Dad."

"Hm. I'm just thankful your dad could talk to them and explain the situation. I'm sure my French wouldn't be up to it."

"Mine wouldn't either."

We both dozed. An hour or so later I came to, and now I was too hot under the blanket. Without disturbing Jasper I threw it off, went into the kitchen, and did the washing up. I made some coffee, thinking that when Michael rang I needed to be reasonably alert.

The hours dragged. I let Dulcie out, and watched her, shining a torch on her as she rooted around. I brought her back in and she went to sleep with what sounded like a disgruntled sigh. I tried to read, but the print wouldn't stay still.

It was almost midnight when the phone rang. I must have been dozing because its shrill sound made me jerk and I felt my heart lurch. Jasper opened his bleary eyes. "Whassup?"

I struggled to my feet and answered the phone. It was Michael. "Can you come and get us? If Jasper's asleep, wake him up – you'll need him to tell you where to go."

"Right. How's Gérard?"

"As far as we know, he's all right. Sedated. We'll know more over the next couple of days."

"We're on our way."

Michael and Marie-Claude were waiting for us in the hospital's reception area. Marie-Claude was asleep, her head on Michael's shoulder. Michael gently shook Marie-Claude awake, and when she saw me she lumbered to her feet and threw her arms round me, weeping and talking incomprehensibly.

"She's just saying thank you," Michael said quietly. "Let's get her home."

Marie-Claude sat in the back with Jasper and Michael took the front passenger seat. The roads were deserted.

"Did they find anything?" I asked as I drove carefully down the winding lanes.

"Nothing definitive," Michael said. "But he'll need to make some big changes: lose weight, drink less – a lot less." He looked at me sideways. "I'm sorry it took so long. They had casualties from a road accident come in while we were there. You must be exhausted."

"We're all weary. Is Marie-Claude all right?"

He nodded. "She rang her sister-in-law, Gérard's sister, from the hospital; Angeline's going to drive up and be with her for the time being. She should get here late tomorrow. Meanwhile I'll take Marie-Claude to see Gérard in the morning." He smiled. "She thinks you're a heroine, incidentally."

"Anyone would have done the same."

He shook his head. "Most people would want to help, but they don't usually know what to do. You did, and you acted quickly. I'm proud of you, Rachel."

I shrugged. "Thank you. But I'm a doctor, even on holiday – as are you."

Marie-Claude insisted she was all right to go home by herself.

We delivered her to her door, returning her keys, and Michael promised to call in the morning and arrange to take her to the hospital once she had rung to see how Gérard was. Michael ate some of the meal he'd so carefully prepared the day before. Then, without much more talking, we all went to bed.

When Michael came back from taking Marie-Claude to the hospital the following morning, he had little fresh news to tell us. Gérard was conscious and awake, but seemed – not surprisingly – a little shell-shocked. Tests were still being run and the results analysed.

"Depending on how long the heart was out of action," Michael said, "there could be some cognitive impairment. I'm sure Marie-Claude rang as soon as he collapsed, but it was a few minutes before we got to him. It's still a bit early to tell. They've found a leaky valve," he continued, "but would that account for cardiac arrest?"

I shook my head. "Not normally, no. We'll just have to wait and see."

The next few days were dominated by Gérard's condition, which continued slowly to improve. On Friday Marie-Claude was taken to the hospital by her sister-in-law, a bustling lady built very like her brother, if on a slightly smaller scale. Angeline seemed a pragmatic sort of person, a good antidote for Marie-Claude, who was inclined to have the vapours and collapse weeping. On Saturday Gérard was well enough for us all – Michael, Jasper, and me – to visit, and we'd been told he'd specifically asked to see the three of us.

We found him propped up in ICU, sprouting wires and drips but looking remarkably hale for one who'd effectively died a few days before. He grasped Michael and Jasper by the hand, and embraced me warmly. "Ma chère Rachelle," he said in his gruff tones, "vous m'avez vraiment sauver la vie. Mon pauvre coeur vous remercie."

"Je suis bien heureuse de vous voir en si bon état," I replied carefully, "very happy indeed."

He held on to my hand while he spoke to Michael at some length. At one point he looked at me and said something I didn't catch, laughing his rumbling laugh into his moustache, and then he waved his free hand and said something I didn't get at all, but finally we said goodbye and left him to rest.

"What do you think, Dad? Does he look OK?" Jasper wanted to know as we pulled out of the hospital car park.

"Ask Rachel – she's the heart specialist."

"It's odd that they haven't found out yet why it happened," I mused. "If he had a heart attack there'd be clear signs. But yes, he looks pretty good, considering."

"What was he saying to you, Dad? Just then, before we left?"

Michael swerved to avoid an elderly cyclist who'd wobbled into the middle of the road. "Good grief," he muttered, "that was close." He straightened the car up. "What, when he was waving his arm about? I thought he was going to dislodge his drip. Oh, he was saying he thought we were a good team."

Jasper smirked. "Just what I said, wasn't it, Rachel?"

"Among other things," Michael added, giving Jasper a warning look, "that are probably best left unsaid."

I'm sure I wasn't alone in hoping that things would quiet down for the remainder of our stay. First Dulcie going missing, now Gérard taken ill – after days of anxiety we were all feeling weary. We went to church on Sunday and I noticed, with some amusement, how people there treated the three of us – four, if you counted the dog – as a kind of family unit, rather than seeing me as an individual, a colleague, and a guest. I supposed it might be something to do with St Luke's being not just the centre of worship but also the focus of social life for a congregation made up chiefly of expatriates. Looking at the list of activities planned for September I noted – as well as services and study groups – outings, fund-raisers, walks, meals, library opening times, and a host of advertisements, from tree felling to washing machine repair. I knew that they weren't a ghetto – the majority made an effort to integrate and speak French and take part in local affairs – but even so they were a little community within the wider one. The chats over coffee demonstrated the breadth and depth of their commitment to one another, such that I too, even though only a visitor, was gathered up under the family umbrella. There was a time when this notion would have met with scornful indignation from me; the fact that I looked on it with equanimity, even a cautious welcome now, showed how far I had come. Was it possible that under my carefully constructed persona lurked a proper human being? Was this perhaps the benign influence that Michael had referred to, all those weeks ago in England?

After lunch we lolled in the garden, lazily discussing what we might do for the next week. Michael and Jasper had another fortnight in France before Jasper had to return to the UK to prepare for school. I hadn't decided when to go back and I didn't want to think about it. There was still time.

An unfamiliar sound came from indoors. "Isn't that your phone, Rachel?" Jasper said.

"I guess it is," I said. "I've forgotten what it sounds like! I don't think it's rung once since you two got here." I heaved myself out of the chair and went in search of my phone, but by the time I located it whoever it was had rung off. I put it in my pocket and went back outside.

"Someone trying to sell you something?" Michael said. "A new driveway, perhaps? A sofa?"

"I've no idea," I said. "I didn't find my phone in time. It was under a pile of laundry. They'll probably ring back if it's important."

I forgot about it; but fifteen minutes later it rang again. A vaguely familiar voice said, "Ms Keyte? It's Patricia Nettlefield here – the manager of your mother's accommodation. We have met, but it was a while ago." I remembered her: a tall, well-dressed woman in her fifties. The sun was warm, but I felt a chill run up my arms. "Your mother is ill," she said. "Quite seriously so, I'm afraid. I tried your landline, but there was no answer."

"I'm not in the UK at the moment. What's wrong with my mother? She seemed well when I saw her last."

"It was most unfortunate. She went into the garden, just to take the air and admire the flowers, and she stumbled and scratched her leg on a rose. One of the other residents was with her – that's how we know."

"When was this?"

"On Tuesday. But on Thursday she complained of feeling unwell, so we called the doctor, and it turns out she's developed cellulitis. Her leg is in a bad way: swollen and badly infected."

"Where is she now?"

"Oh, she's in hospital. They're worried, of course, in case septicaemia sets in." *No. Not again.* "They want to save the leg if they can, but I hope you see there may be very serious decisions to be made. I wouldn't have disturbed you for anything minor – we can usually cope – but I think, in the circumstances, we need you, Ms Keyte."

I took a deep breath; for a moment everything I could see had gone out of focus. "Thank you, Mrs Nettlefield. If you don't mind I'll call you back in half an hour. I have your number." I ended the call and dropped my phone into my lap. I looked up: Michael and Jasper were both staring at me, aghast.

"What's wrong with your mum, Rachel?" Jasper whispered.

I rehashed what Mrs. Nettlefield had told me, and heard Michael groan softly. He would have made the connection with Craig Rawlins. "It looks like I will have to go home. It has to be me, I'm afraid – as far as I know my brother's still in New Zealand."

For a moment there was silence. Then Michael said quietly, "Would you like me to organize the ferry?" He looked suddenly haggard. "You can take the western crossing – it's longer, but it'll get you straight into Porton."

"Yes, please." I got up from the chair, and a wave of misery hit me, so intense I almost gasped. There was no time to analyse it. I would have to pack my things straight away. I swallowed. "It's Sunday – are the lines open?"

Michael stood up. "Yes, until this evening. The only trouble is there's often only one crossing, and it may be full. I'll try them now." As he passed me he laid a hand briefly on my arm. "I'm very sorry your mother's ill."

"Thanks."

"Look, why don't you come in with me now? I'll check what's available online, then you can say what you'd prefer."

He booted up his laptop, and I leaned over his shoulder. After a few minutes he said, "OK, looks like you have a choice: either eight thirty in the morning, getting in at one-fifteen, or five in the afternoon, docking at half past nine. You'd have to get up very early for the early one, but at least you'd get to your mother quickly."

"Let's go for the early one."

"All right; I'll phone them now."

I wandered back into the garden. Jasper was doing something on his phone, but he looked up as I approached. "This is horrible, Rachel," he said. "First Gérard, now this. I really hope your mum will be OK. Is she quite old?"

"Seventy-two."

"You've not ever said much about her."

"We don't see eye to eye, Jasper. Never have."

"Oh." He hesitated, then he said in a rush, "I really wish you didn't have to go. Will you come back?"

I shook my head. "I don't imagine I'll be able to. I'll have to stay until she's better, and who knows how long that will take?"

There seemed nothing else to say, and we both fell silent until Michael came back. "I've booked a crossing on the early ferry," he said.

"Right, thanks." I could not look at him. "I'd better go and get ready, pack my things." I wrapped my arms round my body, as if to hold something in, and went into the house without another word.

There was no real need to pack so soon. All I had to do was empty the wardrobe and pile my clothes into a suitcase, rescue my clean laundry from the stack, and scout around the house for any items of mine that were scattered about; but I felt an urgent need to be alone, away from the sad, anxious eyes of the Wells men.

I rang Patricia Nettlefield, told her my plans, and found out what ward my mother was on. For a while I sat on the edge of my bed, unmoving. I wondered what it would feel like to be hit by a speeding train. Stupid question: you would be dead. But if you survived, every bone would be broken; the pain would be unimaginable. I shook myself, hearing my mother's waspish voice: *Self-dramatizing again, Rachel? When will you learn: nobody cares.*

Wrong, Mother. I care. I wish I didn't, but this place, these people, have made me wonder, and question, and open up, and trust. Here I feel safe, and valued – for more than just my skill for once. I knew it was dangerous, didn't I?

At numerous times in my life, people have told me how clever I am. They admired me for my intellect, my ability to store knowledge, my unwavering purpose, my self-denying focus, my sheer speed of thought. They were all wrong: I am *stupid*. I am blind. I know nothing. There is no such thing as self-sufficiency. My whole life has been founded on a fallacy: a toxic, wrong-headed self-deceit. And when I think of my father, I know he'd be shaking his head in sorrow. I may have achieved many things of which he could be proud, but there is no way he could be proud of the person I've become.

Why all this breast-beating? Because I had to go home and cut short a holiday, all because of a mother who undoubtedly wouldn't care if I was there or not? No: because I found I wanted to belong, and of course I didn't, and couldn't. I was ashamed of my weakness, but I didn't know now how to rebuild my shell.

Somehow I managed to pull myself up and ram a lid down on my chaotic thoughts. Mechanically I took my clothes out of the wardrobe and folded them in my suitcase. My chest felt tight, and I wanted to howl and weep; but I didn't. Instead I crept downstairs and looked around the dining room for things that belonged to me, and sorted out the clean washing. I could hear the TV in the other room and hoped both Michael and Jasper were watching. But as I made for the stairs again, making no sound in my socked feet, Michael emerged from the kitchen. His shirt-sleeves were rolled up.

"I'm making some dinner," he said. "We'd better eat early so you can get to bed in good time. You're going to have to be up in the dark."

I nodded. "Please don't feel you need to get up early too. We'll say goodbye tonight." He stood looking at me sombrely and inclined his head. "I just want to say," I stumbled on, "how good this time has been. This last month... I've been happy. Maybe that sounds ordinary to you; well, it's not for me. Being here with you and Jasper... and Gérard and Marie-Claude... and the people at St Luke's... I don't know how to describe it, but I feel different. And I... I just don't want to go. Thank you for everything. I can't believe, sometimes, how kind you've been to me." I tried to smile, but I didn't really succeed. He just stood there, a small frown between his brows, and said nothing. I turned and bolted back up the stairs.

"What are you going to do, Rachel," Jasper asked at dinner, "after you've been to Porton, and when your mum is getting better? You'll come back to Brant, won't you? We'll see you there?"

I nodded. "I have to. There's a lot of my stuff in Peter and Angela's flat. And I'm still working for the hospital, officially, even though I'm signed off sick. I have no idea what my employment situation is. I don't know what's going to happen next, so I'm just thinking about tomorrow, and the day after. Anything more is too complicated."

I excused myself as soon as I could after we'd done the washing up. I put my belongings in the boot of the car, and Michael set up my sat nav. "It's a straight run, well signed," he said. "There shouldn't be much traffic that early in the morning. Please let us know you've arrived safely, won't you?"

"Of course," I replied, then went to my room. I read a little, and dozed, and tried not to think. My facial muscles felt stiff with the effort of not crying. I set an alarm. Then I heard a quiet tap on my door, and opened it to find Jasper hovering there.

"I'm going to bed, Rachel," he said. "I don't think I'll be awake at five in the morning, so I came to say goodbye. Please say you'll come and see us as soon as you can." He threw his arms round me and hugged me. "I'm going to miss you," he said, his voice muffled.

I disentangled myself, smiling at him. "I'll miss you too," I said. "Will you say goodbye for me to the people at church – especially Letty?"

"Sure. Have a safe journey. Hope your mum's OK. Goodnight, Rachel."

"Goodnight, Jasper." I hesitated, then swiftly kissed his cheek. "Look after your dad."

He looked puzzled for a moment. "I always do."

I got up stealthily at a quarter to four. I was already dressed, and had barely slept. My things were already in the car; all I needed was my handbag. I crept down the stairs. Dulcie shifted in her basket, yawned, and looked at me sleepily. I squatted down beside her and stroked her warm, smooth head. "Goodbye, Dulcie," I whispered. "Thank you for keeping me company." Standing, I looked all around, committing the house to memory. Everything was peaceful. I left a note on the dining room table, weighted down by a vase: "Please forgive me for sneaking off. I found I couldn't say goodbye after all. Thank you. I'll miss you. R."

I padded to the front door and let myself out. A mist had settled round the trunks of the apple trees in the orchard, but above them the moon shone, remote and serene. I opened the gate and drove through, shutting it behind me. I repeated the process with the outer gate. For a moment I looked back at the house; it was still in darkness. I strapped on my seatbelt and took to the road.

PART FOUR

HOME

The sky was low and threatening with dark clouds when I rolled off the ferry, and before I drove up onto the bypass it was raining in vertical sheets, propelled by a brisk wind. Summer was over, in more ways than one.

Unsure of the severity of my mother's emergency, beyond what Patricia Nettlefield had told me, I made directly for the hospital, and parked in the staff car park as I always had. As I'd said to Jasper, I had no idea of my status at this hospital, or even if I had any status at all.

The hospital was the same as when I'd left it five months before, but it seemed strange to me, as if there had been some secret dislocation in time. No doubt I was seeing it with different eyes. I made my way up to the fifth floor and the ward where my mother was, only to find that it was closed to visitors until three o'clock. It was now half past two, and I'd been travelling since before five o'clock that morning. I was tired and felt my temper rise, but I told myself that rudeness would get me nothing but obstinacy, and summoned up what shreds of charm I could manage. I pressed a buzzer on the outside wall, and after a moment a tinny voice answered. "Visiting time begins at 3 p.m."

"Yes, I know, but I've come from abroad to see my mother, who is seriously ill, and I've been travelling since four o'clock this morning. I'd very much appreciate it if you could let me see her."

"Who have you come to see?"

"Frances Keyte – or she may be calling herself Chester."

"Wait a moment, please."

The tinny voice clicked off and I waited. It was at least ten minutes before someone came to the door and let me in.

A middle-aged nurse in a blue uniform ushered me inside. "I'm sorry, Ms Keyte. We're having a bit of a crisis. Please, follow me."

As I walked alongside her through a typical hospital corridor – brightly lit, neutral paint, scuffed vinyl floor – she turned to me. "You used to work here, didn't you?"

"Yes."

"You probably don't remember me, but I was a theatre nurse for a while, and I assisted at some of your operations."

"No, sorry; I don't remember."

"No reason why you should, I suppose. But I remember you, because of that awful business with the young boy who died."

"Oh."

She said no more, but I wondered then if there was any way I could come back to this hospital. Did everyone remember me because of Craig Rawlins and his mother? Did they all know what had happened to me at Brant Lyon? How could I work like this? I'd had no idea anybody at all had been talking about me, and I felt oppressed. It was as if a door had clanged shut in my face.

"Here we are."

She'd brought me to a four-bedded bay. Only two beds were occupied. In one an elderly woman lay prone and still, her face almost as white as the pillow. If I had not seen the slight rise and fall of her chest I'd have thought her dead. The other bed was screened off.

"I don't know if she'll recognize you," the nurse whispered. "She's very poorly. She's on an antibiotic drip, but she's still feverish and not really with it."

She pulled back the screen, and the smell made my nose wrinkle. "The leg is oozing quite badly. But we only changed the dressing about twenty minutes ago."

My mother lay in bed propped up on a mound of pillows. She was wearing a pink nightdress that I recognized. Her right leg was swathed in bandages, but they were seeping with a greenish secretion that was the source of the stench. This did not bother me in itself; I was used to blood and pus. More shocking was how she looked. Her coppery hair – from a bottle, of course – was dry and straggly, the roots beginning to show grey. Her skin, without makeup, was white and powdery, her wrinkles cruelly etched.

Her hands lay on the sheet like claws, without their usual pale pink nail polish. She looked old.

I wanted to protest. *This isn't my mother. She's glamorous, in control, perfectly groomed. She's a witch, but she's a classy one. This woman's a mess.* She was pitiable, and I surprised myself by feeling just that: pity, and indignation.

I lowered myself into a hard chair beside the bed. "Mother." Other than a slight fluttering of her eyelids, there was no response. I looked up at the nurse, who was still hovering. "How long has she been on the IV antibiotic?"

"Er, four days."

"Has there been any improvement?"

"Maybe a bit. Not as much as we'd like. But it does sometimes take longer for a response, especially with a deep infection. Her being diabetic doesn't help, though."

I felt sweat prickle my forehead. "What? She's diabetic? Why did I never know that?" The nurse shrugged helplessly. "Well, knowing my mother, she probably made sure nobody told me. She hates any kind of illness." I sighed, remembering my father. "Who's in charge of her case?"

The nurse named a doctor I'd never heard of.

"I'd like to speak with him. What time will he be here tomorrow?"

"I'll find out," the nurse said, scurrying off.

Gingerly I took my mother's inert hand. It was rough and scaly. "Mother. Open your eyes."

A moment later her eyelids moved and her eyes opened. My mother normally had brown eyes, with clear whites; now they were dull and bloodshot. With an obvious effort she turned her head towards me.

"Rachel?" Her voice was little more than a scratchy whisper.

"Yes, it's me."

"Where have you been?" She seemed bewildered.

"I've been on holiday. I came as soon as I could."

She frowned. "On holiday?"

"Yes, in France."

"Oh, France… I went to France once. But where's Martin?"

"He's in New Zealand, as far as I know. Later on I'll send him a message to tell him you're not well."

"In New Zealand? What's he doing there?" Her voice was slurring.

"He's working."

"Working. Oh." Suddenly, without warning, her eyes closed. She was asleep.

There was no point in my staying. She was making little sense, clearly addled from the toxins coursing through her body. I was dead tired: physical exhaustion from the journey and the early start, but also a spiritual weariness, all joy and energy drained away.

I walked slowly down the corridor to the nurses' station. The nurse who'd accompanied me earlier was on the phone; she waved to me, indicating that I should wait. After a few moments she hung up.

"Sorry, Ms Keyte," she said breathlessly. "It's Dr Abadi, as I told you, and he'll be here just after ten."

"Right, thank you. I'll be back."

Looking out of a window on the corridor leading to the ward, I saw below me a small garden that I hadn't known existed in all the years I'd worked at the hospital. Down several flights of stairs and after a few false turns I managed to locate it, and for a moment sat on a damp bench and sent a text to Michael: "Arrived safely. Mother quite unwell." I thought I'd better text my brother as well, though there was nothing he could do from so far away. "Mart, am back at Porton. Mother very unwell, cellulitis. R x."

Now there was nothing to do but go to the place I had once called home. Reluctantly I made my way back to the car park. As I approached my car I felt my stomach lurch: there was something on my windscreen. For a moment I was back wiping away sticky blood, but then I saw it was a note stuck under one of the wipers: from a surgeon annoyed that I had commandeered his space. No doubt this was an understandable reaction, since he had no clue who I was or that I had once occupied that space legitimately. I took a note of his name and thought I had better apologize, but in my low state it seemed yet another small but telling piece of evidence that I belonged nowhere.

I drove the once-familiar roads to my flat, stopping on the way to buy some supplies at a supermarket. Before I let myself in I knocked on the neighbours' door. Mrs Chilton answered it.

"Oh! Hello, Rachel! You're back. How are you? We heard about what happened. Wasn't that dreadful!"

Her husband joined her at the door, beaming. "Good to see you," he said. "Are you all right now?"

I was astonished that even they knew what had happened to me. "Yes, much better, thank you, but unfortunately my mother isn't." I explained my reason for coming back.

"Ooh, nasty," Mrs Chilton said solemnly. "Well, dear, you know where we are if you need anything."

"Thanks," I said. "I thought I'd better let you know it's me banging about next door, not a burglar."

I let myself in. There was a scattering of post on the doormat, none of which looked significant. The air in the flat was stale; the place felt unwelcoming. I opened all the windows, turned on the water, reconnected the fridge, and stowed my meagre shopping, thinking with a pang of the food we had eaten in France: the tomatoes warm from the garden, the bread and the fruit, the beef, the wine and the cheese. Well, now it was back to the rations of someone who couldn't be bothered to cook. The thought made me flinch. That was the old Rachel, someone I didn't want to remember, let alone keep company with; but the new Rachel, if she existed, was fragile and wispy in the face of a lifetime of grim habit.

I made a cup of coffee and plugged in my laptop so I could

check my emails. I deleted about twenty bits of junk mail and noted a message from St Luke's with the church magazine attached, something I'd forgotten signing up for. I opened the attachment and skimmed the pages, stopping at a report of the Bowmans' barbecue. Someone had been busy with a camera and there was one of me, stretched out on a sun lounger in my red swimsuit, with Dulcie lying beside me. It seemed as distant and unlikely as a work of science fiction.

Scrolling down I found a message from one "HarkerRJ". I frowned as I opened it: what could Rob want to say to me?

> Hi Rachel,
> I wanted to make sure you heard this from me, rather than on some hospital grapevine. Maybe you aren't bothered anyway, but what the heck. Sammy and I are making it legal this Saturday, August 25, at the Town Hall. She didn't want to wait any longer as she's 27 weeks and getting pretty big. Things are OK with us, and I hope for you too. I do think of you often. Wish us well.
> Rob x

There was no reason for me to feel in any way dismayed or bitter. I didn't want him in the long term, did I? But now, coming when everything seemed so bleak and the present and future so utterly uninviting, it was a blow. And I couldn't but be aware of the date, being my father's daughter: 25 August was the birthday of his idol, Leonard Bernstein. I swallowed down the well of tears and savagely told myself not to be so pathetic.

I'd eaten an early lunch on the boat: just a sandwich, but I wasn't hungry. I wondered how to get through the rest of the day, and I thought of visiting the Harries, but when I rang there was no reply; even the answerphone had been disconnected. I read for a while, made a bowl of pasta for my dinner, and went to bed early. There had been no reply from France. Perhaps they were pleased to be on their own again, free of their awkward guest.

Very early the next morning it was my phone bleeping, signalling an incoming text, that woke me.

"Hello Rachel, So sorry not to reply sooner, lost my phone, hunted for hours, just found it and your message in Dulcie's basket. We miss you and are thinking of you. M and J xx."

Tough times I could withstand, just about. Through the years I had hardened myself to keep my feet whatever happened, and even now, when things had altered so much inside my head, I could meet challenges with chin up – more or less. It was kindness that did for me, and as I read Michael's words over and over tears poured down my cheeks unchecked.

Rachel, you have become a soft, soggy, useless mess. Just imagine what your mother would say, if she were in her right mind. Get a grip.

I was in my mother's ward promptly at ten, and greatly to my surprise Dr Abadi arrived five minutes later. I'd been prepared for a long wait. He was a small man with black hair and a neatly clipped moustache, wearing a white coat that was dazzling in its freshly laundered brilliance and beneath it a pair of pin-striped trousers with a crease that could have sliced pizza. He introduced himself and reverently shook my hand. His voice was deep and rich; it didn't seem to belong to his body.

"May I ask, Ms Keyte, is Mrs Chester your biological mother?"

"So she tells me." I laughed weakly.

"She does not use the family name, I see. Just so we know."

"She likes to use her stage name."

Dr Abadi frowned. "Stage? Please explain."

"Decades ago my mother was a minor star of stage and screen," I told him. "Made a few films, some of which were well known at the time."

His eyes widened. "I see – a lady of talent."

284

"How is she, Dr Abadi? When I visited yesterday, she didn't seem to be doing very well."

"I'm afraid that is so." His English was impeccable, but all the more quaint for that. "I am hoping that in the next twenty-four hours we will see some definite improvement as the antibiotics start to work. Of course we are monitoring her closely. Sepsis is always to be feared."

"Indeed it is," I said grimly. "Are you worried she might have to lose the leg?"

He looked shocked. "That would be a most extreme solution, Ms Keyte. One I will strive to avoid, but cannot rule out."

"To be honest with you, Dr Abadi, I think she'd rather die than lose her leg."

"You must be jesting with me, Ms Keyte!"

"I assure you I'm not. Please do your best to save her leg. I'll go and see her now. Good to have met you."

Dr Abadi called after me as I made my way to my mother's bedside. "I am fearful she may not be quite as lucid as we might wish."

I said over my shoulder, "Well, she recognized me yesterday."

He almost ran to catch up with me. "But that is excellent! That is progress! When I tried to examine her a few minutes ago she was unresponsive."

I couldn't help but smile inwardly. "My mother never actually gave up acting, Dr Abadi. She probably didn't want to have to speak to you."

I tapped on the metal frame of the curtains screening my mother's bed. "Mother, it's Rachel. Are you decent?"

Her voice was much stronger today and I heard her typical haughty and dismissive tones through the rough crustiness of her voice. "Has that perfectly ridiculous doctor departed?"

"No, he's right here."

I heard an unrepeatable expletive and some muttering. "I don't want to be poked and prodded. *You* can come in."

I slipped through the curtain, leaving Dr Abadi outside, shaking his head in evident bewilderment. A moment later I heard his retreating footsteps.

I folded my arms and looked down at my mother. "Are you feeling better?"

"Better than what?"

"Than yesterday. You look better, and I assume your brain is functioning normally again, seeing as you are being difficult and making yourself unpopular."

There was a definite gleam in her eye. "I don't know what you're talking about."

"Dr Abadi seems a good man," I said. "Skilful and attentive. Worried you might develop septicaemia."

"What nonsense."

"So it would seem." I sat down at her bedside. She still looked bad: her skin had a grey tinge and her eyes were red-rimmed. I felt her forehead, and she flinched. "Please, Mother. I am being a doctor." I felt her pulse; it wasn't strong, but it was steady. "Looks like you might live after all."

"I have every intention of surviving. Things might be a little more bearable if I could get my hair done. Could you arrange it?"

I smiled and shook my head. "Not today, I'm afraid."

I heard footsteps approaching, and a polite cough. Dr Abadi appeared, with the nurse I'd met the day before.

"Please excuse, Ms Keyte."

I got up. "Look, Mother, I'll come and see you at the proper visiting time this afternoon. Do your best to cooperate – it'll be the quickest way out of here."

"Ha!" She glowered, then relented. "All right. Until this afternoon."

I decided to see if Malcolm Harries was in the hospital. From my mother's ward to the cardiothoracic suite was a long trudge down corridor after corridor, lift after lift. I'd forgotten just how big a hospital Porton West was, especially as I'd rarely visited any part of it but the operating theatres. His door was ajar. I tapped and put my head round. Sefton Chalmers leapt up from Malcolm's chair behind the desk. "Rachel! What a surprise! Are you back?"

"Yes and no, Sef," I said. "At the moment I'm just visiting my mother in Gladstone Ward. Who's this?" A dark, gloomy-looking man, tall and bald, occupied the other chair. He got up and shook my hand. "Oliver Jacobs," he said, his smile revealing over-large teeth. "You must be Ms Keyte. I'm your replacement – temporary, of course."

"Ah. You must be the person who left this note under my windscreen." I produced it and waved it at him. "Sorry for stealing your space. I was in a hurry to see how my mother was. And old habits die hard."

"Oh! I didn't realize it was your car," he said, a slow red stain creeping up his long neck. "Sorry – if I'd known…"

"Not a problem." Despite my former resolve to apologize, my gracious demeanour would have fooled no one. I decided I didn't like Oliver Jacobs. Perhaps I wouldn't have liked anyone who'd got my job and my parking space, and was making free with my boss's office. "So, where's Malcolm?"

"On a cruise," Sefton said. "He and Bridget left last Friday."

"In that case I'll leave you in peace," I said. I turned to my supplanter. "I'll make sure I find a different place to park, Mr Jacobs."

As I made my way down to ground level, I thought about this little interchange, and I realized that I was probably not missed at my old place of work. Sefton was making the most of Malcolm's absence, and I supposed Oliver Jacobs was performing the surgery that would have been mine. More and more I felt like some kind of alien – an interloper, a non-person, already discarded. How did this square with my years of hard work and study and self-denial? Had it all been for nothing?

I'd just got to the revolving exit doors when I heard my name called. I turned to see Sefton running after me, red-faced and panting. "I'm sorry, Rachel," he said. "That Jacobs fellow is a bit lacking in social skills. I didn't have a chance to ask you how you are – after that awful attack."

"I'm a lot better, thanks."

"Are you working again yet?"

"No, I'm signed off sick for now."

"So will you be..." he coughed apologetically, apparently unable to find the right words.

"What? Able to operate?" My voice was cold. "I don't know. I haven't tried. And I don't know where I'll be working. But you're fully staffed here, aren't you? I must be going. See you, Sef."

I left him standing in the doorway, looking embarrassed, with people going in and out around him. *Seems Oliver Jacobs isn't the only one lacking in social skills.*

I changed my mind about leaving the hospital, and found the little garden space again, and sat on the bench. It was a small area, damp and hemmed in by tall buildings. Little light seeped down to ground level; it was just the sort of place to make a depressed person ten times worse, but at least I had it to myself. I looked at the sun-starved saplings and straggly bushes, and I thought they looked as miserable as I was feeling.

Sitting there alone, I asked myself the same question as I had when I first realized how damaged my hands were: *What am I good for?* Unexpectedly an image dropped into my mind, of Letty Wetherly in the Bowmans' pool, and being tenderly pulled out by her father. What was Letty good for? My spirit revolted at the notion of Letty being good for nothing much, and yet it was the standard I applied to myself. *Ah, but Letty is much loved. By her parents, by her friends at St Luke's. She doesn't need to be useful. But who loves me?*

One gleam of light during those dreary, doubt-filled days was the continuing improvement in my mother's health. Defying all the odds – which really shouldn't have surprised me – when I visited her towards the end of the week she was beginning to look and sound like her old self. Much as I had, at times, dreaded my monthly visits to Mother, I always thought she was nothing less than invincible. But seeing her in such a weakened state had shaken me – maybe even made me think about Dad in his final days – and I knew that there were some things I needed to say. So when I sat by her bedside that Friday I tried to swallow my pride and remember that she was, for better or worse, my mother. And I had grown up enough in recent months to be able to speak to her honestly, as an adult.

"Ah," she began. "Tomorrow's a significant day – did you know?" I said nothing, merely raised an enquiring eyebrow. "The birthday of one of your father's idols: Leonard Bernstein. I could never see what he saw in his music, myself. But your father had all sorts of unaccountable passions."

"Presumably one of them was you," I said, and even I could hear in my acid remark an echo of her own voice.

"Excuse *me*," she said in mock-disgust. "It was hardly unaccountable!"

She was obviously in a good mood – perhaps something to do with having confounded the expectations of her doctors – so I stuck my neck out. "Mother, if you don't mind me asking, do you regret getting married? You were very career-minded, after all."

"I was," she said thoughtfully, after a moment. "Just like you, eh? But no, I don't regret it, on the whole. There were moments when I did, of course, but overall, no. Your father and I had some good times." She closed her eyes, remembering. She looked much more like her old self. Someone must have combed her hair and helped her freshen up, because some colour had returned to her face.

"And all that was ruined by having children?"

She smiled knowingly. "Yes, sometimes it felt like that. I think that many women feel the same, but they don't dare admit it.

Whatever else I was – indeed am – it was honest. Perhaps you have had experience of that too – people don't much like honesty. It makes them uncomfortable. But, my dear, it may surprise you to know that now I am getting older, and clearly not invincible, as I once thought, I am quite pleased that I have adult children." She looked at me sideways, a definite gleam in her eyes. "Even if one of them is usually on the other side of the world and the other regards her parent as nothing but a tiresome duty." She pressed a button on the side of the bed, raising it up slightly so that she was sitting more upright.

I opened my mouth to protest, and closed it again. What she'd said was true. Oddly, though, it was beginning to be less true. "As it happens," I said slowly, wondering how she would respond – if, as would so often have been the case, she would shoot me down with scornful words disguised as humour – "I have changed a lot over the last few months. I wonder if we, you and I, could start again somehow. Not so much as mother and daughter, with all the baggage that goes with it, but just as two women. You never know – in time we might actually be friendly."

My mother threw back her head and laughed uproariously, slapping her hand against the bedsheets, till her eyes dripped. "Oh, Rachel," she said, "do try not to be so rash." I bit my lip, but inside I was laughing too.

"Pass me a tissue, will you," she said. She dabbed her eyes and sighed. "So, what has caused this change, if I am not being too nosy?"

"Maybe," I said hesitatingly, "it started with the attack. No, it must have been before that, when I had to leave here after all her – Eve Rawlins' – threatening behaviour."

"Wait." She held up a hand. "I only know you were attacked. It was all over the papers, as I told you. I don't know about the rest."

I told her what had gone before, and she listened, sometimes shaking her head, or sucking in her breath. "Good grief. How ghastly."

"Yes, it wasn't great. But as you might imagine, my main worry was whether I'd be able to work, or whether she'd damaged my hands too badly. That was the worst of it: my career threatened. You might understand that."

She paused. "Hm, sort of, but I don't think I was ever quite as obsessed as you."

"Really? That's news to me! I remember you as never being there, always at auditions, or chasing some plum part. I always thought of work being your focus, with children, especially me, coming a very poor third after Dad."

"It's odd, isn't it?" she mused. "The same set of circumstances, yet so different depending on who is looking at them. Perhaps my memory is at fault." She looked at me keenly. "So what you are saying is that you felt unwanted, is that it?"

"By you, yes. Not by Dad."

She was silent for a moment. "He wasn't perfect, you know."

"Maybe not. But at least he didn't want to abort me." I had to say it.

Her eyes flew wide. "Did I say that?"

"Yes. I was nine."

"My dear, how awful." She sighed. "And you've held it against me ever since."

"I'm trying not to, but it's a tough call."

She tapped her teeth with one long fingernail. "I think it's time to forget it, Rachel," she said softly. "I shouldn't have said it, and I certainly didn't mean it. I expect I spoke in a moment of anger. I'm sorry."

I'd expected her to wipe the floor with me. Once she would have done just that. "Maybe you've changed too, Mother."

"Well, being potentially at death's door does rather concentrate the mind," she said. "Speaking of which, I gather I have you to thank for the fact that I still have two legs." She wiggled them slightly beneath the sheet.

"Pardon?"

"Did you not say to that strange little doctor that I'd rather die than have my leg amputated?"

"Oh, yes. Was I right?"

"Absolutely."

"Actually, though," I said, "to be fair to Dr Abadi, he was horrified by the very idea, and was committed to saving the leg if it was at all possible. He's done well by you, you know. You shouldn't be so dismissive."

"I expect you're right." She pursed her lips. "Mind you, he did say the leg might never go back to normal. It might always be fatter than the other one."

"You'll just have to spearhead a fashion for long flowing skirts," I said. "All the other ladies will follow you slavishly."

"Such sarcasm!" She smiled. "I wonder where you get it from? But enough about me… What about you – your career? Will you be able to resume it?"

I shook my head. "I don't know. I'm still signed off sick."

"Hm. And is that all there is to it – this change in you that you mentioned?"

"No, there's more." I paused, steeling myself to carry on what I'd started. There was no turning back now. "And maybe you won't like this," I continued, "but Dad instilled something in me when I was very young, and I think, tentatively, I am coming back to the faith that he taught me." I watched for her reaction, but she was impassive. "I haven't told anyone about that till today," I said. "I've barely admitted it to myself."

She frowned. "I don't know why you think I wouldn't like it," she said. "I may not share it, but your beliefs are your own. Did this result from what that wretched woman did to you as well?"

"Not entirely," I said, feeling my way. "Not being able to work made me rethink my life. I saw how poor it actually was, how few friends I had, and how little I prioritized time with the ones I did have. Yes, I was focused on saving lives, but I think I lost some of my humanity in the process."

She sighed. "And yet you have done what many people might dream of," she said, straightening up in her hospital bed. "You have made a difference to a lot of sick people. I don't suppose it's been easy."

I raised my eyebrows. "Crikey, Mother, you almost sound sympathetic! And to think you laughed when I told you I wanted to be a heart surgeon!"

"Me, sympathetic? Perish the thought," she said. She spoke in jest, but it sounded so like the old mother that I hooted with laughter.

"So, you've been examining your life," she said. "Not something you've had much time for before, I imagine."

"Not something I wanted to think about, I guess."

"Nor, I suppose," she continued, a twinkle in her eye, "have you had much time for any kind of love life."

"Oh, I don't know," I said. I smiled wryly. What would she make of this? "I was going to get married once."

"What! You never said a word."

"Just as well. It came to nothing."

"Whose fault was that?"

"Mine. I gave him the elbow. But it was ages ago, and now he's married to someone else. A lucky escape for both of us."

She looked at me intently. "Do you really mean that?"

"Yes."

"And since then?"

"Well, as it happens, I had a bit of a fling quite recently. With a young man who tomorrow is getting married to his pregnant ex."

"Oh! You've been busier than I realized, Rachel." Her voice softened. "But I'm sorry – that must be hurtful."

"You know what, Mother? It's fine. Yes, I feel a bit sorry for myself. But it would never have worked, so yet another lucky escape."

I spoke lightly, but she, with her usual eagle-eyed acuity, was not to be fooled. "I'm not sure whether to believe you or not," she said slowly.

"I promise you," I said, "I don't have a broken heart. Certainly not on his account. And that, dear old snoop, is all I am saying. I've told you quite enough already. I can't think how I have been so frank. It must be the relief at knowing you aren't about to snuff it."

"Charming."

"I've also come to realize just how like you I am – a bit of a shock, to say the least."

"Of course you are like me, dear. Just without the stunning looks, elegance, and good taste."

"Ha, ha. Thanks very much."

I would never have believed it possible, before I walked into the ward that afternoon, that there could be any occasion when my mother and I would be sniggering like schoolgirls. Something had definitely changed.

It had become a bit of a habit for me to sit in that sad little garden after visiting my mother. Today, though, it was raining. I had no wish to hurry back to my soulless flat which felt like just a roof over my head, and no kind of home. I huddled in my car, feeling as if someone without mercy was stirring up my insides with a sharp-edged spoon. I had told some kind of truth to my mother, but it was partial, and guarded, and I felt the need to commune with someone, or something, I scarcely knew what. Even a dog would have been some comfort, and I thought of Dulcie and her bright brown eyes that spoke of unhesitating trust. Ruthlessly, I cut my thoughts off there: to have imagined Michael and Jasper in Roqueville happily carrying on without me would have been too much to bear.

There was someone I could approach, I supposed. Having admitted to my mother that I was (cautiously) coming back to faith I should, in all honesty, sign in. But prayer was something I don't understand. I had prayed so fervently, all those years ago, for my father to get well, and yet he had died, that long, slow, agonizing death. I had prayed for Dulcie to return safely, and we'd got her back. I'd listened to Michael's prayer as I pumped Gérard's chest, and Gérard was alive. Many prayers were answered, and many were not, and I couldn't see any reason for either. But maybe prayer was a mystery not to be grasped by the logical brain. Maybe I should just plunge in and trust – not something I would ever find easy.

OK, here goes. I should start by saying thank you. Mother isn't going to die yet, so it seems – and I'm glad. Thank you for the opportunity, and for her willingness to talk. Perhaps we have built a little bridge today, something we can build on, carefully. And I should also say I'm sorry – for the years I have put you to one side, ignored you, relied solely on myself, as if I knew better. I hope you will forgive me; they say that's what you do, those who know. But I am floundering – at a loss, worried and miserable. You know why – I don't have to rehearse it. It hurts, but I can admit to you how lonely I am, how weak I feel, how vulnerable and frightened. I can bring out to the light my longing to be part of a tribe – and I can see my shame for what it is, a stiff-necked stupid wish never to depend on anyone. I am the victim of a delusion, one that I have fed over many years. The new Rachel needs to have some acknowledged place in the world, whether or not she gets back to work. Oh, how I'd love to go back to Roqueville, on the next available boat! To see Michael's and Jasper's faces as I roll down the drive, to be licked to death by Dulcie! But that's over; it's just a happy memory. Now it's me, and Mother, and whatever I can salvage of Rachel the heart surgeon. But, if I'm to go on, I need guidance. It may be that I have it in me to nurture others, to see needs, to empathize, but I need you to show me how. More than that: I need you to show me how to live.

I hadn't realized I'd closed my eyes – something left over from childhood, or maybe just the need to shut out distractions. When I opened them, I half-expected a thin beam of light to be breaking through the heavy raincloud and shining on me, but clearly this was not how God worked, and I certainly didn't deserve such symbolic singling-out. Sighing, I started the engine; and then a thought came to me as if from nowhere, so perhaps God was, after all, prompting my sluggish brain to action. Malcom and Bridget were out of reach, but I still had friends in Porton. With the car idling I picked up my phone and called Beth.

When she heard my voice Beth almost shrieked. "Rachel! Wow, it's you! You haven't phoned in ages! Where are you?"

"About three miles away."

"You're in Porton?"

"Yep."

"You *must* come over. It's time you met Amelia. Come now, Rach, if you can. Stay and have some dinner."

I drove into the city centre, and found a shop which sold baby things. I had to ask the assistant what sort of size the average four-month-old would be and she condescendingly directed me to the appropriate rail. I found a tiny dress in lemon yellow that I thought might suit, and a matching toy rabbit. I stopped at a mini-supermarket and picked up some wine and a box of Beth's favourite chocolate. I assumed she'd still be breastfeeding and so wouldn't want the wine, but I felt sure Jimmy would enjoy it, and I could keep him company with just one glass.

I drove over to Beth and Jimmy's and before I could ring the bell Beth opened the door and enveloped me in a hug. "It's *such* a long time since we've seen you," she said. "And what a lot you've been through. Come in."

Her sitting room was transformed – from a comfortable and well-ordered room it had become a baby's paradise. There were toys everywhere – far more, I thought, than such a small child could use. Amelia herself was lying on the rug, with some kind of multi-sensory thing above her, so that she could reach things that felt interesting or made a noise. Beth scooped her up. "Look who's come to see us, poppet!"

I know all parents think their offspring are exquisitely

beautiful and stunningly clever, but I had to admit that Amelia was a pretty baby. Her skin was light brown, smooth and peachy, her cheeks pink, and her eyes were dark and huge, fringed with long black lashes. Her hair – what there was of it – was a brown fuzz. She was chubby and healthy and very – dare I say – *cute*.

"I brought some things for her," I said. "And for you. I guess you aren't drinking these days, but I can't believe you'd ever give up chocolate."

"Not likely!" Beth said. "Thanks, Rach, that's very kind."

"These are for Amelia. I hope the dress fits." I handed her the bag, and she passed Amelia to me, as if it was something she did every day. I was surprised by the baby's solid weight. She looked at me solemnly, then stretched out her arm and patted my face. "She's lovely, Beth."

"Oh, and so is this little dress! Thank you so much, Rach. Look Amelia – a yellow rabbit!"

Jimmy came home, played with his daughter, and bathed her while Beth cooked. Beth chatted away while she chopped and stirred, asking me about the attack, my recovery, and life at Brant, and telling me all about the things that filled her days, most of which were baby-oriented. Jimmy came down with Amelia in his arms, her hair still damp. She was wearing a soft sleepsuit decorated with jungle animals.

"Time to say goodnight," Jimmy said. "Goodnight, Mummy. Goodnight, Rachel."

The baby was copiously kissed and hugged and then Jimmy whisked her off to bed. I opened the wine, Beth put bowls of pasta and sauce on the table, and we all sat down to eat.

"So, Rachel," Beth said between mouthfuls, "did you ever get to meet our friend Rob?"

"Yes. We even had a bit of a… well, a fling, I suppose."

Jimmy and Beth looked at one another in consternation. "Oh," Beth said, and bit her lip.

I smiled and shook my head. "It's OK, I know about the

wedding. Don't worry, Beth, it was never a big deal, Rob and me. Honestly."

"Phew!" Beth said. "I thought for a moment…"

Jimmy poured himself a top-up and offered me the bottle, but I shook my head. "I met Sammy once," he said. "I thought she seemed a nice girl, very level-headed. It's about time Rob grew up – he's always been a bit of an overgrown boy. Having his own child will probably be good for him."

"I'm sure it will," I said, with a heartiness that was altogether false.

We took our coffee into the living room, and Jimmy excused himself, saying he had work to do.

"You guys seem happy," I said.

"Yeah, we're OK," Beth said softly. "We've been lucky. We don't have much money, but Amelia's a healthy baby and Jimmy's a great dad." She sipped her coffee and looked at me. "What about you, Rach? Are you OK, after all that awful business? I have to say I can barely see any scar."

"I was sewn up by an expert." I thought of Michael then, gloved and masked, putting me back together, and my stomach seemed to twist in a painful knot. "I'm sorry I've been such a rubbish friend," I said. "You had to find out what happened from the press."

"Well, I guess it's not been an easy time for you," Beth said. "You've had a lot of adjusting to do. Where is that terrible woman now?"

"I don't know," I said. "In some centre awaiting trial, I guess."

"What about your hands? Are you going to be able to operate OK?"

"I don't know that either."

She fell silent for a moment, clearly feeling awkward. Then she frowned. "So why are you here, anyway? In Porton?"

"My mum's in hospital – our hospital, Gladstone Ward. Cellulitis, quite badly." I heard Beth gasp. "It was nasty, but she's improving. She's almost back to her old self. I expect by tomorrow she'll have the nurses running round in circles. She'll get what she wants, as usual, by her own unique blend of bullying and charm."

Beth giggled. "Your mum's a character."

"She is that."

"So you're not here for long?"

"Until she's better – then I'll have to go back to Brant and see what happens. It's all a bit foggy, my future."

"Are you all right, Rach? You seem different somehow. A bit sad."

"No, I'm fine. Don't worry about me. Anyway, I should be going – you'll need to get to bed too. I guess little Amelia gets you up early." I stood up and stretched. "It's been great to see you. Thanks for dinner."

She followed me to the front door. I called out goodbye to Jimmy, who was working upstairs.

She reached up and kissed my cheek as I left. "It would be nice if you could meet someone, Rach. But you're always so busy."

"Well, who knows?" I said, smiling. "One day, maybe. Bye, Beth. I'll be in touch."

That drive back to my flat, in the dark, with the rain drizzling half-heartedly down, felt to me like a particularly low point. I thought of Rob and Sammy, their celebration the next day, presumably with some family and friends, and with the added expectation of parenthood. I wished them well, sincerely and without reserve. I thought of Jimmy and Beth, their warm, modest home, their sweet child, and I was thankful for them, and for their continuing, if mystifying, friendship towards me. Did I want the things they had? I hardly knew. I did know that my yearning to get back to operating was becoming stronger all the time, even if with it came the dread that it might not succeed. I knew I had to try, and soon. I smiled to myself, a bleak little smile, as I turned the corner into the rain-washed, lamplit street where I presently camped. I would have to consult my plastic surgeon, I supposed, to see if my hands were up to the demands of surgery.

As I approached my front door, my eyes widened and I stretched forward, gripping the steering wheel. I turned the windscreen wipers to maximum for greater clarity, and felt my scalp prickle. Parked at the kerb was a familiar dark blue estate car, complete with dog guard.

For a moment I found I could scarcely breathe. Then I shuddered to a halt, flung open the driver's door, and scrambled out, feeling as if my heart was unnaturally high in my chest, making me gulp for air. Who was in the car? There was no sign of either a dog or a passenger. I crossed to the kerb and peered into the dark interior. There, alone, was Michael, asleep, his head slumped forward awkwardly resting on his arms which covered the steering wheel.

I stood on the pavement, oblivious of the rain, my thoughts and feelings so chaotic I hardly knew whether to whoop for joy or burst into tears. I did neither. As I calmed I looked at Michael, and seeing him sleeping, looking younger and without defence, I felt a wave of tenderness that I can honestly say I had never felt for anyone before in my adult life. He was outside my house – he was alone. What else could it mean? He had come for me, and I had not been forgotten. It was a moment almost out of time.

Gently I tried the door handle, but of course, sensible man, he had locked it. I tapped on the window. He seemed to frown a little, then his eyes opened, and when he saw me his smile lit up his whole face. He released the door; I opened it and slid into the passenger seat.

"Rachel. There you are, at last." His voice was husky with sleep. He reached across and gathered me up, wrapping his arms around me, and for a long moment I said nothing, and neither did he.

But the gearstick, the handbrake, and the steering wheel soon made themselves felt, and we broke apart, laughing.

"You're wet," he said, running his hand over my head.

"Yes, it's raining. How long have you been here?"

He scratched his chin. "Oh, I don't know, a while. An hour or two, maybe more. I went to the hospital, but they said you'd been and gone. I didn't know where to look after that, but I figured you'd have to come back to your flat some time."

I frowned. "How did you know where I lived?"

"After we docked I went back to Brant, and left Jasper and Dulcie at the house. I asked the Axtons if they had your address, but they didn't. Angela said she'd ring her friend Bridget Harries, but they weren't there. So I did the obvious thing, and looked in the phone book. Not many people in Porton called R.E. Keyte – nobody, actually, only you. And here I am."

I looked at him as if I needed to memorize his every feature. "I can't tell you how glad I am that you are. Shall we go in? You look exhausted."

We got out of the car, and he collected a small bag from the back seat. When he'd locked the car I took his hand and led him to my door. Inside, I snapped on the light. "I don't have any tea, I'm afraid."

"Never mind that – eating, drinking can come later. There's something I want to say to you."

I suddenly felt weirdly, uncharacteristically shy. "Can't it wait? We haven't even left the hallway."

"No. I need to know your thoughts – everything depends on that." He sounded serious, determined not to be deflected by my flippancy. I opened my mouth to speak, but nothing came out. He was gazing at me, frowning, as if trying to decide what to say. "When you left that morning – was it just last Monday? – and you hadn't even said goodbye, I was gutted. I don't think I've ever before felt so utterly devastated, not even when Alison left and took Jasper with her, though God knows that was bad enough. Of course at some level I knew how I felt about you, but I was afraid to face it. That day it came home to me like – I don't know, like a giant wave, and it knocked me over. I was in a terrible mood all day. Poor Jasper! In the end, wise boy, he sat me down and poured me a glass of wine and said, 'Dad, you're a mess. You can't go on like this. We have to go home.' At first I protested, but he wasn't letting me off the hook. He said, 'I don't know much about love. But it looks like you are suffering, Dad. We don't know for sure how Rachel feels. But you have to find out, one way or another.' And he was right. Without you everything lost its colour. As soon as you left it felt as if nothing meant anything. I didn't want to be there; I didn't want to be anywhere that you weren't. Remember the story of Ichabod?" He took a deep breath. "So right now my most urgent issue is persuading you to stay with us – with me."

In the end it was quite simple. I tried to stop myself grinning idiotically or crying like a fool, and failed at both. "I don't need persuading. It's what I want." In a moment he pulled me close, so tight I thought my ribs would cave in. "Oh, Rachel," he said, his voice muffled by my hair. "You wonderful woman. Thank God."

There was so much to say, to tell, to explain, to ask; there was a lot of hugging and kissing and laughing and a few tears as well. I made him a sandwich and a pot of coffee, and he began to revive.

I said, "When you didn't call or text I thought you'd forgotten me."

He groaned. "I should have, I know I should, but I didn't know what to say, and I was scared you would tell me there was no hope before I even got to see you! And things were a bit crazy – it all seemed to take so much time – changing the crossing, packing our stuff, letting people know, driving to the port, then getting Jasper and Dulcie settled, buying some supplies – I was frantic with impatience. Anything could have happened in the meantime."

"I know what you mean, though," I said, "about not wanting to face how you felt. I was the same. I thought of my life like a little leaky boat, barely seaworthy. If I'd admitted to myself what I felt about you I was convinced it would sink without trace."

"How daft we are." He smiled so warmly my stomach contracted. We were flopped on my sofa, surrounded by plates and cups. He drew me into his arms and held me close, and I stayed there, not wanting it to end, resting my cheek on his shoulder, taking in the particular scent of his skin.

I yawned. "It's very late. I'm knackered and so are you. Isn't it time to go to bed?" Suddenly I felt almost shy – me, Rachel, always so forthright with my men friends!

He pulled away and looked at me, and I noted his eyes baggy with weariness, and that feeling of wanting to nurture him returned. Given what I used to be like, it was a revelation.

"I can crash on the sofa."

"You'll do no such thing. It isn't long enough for a man your size." I fought a little with my novel sense of delicacy, and won. "Michael, can I be scarily direct?"

"Go on."

"Do you want to marry me? Because if so, how about you propose, I'll say yes, and then we'll be betrothed – a done deal, a binding promise. And then we can sleep in the same bed without paining your tender conscience."

He collapsed on the back of the sofa and laughed uproariously, laughter full of sheer exuberant joy. "It's not quite how I'd have chosen to do it! But, you win," he said. "I'm too tired to protest." He wiped his hand across his face, making his stubble rasp. He took both my hands in his. "Rachel, my dearest love. Will you marry me?"

"Yes. Now let's go to bed."

That night I gave Michael first turn in the bathroom, and by the time I'd washed and cleaned my teeth he was asleep, flat out in my bed, face down, his hand trailing on the carpet. I sighed, smiling inwardly: this was not working out quite as I'd anticipated. But I told myself we had, God willing, years ahead.

By the time we decided it was now day and we should be getting up, it was almost ten o'clock. I made some coffee and took it in to him as he sat propped up on my pillows.

"I have to go back to Brant today," Michael said. "I can't leave Jasper on his own for too long. Give me a few days to get things sorted and I'll be back."

I sat cross-legged on the bed beside him. "You could bring him with you."

He stretched out a lazy hand and ran his finger down the long silver scar on my face. "Not this time. He'd cramp my style." His hand strayed down to my neck, gentle and tantalizing, and a shiver ran down my backbone. "I'll have to take him back to London soon anyway, to get ready for the new school term. What about you, my darling? What are you going to do?"

I sighed. "I have to stay here for the time being. See my mother every day, until we know what's going to happen with her. If she keeps up this improvement she'll go back to her old place eventually, I guess. But there may well be a few weeks in between where she needs to be in some kind of nursing home. And I'm the one who'll have to organize it."

"As I'm here, do you think I should come with you to the hospital this afternoon? Meet my future mother-in-law?"

"Absolutely not! She'd never forgive me if I brought you along before she'd had the chance to have her hair done, get her nails painted, and put on her makeup! No, I'll tell you when." I settled down beside him and he put his arm around me. I gave him a stern look. "Don't start getting ideas, because there are a few things I need to talk to you about."

Michael sighed. "If you must."

"You said last night that Gérard was going on all right, but have they found out yet what caused him to arrest?"

"Not that I know of."

"I've been thinking about it quite a lot. There are a few conditions which can cause someone to drop dead – electrical faults in the heart. But I'm sure he would have known about them: someone in his family would probably have had a similar problem, and I can't believe Gérard would have got to his age without ever having an ECG, in which case most conditions would have been picked up. He'd have been on medication, or had a device fitted, and his doctor would have advised him what to do and what to avoid. But there is one condition which can kill you without warning. It's rare, but I wrote a paper on it years ago – it's called Brugada Syndrome. The symptoms can come and go and may be absent at the time an ECG is taken."

"So if that was diagnosed, how would they treat it?"

"They'd give him an ICD – an Implantable Cardioverter Defibrillator. It paces the heart, corrects most life-threatening cardiac arrhythmias."

"I have an idea that's what they're going to do anyway, even if no one has actually named the syndrome. But you're right," he said thoughtfully. "Gérard obviously didn't know he had any issues. The French tend to talk about their health or lack of it, their medications and tests and operations, just like the British talk about the weather. Especially knowing I'm a doctor, I think he'd have said something if he knew he had a heart problem."

"When will they send him home, do you think?"

"I don't know, but what I forgot to tell you last night was a really good piece of news: remember I told you about their daughter Pascale? Well, because her father's been ill she's decided to come home and live with them, to help Marie-Claude look after him. She's bringing her little son with her, and I know they're both hoping she's coming back permanently."

"Oh, that would be good."

He finished his coffee and stretched out, winding his arms round my waist, trying to pull me down as well, but for the moment I resisted. "Wait," I said. "I have to tell you I've made a decision."

He closed his eyes. "OK, what?"

"Your friend, John Sutcliffe. I want to have some consultations with him. There's a lot of garbage in my head about my past I need to deal with. I don't want to be your mad burden."

His eyes flew open, and he pushed himself back up into a sitting position. "My darling, you are not mad and you could never be a burden, not to me. You make yourself sound like Bella Mason to my Mr Rochester."

"Who?"

"Oh," he sighed. "I forgot you're a bit of a literary ignoramus. Jane Eyre. The mad woman in the attic."

"Oh, yes. I kind of remember reading it at school. OK, so maybe I'm not mad, but it wouldn't do any harm, would it?"

He turned to me and took my face in his hands. "Look, for my money you're wonderful just as you are. But if you want to talk to John, I can arrange it. You wouldn't necessarily have to see him as a psychiatrist, and maybe that's not so appropriate in the circumstances. John is also a steward at Brant Abbey, as well as a trained counsellor. You could chew over all your spiritual issues as well. He's a good man."

"I have spiritual issues?"

"Well, don't you?"

"I'm not sure I'd recognize a spiritual issue if one came along and hit me with a wooden spoon."

He groaned. "Rachel, you're impossible."

I slithered down and slipped my arm around him, grinning. "I know. But you can help."

"Tell me how."

"By loving me despite my peculiarities."

"I am looking forward to doing just that, for a very, very long time."

Finally after lunch Michael dragged himself reluctantly away.

"I'll miss seeing Jasper," I said as he hugged me for the sixth time before going out of the front door. "And Dulcie."

"You'll see Dulcie soon enough," Michael said, "and when she gets the plaster off her foot you can show me how well trained she is these days."

"She's probably forgotten everything I've taught her."

"I doubt it. As for Jasper, he'll be back in Brant again one weekend soon, I expect. Meanwhile, why don't you ring him? He'd be very pleased to hear from you, and you can tell him what we have decided. He'll be tickled pink."

"I hope so."

"Of course he will!" Michael exclaimed. "He's the chief plotter in this scenario, don't forget." He sighed. "I have to go. I don't want to, but I have to." He bent and kissed me. "I'll ring you later."

"I don't want you to go either," I said, pulling away. "But if you don't, absolutely nothing constructive will get done. Go on, vamoose."

I watched his car roar away until it turned the corner and was lost to sight. Then I went back indoors, picked up my phone, and keyed in Jasper's number.

"Good afternoon," he said in a very correct tone, having obviously recognized my number. "This is the Jasper Wells Dating Agency."

I stifled a giggle. "This is Ms Rachel Keyte, and I'd like to cancel my subscription."

"May I ask why, Madam? Have we not given satisfaction?"

"As a matter of fact, you are the victim of your own success."

I heard him whistle, and normal Jasper was back. "Well, don't leave me in suspense, Rachel!"

I pretended to be very severe. "Look, young man, enough of this insubordination! Since I am going to be your stepmother, you'll have to get used to behaving better!"

All I could hear at the end of the line was hoots of laughter. I listened patiently for a while. "Jasper, calm down. You sound as if you're having convulsions. I realize it might take some getting used to, but you might as well start now."

"Oh, Rachel!" I could hear him gulping down his hilarity. "It's great news – the best. I'm going to raid Dad's so-called cellar and put some bubbly in the fridge for when he gets home. Is he still with you?"

"No, he left a few minutes ago."

"Oops, time I tidied up a bit then. Will I see you before I have to go back to London?"

"I don't think so, Jasper. That's really why I'm ringing you now. I have to get things sorted for my mother."

"I'll try to be a nice stepson."

"Just go on as normal. That'll do just fine."

"I'm really happy, Rachel. *Really* happy."

"Yeah. Me too. I don't know what your dad sees in me, but don't tell him I said so."

"Rachel, you're nuts," Jasper said. "Dad adores you, in his own non-sloppy way. He just needed me to take his blinkers off."

I wish I'd taken a photo of my mother's face when I told her I was going to be married, but she wouldn't have thanked me. In fact she was almost cross, berating me for being a dark horse. She wanted to know every detail about Michael – his family, his work, our plans – until I felt quite exhausted. "Look, Mother, nothing much has been decided. When it is, you'll be the first to know. You need to concentrate on getting well – you don't want to be an old crock in a wheelchair at my wedding."

She was sitting in an easy chair beside her bed, her bad leg resting on a cushioned stool, and she drew herself up with her accustomed hauteur. "Wheelchair? Perish the thought. Actually, they are talking about discharging me. But given my circumstances I can't go back to my flat, not yet."

"Of course you can't. And my flat's not big enough for the two of us. Um, how would you feel about me finding you a nice nursing home to recuperate in?"

To my surprise I met with no resistance. "Very sensible," she said firmly. "Not too far from my own home, then my friends can visit. I know of a very nice place, actually. Doris spent a few weeks there when she broke her hip. I think it's called Marigold Lodge, or possibly Mimosa."

"I'll look it up," I said. "I'll need to check it out, see if it's suitable."

She looked worried suddenly. "The only thing is, it's private, and probably quite expensive. I don't have much in the way of funds these days."

"Whereas I," I said, "have more than I need. Don't give it another thought."

"Well, Rachel," she said, shaking her head. "That's good of you, but why should you spend your hard-earned money on me?"

"Because if you went to some grotty hole where they beat you up it'd be on my conscience. Because if it wasn't up to standard I'd be inundated with complaints. Because you're my mother. Take your pick."

"Thank you, dear." This was something: the second time she'd called me "dear".

"You're welcome. There's just one condition."

"What's that?"

"I don't want to hear you've been bullying the staff."

"I don't know what you mean," she said innocently, a definite glint in her eye.

When Michael rang that evening I had news. "It was all a lot easier than I expected. She didn't argue at all! Amazing. I rang a couple of places and found two which had room for her, so I went and had a look. The upshot is she can move into Magnolia House early next week. It'll be work for me, getting her stuff together and so on, and I dare say it'll cost an arm and a leg, but I hope it won't be for too long."

"I can help with that."

"Don't be silly – she's my responsibility."

I heard him sigh. "This sounds all too similar to the set-to over Dulcie's vet bill. For heaven's sake; she's going to be related to me some time soon!"

"Whatever. Let's not fall out over it, OK? What it means is I can come back to Brant sooner than I thought."

"Good. We have to sort out your work situation too." He was silent for a moment. "I miss you, my mad woman. I can't wait for you to come back."

Relations with my mother had definitely improved – perhaps there was only one way to go. But before long she had cause to find fault, as was probably inevitable.

The day before she was due to leave hospital we were discussing my impending nuptials, a subject of which she never seemed to tire, perhaps because she had never believed such an event would ever happen.

"What a pity your father isn't with us," she said. "Who can you ask to give you away? There must be someone."

I was prepared, and I spoke without heat. "I'm sorry he isn't here too, and not just for that particular function. But as it happens, even if he was, I wouldn't be asking him, or anyone else, to give me away."

She sat bolt upright. "Why ever not?"

"Well, Mother, you know, it's always seemed a most unfortunate phrase, as if the poor bride is a piece of clothing destined for a charity shop, surplus to requirements."

"What nonsense!" she snorted. "It's a charming traditional custom, one which every father of a daughter looks forward to."

"Maybe they do," I said, very quietly. "But in my book it's anything but charming. It dates from an era when women weren't educated to be economically independent. When they were passed from the protection of one man, their father, to another, their prospective husband. I've been looking after myself for almost twenty years. Why should I suddenly pretend to be economically useless?"

She goggled at me and opened her mouth to protest, but nothing emerged.

I ploughed on. "You might say, with some reason, that it represents the passing from one family to another, a symbol of sorts. I could go along with that. But it's one-sided – isn't the groom also changing his life, passing from one family to another? So why doesn't someone give him away? What it says is that he is a free, successful, independent individual, simply by virtue of his gender, while she is a helpless nobody in need of some man to look after her. What a load of utterly insulting rubbish." I smiled sweetly. "I would have thought that you, of all people, would have agreed. Did your father give you away?"

"Certainly not!" she said. "My father, your grandfather – whom I am happy to say you never knew – was a drunk. He would have let the side down to my eternal public shame." She looked at me, her eyebrows knitted together in formidable frown. "So what does Michael say to all this?"

I laughed. "After a moment's thought his words were: 'Fair point.' So there we are."

She shook her head. "I suppose I have to concede that you are more like me than either of us ever thought."

"Sorry about that, Ma."

She shuddered. "Don't call me Ma! It makes me feel about a hundred. So what, then? Are you going to walk up the aisle alone?"

"No. We are going to meet at the top of the church steps and stroll up together. If it's symbolism we're talking about, that suits me fine."

***

311

I didn't quite get to be a consultant by the time I was forty, and there were reasons for that other than the career break necessitated by my recovery from injury. It took me another year, but I was content. As it turned out I could still operate with skill and confidence, perhaps not quite as I had before the attack, but competently and without unnecessary risk to my patients. As well, between Michael and John Sutcliffe I came to understand that I had abilities and gifts other than cutting and stitching, however much of a whizz-kid I had been at both. "You know," Michael said one evening that autumn, "there comes a time in most people's careers when they move away from the coal-face and start thinking about what they have to pass on. I'm doing a lot more supervision and lecturing and speaking at conferences now than I did five years ago. I'm not as quick as I used to be."

"And," I said, "shock, horror: you are going to have to wear glasses."

"That too. But I, and you, have a lifetime of experience which is invaluable to the younger surgeons coming through the system."

"I suppose. But I'm not as old as you."

He chuckled. "As you often like to remind me. But think of it as the best of both worlds: you can do what surgery you choose, without the pressure of having to live up to someone else's expectations."

"Just my own, and the patient's."

"But that's always the case," he said gently.

Over the months before my marriage I had several sessions with John Sutcliffe, and I like to think that by the end of it he was as much my friend as Michael's. We spoke of many things: my strangely lopsided childhood, my truncated relationship with my father, and the trauma of his illness and death at a time when I was particularly impressionable; my past and current relationship with my mother; my life in surgery. More telling, perhaps, than all of this was that he guided me to think about my spiritual life, and challenged my habitual ways of thinking without ever making me feel I had failed. I took much away from those sessions, and pondered.

"You know," he said on one occasion, "I sometimes think that having a powerful intellect, talent, or personality can be a mixed blessing, because it's all the more frustrating to see it restricted by external circumstances. You say you and your mother are – to some extent at least – cut from the same cloth, but you are more open to faith than she is, perhaps because of your father's influence on you early in life. From those I have spoken to over the years it does seem harder for some people to admit that they can't do it all by themselves, that we are all limited. And yet to do so is simple realism: whatever an individual can achieve through personal effort and sacrifice, death destroys it all in the end – or so it seems to our human understanding. Your father, from what you have said, taught you to love and revere creation, which was his way of acknowledging and praising God. Seeing God as Creator must surely lead to the notion that everything you have – life itself, health, brains, good genes, education, and so on – are all from his hand; he is the origin and instigator of all good." He paused, smiling kindly at me. "I dare say you have had these thoughts already, and have realized that you can't refute them by mere logic. But that's a different matter to learning to live by what you believe intellectually – that can be a lifetime's work."

"I know that I am far from perfect and also that I can control very little," I said. "But as you say, it's a matter of altering my habits of thinking."

"You see, Rachel, because we are of necessity limited as individuals – because we have no control over when, or where, or to whom we are born, for instance, not to mention all the other limitations we experience – we must rise to life's challenges *within God's will*. If we refuse, our nature being what it is, before long even our best impulses become corrupted, and we end up serving only ourselves – even if this is hidden beneath a veneer of philanthropy."

"And it is so easy to fool yourself," I said soberly.

He nodded. "Yes, we are good at that."

***

Michael and I married on a cold, still day in mid-December, when fog lay on the river like a blanket and shrouded the lower parts of the trees, so that their crowns seemed to be floating. He was at the church steps a little before me, having found a nearer parking space. I was camping in the Axtons' flat at the time, because although I had been more or less living at Michael's since returning to Brant I'd been banned for a few days while the room that was to be my study and hideaway was decorated and refurbished. We'd decided, for the time being at least, to keep the house on, as much for Dulcie's and Jasper's sakes as anything, and it was anyway very convenient for the hospital.

Having got myself ready I listened out for the Axtons' Mercedes rolling down the drive before I gave it five minutes and left myself. My mother was staying with the Axtons, who had taken pity on her and saved her from a longish journey from Porton on the day of the ceremony. Others, such as Jimmy, Beth and Amelia, and Bridget and Malcolm, had arrived at midday.

I parked the car, and looked at my watch. I was on time. The service was to take place at Michael's church in Brant, All Souls, a middling-sized Georgian building. I'd been attending with him for a couple of months and was beginning to feel I might one day be part of the family there – though it was nothing like St Luke's with its exuberant welcome. Michael was waiting at the top of the steps, and when I saw him in his well-pressed dark suit and white shirt – with, I noted, smiling to myself, a red tie – I felt strange, as if I had landed on another planet. He saw me and a smile lit up his face, as he stretched out a hand to me.

"Wow." He looked me up and down. "That beats a white confection any day."

I'd only told him my outfit was red, so he could match it with his tie. There could have been no other colour, not since he'd confessed to eyeing me up appreciatively when I wore the red swimming costume at the Bowmans' barbecue. The dress was made of some light woollen material, reaching to just below the knee and flaring slightly at the hem, and the jacket, which sat snugly above my hips, was piped in black. "Glad you approve. You're looking pretty fine yourself. Almost handsome, in fact."

He grinned. "That brings back a memory of your dear mother."

We both laughed, remembering the day when we'd moved her from the hospital to the nursing home at the end of August. I'd introduced her to Michael, and he was ahead of us, carrying some of her stuff. She was leaning on my arm as we followed, and she hissed, in the loudest of stage whispers, and quite deliberately, "Rachel! You never told me he was so good-looking!" I'd looked at Michael's retreating back and down at my mother with a puzzled frown. "Oh! Is he?" At which she slapped my wrist.

"My mother is incorrigible," I said. "Ever the actress. Shall we go in? I'm freezing. Fancy clothes are never very warm."

I took his arm and we turned towards the church door – closed to keep in the heat. But then I heard a screech of tyres and turned to the road where a taxi had pulled up at the kerb, its engine throbbing. A man was leaning in at the window, presumably paying his fare, and when he turned I screamed. "Michael! It's Martin – my brother!"

I flew down the steps, almost breaking my neck because of my unaccustomed shoes, and fell into my brother's arms.

"By heck, Lizzie, steady on, girl!"

I stood back and looked at him, and to my shame tears oozed from the corners of my eyes. *What a crybaby I am becoming.* "I thought you couldn't come! Why didn't you tell us?"

"No time," he said. "Schedule got changed, and I managed to find an earlier flight. I've come straight from Heathrow."

"You have an Antipodean twang. And you look more like our father than ever."

"Do I? You look different – I like the short hair. And you're not quite as skinny. So am I in time – it's not all over, is it?"

"No, we were just about to go in. They'll wonder what's happened to us. But come and meet Michael."

The two men shook hands at the top of the steps.

"Mart, we can't let you just stroll in. Mother might have a heart attack. We must warn her."

"How is the old battle-axe?"

"Much better… but you can see for yourself."

"I'll slip in discreetly," Michael said, "and have a word with Peter. Wait here a moment."

Martin and I leaned on the parapet of the steps, arm in arm. I took him in, all six feet and blond beard and blue eyes, his skin tanned from the New Zealand sun. "You OK, then, Lizzie?" he said. "You look pretty OK."

"I am very OK, thanks," I said softly. "Never better."

"And your hands?"

"Functional. I'm working again. The transfer to Brant's permanent now, and I –"

I was cut short by the church door opening, and my mother appeared, leaning on Michael's arm. When she saw Martin her hand flew to her mouth and tears filled her eyes.

"Hey, Ma," he said as he strode forward and hugged her. "Looking good." For once she was speechless.

"Shall we go in?" Michael said. "There's a bemused congregation and a slightly anxious vicar in there."

"Yep," Martin said. "Come on then, Ma; you can lean on me. Nice dress, by the way, but not warm enough for outside in December." He took her back inside and pulled the door to.

"Darling, you won't want to be seen looking like a panda,"

Michael said. He pulled out a handkerchief and wiped away the mascara from beneath my eyes. I was still in some shock. "Come on," he said, tucking my hand into the crook of his arm. He brushed a stray hair from my forehead and kissed me. "There's something going on in this church today, and for some reason they won't start without us."

"What I want to know is," I said, wrinkling my nose, "how come *he's* allowed to call her Ma?"

We'd talked about going away somewhere once Christmas and New Year were over and Jasper was back at school.

Michael was leaning on the kitchen worktop, buttering a piece of toast. "Somewhere warm, maybe?"

"If that's what you want, but if you're asking me..?"

"I'm asking you."

"I'd like to go to Roqueville for a week or two."

He grimaced. "It'll be freezing in January."

"You've got plenty of logs in that outbuilding," I said. "We can rest. Read by a roaring fire, eat, drink, sleep. Etcetera."

"Mm. I like the sound of Etcetera."

"Ha! We'll see if you can keep up."

He laughed. "I'll give it my best shot."

"And," I said, "we can see how Gérard is, and catch up with the folk at St Luke's."

"What about Dulcie?"

"Take her, of course. She'll be happier with us than in kennels, and we'll have to take her out for walks which will save us from becoming obese hermits."

"OK, if that's what you really want to do."

"I associate Roqueville with simply being happy – no pressures, no obligations. Even if there were a few disasters – like almost losing the dog. And Gérard."

Michael washed his hands at the sink, finished his coffee, and shrugged on his jacket. "Roqueville it is, then. Saves having to book anything except the ferry. Now I must go to work." He ruffled my hair as he passed and picked up his briefcase. "See you." He was whistling as he left the house.

First Christmas had to be endured, and I was not looking forward to it. I had of course met Michael's wider family at the wedding, but that provided little opportunity to get to know anyone. It was arranged that we would spend Christmas Eve and Christmas Day with Michael's mother, Barbara, who lived on her own since the death of her husband eleven years before. Jasper would spend Christmas with his mother and then Michael would go to London early on Boxing Day and bring him down to join the family – including Michael's solicitor sister Sarah, her husband Brian, and two young daughters. They lived just a few miles from Barbara, but we were more than two hundred miles away and Michael saw his family rarely. As for me, I was determined to do my best to get on with everyone for Michael's sake, but I hadn't realized quite how problematic this was going to be. My experience of family life was sketchy, and for the past twenty years practically non-existent. I was not well-grounded in how to live with strangers in close proximity. The house was too hot, we ate and drank and lounged about too much, and the girls, aged ten and eight, were soon bored with adult company. I managed to offend my sister-in-law even before the turkey was on the table. The girls called Michael "Uncle Mike", and referred to me as "Aunt Rachel". "Please," I said, smiling, "call me just Rachel. You make me feel old."

Sarah's expression was challenging: chin up, eyes staring. "It's what I said they should call you. It's what you are, isn't it? Their aunt? By marriage, if nothing else."

I tried to answer pleasantly. "I'd really much prefer to dispense with the honorifics."

"Aren't you encouraging them to be disrespectful?" Sarah's

tone was sharp, and by this time heads were up and people, including the children, were listening.

"I don't think giving me a title is a sign of respect," I said quietly. "And surely I'm entitled to say what I'd prefer?"

She made no reply, but her pink face gave away her annoyance.

"Did I mess up?" I said to Michael later when we escaped to walk Dulcie. "I'm afraid I'm not very good at family life."

"You were perfectly within your rights," Michael said, "and Sarah likes her own way. But when we're only here for such a short time, and for my mother's sake, it might be politic to keep your own counsel, back off a bit."

"Sorry."

He took my hand and squeezed it. "Not your fault."

I thought things might be better when Jasper was there to take eyes off me for a bit, but they weren't. He teased the girls, insisting on calling them George and Charles, and they retaliated by calling him Jasmine, and things got loud and Brian became tetchy. I surprised myself by being irritated by Jasper as well as with Georgina and Charlotte who, I thought privately, were spoilt and whiny. I thought Jasper at least should have known better. On Boxing Day afternoon we were finally free to go home, and we drove to London and dropped Jasper off en route. I felt sorry for Barbara and a little guilty, because she had made an effort with the Christmas preparations and she didn't see Michael or Jasper very often. I knew Michael rang his mother regularly every week, but until now I hadn't really thought about how I was going to get on with his family – if at all. All this gave me much to think about, and I stored it up.

We had ten days at the house in France, and they were like a glimpse of heaven. We did just as we pleased, which was very little except be happy in each other's company.

"If only it could be like this all the time," I said.

Michael said nothing, just looked at me over his new glasses, smiled, and went back to whatever he was reading: I suspected, something to do with his work. But as soon as I'd spoken I realized the folly – selfishness, even – of my thought. Compared to many we had so much, and yet I was demanding more. Not only that, but I had taken on not only one man but all that went with him. "It can't be, though – can it?" I said abruptly. "And maybe it's not meant to be that way." He looked up, one eyebrow raised enquiringly. "I've had a thought. What do you say we take a week off at Easter, invite Georgina and Charlotte down for a few days, take them to London perhaps?"

He frowned. "I thought you didn't much care for them."

"I was hasty. I hardly gave them a chance. And Christmas isn't the best time." I took a deep breath. "And," I said, "I'm going to mend fences with Sarah."

"How are you going to do that?"

"When we get home, I'll ring her. Apologize. Mount a charm offensive."

He laughed, then sobered. "You know, you and Sarah have more in common than you may realize."

"Oh?"

"I live too far away from them for frequent visits; Sarah's down the road from my mother. I know both she and Brian do a lot to help her. I go up there and am treated like the Prodigal Son. Your brother has been constantly overseas for some years, apart from flying visits. So you and Sarah tend to get the messy end, and I guess aren't always appreciated. Or that's how it feels."

"All I ever did was dutifully visit my mother regularly and take the flak. But I see your point."

"Perhaps it might be of use in your charm offensive." He took off his glasses and rubbed his eyes. "But as to the girls, yes, by all means. I know Sarah and Brian have problems knowing what to do with them during the school holidays."

"We could drive up to collect them and see your mum at the same time."

He got up, crossed the room, and sat beside me on the sofa, sliding one arm round my shoulders. "One of the many things I love about you," he said, "quite apart from the obvious and carnal, is your directness. And positive thinking."

"Oh. Well, thank you. And one of the many things I love about you," I said, trying and failing to keep the laughter out of my voice, "is the way you look in those glasses. The wise owl look. It's strangely sexy."

Later that evening, as we chopped vegetables in the kitchen, Michael said, "Speaking of Martin, where has he disappeared to? Did he tell you?" Martin had spent Christmas with my mother, but we hadn't seen him since.

"Ah. Yes – he was a bit secretive and sheepish about it, but he went to spend New Year in Hamburg. He met a German girl in New Zealand while he was working there. She specializes in underwater photography, so they've got plenty in common. You never know with Martin, but I got the impression he was seriously smitten."

"I know how he feels," Michael said, sighing.

"Oh, really? Who's the lucky girl?"

"Can't remember her name now. Tall, lanky sort of woman, a bit weird."

"Cheeky."

We were in France for just one Sunday. We arrived at St Luke's to a reception even more welcoming than ever – almost embarrassingly over the top, it seemed to me, as they expressed their delight in seeing us together and happy. The congregation was diminished, because now only those resident in France were there, and of them only the hardiest, since the church was chilly and the weather forbidding. But as I looked around covertly during the sermon, watching the attentive faces, I suddenly felt my heart warm. To me these people were like pinpricks of light, such as you might see when looking down from an aeroplane at night as it circles above a city, waiting to land. I thought too of those who had quite unobtrusively modelled the Christian life for me: Bridget, Jasper, Father Vincent, the folk at St Luke's and All Souls, and of course, every day, Michael himself. *Thank you, God, if this is, as I suspect, your work.*

Of course we went next door to see Gérard and Marie-Claude. We were introduced to Pascale, a quiet woman with long, lank fair hair and a strangely shuffling gait. Her little boy seemed like her, oddly quiet for a three-year-old. Gérard was himself as ever, apparently little the worse for his waltz with death. He pulled back his shirt to show me where they'd put his ICD and grinned knowingly. What he said I couldn't quite catch: something about being a robot. Michael asked Marie-Claude privately if she thought Gérard had changed since his illness: had his thinking been affected? She said he was even more forgetful than before, especially when it came to losing his glasses and his car keys, but that having their young grandson in the house kept his spirits up. It was far better than it might have been.

***

Michael often remarked that I constantly surprised him.

"For example?" I said, frowning.

"Well, the way you handled Sarah and the girls," he said, "when we went up to visit. That could have been a source of friction."

"Which I really didn't want," I said, "and I felt it was down to me to put things right, seeing as I'm the new girl. Also, I thought I could afford to be gracious."

"My mother was pleased."

"Then so am I. If you can cope with me, I can do my best to cope with them."

Oddly, though, Michael rarely *looked* surprised. Perhaps he felt it, but it didn't reach his face. He was habitually calm and measured; perhaps that was what Alison had interpreted as *no fun*, but it was fine by me. He was cautious in the expression of his feelings, but I sensed they ran deep.

One gloomy morning in November we were both due at the hospital to operate, and we were running late. I grabbed a coat and joined him in his car, throwing my briefcase on the back seat. He turned the car round and headed for the city.

"I've been meaning to ask you," he said. "What do you want, or want to do, for your birthday?"

He couldn't have foreseen my answer, but he still managed not to look surprised.

"I'd like a baby," I said.

It wasn't the first time the subject had arisen; it had been aired in a vague, general, maybe-later-or-not-at-all kind of way. But the previous summer it had been mentioned quite publicly. We were in France, just Michael and me and Dulcie; Jasper was somewhere at a music festival, camping with friends.

As soon as we walked into St Luke's before the service that summer morning I was gleefully accosted by Letty Wetherly. Janet had parked her at the end of a pew while she fetched something from her car.

"Rachel, it's you!" Letty crowed.

"Hi, Letty. How are you?"

"Got a sunburned nose."

"So you have. Did you forget your hat?"

"No. Mum forgot my sunblock." She looked me up and down with a critical eye. "That's a pretty colour," she said of my blue and cream striped top.

"Thanks."

Letty's voice was rarely quiet, and that day it was louder than ever. "You know what I think, Rachel," she said. "I think you should have a baby."

People heard, and heads turned. There was some laughter, but not from Michael, who was behind me, nor from Janet, who was just coming to join us. "Colette!" she said. "How many times have I told you not to be so personal! That's Rachel's business, not yours."

"And Michael's," Letty said with a sly giggle.

"Well, yes, of course, but –" Janet's face flushed pink.

"*Because*, you see," Letty went on, her voice rising higher and higher, "I know how you make one. A baby, I mean. Danny told me."

Now poor Janet was utterly mortified. The service was about to begin, and Letty was in no mood to be hushed. I put my finger to my lips and bent down, so that my head was on a level with hers. I beckoned her closer, with what I hoped was a conspiratorial expression on my face, and whispered in her ear. She grinned, and put a finger to her lips, copying me. For the next hour she said nothing more. She joined in all the hymns, singing random words as usual, and occasionally exchanging grins with me.

That service was memorable for another reason. A visiting clergyman was preaching on 2 Corinthians 1, verses 19 and 20. "For Jesus Christ, the Son of God, who was preached among you by Silas, Timothy, and myself, is not one who is 'Yes' and 'No.' On the contrary, he is God's 'Yes'; for it is he who is the 'Yes' to all God's promises." I had heard this, or something like it, many years before; I couldn't recall when or where. As the preacher unpacked the references to Jesus in the Old Testament, applying various prophetic sayings, I tried to remember, but it eluded me.

Afterwards, as we were drinking coffee in the hall, Janet Wetherly came up to me. "I'm so grateful you managed to shut Letty up," she said. "She can be a pain, and I'm sure she knows it will embarrass me and does it all the more. However did you do it?"

"Ah," I said, "I'm afraid I can't tell you – it's a secret. Letty has been sworn to secrecy too."

Much later, as we sipped a cool aperitif in the garden, Michael asked me the same question.

"Seeing as Letty isn't here, glowering at me, I can tell you. I said if she kept it a deep, dark, sacred secret, we'd make the effort."

"To do what?"

"Procreate."

Now, in November, all he said was, "Are you sure? Thought long and hard?"

"Yes, as far as I can. I don't see how you can prepare for parenthood, actually. No two babies are the same, are they? We could have a grumpy one, or a cheerful one, for example. I could manage well, or not. But, my love, you have to buy into it too, for your own sake, not just to please me."

"I always wanted more children, as it happens," Michael said.

"So why didn't you?"

He sighed. "When Jasper was born Alison was quite ill. She couldn't look after him for the first eight weeks of his life."

"Ill physically or mentally?"

"Both, poor thing."

"So who did look after baby Jasper?"

"I did. Took time off. I couldn't let anyone else have him when he was so tiny."

"Does he know?"

Michael shrugged. "I haven't told him, and I don't suppose Alison has – she wouldn't want to remember such a horrible time. My mother may have mentioned it, but he's never said anything."

"How do you think he'll feel about the prospect of a sibling?"

Michael swung the car into the hospital approach road. "He'll love it. Besides, he's at university, rarely home. He'll only have the fun part of being a brother."

"So you're quite happy to go along with my crazy plan?"

He looked over at me, the merest hint of a smile twitching his lips. "If you're certain," he said quietly. "Would you like to put your plan into action straight away?"

"Ha! Wouldn't that be a bit ill-advised? Seeing as we're fully clothed, in a moving car, and on our way to do a day's work? Soon, though."

I conceived straight away, had a trouble-free pregnancy, and was walking Dulcie when my waters broke. Labour was long enough and quite tedious and wearing, but on 24 August – *not quite Bernstein's birthday: sorry, Dad* – Jonathan Frederick Wells saw the light of day, a neat, compact baby with a shock of dark hair and a prodigious gummy yawn. He was perfect.

Jonathan is seventeen months old now, and runs around the house on his sturdy little legs, chuckling and burbling all sorts of random almost-words, usually followed by a watchful collie. He is a cheerful child, free with smiles, and apart from having my blue eyes, he's eerily like his father, who adores him (quietly, of course). It seems to me that my life has done several somersaults in the last four years; becoming a mother has stood it on its head yet again. Clearly Michael's life has also been taken apart and put together again in a different order. "How can it be," he mused one evening as he poured water over Jonathan's head in the bath, "I have one son at university and another one in nappies? What was I doing in between?"

Taking my husband at his word, I gave thought to the idea of another child. Michael told me we should get a move on, with me forty-one and him fifty in May. But I knew there was something I had to do first, something I'd been brooding on for some time. The New Year with all its hysteria was over, leaving a trail of party-poppers and broken glass; the lights and baubles and tinsel had all been stowed in the attic. It was time to put my plan into action.

JANUARY 2016

I phoned my old mentor and friend Malcolm Harries, but he wasn't there. So I had a long chat with Bridget, who asked me a few questions, mainly on the progress of my son, but also bemoaned the fact that I was no longer on the Porton West team. "You're greatly missed," she said. "At least that Oliver Jacobs fellow has moved on. Malcolm is relieved about that, I know. He said he was competent enough, a safe pair of hands, but nobody seemed able to get on with him. He ruffled a few feathers, quite unwittingly, I believe: it was just his manner, the way he spoke to people." (I didn't say so, but I was surprised that I could come out best in a civility contest with Oliver Jacobs. Either Malcolm's memory was faulty, or Jacobs must have been singularly charmless. I guess I have mellowed – but not that much.)

"What is it you wanted to talk to Malcolm about, my dear?" Bridget asked finally. "Is it urgent? Should I ask him to call you back?"

I had changed my mind, and prevaricated. "No, that's OK, Bridget. It'll keep. Just give him my best. I'll be in touch."

I'd decided there was, after all, no need to involve Malcolm. I hunted around on the internet and found contact details for St Joseph's church. I left a message on the answerphone, with my own details, and the same evening Father Vincent rang me.

"Good evening, Ms Keyte – or should I call you Mrs Wells?"

"Either will do, and Rachel is fine too. I see you've been keeping up with me."

"I talk to Professor Harries from time to time. He likes to discuss theology."

"Does he? How surprising people are." I thought about this for a moment, and then set it aside. "How are you, Father?"

"In a lot of pain from arthritis," he said. "It's time I retired properly."

"I'm sorry to hear that."

"What can I do for you?" he asked gently. "I don't imagine you contacted me just to enquire about my health."

"Ah, yes. Thank you for ringing back so promptly. I… actually, I need your input. I want to visit Eve Rawlins."

There was a long silence at the other end. Then he said, "May I ask what has inspired this? You understand I have an interest in defending her."

"I understand, and applaud. I've been thinking about it for some time, and it's been getting stronger, the notion of unfinished business. Also the anniversary is coming up, really soon – the day Craig died. If nothing else, and even if she refuses to see me, she'll know that someone else remembers and thinks of it as significant."

"What is it you'd like me to do?"

"I'm assuming you visit her from time to time – is that right?"

He cleared his throat. "Yes, I go to the prison regularly and we pray together."

"I wondered if you'd ask her on my behalf – whether she'd be willing to talk to me. I don't want to just turn up unannounced. I guess someone in her position has few choices, but at least she can have the option of telling me no."

"I'm due to visit her, as it happens, on the 12th. The anniversary. I can telephone, see if she would be willing for you to come as well. If so, I'll come with you, but I'll remain in the outer room. If she agrees, this can be your visit."

"Thank you. But if not then, if that is just too sensitive, perhaps another day."

"All right, Ms Keyte. I'll see what I can do, and I'll get back to you."

I hesitated to tell Michael of my plan, simply because I thought he would be anxious. I said nothing for a few days.

But somehow he knew. He looked up, over the top of his glasses – a new pair, as it happened – and said, "Something bothering you?"

"Uh, yes. I have to tell you something and I'm not sure how to do it."

He raised his eyebrows. "Since when did you turn into a shrinking violet? Anyway, I think I know."

"You do? Since when did you turn into a mind-reader?"

He laughed. "I've been honing my mind-reading skills over the last couple of years, actually." We were sitting on either side of the breakfast table with Jonathan in his high chair between us. Michael stretched over and took my hand in his, sticky spoon and all. "It's that time of year," he said softly, "when you go into a sort of gloom. I can almost see the dark cloud hanging over you. Happens every January."

"I didn't know I was so transparent." I heaved a sigh. "I'm thinking of going to see Eve Rawlins in the prison."

"Of course you are."

"It doesn't bother you?"

He shook his head. "I can't see that there is much likelihood of you being in any physical danger. If I had a concern it would be the possible psychological effect, but I trust your judgment. When are you thinking of going?"

"The 12th – the anniversary. I'll drive down to Porton and pick up Father Vincent. I thought I'd combine it with visiting Mother, and call in to see Bridget and Malcolm. Maybe if I stay over I can fit in Beth and Jimmy too. But that depends on who's going to take care of His Lordship." I waved a hand in the direction of our son, who was eating fingers of buttery toast and singing at the same time.

"I can look after him," Michael said, "and if there's some emergency at the hospital and it has to be me that deals with it, I'm sure Angela would step in for half a day. Go, love. You need to do this, I think."

"Thank you – for understanding."

I left early in the morning, and as I headed west the heavy cloud that had persisted ever since New Year lifted, and a weak wintry sun blinked through. I was apprehensive; Eve Rawlins remained a mystery to me, someone I found hard to fathom. I thought of her in the hospital before Craig's surgery, taciturn, tense, controlling some vast and difficult emotion. I thought of her like a demon, or a harpy, when I went to see her the day he died, and the out-of-control maniac at his funeral. Worse, I saw the deranged knife-wielding attacker, full of hatred. The only other time I'd seen her was briefly at her trial, the day I was called to give my witness statement. Then she had been completely different: pale, almost bloodless except for the birthmark, unnaturally calm, her hands folded in her lap, and answering questions so quietly that she had to be asked to speak up. A statement was read on her behalf by her defence – a plain, unemotional statement of deep regret. As I lay in the hospital after the attack, I was in no frame of mind to think about what had happened from anyone's viewpoint save my own. Father Vincent's visit was much too soon, though I knew he had come at her request. But later I came to see that she had, as he claimed, seen what she had done; that in the moment of my terror and anguish her own fury had leached away. Now she was paying the price exacted by the law for her months of cold calculation fuelled by rage and despair, culminating in an act of violence that was entirely foreign to her beliefs. Because I was beginning to take on these beliefs for myself, I was willing to accept that she felt then – and perhaps still felt – a profound sense of failure and shame. And yet… what had she really done? Would I have responded differently in her place? These were questions that could not be answered; one question that I hoped she could answer was why she focused on me. Why not Malcolm? Or the anaesthetist? Or the hospital? She was no fool. She knew that any operation was the work of a team of specialists, any one of whom (or none) could have introduced into Craig's body the toxic agent that killed him. Why me?

I parked outside Father Vincent's vicarage a little before half past ten. He was waiting for me, and had a pot of coffee brewing. After a longish drive I was grateful. I noticed how he seemed to have aged in the time since I'd last seen him, and how he walked carefully, stooped and leaning heavily on his stick. His face was more lined, and his pallor spoke of constant pain.

We were due at the prison at midday. On the way, as I drove, I asked him what Eve's life in prison was like, and how it had changed her.

He reflected for a while, then he said, "She has tried to make the best of it. As I tried to tell you, she is a remarkable woman in many ways: accepting the burden of a sick child with selfless devotion, working in hard and unpleasant jobs, when in fact she is qualified to do better. I suppose I am not really surprised. Prison has brought out a calmer, yet more determined woman. She has found a role in the prison library, and in a quiet way she is supporting some of the other women, often younger and disadvantaged. She is trying to turn something bad around and wring some good out of it."

"I was going to ask her... but perhaps it would be better if I asked you. I don't want to cause more distress. I've wondered – why did she pick on me? I've always felt there was something personal in her revenge."

"I agree," Father Vincent said, shifting his bulk in the seat, trying to find a less painful position. "And I'm glad you asked me, rather than her, because she would be very embarrassed. I think, right from the beginning, when you went to introduce yourself as the surgeon, she took against you – for no real reason, except that she envied you."

"Why?"

"She saw you as successful, free of constraints, able to choose your own path, respected, perhaps a little arrogant; the sort of woman she would like to have been, if life had not dealt her a couple of bad hands. As you might imagine, even though she never mentions it, that birthmark has always kept her in the shadows. And then there were the circumstances of how Craig was conceived... But she knows – maybe she knew even then –

that her vendetta wasn't rational. Perhaps it provided a desperate sort of distraction from the overwhelming devastation she felt when Craig died." He looked out of the car window. "We're almost there. Take the next left." As I swung in and started the long approach, he said, "I believe that's what grates on her even now – that she let such an unworthy feeling drive her. That's why all her rage evaporated when she saw you bleeding: you were no longer someone far above her, but a vulnerable and hurting human being." I brought the car to a halt. "Tell me, Ms Keyte – Rachel. Why have you come today?"

I turned to look at him. "I need to tell her something, and it needs to come from me, not second-hand. And I need to ask her something too, if I can find the courage."

My meeting with Eve Rawlins, which I had imagined, on and off, for a long time, was curiously understated. Perhaps this was unsurprising. She sat opposite me, very still and calm, and answered my questions in a low, unemotional voice. She told me about her work in the library, how her old skills had come back to her, how she loved to be among the books, and how she was trying to encourage reading in some of her fellow-prisoners; as well, she was running a literacy course for those who had never learned to read with confidence.

There was a silence, then she said abruptly, "Did you come today hoping I would ask your forgiveness for what I did?"

I shook my head. "No, that's not it at all. If it's what you want, you have it. No, I wanted to say something about Joseph."

She frowned. "Joseph who?"

"Joseph son of Jacob. It's been on my mind, that story. You must know it well. It's the bit where he reassures his brothers. He says, 'You plotted evil against me, but God turned it into good.'" I paused, considering the verse. "I think God may have done the same with you and me."

She leaned forward, and I saw her hands clench into fists, as if she was trying to hold something in. "What do you know about God?"

"Maybe not much. But more than I did."

She relaxed, perhaps with an effort of will, and a small smile twitched her lips. "Well, that's good, I suppose. So tell me what good has come out of my wickedness."

I took a deep breath. "When I look back, I see I was living half a life. I lived for work. My work was, is, important: saving lives, making lives more bearable. That bit hasn't changed. But it was obsessive. I did little else. On my free days I read whatever I could lay my hands on to advance my career, to further my knowledge, to be better than any of the competition. I guess I was arrogant, but I didn't see it that way. But also I didn't really see patients as people. I didn't dare to wonder what they must be feeling, because it would have made me vulnerable. Empathy is painful, as I've found out." I paused, trying to gather my swirling thoughts; she sat very still, her eyes on my face. "A lot has happened, in my life and in my head, and I think I am a better, kinder person now. And happier. If you feel like beating yourself up at any time about what you did, don't, not on my account. I can still work – maybe I am not as quick as I used to be, but I am still a heart surgeon, which is all I ever wanted – until recently."

She looked at me wide-eyed for a while, saying nothing. Then she said, almost in a whisper, "Are you actually *thanking* me for what I did?"

I smiled. "Not exactly. It was a very bad time, and I wouldn't want ever to go through it again. But perhaps it had to happen. You were an agent of necessary change. I can't complain, and I don't. You made a terrible mistake, and you're paying for it. I suffered a black time, but I survived and I'm learning how to live. I wanted you to know."

She nodded slowly. "Father Vincent told me you have a son now."

"Yes."

"He is a blessing to you."

"Yes, indeed."

She was silent for a long moment, then abruptly she got up. "Thank you for coming to see me," she said formally. "You've come a long way. It was good of you." She took a step back.

I stood up too, scraping the legs of my chair on the dull blue vinyl floor. "Ms Rawlins – Eve – may I call you Eve?" She stopped, nodded warily. "Please, there's something I want to ask you."

She seemed poised to leave. "What is it?"

I hesitated, then spoke in a jumbled rush. "I hope you won't be offended... My husband is a consultant plastic surgeon – one of the best in the country, so they say. When you get out of here, he could look at your birthmark. There may be something he can do, if not to get rid of it, to reduce it. If you would like that."

I had no idea how she would react. Would she be angry that I'd had the presumption even to mention it? She bit her lip, and for a moment I saw, beneath the proud veneer of control, a woman who daily endured an unbearable hurt.

"Thank you," she said at last, her voice low. "I'll think about it." She began to walk away, to the door where a heavy-set female prison officer stood impassively, and then half-turned back to me. "Goodbye, Rachel."

As I drove away from the prison that afternoon, Father Vincent sitting beside me tactfully silent, it came back to me: the thing I had tried to remember at St Luke's, when the preacher was talking about Jesus being the "Yes" to God's promises. I laughed aloud. How could I have forgotten? It was one of the things my father had liked to quote, one of Leonard Bernstein's reputed sayings: "I'm no longer sure what the question is, but I do know that the answer is Yes."

Book club questions

1. How far did you feel empathy for Rachel at the beginning of the story? Did your attitude change as things developed?

2. What effect did the act of revenge – at the time and later – have on Eve? To what extent do you think this story is about women other than Rachel, such as Eve and Rachel's mother, Frances?

3. In general, did you find it easy to empathize with the characters? Was there anyone in particular you did or didn't like?

4. How did you feel about the faith element in the story? Did it enhance the plot, detract from it, or make no difference?

5. Were there any minor characters you would like the author to have developed more fully?

6. We're not told exactly how Eve tracked Rachel down as she planned her revenge. Would this knowledge have added anything to the story? In general, do omissions like this matter?

7. What is your favourite scene?

8. How did the time in France contribute to Rachel's development?

9. If you could ask the author a question or make a comment, what would it be? You could tweet @SueLRussell, or leave a comment on her website: www.slrussell.net

10. Have you taken away anything of value from this story? If so, what?